In Freedom's Shadow

Robert Hilliard

Published by Robert T. Hilliard, 2023.

IN FREEDOM'S SHADOW

First edition. November 17, 2023.

ISBN: 979-8218289362

Written by Robert Hilliard.

To my wonderful wife Pamela. I can never thank you enough for your patience, insight, and support throughout this project - and in life.

The true history of this war will show that the loyal army found no friends at the South so faithful, active, and daring in their efforts to sustain the government as the Negroes. Negroes have repeatedly threaded their way through the lines of the rebels exposing themselves to bullets to convey important information to the loyal army of the Potomac.
- Frederick Douglass

⸻ ● ⸻

The chief source of information to the enemy is through our Negroes.
- Robert E. Lee

CHAPTER 1

October 22, 1861

He was terrified of the river crossing.

It frightened him only barely less than the thought of being captured. John Scobell knew that the cold, dark depths of the Potomac River were not only the last obstacle he would face on his journey to freedom, but they were also the most dangerous. At least for a man who couldn't swim.

Scobell had been running away from the war between the North and South for days. He'd spent the entire time dodging Confederate pickets, eluding the dreaded slave patrols across the Virginia countryside, and hiding in the brush like a wild beast. He had edged his way farther from the gray-coated web that sought to ensnare him and wove his way ever closer to the North...and freedom.

Now, he crouched in a dank, cold swamp, just a few hundred feet from the Potomac River. On the other side lay Maryland, a Union encampment, and most importantly, precious liberty. For most of his twenty-seven years, Scobell had thought of little else.

The plan was simple: get to the bank of the river and find a couple of logs to help him float across. He would maneuver under the cover of darkness, making the execution even more dangerous. But that hardly mattered now. It was his only chance to make it across the Potomac alive.

He'd arrived at the crossing point the day before, and nearly blundered into a fight between the two armies. Concealed in the swamp, he watched the Confederate soldiers encircle the outnumbered Federals, pushing them back to the river's edge. The gray noose tightened inexorably around their position until they could hold out no more.

Blue-coated soldiers jumped or fell down the cliff that formed the riverbank here. With the Rebel soldiers firing down on them from above, a few lucky Union men climbed into waiting rowboats to escape. The rest milled about on the shore like panicked cattle or dove into the Potomac to swim for safety. Scobell watched as several of them sank out of sight into the river's murky waters.

Today, though, the fighting was over. Pickets on both sides of the river had pulled back nearer their camps and the search parties along each bank had ceased. It was time for Scobell to cross the last – and most dangerous – hundred yards separating him from a free life.

Loose rocks and boulders jutted randomly out of the steep, brushy hillside leading to the river. Scobell lowered himself slowly, clinging to each branch until he could find another strong enough to hold him. Twice, the earth under his feet gave way, sending him skidding precariously down the face of the cliff. Each time, he clawed at passing trees until he grasped one that stopped his fall.

At last, panting and sweating from fear and exertion, Scobell reached the narrow flat at the bottom of the bluff. He hid for a few moments to be sure no one had detected his movements, then began searching the bank for pieces of wood that would suit his purpose.

It took him nearly two hours, far longer than he had planned, to drag together three logs that he hoped were large and sturdy enough for him to paddle across. He had no way to bind them together, so he wove his arms through branching limbs and waded into the cold water, pushing the logs ahead of him. As the water reached his waist, the chill seemed to suck the wind out of his lungs.

Scobell gave one final push off the muddy bottom and launched himself onto his makeshift raft. His chest landed on the logs and his powerful arms crushed them tightly together, his grip made even stronger by terror.

Scobell's feet thrashed below the surface, but his panicked kicking resulted only in agonizingly slow forward motion. He continued to struggle, fueled equally by his fear of drowning and of being captured.

After several minutes, his thrashing slowed from exhaustion and cold. As he slackened his effort, however, his progress improved slightly. He found that relaxing his hold on the logs eased the cramps forming in his arm muscles, and that slow, more controlled kicking pushed him through the water a bit more smoothly.

Still, progress was slow. The cold and the current both fought his every stroke. Scobell guessed that a half-hour had passed since he pushed off and a quick glance around told him he wasn't even halfway across.

At one point, something brushed his right leg and panic rushed back into him. His feet churned the water even harder than before.

Scobell had been in the water for nearly two hours. His teeth rattled uncontrollably and, with his grip finally weakened by exhaustion and cold, he had lost two of his logs. Though he strained to control his muscles, he could no longer move his legs.

He was adrift, clinging awkwardly to the last remaining log. It dipped so low into the black water of the Potomac under his weight he could only keep his face above water by turning it to one side. Still, an occasional small wave splashed over his nose and mouth, resulting in a fit of choking coughs.

His legs had long ago gone numb, so it took a few moments to register that his feet had caught on something. His slow drift had stopped. With a massive strain, Scobell lifted his head and peered out of the water. Pink light softened the gray sky overhead.

There it was. The eastern bank of the Potomac was just a few feet ahead. He had come to a stop in the shallow riffles along the shoreline.

Mustering his last reserve of strength, Scobell crawled out of the water and pitched forward into the brush on the bank. The hill on this side was only a few yards high, but it would still have to be climbed. The slow realization that he had reached the goal of a lifetime gave him a last burst of adrenaline, allowing him to drag himself upward.

He paused just short of the top. One more push and he could heave himself onto flat ground. There he could rest, just for a bit.

Suddenly, Scobell felt something hard jab against his temple. A tree branch, he thought, and he reached his hand up to push it away.

"Hold it right there," said a voice from above him. Scobell heard the metallic click of a hammer being cocked. "If you even think about touching this rifle, I'll blow your head clean off," said the voice.

All the remaining strength drained out of Scobell's body and he sagged facedown into the muddy knoll, shivering uncontrollably.

"Just what do you think you're doing, sneaking around here, boy?" asked the man standing over him. "Where do you think you're heading?"

Scobell didn't have the energy to lift his head. The most he could do, with a massive effort, was twist his face slightly toward the voice.

From that position, he could see black boots covered by dark blue pants. A Union soldier.

"What's a matter, boy? You deaf?"

Scobell could hear anger creeping into the soldier's voice. He forced himself to speak. "N-n-no," he rasped through rattling teeth. "N-no, s-s-suh."

"Then you better answer me, boy, when I ask you somethin'. You better speak when spoken to, you hear me?" The soldier punctuated the last statement by jabbing the barrel of his rifle sharply into Scobell's left ear.

"Y-yes, s-suh," Scobell said, still wracked by shivering.

"Now tell me what you think you're doin' here? I s'pose you're runnin' away? Trying to get free?" He spit out the last word in a mocking tone.

"Y-yes, suh," said Scobell. "F-f-free."

"You know, we jus' fought them Rebs across the river the other day. Lotta good men died in that row, boy. Lotta good white men who ain't never gonna get home again. Even lost our colonel." The soldier's voice trailed off slightly, then quickly hardened again. "But I'm s'posed to let you, some nigger who ain't never lifted a finger to help nobody, jus' waltz right in here?"

The soldier crouched so that his face came close to Scobell's ear. His breath smelled of tobacco and stale coffee.

The man's voice dropped into a sinister growl. "I don't think I'm gonna let that happen, boy. I think I'm jus' gonna put a ball in your head and roll you back in the river where you came from. Then you can keep some of our boys company, them that didn't make it across."

Scobell let out a low groan. He had come so far, run so hard, to be free. His lifetime dream was going to end here, on a muddy bank of the Potomac River.

The soldier stood again and poked the muzzle of his gun against Scobell's temple. "So long, ni-"

"What the hell's going on here?" a second voice shouted. "Peiffer, what the hell are you doing?"

"This is none of your business, Wyant. I'm just puttin' this here buck back in the river where he belongs," Peiffer replied.

Scobell forced himself to turn toward the second voice. The newly arrived soldier quickly strode over to confront Peiffer. When they were about a yard apart, Peiffer swung the rifle away from Scobell and pointed it at Wyant.

"Stop right there," Peiffer demanded. "I told you this is none of your business, dammit."

Wyant stopped short. He was nearly a head taller than Peiffer and had to tilt his chin to look down at the man holding the gun.

"You know damn well what our orders are here. Any Negroes coming across are supposed to be brought to the commanding officer," said Wyant evenly. "You need to put that gun down and we'll take this man back to the camp." Wyant didn't look the least bit frightened, despite the rifle pointed at his midsection.

"Yeah, well, Colonel Baker's dead now, ain't he?" said Peiffer. "Can't report nothing to him. A lot of our other boys are dead now, too. And you wanna let this buck jus' walk in like it's nothing? If it weren't for all the darkies, our boys would still be alive. Hell, we wouldn't even be here!"

"So, you're making the decisions now?" asked Wyant. "You have orders, soldier. What you want or I want, that don't mean nothing. You know damn well the army's claiming the Negroes coming across the lines as contraband and we're s'posed to bring them into camp. That's it."

Peiffer looked uncertainly between Wyant and Scobell. "This buck doesn't deserve to live when all our good boys in blue are dead," he said, although his conviction seemed to be ebbing.

Wyant took a step closer. "You gonna shoot me too?" he asked the smaller man. "'Cause I'll tell you what, you're gonna have to if you kill him. Either that or I'll give you the whipping of your life and drag your ass back to camp as a prisoner."

Peiffer suddenly looked even less certain. He glanced down at Scobell again and took a half-step back from Wyant.

"Or," Wyant pressed, "you can just walk away and leave this man alone. I'll take him in and forget all this ever happened."

Peiffer considered the situation, looking back and forth between Scobell and Wyant once more. Then his shoulders sagged, and he lowered the rifle barrel toward the ground.

Wyant quickly stepped forward to help Scobell, brushing past Peiffer as if he were no longer there. The smaller man edged back a few steps, then turned and trudged slowly away.

Grasping the black man under each arm, Wyant swiftly pulled Scobell the rest of the way up the bank until he was seated on flat ground. "Are you alright?" he asked.

"Th-think so," said Scobell, still shivering uncontrollably.

"We need to get you warmed up," said Wyant. He quickly stripped off his coat and draped it around Scobell.

"Can you walk?" the soldier asked.

Scobell nodded. Wyant helped lift him to his feet.

He surveyed Scobell for a moment. Though not as tall as Wyant's six-foot frame, the man's muscular shoulders stretched the soldier's coat to its limit. Stinking river water still dripped from his ragged cotton shirt and leaked from the torn cuffs of his pants onto bare feet.

"You look like you've had a rough go of it," said Wyant.

"Yes, suh," Scobell replied, his chills finally subsiding under the warmth of the coat and the morning sun. He looked back at the muddy Potomac swirling below them. "Don' think I wanna go swimmin' agin soon."

Wyant chuckled. "No," he said, "I don't s'pose you would. You got a name?"

"John, suh. John Scobell."

"John, I'm Henry Wyant." The soldier stuck out his hand to shake. "And you can stop callin' me sir. I'm only a private. Jus' call me Henry."

"Fair 'nuff, Henry," said Scobell, mustering a slight smile.

"Now, let's go get you in front of a fire and into some dry clothes," said Wyant. He grinned slyly at Scobell. "Too bad you're so big in the arms. We mighta borrowed some clothes from Private Peiffer."

CHAPTER 2

Scobell spent the next few days working in the Union camp. He helped where he could and even earned a few coins by running errands and cleaning uniforms and boots for the men. At night, he slept on the floor of Wyant's tent, wrapped snugly in a US Army-issued wool blanket.

The familiar dream came to him more than once there in the camp. He walked through a dark forest, then emerged into a rolling meadow. He strolled easily up a knoll, trailing his hands across the tops of the lush grass as he went. At the top of the hill, he turned to look across the fields below and knew that they belonged to him. His own farm, stretching to the horizon. Honeybees buzzed around a clump of yellow flowers just a few feet away. Scobell inhaled deeply and smelled the earthy greenness of the plants growing in the field. His field.

Each time he awoke from the dream, he felt a gladness deep inside. What had once been just a tiny spark of hope for a life away from bondage was now flickering into a warming flame.

He hadn't quite earned his freedom yet, though. Like the other escaped slaves who had crossed from the South, they labeled him as 'contraband,' captured goods of the Confederacy.

Being a contraband conveyed an odd status: not quite a slave, but not quite free. He could move around camp as he pleased and didn't have to do any work that he didn't want to do. Further, he got paid for whatever tasks he elected to do, which was a rather pleasant development.

But he also couldn't leave the camp, at least not legally. While he wasn't under guard, running off would leave him roaming the Maryland countryside unprotected. Despite its neutral status in the war, Maryland remained a slave state. Slave catchers still roamed the countryside and under the Fugitive Slave Act, they could legally return escapees to their owners to collect a bounty.

Scobell wasn't quite free. Not yet.

In between odd jobs, he chatted with Wyant and some of the other soldiers. Scobell learned that the fight he'd stumbled into was being called the Battle of Ball's Bluff, named for the steep hillside at the edge of the river.

Well over one hundred men had died in the clash, including those that Scobell had seen drowning in the river. Among those killed was Colonel Edward Baker, who was also a US Senator. Baker died from a single bullet to the head during the fight.

Wyant was part of Baker's regiment, the 1st California. Despite the name, most of its soldiers had never been west of the Ohio River. The regiment was created to encourage men from California to volunteer, but distance and a small population in that state worked against filling the ranks. The balance of the troops were native Pennsylvanians, like Wyant.

The other Federal troops in camp represented Minnesota, New York, Michigan, and Massachusetts. Scobell noticed that losing a commander who was also a senator – who was, in fact, a close friend of President Abraham Lincoln – seemed to have soldiers from every state on edge. Coming so soon after the Union loss at Manassas, a second defeat, albeit much smaller in terms of numbers, was worrisome. Realization was dawning on the Federal soldiers that this might not be the quick fight against a rag-tag opponent they initially supposed.

In the evenings, Scobell would sit with Wyant and some of the other soldiers around their campfire. He liked to listen to them talk, noting the different accents that men from different parts of the country carried. Having never heard anything but a Mississippi drawl or a Scottish burr for the prior 27 years of his life, the new inflections and occasional unfamiliar words were funny to him.

"How come you don' talk like these other fellas?" Scobell asked Wyant one evening.

Wyant laughed and nodded his head toward some of the other soldiers ringed around the fire. "You mean these Bah-ston boys?" he asked, mimicking their accent. "They do kinda talk funny, don't they?" he said, raising his voice to make sure his intended targets had heard him.

"Listen to the pie-eater," replied one of the young men, pretending to be offended by the comment. "He wouldn't know the inside of a schoolhouse from the inside of an outhouse, and he says we talk funny?"

The entire knot of soldiers laughed this time, including Wyant.

He turned back to Scobell and said, "These boys are with the 19th Massachusetts. They're from way up in New England, most of 'em city boys from Boston. I'm from Pennsylvania, over in the western part of the state. Out in the sticks, no place you ever heard of."

"Nice there?" asked Scobell.

Wyant shrugged. "Nice as any place, I s'pose. It's in the country, which I like. I ain't cut out for city life."

"Whatcha do when y'all ain't soldierin'?" asked Scobell.

"Work at whatever I can," said Wyant. "Fixing wagons, working at the sawmill. I got a wife and a little girl at home so I do what I can to take care of 'em. How 'bout you? You got any family?"

Scobell stared straight ahead into the fire. "Had me a wife for a time," he said. "But she done got sold away."

Scobell felt Wyant looking at him, but the black man continued to gaze into the flames. He'd closed that door years ago. He wasn't about to reopen it now.

"I'm sorry to hear that," Wyant said at last.

When Scobell didn't respond, the Pennsylvanian finally said, "I'd like to get me a little farm when this fight's over. Someplace to call my own."

"Me, too," said Scobell, lifting from his reverie. "Like to have me a patch to work someday. Takes money, though. Man like me, don' rightly know if that'd ever happen."

"Money doesn't come easy to any man," said Wyant. "Least, none that I ever met." He turned his gaze from the fire to look directly at Scobell. "You don't seem afraid of work any. We get busy and win this war, you might get your chance."

"That how it is where y'all come from?" Scobell asked. "A Negro man can have 'is own farm?"

"Don' know why not," Wyant replied. "You jus' gotta be willing to work hard enough. Like my dad says, ain't no man ever fell up a mountain."

"I always heard that all Negroes were lazy as sin," piped up one of the Massachusetts soldiers. "But you don't seem so bad."

"Ain't no such thing as a slave 'fraid of hard work," said Scobell. "You pick a couple hunnert pounds a' cotton a day, in that hot Mississip' sun? Ain't no work harder'n at."

"What if you didn't?" asked one of the younger soldiers, with sudden interest. "Did you get whipped?"

"Doyle!" said Wyant sharply. "What the hell's the matter with you?"

Doyle opened his mouth to protest, but Scobell chimed in, "Yeah, I been whipped a few times. We all been whipped. First day pickin' cotton, that overseer'll whip you sumpin' awful so's you won't slow down. Then they know how much you can pick. Any day after that you don' pick as much gets you another whippin'."

Wyant looked at Scobell in silence. Doyle let out a low whistle.

"Damn," he said. "You evah try to run off?"

Scobell nodded. "When I's a young 'un, yeah."

"What happened?"

"Didn' get far," Scobell said. "They done caught me an' beat me till I's near killed."

Another soldier, who had been quietly pulling long draws from a flask up to now, suddenly spoke up. "The way I hear it, whippin's about the only way you can teach a nigger anything. They ain't smart enough to learn, 'less you beat it into 'em. That's why none of 'em can read or write, 'cause you can't teach that with a whippin'."

"Jesus, O'Toole!" barked Wyant. "Are you tryin' to start a row?"

"I'm just tellin' you what I've heard," answered O'Toole, shrugging nonchalantly and taking another deep swig from his flask.

Scobell realized that the entire group awaited his response. The last thing he wanted was to start a fight here in camp, where it would be at least twenty against one. He took another tack.

"Ain't no nigger smart 'nuff for readin' and writin', you say?" Scobell asked. "You sho' 'bout dat?"

"Damn right," replied O'Toole.

"Well, my good man, I'll have you know that you're looking at one who can read and write as well as any white man you know," said Scobell.

Several seconds of stunned silence passed after the sudden speech transformation. Finally, Wyant, who had been gaping at Scobell with his mouth hanging open, laughed uproariously. It was instantly contagious and within seconds, the other soldiers around the fire all roared with laughter as well. Even O'Toole guffawed along with the rest.

"Well, I will be damned," said Wyant when he finally recovered his senses. "You talk better English than any man here! And you can read and write, too?"

"Yes, I can," said Scobell with a smile.

"Now this I gotta see!" yelped another soldier, rushing off into the dark. In less than a minute, he returned with a Bible from his tent and handed it to Scobell. "Here, read us a passage from the Good Book. I want to hear it!"

Scobell moved closer to the fire so he could see more clearly. He thumbed through the pages for a moment, then stopped and said, "This is one of my favorites. It's from the Book of Isaiah."

In a clear, deep voice, he read, "The Spirit of the Lord God is upon me, because the Lord has anointed me to bring good news to the poor; he has sent me to bind up the brokenhearted, to proclaim liberty to the captives, and the opening of the prison to those who are bound."

He slowly closed the Bible and handed it back to the soldier who had retrieved it.

There were several more seconds of silence among the group. Then Wyant repeated in a barely audible voice, "Well, I will be damned."

CHAPTER 3

The following night, Scobell lay curled on the floor of the tent. Wyant's bunkmate, a soldier in his early twenties from Philadelphia, was snoring loud enough to shake the wooden tentpoles.

"You awake, John?" Wyant asked.

"Who could sleep with all this noise?" Scobell replied. "That boy snores louder than cannon fire."

"Don't I know it," said Wyant. "We've been bunking together for two months now. I considered shooting him, but it turns out they frown on that sorta thing here."

"You wouldn't get any argument from me. Or anybody else for about a mile around."

Wyant chuckled. "No, I don't s'pose I would."

After a minute of silence, Wyant said, "So how'd you end up here anyway? I mean, I know you crossed the river. But how'd you make it to there?"

"My master brought me north from the plantation in Mississippi when the war broke out. He was a captain in a volunteer unit. At first, he just had me looking after his gear, but when they asked for slaves to work on the defenses, he lent me out."

"What did they have you doing?"

"Digging trenches, piling dirt, and stacking logs on the embankments around the camp. First, we were cooking in the heat during August and September, then freezing our asses in the wind and rains when October came."

"How'd you get out?"

"One day, I decided I'd had enough. I've been slave since the day I was born." Scobell paused, staring up at the ceiling of the tent. Out of nowhere, he could feel a wave of emotion welling inside him. A single tear leaked out of the corner of his eye and trickled across his temple.

He cleared his throat. "I once read that all men are created equal. I was going to find a place where those words mattered."

"Can't say I blame you," said Wyant softly.

"The next rainy evening, I grabbed my chance. The soldiers called all of us in when it got too dark to work. I stayed at the back when the slaves formed their line."

He paused again, considering the significance of that moment. "It was dark by then and storming pretty hard, so it was tough to see. I ducked behind a pile of logs we had stacked nearby. Then, when it was full dark, I just slipped off into the forest. It was still pouring rain, which made it easier to disappear."

"Just like that?" Wyant asked.

"Yep, just like that. Hard to believe it was that simple, after all those years. 'Course, escaping from Virginia to Maryland is a little easier than getting North from Mississippi."

"Yeah, I imagine so. How'd you get all the way to the Potomac then?"

"Traveled at night, and stuck to the thickest cover I could find. I made my way out around the Rebs at Leesburg, and snuck through the woods until I made it to the Potomac."

Both men were quiet for a moment. Even the thunderous snoring subsided when the Philadelphia soldier rolled onto his side.

"That's a hell of a run," Wyant said at last. "I'm glad you made it out."

"Trust me," said Scobell, "You're not nearly as glad as I am."

⟢ ◉ ⟣

Two days later, a sergeant from the camp commander's staff called Scobell out of the tent.

"There's a wagon leaving today at 10 AM," the sergeant told him briskly. "You be on it. We have orders to move all the contrabands to Washington."

"Yes, suh," Scobell replied, and he hurried off to collect his things. He didn't know how far word of his eloquence had spread, so he still relied on his slave speech when talking to most of the soldiers in camp. Being underestimated could be an advantage.

Wyant strolled up as Scobell was gathering his few newly purchased belongings from the tent. "What's going on?" the tall Pennsylvanian asked.

"I have to go," said Scobell, gesturing to the small bundle under his arm. "They're shipping all the contrabands to Washington."

"What for?" asked Wyant.

Scobell shrugged. "It's the Army," he said with a smile. "They didn't say, and I didn't ask."

Wyant looked down at his boots for a moment. Then he took a deep breath and extended his hand. "You're a good man, John, not to mention one that's full of surprises," he said. "I'm gonna miss having you around."

Scobell shook his hand. As he tried to let go, the soldier's grip lingered for a moment. Wyant looked like he wanted to say something, but no words came out.

Wyant's gaze shifted from Scobell to a point somewhere in the distance over Scobell's shoulder. Before it did, Scobell thought he saw tears welling in the white man's eyes.

The Pennsylvanian's reaction confused Scobell. They'd shared meals and campfires and tent space for the past two weeks, but it wasn't like they were friends. Scobell didn't have any friends.

"Wait," said Wyant after a moment, "I have something for you." He ducked into his tent and emerged a few seconds later with a folded woolen blanket. It was a basic gray color, with a darker gray stripe across each end.

"It's gettin' colder now," Wyant said. "I notice you don't have much to keep you warm. This'll help some." Looking down at his boots again, he added, "They make 'em up in Pennsylvania so you know they're good."

Recovering from his confusion, Scobell thanked him for the blanket. Then he added, "Still trying to save my life, I guess."

"Yeah, I s'pose so," replied Wyant. Though the taller man was now looking down at the ground, Scobell thought he'd caught another glimpse of shiny tears in his eyes.

"I hope you get that farm someday," said Scobell.

As Scobell walked off toward the waiting wagon, Wyant said quietly, "You too."

CHAPTER 4

A dozen black men walked side by side through the streets of Washington, D.C., led by one blue-coated solider in front and followed by one to the rear. They walked slowly, heads down, staring at the muddy footprints and hoofprints that chewed up the street ahead of them. Scobell was the only one who occasionally looked up at the busy streets, soldiers marching, and carriages hustling in all directions.

The lead soldier stopped suddenly in front of a two-story brick building on I Street, just a few blocks from the White House. He turned to his charges and said curtly, "In here," motioning them up the stairs to the double door.

Once inside, the group walked down a long hallway lined with offices on each side. As near as Scobell could tell, most of them were empty. In fact, the building itself seemed nearly deserted and the echo of their footsteps, along with the clinking rattle of the soldiers' uniform straps, sounded almost obscenely loud in the quiet surroundings.

At the end of the hallway, the lead soldier motioned to two wooden benches facing each other across the hallway. "Sit," he commanded quietly.

He then stepped through a doorway near the benches, announcing in an official tone, "Contrabands here for questioning."

"Very good," came the reply. "How many?"

"Twelve," the soldier answered.

"Very good," the man in the office repeated. "Mr. Allen will be ready to see them shortly."

The soldier returned to the hallway and took a seat next to the other soldier on a bench farther down the hall. The two of them glanced back at the group of black men occasionally, but mostly they busied themselves rolling and smoking cigarettes, and complaining about their platoon sergeant.

From his seat on the opposite side of the hallway, Scobell could glimpse the man in the office: young and thin, with pince-nez glasses perched on the end of his nose. Wearing a dark suit, definitely not a soldier. If it wasn't an army office, then what was this place? And who was this Mr. Allen?

After about twenty minutes, the young man emerged from the office. Without expression, he pointed at the man next to Scobell and said, "Follow me, please."

The black man, a scruffy, old runaway who had given his name as Joshua during the ride to Washington, fairly hopped out of his seat and ambled off down the hall, being careful to stay two full strides behind the white man. Force of habit, thought Scobell.

At the end of the hallway, the two men went through another double door and then turned out of sight. Scobell could hear their footsteps as they climbed an unseen set of stairs. He heard a door open and close on the second floor, but then nothing else.

He turned his attention to the rest of the group seated on the benches. They ranged from men in their teens to much older men, maybe 60 years old or more judging by their white hair and stooped posture. He wondered whether any of them were freemen or if they were all runaways who'd made it out of the Confederacy to the safety of Federal lines.

The man on the bench directly across from him began fidgeting. Barely more than a boy, perhaps 16 years old, the youngster had been wearing a bowler hat. He now held the hat between his knees, rapidly turning it in circles by the brim as he looked up and down the hallway.

When they made eye contact, the younger man couldn't restrain himself any longer. "What you think they want wid' us?" he said, keeping his voice low so as not to attract attention from the two soldiers conversing farther down the hall.

Scobell shook his head and shrugged slightly.

"Don' think they gonna sen' us back, do ya? I mean, we's free up north heah, right?" His bowler continued to rotate in his fingers as he talked.

"Don' rightly know," Scobell replied.

For an instant, he worried that the younger man might panic and cause a scene, but just then they heard the door from the second floor open and close again, and more footsteps on the stairway. In a moment, Joshua and the man in the suit reappeared at the end of the hallway. They had barely been gone ten minutes, Scobell observed.

The man in the dark suit motioned for Joshua to be seated again. He then pointed to another from the group on the benches and said, "Follow me, please." Once again, they paraded down the hall with the black man trailing behind, then disappeared around the corner and up the stairs.

The second they were out of sight, the young man with the bowler turned on Joshua. "What dey say? What dey gonna do wid us?" he asked eagerly. Every other man on both benches leaned in to hear the response.

"It were jus' one man," replied Joshua amiably. "He jus' axed me a few questions, is all. Jus' axed ol' Joshua some questions."

"Wha'd he ax?" quizzed the youngster. The bowler stopped rotating when Joshua spoke, starting back up again when he stopped.

"He 'uz nice 'nuff. Jus' axed where I bin, where I come from an' such," said Joshua. "Axed how many Johnny Rebs I seen."

"What y'all say?" asked another man. "Y'all tell 'im what you knew?"

Joshua cackled. The sound reminded Scobell of an iron gate that needed grease.

"Why, I tol' that feller that ol' Joshua don' know howta count. Don' know howta count one bit."

He guffawed again. "Told 'im there were a big ol' bunch of 'em, though. Mebbe at least a hunnert or a thousan'."

"Tha's it?" asked the young man with the bowler. "Tha's all?" Scobell could read both relief and doubt in his face.

"Yep. Tha's it," Joshua replied. "Tol' me, 'Thank you for your time,' and sen' me back down heah," he announced with a satisfied grin.

Scobell had a clearer picture now. The opposing armies were massed just a few miles apart, but knew little about each other's size or strength. What better source of information than blacks escaping from the South, some of whom had traveled hundreds of miles through Confederate territory to get to freedom in the North? They couldn't have avoided seeing Confederate troops and fortifications.

This man, Mr. Allen, was asking the dozens of refugees that streamed in from the South each day to supply that critical information. Knowing the number and location of Rebel troops would be invaluable to US military leaders. Assuming, Scobell thought to himself, *your observers could count.* He smiled inwardly at the irony.

Shortly, they heard the upstairs door open and close again, and the man in the suit returned to the hallway with the black man following behind. The white man gestured for him to be seated on the bench and then turned to Scobell.

"You," the man in the suit said, pointing to him. "Follow me, please."

Scobell complied. They walked to the end of the hallway and through the double doors, then mounted the stairs. At the top of the stairs, they came to a door, which the young man in the dark suit opened. He waved Scobell through, then led him down another long hallway. Near the far end, they turned into an open door on their right.

They came to a stop in front of a man seated behind a large oak desk. He was hurriedly scribbling on a piece of paper atop the desk and did not look up when they entered.

"Another black dispatch, Mr. Allen," said the man who had escorted Scobell upstairs.

"Yes, thank you, Mr. Bangs," replied the man behind the desk in a Scottish accent. He never glanced up from his writing. "I'll call you when I'm finished with the interview."

Bangs gestured for Scobell to sit down in a wooden chair in front of the desk. He then wheeled and exited the room, closing the door behind him.

Scobell took in the room. It smelled of cigar smoke. Behind the desk, there was an enormous window, allowing a sweeping view down onto I Street. There were large bookshelves along the wall on his left, lined with leather-bound ledgers and stacks of paper. Along the right wall, several packing crates had been cracked open to retrieve an item or two, but never completely unpacked. Though tidily arranged, the room looked like someone with much work to do inhabited it, someone so busy that they had never taken time to settle in.

He turned his attention to Mr. Allen, who was still composing furiously. Like Bangs, he wore a dark suit with a pressed white shirt and a bow tie. He had a dark brown beard, neatly trimmed. His brown hair, though thinning, was precisely parted and carefully combed.

With his full beard and the abrupt movements of his head and hands, the Scotsman reminded Scobell of the small terrier that lived on a neighboring plantation. The dog rode everywhere in its master's buckboard, barking at everything in sight and growling constantly at anyone who came near the wagon.

Once, after a visit from the dog's owner, John asked Master Scobell, "What good's a little dog like that? He don' do nothin' but make noise."

Master Scobell smiled. "He makes a lot of noise, I'll give you that. But that dog's a terrier, bred to kill vermin. I once saw him clean 17 rats out of a cotton barn in under an hour."

John whistled.

"Another time, he killed a rabid raccoon that had their little girls cornered in the henhouse. Neither the girls nor the dog got a scratch," said Master Scobell. "That's why he gets to ride up on the wagon."

Mr. Allen had finished his important writing and set it to the side of his grand desk. Then, pulling a fresh sheet of paper from a drawer, he dipped his pen in an ink jar. Without looking up from the paper, he snapped, "Name, please."

"John Scobell." Then, playing a hunch, he added, "S-C-O-B-E-L-L."

Allen finished making his note, then looked up at Scobell for the first time. "Do you know how to spell anything besides your name?"

"Yes, I can read and write." said Scobell. "And count," he added.

Allen showed no hint that he got the jab. "Very good," he answered, making another note. "And where did you learn these skills?"

"My master," Scobell lied. "His name was James Scobell." Guessing that a little flattery wouldn't hurt, he added, "He was a Scotsman, like yourself."

Allen looked directly at Scobell for a moment. A hint of a smile played at the corners of his mouth. "Scottish, eh? I see. Yes, quite good." Another note on the paper.

"So, you ran away from this Master James Scobell's plantation then? And where was this plantation located?" Allen asked the questions in rapid succession.

"No, sir," Scobell replied. "That is, the plantation was in Mississippi, but I didn't run away. My master gave me my freedom." Another lie.

Allen scrutinized Scobell for a moment from across the desk. "I see, yes," he mumbled. He scribbled another note.

"So then, how did you come to be here in the North?" Allen asked.

"Master Scobell volunteered for the army when the war started," Scobell began.

Allen interrupted suddenly, "What regiment?"

"Master Scobell volunteered for the Minute Men of Attala County, Mississippi," Scobell recited. "When we got to into Virginia, they became Company D, then later Company I of Col. Barksdale's 13th Infantry." He added almost apologetically, "They fought at Manassas back in July."

Allen stopped writing and peered across the desk. His penetrating gray eyes locked onto Scobell's and silence descended on the room. Allen seemed to be fully considering the man across from him for the first time.

After a few moments passed, Allen picked up his pen, dipped it in the inkwell, and started writing again. "That was the 11th Infantry?" he asked.

"13th," Scobell corrected. "Under Col. Barksdale."

"Yes, of course," Allen nodded. "Barksdale's 13th." He regarded Scobell again. "And when did Master Scobell choose to set you free?"

"Four days ago."

"Why did he choose to do so now, after all this marching and fighting?"

Scobell couldn't resist a grin. "General Beauregard turned us loose."

Allen looked at him quizzically. P. G. T. Beauregard was one of the most well-known Confederate generals, acclaimed as a hero at both Fort Sumter and Manassas.

"Apparently, the officers who didn't have slaves with them in the Rebel army were causing trouble with the ones who did," explained Scobell. "I guess General Beauregard finally got fed up and told his men that they couldn't keep personal slaves anymore. They put most of us to work building fortifications, but Master Scobell chose to set me free instead. I suppose he had his reasons." The falsehoods were piling up.

"Yes, one supposes," said Allen, contemplating this for a moment.

"Now," he continued, "What can you tell me about Rebel fortifications between Richmond and the Potomac River? How many encampments and forts do you know of? How many men did you see at each?" Allen had returned to his rapid-fire questioning style.

Scobell listed the location of each Confederate fortification that he had encountered, as well as those he hadn't seen personally but had heard discussed. He described those he had seen, including the number of soldiers at each.

Since he'd traveled with the Rebel army for so long, he knew artillery models by sight and gave a careful accounting of those to Allen as well. He was careful not to exaggerate and to distinguish in his responses between what he had seen with his own eyes and what he had only overheard.

When Scobell finished answering the extensive list of questions, Allen put his pen down and folded his hands atop the desk. Once more, his gray eyes seemed to bore into Scobell's as Allen regarded him in silence.

"Mr. Scobell," Allen began after a few moments, "I would like to make you a proposal."

Scobell nodded slightly, keeping his gaze locked on the Scotsman's.

Allen reached into a desk drawer and pulled out a fresh piece of paper. As he wrote on it, he again spoke to Scobell without looking up. "I should like you to take this letter across town to an associate of mine, a Mr. Broughton, then await his reply and bring it back to me. His office is near the intersection of Third Street and Indiana Avenue. You're new to Washington, so my secretary, George Bangs, will give you directions."

Allen finished writing and fixed his gray eyes on Scobell again. "If you do this task for me, I will pay you $10, five now and five upon your return with Mr. Broughton's reply. As you may know, colored men working for the Union Navy are currently being paid eight dollars each month, so this is a substantial sum of money."

He paused for a moment. "Will you complete this task for me, Mr. Scobell?"

Scobell also paused. He had no home, no job, and no prospects at all for his own future – and now the animated man across the desk from him was offering a month's pay to walk across town and back?

"Yes, sir," he replied, in the calmest voice he could muster.

"Excellent," said Allen. He popped abruptly out of his chair and strode around the desk to hand the letter to Scobell. As he did, Allen said, "I've forgotten my manners. I am Mr. E.J. Allen." He extended his hand and shook Scobell's vigorously.

"It's a pleasure to make your acquaintance, sir," said Scobell.

"Likewise," replied Allen. "Likewise."

He called for Mr. Bangs, who quickly opened the door and stepped in from the hallway. "Bangs, please give Mr. Scobell here directions to Broughton's office. I've asked him to deliver a letter for me and bring back a response. Also, please give him five dollars for his trouble. He will receive another five when he returns."

Bangs nodded hastily and said, "Of course, Mr. Allen," then ushered Scobell out of the room. They hustled downstairs to the secretary's office, where he provided Scobell with the directions and five dollars in gold coins.

As they stepped back out into the hallway, Bangs said, "You best hurry. Mr. Allen doesn't like to be kept waiting."

Scobell nodded and turned to leave the building. In doing so, he had to walk between the two long benches where his temporary companions still sat. They looked at him searchingly, their quizzical expressions asking why he was leaving and to where.

Scobell kept his expression blank, except for a quick nod as he passed between them. And then they were behind him as he pushed open the front door and strode down the steps into the late morning chill. He turned left, then hustled across the street. As he strode hurriedly up I Street, he glanced over his shoulder.

He couldn't be sure, but for a moment, Scobell thought he saw E.J. Allen gazing down at him from the second-story window.

———— ◉ ————

As Scobell hustled across town to the address Bangs had given him, he gawked at the bustle of activity around him. Uniformed soldiers marched on every street, interspersed by men in suits and top hats hurrying off to some critical appointment or other. Women in bonnets and dresses trimmed in lace trod the brick sidewalks, some accompanied by their slaves. Other free black citizens went about their daily business as well.

Few of them paid a second's attention to the two and three-story brick buildings that surrounded each street. But Scobell did. He had never been in such a large city before, nor seen a building taller than two stories, not counting the occasional church steeple.

When he rounded a corner and saw the massive edifice of the Treasury Building, he stopped and stared in amazement. The five-story building was taller than anything he'd ever seen. It seemed to stretch endlessly along Pennsylvania Avenue, dwarfing every other building in sight. Scobell stood gaping at the towering granite columns. At last, remembering his mission, he forced himself to look away from the towering edifice and start moving forward again.

As he strode quickly down the busy streets, Scobell's thoughts turned again to E.J. Allen. Who was this man? Something obviously tied him to the military and yet, he was not in the army himself.

What was Allen's interest in Scobell? Why was he willing to pay so much for a simple errand across town – not to mention giving half of the payment in advance?

Scobell felt the weight of the coins in his pants. He put his right hand in his pocket to touch them as he turned these questions over in his mind.

When he was about a block from his destination, the realization dawned on him. This was a test. Allen paid him upfront to see if Scobell would actually deliver the letter or simply take the money and walk off. Half a month's salary would be a great temptation for some men, and it would be easy to disappear with it.

Scobell picked up his pace as he approached the corner of Third Street and Indiana Avenue. He was anxious now to complete his assignment, temporarily forgetting the five-dollar incentive. He was now fixated on a single question: Who in the hell was E. J. Allen?

Scobell entered the office and told the secretary that he had a letter for Mr. Broughton from Mr. E. J. Allen, and that he was to wait for a reply. At the sound of Allen's name, the secretary perked up suddenly and hurried off to locate Broughton. In a moment, both men returned.

Scobell repeated his message and handed the letter to Broughton. He took it slowly, looking Scobell over skeptically as he did so. Broughton walked to a desk at the back of the room, cut open the envelope, and spread the letter on the desk to read it. When he finished, he looked up at Scobell, who still stood near the secretary's desk at the front of the room.

"Do you know what this letter says?" asked Broughton brusquely.

"No, suh," Scobell replied.

"Did Major Allen give you any other instruction?" Broughton inquired.

Major Allen? "No, suh. He only say I's to give it to you, then give him back yo' reply," said Scobell.

Broughton fixed Scobell with an odd look, then shook his head slightly. He bent over the desk, penned a few words, and after drying the ink for a few seconds, sealed it in another envelope and handed it back to Scobell.

"Here is my reply," Broughton said. "Please take it directly back to Major Allen. I do not want you stopping anywhere on your return trip, nor are you to open the envelope under any circumstances. Nor should you give it to anyone except Major Allen. Do you understand me?"

It was clear to Scobell that whatever trust Allen had placed in him, Broughton did not share in the slightest.

"Yes, suh," Scobell replied. "Straight to Massa Allen."

"Very well. You best be on your way," said Broughton. As Scobell turned to leave, Broughton added cryptically, "Major Allen certainly has his own ideas about things." Scobell decided that this didn't require a response and walked out the door without looking back.

When Scobell arrived back at the building on I Street, he was immediately ushered upstairs to Allen's office. He handed the letter to the Scotsman, who looked exceedingly pleased at Scobell's reappearance.

Motioning for him to sit in the chair in front of the desk, Allen said, "Let us see what Mr. Broughton has to say."

Allen read the brief reply and chuckled. "Well, let's hope he is incorrect," he said, still looking down at the letter.

Allen then looked up and fixed his gray eyes on the man across the desk. "Mr. Scobell, you have done precisely what I have asked of you this afternoon. You ran this important errand and returned promptly, which I respect and for which I owe you another five dollars."

Scobell nodded slightly in response, but did not reply.

"I gleaned from our earlier conversation that you are an intelligent man with a keen eye for observation. You obviously have had some education, notably so for someone of your race who dwelt in Mississippi. And your activity this afternoon has shown me you are also a man to be trusted, one who can carry out an assignment as instructed."

"Thank you, sir," said Scobell.

"Being a clever and observant man, you are no doubt wondering about the purpose of today's exercises. In short, you are probably asking yourself who I am and what my role is, correct?" inquired Allen with a hint of a smile.

Scobell nodded. "Yes, those questions had occurred to me."

"Very well," said Allen, his smile disappearing. "To this point, Mr. Scobell, I have not been forthright with you. This was, as you shall see, completely necessary given the essence of my work."

"In truth, my name is not E. J. Allen. That is merely an alias that I have assumed for the purpose of my current role. That role, Mr. Scobell, is the chief of the Secret Service of the United States. I am charged with gathering intelligence to help the Union win the war against the secessionists."

"My real name," Allen said, pausing slightly for effect, "is Allan Pinkerton."

Scobell had never heard the name before. He continued to contemplate the man across the desk from him.

"Yes, well," continued Pinkerton, clearly perturbed at Scobell's indifference to his announcement. "In some areas of the country, my name is quite well-known as the chief of a successful detective agency. Though not, apparently, in Mississippi."

"At any rate," Pinkerton went on, "In April of this year, I was called to the service of this great country by General George McClellan, who requested that I organize a secret service on his behalf. The purpose of this service is the gathering of intelligence to aid the war effort. Specifically, the general asked me to send scouts to gather observations within the Rebel lines, and secure information on the troop distribution, equipment, and intentions of the enemy."

"Since that time, my operatives have been completing missions behind Confederate lines, gathering critical information that we relay to General McClellan. As I'm sure you can understand, none but intelligent, reliable people can be called upon for such service."

Scobell nodded, now wondering where this discussion was heading.

"Mr. Scobell, I believe you are such a man. In fact, the letter you carried to my associate Mr. Broughton today detailed my beliefs to that effect and stated my proposal to make you an operative of our secret service. The fact that you carried out that errand quickly and correctly further confirmed my assessment of your potential."

Scobell was stunned at Pinkerton's comments. After considering the correct reply for a moment, he asked, "What was Mr. Broughton's response?"

Pinkerton picked up the letter and read aloud, "Enacting this proposal would be a mistake. Using a Negro in this manner would be ruinous to our effort."

"He doesn't believe a Negro can be a spy," said Scobell flatly.

Pinkerton responded with a dismissive wave of his hand. "I prefer the term 'operative.' Besides, Mr. Scobell, should you choose to accept the offer that I am about to present, you will have larger concerns than the opinion of an administrative wage-earner who would no more know what makes a successful operative than what makes a robin sing."

"I have operated a successful detective agency in Chicago for over ten years, using a variety of men – and even women – in my employ. Trust me when I tell you it is the heart, mind, and spirit that makes someone a reliable operative, not their size or class or color."

Scobell said nothing, so Pinkerton continued. "Should you choose to operate in the employ of our secret service, you will receive training in our methods over the next few weeks. We will teach you how to pump informants for information, how to shadow another person while remaining undetected, and the proper way to assume a disguised role to protect your own identity."

"What exactly would I be asked to do?" said Scobell.

"As an operative of the secret service," said Pinkerton, "We will ask you to travel behind Confederate lines and infiltrate their ranks to make observations. We expect you to relay those observations secretly back to me, through methods that we will reveal only if you choose to join us."

The Scotsman paused, and his tone became graver. "I have in my employ several people who have served in this capacity. Each of them risks imprisonment and trial with the possibility of being hanged as a spy should their efforts on behalf of the Union be discovered. The consequences are quite serious."

Scobell blew out a breath. "Mr....Pinkerton?" he began.

The man across the desk nodded. "Mr. Pinkerton, I'm sure your operatives are quite brave and are serving the Union cause well. However, the consequences you mentioned are not the ones that I would face in the same situation."

"How so?" asked Pinkerton.

"Because I am a Negro," Scobell said. "There would be no trial if they captured me. No long incarceration, no offers of a prisoner swap."

"They will kill me," he continued. "Immediately, and under the most excruciating forms of torture you can envision. I know this because I've already seen it happen to other Negroes who went against the Southern system."

Scobell paused, letting his words sink in. "Arrest by the Confederates, on even the slightest suspicion of espionage, would be a death sentence – a slow, painful death – for me."

"I can see how that might be the case," Pinkerton replied. "Still, I believe a man of your talents would be useful to the Union cause – and to the cause of your people."

Scobell's attitude hardened at the detective's blatant change in tactics. "You clearly know nothing of my people. If you did, you wouldn't be asking me to do this."

Pinkerton stared at him, the steel-gray eyes boring into Scobell's own soft, brown ones. "Mr. Scobell," he snapped, "You told me earlier today that your master had set you free."

"That's correct," Scobell asserted, curious at another sudden switch in direction.

"However," Pinkerton went on, "you have no proof of this. I have nothing but your own word that this is true."

Suspicion creeping into his mind, Scobell simply answered, "Yes." It didn't come out as authoritatively as he'd intended.

His clipped Scottish burr picking up speed again, Pinkerton continued. "Being an abolitionist myself, allow me to add a condition to my proposal. Agree to join the secret service and successfully complete the mission I assign you. Upon your return, I will personally sign an oath attesting to your emancipation, which you can use to secure your free papers."

The carrot, Scobell thought.

"Should you choose to decline my offer, you will remain a contraband. Mr. Bangs will see that you're moved to Fort Monroe with the other escaped slaves. There you can earn your eight-dollar monthly wage, tend fields, and make yourself useful as you see fit."

And the stick.

"If our army wins this war," Pinkerton went on, "they may set you free. Of course, who can say how long that might take? Months? A year? More than that?"

Scobell's jaw clenched and the cords in his neck throbbed as he tried to contain his rage.

Pinkerton, seemingly oblivious to this reaction, continued. "And in the tragic event that the South should maintain their secession...well, who knows what might happen to the contrabands? A return to enslavement, perhaps. A return to something much worse, in retribution for their attempted escape?"

He stopped and let the question hang in the air. Scobell remained silent, shifting his gaze away from the spy chief's face and staring out the window behind him instead.

"Before you respond to my offer," Pinkerton said, "I should like you to take this evening to sleep on it. Reflect carefully on my proposition, considering both the opportunity to serve your country and your people in their efforts for freedom. And, of course, the consequences should you decline. Meet me here at eight o'clock tomorrow morning and let me know your answer."

Scobell sat quietly for a moment. "Mr. Pinkerton," he said at last, "I appreciate your assessment of my abilities and the offer of employment. I will let you know my answer in the morning."

As Scobell walked out of the office, he heard papers rustling on Pinkerton's desk behind him. Apparently, the spy chief had already moved on to other business.

CHAPTER 5

That night Scobell slept only fitfully. When slumber finally came, he didn't dream of green fields and yellow flowers. Instead, he clawed through the black, frigid waters of the Potomac once again, this time with no floating log for support.

He flailed wildly to stay afloat, but no amount of thrashing could keep his head above water. When his head went below the surface, he saw dozens of skeletons gliding through the river's inky waters.

Each one wore the blue uniform of a Union soldier.

Their eyes were empty sockets, as black as the water that flowed through them. Their teeth protruded from their bony jaws in frozen, hideous grins.

Horrified as he was at the soldiers' appearance, he was even more terrified when those closest to him reached out to pull him down. Their gaunt fingers clawed at his limbs, dragging him downward with irresistible strength.

Scobell punched and kicked at the swirling ghouls, but it was futile. He was slipping deeper, his arms and legs moving as though they were in molasses instead of water.

Suddenly, a skeleton came face to face with him. Grasping his shoulders, the corpse shoved Scobell downward to the bottom of the river. He screamed, but no sound came forth.

Scobell bounced awake. Peering through the darkness, he realized he was alive, warm and dry, in bed.

His heart hammered, and several minutes passed before his panting breath returned to normal. Another two hours passed before sleep finally came again.

Promptly at eight the following morning, Bangs ushered Scobell again into Pinkerton's cluttered office. The Scotsman, once again without looking up, stabbed an open hand toward the unoccupied chair in front of the desk.

Scobell resumed his position from the previous day. He sat in silence, waiting for the Union spy chief to finish.

Signing a sheet of paper with a flourish and setting it to the side of his desk, Pinkerton looked up to acknowledge him at last. "Mr. Scobell," he said without preamble. "Have you reached a decision?"

"Yes. Although, I'm not sure you left me much of a choice."

Pinkerton looked pleased with himself. "That was my intent."

"I'm sure," said Scobell drily.

"I've risked my life several times to gain my freedom," he continued. "You're asking me to do that yet again."

He stopped, the words sticking in his throat. With an effort, he forced them out. "I will accept your offer and become an operative of your secret service. As long as you swear you'll guarantee my full emancipation when my mission is complete."

"You have my oath on it," Pinkerton responded immediately.

Not waiting to be dismissed, Scobell stood and headed toward the door. As his hand reached for the knob, he turned back toward the man behind the desk.

"You've threatened my liberty, Mr. Pinkerton, the very thing I value most. If I don't survive your mission and never get to live free, that will lie on your head. Forever."

The two men locked eyes once again. This time, though, it was Scobell's stare that pierced more deeply.

Pinkerton blinked, then gave a slight nod. "I understand."

I doubt that, Scobell thought as he turned and left the room.

⎯⎯◉⎯⎯

For the next two weeks, Scobell underwent intensive training with the operatives in Washington, many of whom arrived from the Pinkerton National Detective Agency in Chicago. The agency's motto was "We Never Sleep." To Scobell, it certainly felt that way. He shifted rapidly from one training session to another for up to 16 hours each day and night.

Pryce Lewis conducted Scobell's initial session. Like Scobell, Lewis was in his late twenties. That's where any similarities ended.

A Welshman by birth, Lewis had been working for Pinkerton's agency for just a few months when the war broke out. He had dark, curly hair and enormously bushy sideburns that crowded down toward his moustache and bare chin. About two inches taller than Scobell, Lewis was thin and his ever-present stovepipe hat made him appear even lankier.

Lewis schooled Scobell on assuming a role, Pinkerton's terminology for spying in disguise. "The key is not just to assume the role, but maintain it long enough to gather useful information," said Lewis. "You have to act as your character would act at all times. If pressed or questioned, respond as your character would respond, never as you'd wish to respond yourself."

Scobell hadn't the heart to tell Lewis that he'd spent most of his life doing exactly that. Slaves couldn't afford the luxury of responding as they wished.

"When you go behind Rebel lines, we'll naturally have you assume the role of a slave," said Lewis. "Since you've been a slave most of your life, I assume this is a part you can play with ease?"

"The easiest thing for a black man to be in this country is a slave," said Scobell. "The hard part is being something else."

Lewis looked uncomfortable for a moment, searching for a response. After letting him dangle a moment, Scobell let him off the hook.

"Of course, I can assume the role of a slave. Why, I be the best slave in these heah parts, Massa," Scobell said, a toothy grin suddenly appearing on his face. "Ain't nobody ever work harder or better'n me pickin' cotton, that's fo' sho.'"

Lewis forgot the awkward moment and laughed out loud at the sudden shift in character. "Yes, Mr. Scobell," he said through his chuckle, "I do believe you'll be a natural at assuming a role."

Using Pinkerton's wartime alias, Lewis continued, "Major Allen believes this will let you move freely without arising suspicion. Do you agree?"

"No doubt," said Scobell, a dark undertone in his voice. "They don't look at a black man down south as a person. The Secesh look at him like you'd look at a dog or a horse, meaning they ignore him unless they need him to do some job they wouldn't."

"Secesh?" asked Lewis.

"Secessionists, the Rebels," explained Scobell. "Your Major Allen is right on that point. I doubt they'd think a Negro was smart enough to do them any harm."

"Use that to your advantage then," said Lewis. "The more they think you a fool, the deeper you'll be able to penetrate their inner circles and the more you'll be able to learn."

"Have you done this yourself?" Scobell asked.

Welcoming the invitation, Lewis launched into the tale of his own first adventure in assuming a role. In the summer of 1861, he and another Pinkerton agent named Sam Bridgeman traveled to the Kanawha Valley of Virginia. Their assignment was to scout the area and determine the plans of the Rebel troops who were active there.

"So I put on airs and played the part of an English nobleman," Lewis said, replacing his own Welsh accent with an exaggerated aristocratic British one. "Bridgeman was my trusty manservant," he added with a chuckle.

"It went perfectly at first," said Lewis. "Confederate soldiers intercepted us near the James River, just as we planned. They took us to their commander, a quite genial chap named Colonel George Patton."

Scobell noticed Lewis was continuing to tell the tale in his British nobleman accent. He wondered if that was deliberate or unconscious.

"As I said, you must respond as your character would respond," Lewis said. "When we got to their camp, I started complaining to the good colonel about how poorly they'd treated us and asking why an Englishman should be so roguishly handled."

It took some gall to complain about poor treatment after deliberately being captured, Scobell thought. He said, "What did this Colonel Patton say to all that?"

Grinning broadly, Lewis said. "He started apologizing. Then he ordered us a couple of cigars and some wine, and we had a first-class dinner."

"Did you get any useful information out of him?" asked Scobell, impressed at Lewis's brazenness.

"Oh my, yes," said Lewis. "He gave me the exact location of his camp, the exact number of soldiers he had available, and the precise area his commander had ordered him to defend."

Lewis paused. With a wink, he added, "As I recall, most of that information came out about halfway through the third bottle of wine."

"So how were you able to get the word back to the North?" asked Scobell. "Were they able to use it?"

"It proved quite valuable to General McClellan in his western Virginia campaign," announced Lewis proudly. "Patton released us in the morning and we made our way into Kentucky, with a pass signed by him in my pocket. From there, we rode back north to Cincinnati, where Major Allen was based then."

"McClellan was just moving into that part of Virginia, so the major immediately sent me to the general's field quarters to relay the intelligence."

Scobell noted that Bridgeman had disappeared from the narrative. Lewis had become a team of one, at least in his recollection of events.

"Using the information I gave him on the Rebels' location and condition," Lewis said, "our troops moved around to the southeast and attacked the Confederates from the rear."

"A complete victory," he continued. "The Rebels retreated, leaving Charleston and the Kanawha River in the control of our army. They even mentioned it in the *New York Times*!"

His tone turned wistful. "Of course, there was no mention of where McClellan got his information or why he decided on such a brilliant strategic move." Lewis looked Scobell in the eye. "It must always be so, of course. It's for your safety and the integrity of the secret service...and the Union. Being an operative is both a blessing and a curse. In this role, you accept that you'll never receive credit for your best work."

"I can see that," replied Scobell. He was already quite familiar with the concept.

———◉———

Scobell moved from one agent-tutor to another, with the busy streets of Washington often serving as the classroom. A short, soft-spoken Pennsylvanian named William Ascot taught him the technique of shadowing a target by following them at a safe distance so as not to raise suspicion. Augustus Littlefield, a hawk-nosed man with a beard and mustache so bushy they nearly obscured his face, showed Scobell how to estimate troop numbers. They practiced daily by watching the troops marching around the capitol, with occasional simulated reconnaissance trips to the Union camps outside the city.

Timothy Webster, an Englishman by birth who'd worked as a Pinkerton operative for nearly five years prior to the war, coached Scobell on the art of "pumping." This was Pinkerton's term for interrogating using indirect questions in a conversational tone. Again, Scobell practiced on the streets of the city, striking up conversations with everyone from soldiers to newspaper boys, to see what information he could glean. It surprised him how easily people opened up, especially when he held onto the guise of an ignorant slave.

Toward the end of the first week, Scobell climbed into a wagon with a Pinkerton operative named John Scully and rode northeast from the I Street office to Fort Bunker Hill just outside the city. Scully, a genial Irishman, chatted ceaselessly with Scobell as they rode along. He pointed out interesting locations along the way and regaled Scobell with tales of earlier missions, both before and during the war.

When they got to the fort, Scully hopped down from the wagon and walked around to the back. As Scobell joined him, the Irishman said, "The others have been teaching you how to do your job and how not to get caught. That's good. Those are things you need to know."

"Today," he continued, "I'm going to teach you what to do when things go wrong. You may be great at this spy game, but at some point, everything will turn to shite, you understand? That's when you'll need to know how to defend yourself."

Scobell nodded soberly.

"Ever shot a gun before?" Scully asked.

"No," said Scobell. "A black man with a gun isn't too popular where I come from."

"I suppose that's true," said Scully. "Well, today we're going to make up for lost time."

He opened a long wooden trunk in the wagon's bed to reveal a small arsenal: three rifles and a half-dozen handguns.

"This ought to be enough to get started," Scully said. He pulled out a rifle and handed it to Scobell. "This here's a Springfield rifle," Scully announced. "Truthfully, there's not much call for using a rifle in our line of work, but we're gonna shoot a couple today, anyway."

He gave Scobell a mischievous look, then added, "Mostly just 'cause it's fun."

Scobell had seen plenty of muzzleloading rifles used at home, both for hunting and then after the war broke out. Although he'd never done it himself, he was familiar with the loading process: black powder poured down the barrel, followed by a lead projectile. The Springfield used what Scully called a minié ball, but to Scobell, it didn't look like a ball at all. Cone-shaped on the front and with an indentation on the rear, Scobell thought the minié ball looked like a small, tubular arrowhead.

Scully quickly explained the workings of the gun as Scobell held it in his hands. The Irishman stepped him through loading it, then they walked over to an empty drill area where fresh wooden targets stood. "Believe it or not, that Springfield will knock a man out of his saddle 500 yards out."

Scobell grunted softly, looking down at the rifle in his hands.

"Only problem is, the damn Rebs captured the rifle works at Harpers Ferry, so now we can't make these anymore," said Scully. He pointed to a white target painted on the range. "That's only about 75 yards, so you ought to be able to kill it with no problem at all."

Scobell pulled the rifle to his shoulder tentatively. He tried to line up the sights on the barrel as Scully had instructed, but he was already preparing for the noise and recoil, and the rifle wavered in his hands. His nerves were getting the better of him.

"Easy now," said Scully. "Hold it steady. It ain't gonna bite you. Just a little bang."

Scobell took a deep breath and fired. A loud boom barked from the rifle, followed by a cloud of smoke that enveloped Scobell's head and obscured the target. It surprised him; neither the sound nor the kick of the rifle was as bad as he expected.

"See, I told you," Scully said with a smile. "Just a little bang. It wasn't too bad, was it?"

"No," said Scobell with surprise in his voice. "It wasn't bad at all. Did I hit the target?"

Scully laughed loudly. "Not hardly," he replied. "I hope there wasn't a man 500 yards out there on a horse 'cause you might've done him some damage, but that target didn't get a scratch."

"Let me give it another try," said Scobell eagerly.

"Aye," said Scully. He grabbed the supplies to reload. "That's what we came here for."

The two men continued the process, Scobell firing and Scully coaching. They tried the other rifles from the trunk, switching first to a Sharps and then a Smith carbine. Scobell's aim quickly improved to the extent that he was consistently grouping his shots within a few inches of each other near the center of the target.

"Shoulder getting sore at all?" inquired Scully. They had been shooting for over an hour.

"A bit," admitted Scobell. Truthfully, he'd been feeling pain from the recoil for a while, but didn't want to admit it.

"Don't worry," said Scully amiably. "That happens to everyone, especially on their first day shooting." He walked back over toward the wagon. "Let's switch over to the pistols and give that shoulder a rest."

As Scully explained the intricacies of each handgun, it amazed Scobell to see that a few of them didn't use loose powder or even paper cartridges to load. Instead, they used brass casings that contained both powder and a lead ball.

The Smith and Wesson Model 1 particularly impressed him. It was small – barely bigger than Scobell's hand – but the six-shot cylinders took only a few seconds to load with their brass cartridges. And, as Scully was quick to point out, it was plenty powerful enough to kill.

"This looks tiny," he said, "but it's no lady's gun. It's more accurate than a pepperbox or derringer, and will put a man down at fifty feet. Plus, it's easier to hide than one of those big Colts that the soldiers carry. That's kind of nice in our line of work."

More confident now, Scobell proved to be a quick study with the pistol. Scully took note. "You're damn good for a first-timer," he said with admiration. "Maybe better than me. What's your secret?"

"Just telling myself to stay steady," Scobell replied. "That, and picturing the massa's face on the target."

Scully howled with laughter. "That's good," he said. "At least you aren't picturing me!"

As the two men rode back to the city after the training session, Scully said, "You know, the boys are getting together for a bit this evening at my house. We can't be seen out together, as you'd expect, but we sometimes gather at someone's house for a little food and company. You'd be more than welcome if you'd like to stop by."

"Thank you," said Scobell, looking at the passing countryside. "That sounds nice."

⸺◉⸺

Dinner was, in fact, a jolly affair. None of Pinkerton's female agents were in Washington at the moment, but there were about a dozen men in town and nearly all of them attended – with the notable exception of Pinkerton himself. Scobell wondered if they had even invited the boss, although he doubted, given Pinkerton's stern demeanor, that he would've accepted.

It surprised Scobell at how much friendlier and relaxed some of them seemed here than they had at work. Scully was his usual cheerful self, but some of the other men were almost completely opposite from the taut and serious demeanors he'd seen during the week. He realized that their burden was a heavy one. They bore not only the constant dangers of their critical missions, but also the added stress of maintaining a façade while carrying them out.

Tonight, however, as they gathered after dinner around the glowing fire in Scully's parlor, those concerns seemed to be forgotten. Even Tim Webster, who'd seemed somewhat aloof when Scobell met him earlier, joked and laughed with the other men.

"What are we going to do without our little songbird here this evening?" Webster called out jovially. "Kate's down in Richmond and we've no one to sing or play for us."

"Aye," said Scully. "The lovely Mrs. Warne's hard at work tonight, so we'll have to make do with these rascals instead. Bridgeman here can play the piano, can't you, my man?"

"Yes, I suppose I might pound the keys a bit," said Bridgeman in his British accent.

"But he sings like a crow!" protested Harry Davies, the affable young operative from New Orleans. "I heard him when we worked together in Baltimore. The equipment in an iron works has more musical ability!" The men roared with laughter at this, including Bridgeman.

"We all squawk like crows when we sing," chimed in Alexander Gardner. "That's why we always let Kate do it!" Gardner was a Scotsman with a dark, flowing beard and a high forehead topped by a thatch of long, black hair. He was Pinkerton's photographer, taking both battlefield photos and landscape shots to help the Union topographers with their mapping efforts.

"What about Scobell here?" said Davies, turning to the newest recruit. "We haven't heard him squawk yet."

"What about it, Scobell?" asked Scully. "Can you carry a tune for us?"

"I suppose I can try," said Scobell.

"Can't be any worse than Bridgeman," said Davies. Bridgeman thumbed his nose in reply.

Scobell walked to where Bridgeman sat at the piano. "Do you know the song *Killiekrankie*?" he asked the Englishman.

"Yes, I do," said Bridgeman with mild surprise. "You know that one?"

Scobell smiled. "My master was from Scotland. He taught me a few songs from there."

"A tune from Robbie Burns!" Gardner interjected. "From my beloved land of the thistle. I can't wait to hear this!" He fairly squirmed in his chair with anticipation.

Scobell nodded toward Bridgeman, who played the opening notes of the upbeat tune. Scobell then opened his mouth and sang:

Where hae ye been sae braw, lad?
Where hae ye been sae brankie-o?
Where hae ye been sae braw, lad?
Cam' ye by Killiecrankie-o?

As he continued through the song, the other men in the room looked first at him and then at each other, exchanging glances of shocked admiration. Scobell's deep baritone voice was smooth as glass and seemed to wash over them in tranquil waves.

On the second time through the chorus, Gardner joined in. By the time Scobell reached the last round, everyone in the room was singing the chorus.

When he finished, the men applauded loudly. A couple of them, including Gardner, cheered.

"That," said Webster, "was wonderful! What a beautiful singing voice. Why, I'd venture to say that it's even finer than Mrs. Warne's – and that's no small compliment!"

"Let's hear another!" shouted Davies.

"Another Scottish song!" added Gardner. "Do you know any ballads?"

And so it went for the rest of the evening: Scobell's resounding, melodic voice singing to Bridgeman's accompaniment on the piano. He sang every Scottish ballad he knew then, given the season, switched to Christmas carols. Everyone cheerfully sang along with him to *Hark, the Herald Angels Sing* and *O Come, All Ye Faithful*.

Late in the evening, Scobell stepped to the center of the room and said, "I'd like to sing one I learned down in Mississippi." The room hushed as he sang:

We raise de wheat, dey gib us de corn;
We bake de bread, dey gib us de cruss;
We sif de meal, dey gib us de huss;
We peal de meat, dey gib us de skin;
And dat's de way dey takes us in.
We skim de pot, dey gib us de liquor;
And say dat's good enough for nigger.
Walk over! Walk over! Tom butter and de fat;
Poor nigger, you can't get over dat; Walk over!

A sudden silence replaced the boisterous humor of a few moments prior. Sensing the sudden uneasiness in the room, Scobell immediately launched into a more familiar song, *Nobody Knows the Trouble I've Seen*. The men applauded again when he finished, but the song had broken the spell. He'd reminded them of the troubling life Scobell and so many other slaves had faced. And the frightful war, which had stalled outside the walls of the snug parlor for a few hours, seeped back into their reality once again.

As the evening grew late and the night cold, each of the men, alone or in groups of two or three, took their leave. Each of them thanked Scully for his hospitality and, to a man, complimented Scobell on his wonderful singing.

As Scobell dressed to leave, Scully shook his hand and added his compliments to those of the group. "You've got a lovely singing voice there," said Scully.

"I doubt I've heard anyone who's your equal – and I've heard some charming crooners back in Ireland. But you top them all, Scobell." Scully clapped him on the shoulder.

Embarrassed by the attention, Scobell mumbled his thanks.

"I'll tell you something else," said Scully. "You're going to make an excellent spy."

"Excuse me," he corrected himself, "Major E. J. Allen doesn't like us using the word 'spy.' You're going to be an excellent operative. I admire your bravery, being willing to go back south when you've already earned your freedom."

As if I had a choice, thought Scobell. He nodded and looked into the darkness beyond the doorway. "Thank you again for your kind words," said Scobell soberly.

Scully shook his hand. "Godspeed to you, then."

"And to you," said Scobell. He stepped out the door into the icy December night.

CHAPTER 6

One week later, Scobell found himself back in Pinkerton's I Street office. This time, Tim Webster sat next to him. The two men were receiving their orders for what would be Scobell's first return behind Confederate lines.

As Pinkerton spoke, Scobell glanced over at Webster. He was a shade taller than Scobell and narrower through the shoulders. Though he'd been born in England, his family had moved to New Jersey when he was young and he'd long ago lost any remaining accent. Webster had thick, wavy black hair and wore his beard neatly trimmed. His green eyes rested atop high cheekbones on his elongated face, giving him a perpetually melancholy expression.

Scobell had already heard that Webster was instrumental in breaking up a plot to assassinate President Lincoln before the war. Posing as a Southern sympathizer, the longtime Pinkerton operative had infiltrated a Baltimore group called the Knights of Liberty, whose intent was to murder Lincoln as he traveled through their city on the way to his inauguration.

It was largely Webster's inside intelligence on the situation that allowed Pinkerton and Kate Warne to foil the murder plot by orchestrating Lincoln's clandestine entrance to Washington under the cover of night. It was clear from the way Pinkerton spoke to Webster, and from the way the other operatives treated him, that he had earned their respect – and more important, their trust – through his actions in Baltimore.

Scobell couldn't help but wonder if that was why he was partnering with Webster on this first mission behind enemy lines. It seemed reasonable that Pinkerton would send his best agent to accompany a completely inexperienced man on his first mission.

"Now then," Pinkerton was saying, "I want the two of you to travel together until you reach Leonardtown in Maryland. At that point, you will detach and move separately. Webster, you are to proceed west to

Fredericksburg and then south to Richmond. Scobell, I wish you to travel northwest to Dumfries, Virginia, and then continue north to Centreville."

"You are to gather the most reliable information available on the location and strength of the enemy in these areas," Pinkerton continued. "As always, I expect you to prepare detailed reports containing this information and return them to me with the utmost expediency."

Addressing Webster, Pinkerton said, "You are, of course, quite familiar with the procedures. I think it best that you attempt to renew your acquaintance with Mr. Miller and some of your former Baltimore associates. They may have insight into the current designs of the Rebel army."

Turning to Scobell, Pinkerton directed, "I expect you to rely on your wit and intuition as to the information you will gather. At a minimum, however, I expect troop estimates and artillery counts from each fortification that you encounter, as well as any maps of those forts and their environs that you can create."

"Those are your orders, gentlemen. Questions?" asked the secret service chief.

Webster answered, "No, sir." Scobell simply shook his head.

"Excellent," said Pinkerton. "Please proceed with all due caution and may fortune attend you. I hope that you come home safely."

As the two agents stood, Pinkerton added in a friendly tone, "Mr. Scobell, I hear from a few of the men that you have an extraordinary talent as a singer. Is that correct?"

Scobell hesitated, but Webster jumped in quickly and said, "He's quite wonderful, sir. People in the finest concert halls would pay to hear him."

"That good, eh?" said Pinkerton with a slight smile. "Use that if there's an opportunity, Scobell. Music can make a wonderful distraction and is an excellent tool to disarm people who might otherwise suspect you."

"Yes, sir," replied Scobell.

Both operatives turned to leave, but Pinkerton said, "Webster, I'd like a short word with you. Scobell, you are free to go."

As Scobell headed out the door, he heard the Scotsman say, "I want you to look after Scobell there. He seems like a good man, but there may be trouble along the way..." The conversation continued, but Scobell couldn't hear any more as he walked down the hallway.

Within the hour, Webster and Scobell were walking through Washington, headed to a stagecoach stop on the east side of the city. Once on the stage, they would pretend not to know each other but as they moved through the capitol, they talked freely.

In response to Scobell's queries, Webster filled in a few details of his experience in Baltimore and how he had penetrated the Knights of Liberty. Webster explained how he'd acted as a Northerner who secretly had Southern sympathies, so he might ingratiate himself into the secret network of Rebel operatives. All the while, he reported the activities of the Confederate conspirators back to the US Army through Pinkerton.

No wonder Webster seemed aloof at first. As a former slave, Scobell was a man who understood keeping secrets. The double life had to keep Webster's nerves on edge constantly.

In short order, they reached the station and boarded the stage for Leonardtown. Webster rode inside while Scobell climbed onto the cramped, external bench seat on the rear of the coach.

Across his back was slung a soft bag containing extra clothes. After two weeks of enjoying new, clean garments in Washington, he was back to wearing slave garb. His outfit consisted of a baggy cotton flannel shirt under an equally roomy wool jacket that looked as though he had recently pulled it from a trash heap. His tattered denim pants barely scraped the tops of his scuffed leather boots, and a battered felt hat rode atop his head.

He had kicked all the clothes through the mud prior to donning them in order to achieve a suitably shabby appearance. In his pocket was a pass, written in Webster's hand, explaining that he was on an errand for his fictitious master to bring building supplies from Leonardtown back to Rockville, Maryland.

Perched alone on the back of the rumbling stagecoach, huddled against the biting December wind, Scobell suddenly felt forlorn. Perhaps it was changing from his clean clothes back into the rags that had for so long characterized his bondage. Or perhaps it was the sudden realization that he was leaving the safety and fellowship he'd found in Washington for the danger that lay ahead in Virginia.

Scobell couldn't be sure of the source. He only knew that, in a life baptized in heartache and loneliness, he'd never felt more dismal and alone.

———◆———

When they reached Leonardtown, the two agents disembarked the stage without acknowledging each other's presence. Webster motioned for a porter to carry his bags to the Fenwick Hotel, one of just two in this tiny hamlet on the edge of Breton Bay. Scobell, his pack slung across his shoulders, moved off to find lodging among the local slave population.

Leonardtown was technically Union territory – in fact, a small contingent of the Union Navy occupied it. They made regular sweeps looking for smugglers taking weapons and other goods across the wide Potomac into Confederate Virginia. Still, Scobell's practiced eye could pick out every earmark of a secessionist town, from the obvious presence of dozens of slaves to the furtive glares cast by the white citizenry at the Union sailors.

At the south end of town, he found a plantation owned by the Key family, where he quickly struck up a conversation with a few of the slaves. As Scobell tried out his new pumping skills, the slaves confirmed his suspicions of the predominant local sympathies. They also told him that, despite the Union Navy's presence, there was quite an active smuggling business across the Potomac.

With assurances from the Key plantation slaves that he could stay there for the night, Scobell headed back toward town to relay his information to Webster and find a boat passage across the Potomac.

Scobell had not only changed his clothing and manner of speaking to re-assume the role of a slave, but he had shifted his entire demeanor. He stood with a practiced slouch, looking mostly at the ground, and moved with a shuffling gait that was half his natural pace. Although eager to reach Webster and confer, he reminded himself to shamble along slowly.

When Scobell was within a block of the Fenwick Hotel, he saw Webster walk out the front door and stop to light a cigar. Taking a deep draw, Webster looked up and down the main street, seemingly deciding which way to take a leisurely stroll. For a split second, the pair locked eyes. Webster, giving no sign of recognition, stepped off the sidewalk and headed down Fenwick Street.

Scobell stopped at the next street and turned right, paralleling Webster a block to the south. Although they could no longer see each other, the two men intuitively moved on intersecting paths and, within a few minutes, met up with each other in an overgrown apple orchard at the edge of town. As Scobell opened his mouth to speak, Webster placed a finger on his own lips and then motioned for them to step behind a dilapidated shed to talk.

After a careful look around to ascertain that they were completely alone, Webster looked at Scobell and said, "Go ahead."

"I talked to some slaves at a plantation down by the bay," said Scobell. "They tell me there's a regular smuggling operation running from here to the Confederates on the Virginia side of the river."

"That's good information. I'll put that in my report," said Webster. "Now I've got some news of my own. And I need you to do something important."

Webster quickly relayed a conversation he'd had with Mr. Miller, proprietor of the Fenwick Hotel and a fervent secessionist. "He might even be the one orchestrating this smuggling ring you're talking about," said Webster.

"He told me there's a Union Army doctor here in town. The doctor's from out west, but his family are Southerners," relayed the veteran spy calmly, but quickly. "According to Miller, this Dr. Gurley is ready to desert to the Rebels. Not only that, but he's carrying messages to Judah Benjamin, the new Confederate Secretary of War."

Scobell let out a low whistle.

"That's where you come in," said Webster. "I need you to grab that packet of papers."

The older operative quickly outlined his plan. Dr. Gurley was due back at the hotel later that afternoon. Webster would have Miller introduce him, and they would visit for a while.

"You watch the hotel – without being noticed," he said to Scobell. "When you see me step out the front door and tip my hat, you'll know the man with me is Gurley. He's staying with some friends north of town, so shadow him until you get the opportunity. Then jump him and get that packet."

Scobell nodded his understanding.

"Do whatever you need to do to get those papers," said Webster. "But don't get caught and don't kill him. Either of those would make too much of a ruckus in a little town like this."

"Don't worry," said Scobell with a wry smile. "We'll give the good doctor his medicine."

<hr>

The younger agent, knowing he had a few hours to kill, moved slowly around Leonardtown. He chatted up the black inhabitants he encountered and surreptitiously observed the white ones. As he'd learned from a lifetime of experience, slaves often knew the comings and goings of every person, black or white, in a small town. That was a process he intended to use to his advantage at every opportunity.

Scrounging a meal at a slave quarters in town, he asked in passing whether there were any unknown visitors in the village. Within minutes, one woman volunteered that there was a doctor named Gurley visiting a family that lived just outside of town. With a few more casual questions, Scobell determined the house where Gurley was staying and the best way to get there.

Much to his surprise, he also gathered another critical piece of information regarding secret activities in Leonardtown. He resolved to stow that intelligence away until needed.

After his meal, Scobell set out to scout the route from the Fenwick to Dr. Gurley's guest residence. He noted that the road narrowed considerably at the edge of town, where a thick cluster of trees crowded against it. The leaves had already fallen, so it wouldn't provide the thick cover that he might have wanted, but it was clearly the best spot for an ambush.

By evening, Scobell had stationed himself outside the hotel, slouching unobtrusively on a set of wooden stairs on the opposite side of the street and a few doors down. He hummed to himself, loud enough to be heard by passersby, but not enough to attract undue attention.

Two hours passed with no sign of Webster. Sitting still and unable to abandon his post, Scobell pulled his coat tighter against the bitter December wind howling off of Breton Bay. The light spilling from the hotel's front barroom tormented him with its warm, inviting glow.

A slight movement caught his attention just a few feet away. A scroungy, orange tomcat had slipped out of a window well and was padding along the street.

Scobell liked cats. They went where they pleased and answered to no one. Dogs, horses, even mules, could be trained to serve the demands of people. Cats had no masters.

"Psh, psh," he called, rubbing his thumb and forefinger in the direction of the feline. It came a few steps closer, stopping just out of reach. From there, it regarded him with suspicion, then suddenly darted back toward the window well and disappeared into the night.

At that moment, two figures walked out of the tavern doors and paused on the front porch. Scobell quickly recognized the tall figure of Tim Webster as one of them.

The two men engaged in a congenial and lengthy goodbye. They shook hands, exchanged a few more words, and clapped each other on the shoulders. Finally, the second figure, shorter and portlier than the athletically built Webster, turned away and headed up the street.

Webster stepped to the edge of the porch, looked up at the sky, and removed his hat as though to get a better look at the clouds that gathered across the moon. "There's going to be a shower," he said to no one in particular as he turned and strode back into the barroom. "The doctor will have to walk fast to escape it."

Scobell eased himself off of the staircase and stretched as he stood. His slow movements were partly for show, but also partly because of the stiffness that had set in during hours of sitting in the cold. He unhurriedly ambled to his left, opposite the direction that the doctor had taken, then turned up the next alley.

Once out of sight in the dark alley, Scobell picked up his pace. Reaching the next street, he again turned left so that he was now moving in the same direction as Gurley. Checking carefully that no one was watching, Scobell broke into a quick trot and headed for the woods at the edge of town.

Even the quick glimpse he'd had of the doctor in front of the hotel gave Scobell confidence that he would easily arrive at the forest ahead of the deserter. Gurley was short-legged and stout, and had been drinking with Webster in the hotel bar all evening. The doctor wouldn't be in any great hurry, despite the chill wind at his back.

Scobell still ran faster than intended and was a bit out of breath when he reached the spot he'd selected. He silently cursed his nerves.

He walked to the edge of the trail and peered furtively in both directions. Seeing no one, he ducked back into the trees and found the enormous oak tree he had mentally marked earlier. Its three-foot wide trunk would easily conceal him as he waited.

Scobell stood with his back to the tree, out of sight of the trail. He sucked a long gasp of brisk air into his lungs to calm himself. Still, his breath came too quickly and his hands trembled, even though he was no longer cold.

Frustrated at his inability to relax, he turned his thoughts to the matter at hand. He needed a plan to disable the doctor and safely lift the dispatch package.

It would have to be quick and it would have to be quiet. Scobell couldn't risk having Gurley run off before he could grab the letters and, just as important, he couldn't risk having the doctor shouting for help and drawing a crowd. The nearest buildings in town were too close to risk any kind of uproar.

Scobell had been in plenty of scraps with other slaves on the plantation. With the frustrating humiliation and inhumanity of bondage, fighting seemed almost a natural extension of the captive life. Years of picking cotton from its prickly stems had hardened his fists, and hauling bales and plowing fields had made his shoulders powerful. Brawling allowed a release, however temporary, of the resentment borne of confinement.

Suddenly, however, it occurred to the former slave that he'd never struck a white man. In fact, he'd been taught his entire life that striking someone with fair skin would result in the most severe punishment – whipping, or even death. Yet here he stood, hiding in a pitch black forest, waiting to do exactly that.

An odd sound coming from the direction of town brought Scobell out of his reverie. After a moment, he realized it was the sound of whistling that reached his ears above the gusts of wind.

Peeking around the tree, he spied Gurley about fifty yards away. The traitor physician shuffled drunkenly down the trail with his head tilted back, whistling loudly as he walked.

Scobell pulled his head back behind the oak and took another deep breath. A bead of sweat that had gathered at his hairline suddenly raced down his right cheek, following the front of his ear. The droplet rested briefly at the back of his jaw, then slid slowly down his neck into the collar of his shirt.

As the doctor drew closer, Scobell recognized the song he was blowing through his pursed lips as *Jingle Bells*. The absurdity of the song – of the entire situation – abruptly hit Scobell. He had to forcibly suppress a laugh.

After a few more tense moments, the unsuspecting doctor was close enough for Scobell to hear his footsteps. The operative waited even longer, until he could hear the labored breathing between the whistled bars of music.

As Gurley reached the oak, Scobell spun suddenly from behind it and fired his right hand, low and hard, into the doctor's side. He had hoped to catch the fat man in the ribs, a blow Scobell figured would be instantly disabling. But his fist had instead caught the man's ample belly, penetrating to what seemed an impossible depth before finally coming to a stop. The spy had to wrench his hand back to retrieve it.

Caught completely unawares by the sudden strike, the Rebel sympathizer doubled over, teetered for a moment on the balls of his feet, then pitched forward onto his face. He landed hard in the dirt and gravel, bounced slightly, then rolled onto his left side and lay still.

For a split second, a rush of fear shot through Scobell. He'd killed him, exactly what Webster had warned him not to do. How could it have happened from just one punch? He stepped closer and peered down at the body.

As he did, he heard a gurgle issue from the doctor's throat, followed by a sudden wheeze and a soft moan. Then a hasty rush of air escaped from Scobell's own lungs as he sighed in relief. Gurley wasn't dead; he'd merely had the wind knocked out of him.

Quickly gathering himself, Scobell bent over and patted the doctor's coat to find the package of letters. A hurried glance at the poor man's face told him the doctor would never recognize him: Gurley's eyes squeezed tightly shut, and he launched into a fit of coughing and choking as his breath returned.

Scobell whipped open the doctor's coat and pulled the thick packet of letters from the breast pocket. He quickly tucked it inside his own coat. Then he looked down at the quivering lump of humanity on the road beside him.

For an instant, he considered delivering one more kick to the deserter's midsection. Aside from the doctor, no one would ever know. And after the rush of the first punch he'd delivered, Scobell knew how good it would feel to give him another shot before leaving.

But he couldn't bring himself to do it. As satisfying as it would've been, it wouldn't have been right. And he was tired of what wasn't right.

Instead, Scobell turned and loped off into the darkened woods, carefully clutching the stolen package to his breast as he ran.

CHAPTER 7

Thirty minutes later, Scobell spied Webster, who appeared to be enjoying an after-dinner stroll down Fenwick Street. From a dark side alley, Scobell beckoned Webster to join him.

They hurried to a secluded spot on the outskirts of the tiny village. After glancing around to make sure no one had followed them, Scobell quickly recounted the events in the woods. He added that he'd left the deserting doctor alive, in case there was any question.

"Yes, I saw him when he staggered back into the hotel," said Webster with a smile. "He was alive for certain, but you dented him up pretty well. He couldn't stand up straight and his face looked like he'd been dragged behind a horse."

Scobell suppressed his own grin. "He didn't see me, though?"

"No," said Webster. "All he knew was that he got hit by a thunderbolt and that his dispatches were gone. What's more, the letters were sealed so he didn't know what he was carrying. He can't even pass along a report to his contacts. Which brings us to the matter at hand – what did you get from him?"

As he handed over the packet, Scobell said, "I opened the letters. They're written in some kind of code."

"A code?" Webster repeated, eagerly pulling the letters out of the envelope.

Scobell nodded. "Just looks like a bunch of jumbled letters. But from the spacing and how they're written, I'm certain they mean something. I'm sure our friend Gurley wouldn't have smuggled them down here if they didn't."

Webster stared at one of the letters for several minutes in silence. Finally, he shook his head in frustration.

"These are written with a cipher. It's like a code, but instead of replacing a whole word or phrase with another word, they replace each individual letter with a different one. Makes it damned hard to crack."

He looked up at Scobell. "There has to be a key. Something they're using to replace the message with the cipher and then convert it back when they receive the message. Without that key, we'll never be able to decipher this. It'll be impossible."

"What kind of key are you talking about?" asked Scobell. This was all unfamiliar territory to him.

Webster blew out a long breath. "That's the problem. It could be anything. It might just be a piece of paper showing how the cipher letters match to the real alphabet. Or they could do it some other way. I've seen ciphers done with pieces of wood, where you slide one a few notches to the left or right to scramble the letters and then line them back up. Before we even try to find the key, we're going to have to figure out what it is first."

Scobell's earlier excitement at nabbing the letters quickly faded. "How do we even start? As you said, it could be almost anything, maybe even something we haven't seen before."

"At this moment," said Webster dejectedly, "I have no idea."

They pondered in silence for a moment. Then Scobell asked, "Who do you think wrote the letters? Maybe that could give us a clue about the key."

"That's a good thought," Webster replied. "Let me look closer at these."

He pored over the letters, flipping the pages back and forth as he read and reread them. Then he let out a low grunt. "I will be damned."

"What is it?" asked Scobell.

"I know who wrote these letters," said Webster. "I've seen this handwriting before. It doesn't seem possible, but I'm sure of it."

"What do you mean?"

Webster finally looked up from the letters and locked eyes with Scobell. "These letters are from Rose Greenhow," he said. "The Secesh spy from Washington, D.C."

Scobell immediately recognized the name of the notorious Confederate spy who'd passed information she collected while flirting with senators and Union officers. Her paramours were hardly out her front door before she passed the intelligence to her Confederate co-conspirators.

"How can that be?" he questioned. "Scully told me Pinkerton captured her months ago."

"I know," Webster replied. "I helped catch her. We found letters she was writing to Confederate leaders and other letters sent to her from a Massachusetts senator. Poor buffoon was in love with her and she was just using him to get information. She had notes on our troop sizes and placements, dozens of pages of damaging information for the Union. And that was just the pieces we saved before she destroyed them. She burned quite a few more before we took her into custody."

Webster paused for a moment, then added thoughtfully, "Some of the letters we seized from her that night were in cipher, too."

Scobell nodded, but didn't speak.

"I was one of the agents who read through all those confiscated papers," Webster continued. "This is her handwriting, without a doubt. I'd know it anywhere."

"But Scully said she's locked up in the Old Capitol Prison," said Scobell.

"She must've discovered a way to smuggle out these letters and send them south," Webster replied. "Miss Rose is definitely spying again."

"We've got to get word back to Pinkerton so that they can shut her down again," said Scobell.

"You're right," said Webster. "Or," he added thoughtfully, "let her keep working and monitor her messages. But to do either, we must find that cipher key."

He paused for a moment, looking directly at the black agent. "This material would've gone straight to the Confederate Secretary of War if you hadn't stopped it. That's good work, indeed."

Scobell grunted his thanks, looking down at the ground between them as he did so.

"Now," said Webster, "how are we going to get this back to Washington? You and I need to stay on our original mission. We could give it to the commanding officer of the Navy unit here, but they would want to run it through their channels, which would take forever. We need to get this back to Pinkerton immediately."

Scobell said, "I hope you don't mind, but I already took the liberty. I found someone who can take this information to Washington tomorrow."

Webster looked startled. "Someone we can trust? It needs to get there quickly, but also quietly. I don't have to remind you of the consequences if we're found out."

"No, you don't," Scobell replied, only barely keeping the sarcasm from his voice. "We can trust this man," he assured Webster. "He has his own reasons to travel quietly."

"I'm going to want to meet him first. There's just too much on the line," Webster said.

"I assumed you'd want it that way," said Scobell. Turning away, he said, "Follow me. If we go now, we can still catch them."

"Them?" asked a bewildered Webster as he started off after Scobell. "I thought you said it was one man?"

"Webster, you best prepare yourself," said Scobell over his shoulder. "I'm going to show you something tonight that you've never even imagined."

With that, he led his fellow agent off into the gloomy winter night.

⎯⎯◉⎯⎯

Hurrying through the darkness as quickly as they dared, the two spies came to a dilapidated building outside of town. It was a two-story structure that might've once been a store or a wagon shop. But now rough boards covered the windows and the front door dangled from one hinge. It looked as though it had been vacant for years.

"Around here," Scobell whispered. He grasped Webster's sleeve and led him around the side of the building to a second entrance, this one with a more substantial door on it.

Scobell quietly knocked three times on the door, pausing a moment between the second and third raps. He felt Webster's arm jerk in surprise when the door suddenly and silently swung open.

Scobell stepped through the doorway into the dark interior of the building, towing Webster alongside. They heard the door close behind them and a bolt slide into place to lock it. Unseen forms rustled in the surrounding blackness.

The two men stood still in the shadows. At one point, Webster leaned over to say something, but Scobell quieted him with a firm squeeze of his wrist.

Finally, a low voice came out of the gloom. "Who comes?"

"Friends of Uncle Abe," Scobell replied in an equally hushed tone.

"What do you desire?" asked the voice.

"Light and liberty," said Scobell.

Suddenly, there was a noise from above them and a faint light filtered into the room. It was flickering candlelight, drifting down to them through a trapdoor that had opened from the second story. With barely a sound, a rope ladder unrolled through the hatch.

"After you," Scobell said, motioning toward the rope ladder.

Webster hesitantly scaled the ladder, followed by Scobell, who slipped up the ropes as easily as walking up a set of stairs.

Once their eyes adjusted to the light, Scobell had to suppress a grin at the look of shock on Webster's face.

Though there was not a stick of furniture in the room, there were about three dozen men crammed into it, some standing and some sitting on the floor. A large wooden barrel stood in the center of the room, an American flag draped over it.

"Webster," said Scobell, "Welcome to the Loyal League."

━━●━━

Webster scanned the room, the gaping look of astonishment still affixed to his features. The surrounding men ranged from teenagers to stooped oldsters with white hair and beards. Nearly all of them wore the ragged clothes of slaves, some with blankets wrapped around them to ward off the December cold.

"What the hell is this?" Webster finally asked no one in particular. "Who are all these men?"

"This is Tim Webster," said Scobell to the group. "He is an agent working undercover in Secesh territory, and reporting directly to the head of the Union Army. You'll have to forgive his surprise, though. I didn't tell him what to expect before we came." There were quiet laughs around the room.

Scobell continued, "Webster is working on a mission to gather information here in Virginia. And I have been called into the secret service to help him." Indistinct sounds of approval from the gathering greeted this news.

A tall, slender black man who looked to be in his mid-thirties stood up and extended his hand to Webster. The man had been sitting on a packing crate next to the barrel in the center of the room.

"Mr. Webster, my name is Elijah. I am the leader here. Welcome to the Loyal League." The two men shook hands firmly.

Webster, slowly recovering his wits, looked from Elijah to Scobell and back again.

"Thank you," Webster said slowly. "But I'm afraid you have me at a disadvantage. I've never heard of the Loyal League."

"No," said Elijah with a slight smile, "you wouldn't have. Our group is made of Negroes dedicated to securing freedom for all of our brothers and sisters. We believe in the Declaration of Independence and the Constitution – and that the rights guaranteed by those documents apply to black Americans just as much as whites." There were murmurs of assent from the crowd.

"There are groups like this one that meet across the South," Elijah continued, "In secret, of course, to protect our members. We look for opportunities to get Negroes safely to freedom, identify southerners who might be sympathetic to our cause, and get news to Negro newspapers in the North so they can spread the word. Anything at all we can do to further the effort for liberty."

Then he added, "I first met your friend Scobell at a Loyal League meeting down in Mississippi, nearly a year ago." Webster looked across at Scobell, who avoided his gaze.

"You've found a good man in Scobell," concluded Elijah. "He's smart as an owl and strong as a bull. Plus, he knows how to keep a secret."

"So I gather," said Webster with appreciation.

Scobell quickly changed the subject. "Elijah is headed north to Washington tomorrow to meet with some northern abolitionists who are friendly to the League. He's agreed to deliver our package to Major Allen while he's there."

Webster shot another quick glance at Scobell. Scobell knew he'd picked up on the use of Pinkerton's cover name in the instructions to Elijah.

"I'm honored to help," said Elijah.

"Then it's settled," said Webster. "I doubt we could find anyone better for the job."

Scobell handed over the package of letters to Elijah and gave him directions to deliver it to Major Allen's I Street office. Scobell then turned to Webster and said, "We should go."

"Before you do," said Elijah, laying his hand on Scobell's shoulder, "would you mind saying a few words to our friends here?"

"Well, uh..." Scobell stammered. He took a small step toward the trapdoor. "We really need to get back to town before someone at the hotel misses Webster."

"It would mean a lot," said Elijah quietly.

Scobell hesitated a moment and then stepped back to the middle of the room.

"Men," he said in a quiet, but clear voice, "our time is at hand. For 200 years and more, Negroes have been slaves in this land. I don't need to tell any of you about that. But our chance for freedom is here, courtesy of Lincoln and the Union Army." Sounds of approval again came from the men. A few even clapped their hands.

"I've seen those boys in blue fight. Seen some of them die, too," continued Scobell. "But from what I've seen, they're ready and able to give the Johnny Rebs every bit of fight they want – and more." There was more clapping and a few hoots of encouragement, followed immediately by reminders to stay quiet.

Scobell's voice grew more intense. "But I'll tell you this: those boys won't win this war on their own. There will come a time when every single man in this room will be called upon to help in his own way. When that time comes, what are you going to do?" He slowly turned in a circle, directing his words to every man in the room.

"Are you going to shrink? Will you be able to look your children and grandchildren in the eye? It might be pretty sweet to tell them, 'When my name was called, I stood up. I answered the call.'"

Although Scobell's voice had barely risen above a whisper, his chest heaved as though with exertion. Several men around the room shook raised fists toward the ceiling.

After saying goodbye to Elijah, the two spies crawled down the ladder and headed back toward Leonardtown through the black night. They had walked briskly for several minutes when Webster finally said, "That was some speech."

Scobell shrugged. "I said what they needed to hear. Some of them have been beaten down for so long that they've forgotten how it feels to stand. But there'll come a time when they'll have to step up and fight to get what they want most."

Then he added, "No man ever fell up a mountain."

CHAPTER 8

Since they had arrived on the same stagecoach, Webster and Scobell left Leonardtown separately. It was another extra step to avoid any potential suspicion.

Webster, applying his sympathy like a balm to Gurley's wounds, ingratiated himself with the doctor when the latter staggered back into the hotel bar after Scobell's attack. Convinced that Webster was a loyal secessionist, the deserting doctor invited him along on his covert trip to Virginia. The following night, the two men slipped away together on a boat loaded with goods being smuggled to Rebels across the Potomac.

Scobell remained behind, blending unobtrusively into the black population of the town. He gathered as much useful information as he could through quiet observation and through the pumping skills learned in Washington.

When a few days had gone by and any chance of being associated with Webster passed, Scobell decided it was safe to move on with the next phase of his mission. Through another Loyal League member, he secured a ride across the river on a small fishing skiff.

Just before midnight, he found the raft and its pilot hidden in the reeds along the edge of Breton Bay. It surprised Scobell to see that the pilot was a young teen, barely more than a boy. But he quickly saw from the quiet efficiency of the teen's movements that he was a skilled riverman.

They slipped silently down the bay and out into the wide Potomac, headed toward the Virginia shoreline. Neither man spoke a word for the first hour.

As the youngster poled the raft, Scobell stared into the dark, trying to quell his fear of the cold, inky liquid below. He couldn't help but imagine the skiff as a tiny piece of bark on the open water, one that a single wintry gust might flip at any moment.

Still, he thought as he glanced back toward the pilot leaning on the pole, this sure beats swimming across. In his nervous state, the thought almost made him giggle out loud.

When they were near the middle of the river, the young pilot finally broke the silence. In a low voice, he said, "You know, I taked lotsa Negroes like us 'cross this river. Mebbe three, four dozen jus' since the weather turned cold." He paused for a moment, staring at Scobell. "But they was all escapin' to Mar'land, tryin' to get North. You sure as hell be the first one I taked this direction."

"Yeah," said Scobell, "I s'pose that's true. Don't 'spect you gonna find too many Negroes dumb enough to go South when they's already North."

The young man pondered for a moment, and then said, "Mus' be somethin' you want pretty bad over in Virginny. Bad enough to risk yer neck."

Scobell looked out into the murky gloom surrounding them. "I want the same as them other folks you rowed over. Jus' found me a different way to get it."

The young boatman nodded and pushed the skiff on into the night.

⎯⎯⎯⎯◉⎯⎯⎯⎯

When they reached the Virginia shore, Scobell paid the young man, then set off up the bank. Pinkerton hadn't given him specific directions, other than to scout Rebel camps and note troop strength and fortifications. He realized he needed to scout the most locations possible, yet carry the intelligence back to Washington in a timely fashion.

Consulting a map given to him by a Loyal League member who had once been enslaved in Virginia, Scobell decided his best course would be to walk overland to the Rappahannock River. From there, he would try to catch a ride on a riverboat upriver to Fredericksburg. The fake pass from his Maryland master was worthless here in the Confederacy. He'd have to rely on his wits from here.

Taking a quick bearing from the stars in the pre-dawn sky, he set off to the southwest. Walking smartly, but still cautious of wandering Confederate soldiers, Scobell arrived just after noon at Leedstown, a small port on the banks of the Rappahannock. He spent about an hour scouting the layout of the town. He soon discovered that, given the short winter day, no more boats would leave to go upriver that afternoon.

He needed to get upriver soon, but in reality, he was thankful for the delay. He hadn't slept in nearly three days, hadn't eaten since the previous day, and had just walked 15 miles in the windy cold of January. Scobell was flat out exhausted.

For now, he'd finished asking questions and scouting the landscape. With a few brief inquiries, he found a slave hut where he could bed down for the night and share a few meager bites of food. Sitting on a wooden plank inside the little hut, Scobell hadn't even finished his hoe-cake and salt pork when his head nodded onto his chest. In moments, he was snoring softly.

⎯⎯◆⎯⎯

The next morning, Scobell was at the docks before the sun came up. He learned from the dockhands that a packet boat called the *Celeste*, bound for Fredericksburg, was due in shortly. When the *Celeste*'s gangplank dropped, he grabbed a heavy crate from the dock and hustled it onboard.

He quickly found the captain to ask if he would allow Scobell to work off his passage to Fredericksburg.

The captain, a grumpy man in his mid-fifties with a long clay pipe clenched tight in his teeth, eyed Scobell suspiciously. "So you're lookin' for a free ride to Fredericksburg, is it?" he asked.

"Not a free ride, Massa Cap'n," Scobell replied. "I'll work hard as any man heah."

"And what's so interesting for you up there?" the older man asked. He shifted his pipe from one side of his mouth to the other without using his hands.

"I gotta get back to my massa's plantation. He off fightin' Yankees and I gotta git back to help the missus," Scobell lied. Recalling the name of a town from his map, he added, "I been down Montross seein' some of my kinfolk, but I ain't got no money for to get back."

The captain considered this for a moment. With the war underway, many of the working-class white men from the local area had gone off to fight. Consequently, there was a shortage of able-bodied men to work on the packet boats that shipped their cargo up and down the inland waterways. Scobell could tell by the slow pace of the loading going on around them that the *Celeste* needed more hands.

"Alright then," the captain said, letting out a great cloud of smoke from between his teeth. "It's agin' my better judgement, but I'll take ya."

Before Scobell could thank him, the old crotchet said, "Grab them crates and get 'em on here, quick. When we're loaded, get below and help out the cook." The captain turned and stalked off, but Scobell heard him mutter as he went, "I'll get my money's worth out of 'im, so I will."

Grabbing a cask of molasses, the operative threw his shoulders into the work. Even as he labored, Scobell observed the scrum of people milling about the quay, vigilant for any action or conversation that might provide him useful intelligence – or better yet, an insight to the cipher key.

One man, in particular, caught Scobell's observant eye. Dressed in a long gray coat and matching top hat, the gentlemen appeared to be waiting for someone. And a bit impatiently at that, thought Scobell, as the man glanced repeatedly toward the street.

After about an hour, Scobell saw a Confederate military messenger ride up the street to the dock. Still hauling cargo onto the boat, he watched the rider approach and dismount. Searching the crowd dockside, the messenger glimpsed the man in the top hat beckoning furtively and strode toward him.

As the two men talked, Scobell moved across the dock to grab a crate from the pile nearest them. Feigning difficulty in lifting it, he overheard a few small snatches of their quiet conversation.

"I'm to take them to General Johnston at Fredericksburg, then?" asked Top Hat.

"Yes," said the rider. "He'll have a messenger meet you at the dock there."

As Scobell moved slowly past them, he saw the soldier pull a thick packet from his coat. The crate Scobell carried suddenly crashed onto the dock. It fell about as heavily as he could drop it without appearing deliberate; hard enough for one corner to crack open and scatter horseshoes within a few feet of where the two men conversed.

They glowered at him. "I's sorry, massas. Real sorry 'bout dat," said Scobell as he walked toward them. "Lemme get dese all put up and out yo' way."

With derisive looks, the two men returned to their conversation. Scobell scurried about nearby, gathering horseshoes while on his hands and knees. His aim in dropping the crate had been perfect, but he hadn't counted on how much noise the metal shoes would make as he collected them again. Despite his proximity, he could still only catch shards of the hushed conversation between the two men.

"Orders are in here," said the rider as he handed the packet to Top Hat. The messenger added another comment, but Scobell didn't catch it as the horseshoes clanked in his hands. The two men quickly parted, and Top Hat hurried up the gangplank onto the *Celeste*.

What did he say? Scobell played it back in his head. Chosen tea? That made no sense. Slows the tree? That made even less sense.

It suddenly hit him. The soldier had said key. "So is the key."

A key. The cipher key? In a packet with military orders, it would make sense. If the orders were sensitive, they might use the cipher and would need the key to translate them.

With luck, thought Scobell, it would be him and Pinkerton doing the deciphering. He was already devising a plan to make sure that packet of orders, and its valuable key, would never make it to General Johnston.

⋗●⋖

The *Celeste* started upriver from Leedstown around midafternoon. Shortly after the crew finished their dinner, word came from the pilothouse that there were shoals ahead, exposed by the low tides. They would have to anchor for a few hours until the high tide returned.

Scobell saw his opportunity. With the boat idled in the shallows, he could grab the cipher key, get over the side, and wade to shore with it.

He slipped across the shadowy deck of the *Celeste*, crouching behind stored cargo, edging closer to Top Hat's cabin. Soft lantern light glowed through its window.

Scobell crept to the window and peeked in. Through the small pane of glass, he saw the packet-bearer preparing for bed. Finishing his nighttime routine, the man reached into one of the deep outer pockets of his coat, which lay draped across the cot, and pulled out the leather packet he'd received from the soldier.

He laid it on the foot of the cot, then went to his duffel and retrieved a wedge-shaped wooden box. Sitting on small stool, Top Hat unfolded a pair of wooden flaps on the top of the box to reveal a small desk inside.

Scobell watched through the window as the man removed a thin stack of papers from the leather packet and spread them on the desk. Then he withdrew a fresh sheet of paper and laid it beside a page from the packet. As the officer grabbed a pen, Scobell realized the man was getting ready to transcribe the encrypted orders.

Top Hat peered at the orders for a moment, then reached into the packet once more. He extracted something that Scobell couldn't see at first and placed it on the corner of the portable desk.

Staring down at the orders, the Confederate picked up the object and held it to the light. For a moment, Scobell could see it clearly: a metallic gold disc, about the width of a man's palm. There were markings on its face, although he couldn't make them out.

The man adjusted the disc by twisting it slightly, then set to deciphering the orders. For each letter being transposed, he glanced at the order, then at the disc, and then wrote the corresponding letter on the clean sheet of paper. As the minutes went by, his decryption picked up speed.

Though he couldn't see it clearly, Scobell could tell someone had fashioned the cipher key from two discs, placed one atop the other. That's why Top Hat had to twist it before he started, to align the set of cipher letters with the real alphabet. Then it was simply a matter of matching each cipher letter with its mate and writing the proper letter on the clean page.

The cipher key was actually a cipher *disc*. Scobell felt a rush run through his body. With the disc in hand, Pinkerton's team could decipher Rose Greenhow's letters. If he could grab both, they could decode the Confederate orders as well. It would be an enormous accomplishment, maybe even one that could swing the course of the war.

Suddenly, Scobell felt a clap on his shoulder and a heavy grip spun him around.

"What are you doing there, boy?"

A burly crewman glared at him. "You ain't s'posed to be peeping in folks' windows," he said loudly, accusation in his voice.

Before Scobell could reply, the door to Top Hat's room swept open, and the man thrust his head out. "What's going on here?" he demanded.

"This here buck was looking in your window, sir," said the crewman.

"Is that so?" Top Hat demanded of Scobell.

"Jus' checkin' to see why your light was still on, suh," Scobell lied. "Jus' makin' shore you didn't fall asleep with a candle still burnin'. That's how my massa done taught me, suh."

The Confederate messenger wasn't having it. "Your master taught you it was alright to peek in windows, did he? We'll see about that." Turning to the crewman, the lieutenant said, "This is a matter for the captain. He'll need to hold this buck at Fredericksburg until his master comes to get him."

"My massa be off fightin', suh," Scobell argued. "He won' be able to come git me."

Top Hat swiftly smacked him across the temple. "Apparently, your master didn't teach you not to sass white folks either," he retorted. "I'll not have it!"

The burly crewman grabbed Scobell by the arm. Top Hat stepped back into the doorway so they could pass on the narrow section of deck. "Let's go to the captain," he ordered.

The three men moved forward along the port rail of the *Celeste*. Scobell walked slowly in front, prodded at every step by the boatman, with Top Hat trailing close behind.

Scobell's mind rushed. He couldn't let them capture him. They'd eventually discover that he had no master to come for him at Fredericksburg, and they would treat him as a runaway slave. A severe whipping followed by being sold back into slavery was the best outcome he could hope for.

A much worse fate would befall him if they searched him first. He still carried the Virginia map and some gold pieces supplied by Pinkerton, carefully hidden in the lining of his clothes. If they found those, they'd assume he was spying or acting as a conductor for the Underground Railroad, helping other slaves escape. Either way, the result would be the same: hours of torture and then death by hanging.

The three men were nearing the front of the boat and the captain's cabin. The crewman gave Scobell a shove as they came to a narrow section of walkway. He staggered a few steps, then pitched forward onto the ground.

Scobell regained his feet quickly, grabbing the boat's rail to steady himself. With a glance back to confirm he was beyond arm's reach, he gripped the rail and abruptly vaulted over the side and into the frigid December waters of the Rappahannock.

CHAPTER 9

Splashing into the icy river jolted him like an axe handle jammed into his gut. The stunning cold immediately swept away the breath in his lungs, along with any panic his fear of water might've conjured.

His heavy wool clothes were suddenly a leaden weight, forcing him under the water. For a few seconds, he simply sank below the surface, immobilized by the shock of hitting the frosty river.

At last, his mind started working again. He felt his feet hit the bottom of the river and pushed as hard as he could toward the surface.

Scobell's head splashed out of the water, and he drew in several rapid breaths. The cold was so shocking that it seemed he could only draw in a little air at a time, not enough to fill his starving lungs.

In another few moments, as his senses started to fully return, he realized the river wasn't that deep here. He could stand on the bottom and still barely keep his nose above water. At least he wouldn't drown – yet.

He could hear shouts from the deck above as they raised the alarm of his escape. He reckoned it would be barely a minute before they'd secure lanterns to poles and dangle them over the side to light the water's surface.

Hugging the hull where it met the water, Scobell used every ounce of strength in his legs to push himself upstream. Before the sun had set, he'd noted the position of the shoals that stopped the *Celeste*'s progress. Now, he needed to reach those shallow waters and hurry across them to the relative safety of the shore.

The chilling water quickly fatigued his muscles. His heavy clothes billowed in the current, battling his every step upstream. Scobell clenched his teeth and drove himself forward.

Reaching the bow, he paused. From memory, he calculated it was about thirty yards to reach the exposed shoals and maybe another seventy from there to the wooded shoreline. On dry land, he could cover that in under twenty seconds. Tonight, he'd be hard-pressed to make it in five minutes.

In fact, he'd be lucky to make it at all.

There were already men hanging lanterns over the side of the boat near where he'd jumped. They were working their way forward.

He gave a shove off the bow of the *Celeste* and plowed forward through the icy, black river.

The water quickly got shallower, exposing first his shoulders, then his chest. Though it allowed him to move faster, he knew he was also more visible to the searchers.

As the water receded to his waist, the bitter January wind cut through his sodden clothes. He didn't think it was possible, but he was suddenly even colder than before.

The water was now splashing about his knees. Through the cold and fatigue, each step was an act of will. He pushed himself to go faster.

A shout came from the deck of the *Celeste*. "There he is! Up ahead!"

Scobell told himself that he was dashing toward the shore, but in reality, he slogged through the knee-deep water at barely more than a walking pace.

A gunshot boomed from the deck of the boat. A second shot roared, and he heard the minié ball splash into the water just a few inches in front of him.

There was no way he could outrun the shooters. The darkness had protected him so far, but he was too close to them and moving too slowly. They'd soon find their mark.

Scobell filled his lungs with air and dove forward, just as another rifle shot cracked. He felt the ball tug at his coat as it passed through, missing his back by a fraction of an inch.

He splashed face-first into the water and let his momentum carry him. If he could stay flat in the water, he might stay hidden long enough to make it to shore without being shot.

It was his only chance to live.

He held his breath for as long as he could, then slowly raised his mouth out of the water to take another gulp of precious air. Lowering his face again, he found he could propel himself forward in the shallow water without splashing by pushing off the river bottom with his hands.

More shots rang out from the *Celeste* and Scobell heard more splashes nearby. But he could also hear the shouting from the deck, and he knew they'd lost sight of him again.

The river eventually became shallow enough that he couldn't stay below the surface. Scobell dragged himself the last several yards to the bank on his elbows.

Pulling himself up under some brush, he flopped onto his back and took a deep breath. Gasping for air from the panic and exertion, he peered out at the river through the darkness, looking for pursuers.

Across the shoals, he could see lanterns swinging around the deck of the *Celeste* as searchers peered into the gloomy night. But there was no more gunfire and no sounds of anyone splashing into the water after him.

They'd either convinced themselves that he'd died in the water or decided one runaway slave wasn't worth plunging into the frigid Rappahannock. Either way, it meant no one was following him to shore.

Scobell dragged himself up the bank. The adrenaline was wearing off and a chilling cold settled over him. He needed to find warmth and cover immediately.

Fortunately, he emerged from the Rappahannock at the edge of a large plantation. Within a few minutes, he was wrapped in a borrowed blanket inside the slave quarters, safe among the plantation's black laborers. Scobell, allowing the others to believe they were harboring a runaway, fell into an exhausted sleep.

Arising well before the other plantation slaves the next morning, Scobell slipped away into the neighboring woods. Finding a hiding spot in a narrow stream valley, he stopped for a rest and considered his options.

His orders from Pinkerton were to report on troop positions and strength at Centreville. But now he also knew about the Confederate cipher disc, and its importance in deciphering not only the Greenhow letters, but perhaps intercepted military orders, too. Should he just take that intelligence back to Pinkerton?

An idea slowly dawned. Perhaps there was a way he could do both. If he could penetrate the camp at Centreville, maybe he could locate – and steal – cipher disc. If he returned to Washington with the reconnaissance intelligence and a disc in hand, it would pay his debt. He could walk away from Pinkerton's secret service with his free papers in hand and never look back.

First, he needed to find a way into the Rebel camp. That wouldn't be too difficult. They would never suspect a black man of breaking into a Secesh camp.

Once inside, he'd note the number of troops and their positioning. Then, he'd have to find a cipher disc and somehow get his hands on it. Finally, after casing the entire camp and stealing the most protected item there, he'd need to find a way back out again without being suspected.

That part would be slightly more difficult, he thought with a wry smile.

Worst of all was the fact that it was Centreville. At any other camp, he'd need to guard against alert sentries and suspicious soldiers who might wonder why a slave was so interested in troop placement. But at Centreville, where he'd spent two months before his escape, there were dozens of people who might recognize his face.

If just one of them identified him and raised an alarm, this spy mission would end with Scobell swinging from a rope.

Shaking that thought from his head, Scobell turned his mind to the problem nearest at hand. How could a black man walk right past a line of pickets and into the midst of a camp packed with thousands of Confederate soldiers without immediately being forced back into slave service?

There were two simple answers to that question: sex or food. Scobell couldn't help but smile to himself. It's probably been the same two answers in every war since the beginning of time.

With women in short supply at the moment, food would be his key. With a bit of luck and a convincing story, it would let him walk right into the middle of camp and set up shop. He wondered, though, if he'd be able to walk right back out again.

⎯⎯◉⎯⎯

The next morning, Scobell set out to the northwest. By mid-morning, he reached the town of Stafford. Making the excuse that his missus had sent him to town to get supplies, Scobell used one of the gold pieces he'd sewn into the armpit of his coat before leaving Washington to buy a handcart. Another gold piece allowed him to fill it with pork, chicken, corn meal, tea, fresh vegetables, and apples.

Thus prepared, he pushed on to Centreville. Near sundown the following day, he encountered pickets at the fringe of the Confederate camp. They were posted farther out than when he escaped last fall, a sign that the Rebel encampment had grown since then. This past winter's skirmishes at places like Dranesville, just a few miles north, may have had something to do with that.

Challenged by the pickets, Scobell explained that his master had sent him to cook a fine meal for the troops. "He know'd I cooks good, so he sent me up to make sumpin' for our boys in gray," said Scobell. "That's what he say'd."

"That ain't gonna do us no good," a picket grumbled to his partner as he peeked into Scobell's cart. "Those fellas in camp will get themselves a fine meal and we won't get squat out here."

Producing two apples from the cart with the speed and grace of a magician, Scobell presented one to each of the guards. "How 'bout a nice, fresh apple?" he offered. "Can't get many fresh apples this time of year. These 'uns was kept in cold storage, so they was. Got 'em special fo' you boys."

The pickets snagged the apples eagerly. Taking a bite so huge that he couldn't speak as he chewed, one of them waved Scobell into camp. Juice leaked out of the soldier's mouth and ran down his beard as Scobell rolled his cart forward.

Arriving at the main camp, he moved almost unnoticed among the soldiers, who were just gathering around their evening fires. Selecting an exceptionally overweight sergeant, Scobell explained again that he'd been sent to cook "sumpin' special fo' the boys."

The sergeant grinned broadly. "Well, ain't that a right fine thing?" he declared. "Boy, you just take them vittles right over to that fire there and set yourself up. You can cook supper for the boys of the 17th Mississippi tonight!"

Following the sergeant's instructions, Scobell soon had three large kettles of food bubbling over the fire. As supper cooked, he surreptitiously scanned the camp and listened to the soldiers as they chatted. When they filed past him to receive their first delicious meal in months, he subtly pumped them for information on other units in the encampment.

Scobell also asked about the camp's defenses. "What's them logs you boys done laid out, pokin' over the fences?" he asked one private, as he ladled an extra bit of stew into the man's bowl. "Seen 'em on my way in. You fixin' to run up over them if'n the Yankees come callin'?"

The private laughed loudly. "Them's our Quaker cannons," he said. "General Johnston didn't have enough cannon, so he had us take those big logs, peel the bark down, paint them black, and stick them out over the ramparts. Them Yanks are too damn stupid to know the difference! They think we got three times the guns we really got." He chuckled again as Scobell handed him an extra piece of cornbread.

As the meal wound down, Scobell asked the sergeant, who said his name was Danley, if he could visit the camp headquarters. "My massa done asked me to make sho' the general gets a good meal, too. He sayed the general need a bellyful o' good eats to whip them Yanks."

"I believe General Johnston might not mind a change from salt pork and beans," said Danley, rubbing his own plump belly as he spoke.

"Man that get that fo' him might get made a general his own self," Scobell coaxed.

Sergeant Danley switched from rubbing his stomach to scratching his chin. "I allow he might, at that," he said. "Put the rest of that stew in the cart and follow me. I'll take you to the officers' tent."

Taking care not to spill the kettles, Scobell pushed the handcart along behind the rotund sergeant as they wound their way through the camp. Although it was dark, his eyes swept across everything he could see by fire and lantern light, noting insignias, flags, and numbers of troops along the way.

Arriving at the headquarters tent, the sergeant explained to General Johnston and his staff about the wonderful meal Scobell had made, courtesy of his generous master. The thin, slope-shouldered Johnston looked cautiously at Scobell.

"And just who is this kindhearted benefactor that sent you here?" Johnston asked.

Scobell stared for a moment. "Suh?" he asked.

"Who is your master, boy?" Johnston clarified.

"Why, it's Massa Colchester, suh," Scobell said, repeating the name of the plantation owner in whose slave quarters he'd recently spent the night. "He done sent me to whip up sumpin' special fo' the boys."

"I see," said Johnston. "And did Mr. Colchester provide you with some documentation? A pass, so that you could enter and leave our camp?"

Scobell hesitated again. He slowly reached into his coat pocket and pulled out a folded piece of paper. Handing it to Sergeant Danley, Scobell said, "Massa done give me this pass. Told me to show it to anybody who asked."

Danley, seeing his promotion evaporating for not having demanded to see a pass earlier, handed the note to Johnston without reading it. Then, as if trying to evaporate himself, he drifted a few steps back.

The general unfolded the note. It read, "I have sent my best Negro cook, John, to buy foodstuffs and prepare a fine meal for the soldiers encamped at Centreville. Please allow him passage to the camp and back again to our plantation after he has carried out these instructions." It was signed "William Colchester, Esq."

Scobell was especially proud of the sweeping flourishes he'd added to the signature.

Johnston considered the note for a moment. Then he fixed his eyes on Scobell once again. "Well," he said, "what kind of food did you bring us?"

Sensing maybe he could earn a promotion after all, Danley bustled forward again. He recited the menu Scobell had prepared, emphasizing each item he mentioned by pointing to it.

Wanting to buy some extra time at the headquarters tent, Scobell said, "I believe these vittles done cooled off too much. I needs to heat 'em up again for the general to eat." Without waiting for permission, he stoked the cook fire in front of the tent and started warming the pots.

Scobell prepared the meal as slowly as suspicion would allow, eavesdropping on Johnston and his headquarters staff as he did so. He even made another batch of cornbread, just to delay a few minutes more.

When the officers finally sat down to eat, Scobell faded to the back of the tent. Waiting for them to finish, he visually scoured the headquarters. He attempted to memorize the maps laid out on the table, and strained to read an odd letter or two by the fluttering lantern light without picking them up.

While the maps revealed more intelligence about troop placement, there was no sign of encoded orders or a cipher disc anywhere.

As Scobell cleared away the supper plates and his cookware, he once again prolonged the process as much as he dared. He offered seconds and thirds, and fumbled more than one pot as he loaded it.

Just as he was finishing, a rider pulled up his mount next to the cook fire. "A message, General," the young man in gray announced.

One of the staff officers snatched the envelope from the rider and handed it to Johnston. Quickly opening it, Johnston snapped to the junior officer, "It's encoded."

The soldier walked to the back of the tent, disappearing into the shadows. Scobell could hear the clinking and scraping of a metal lid as a lockbox opened. The officer emerged carrying a leather pouch, identical to the one Scobell had seen on the *Celeste*.

There could be no doubt. It was a cipher disc.

As Scobell dawdled in front of the tent, they spread the letter on Johnston's desk and quickly deciphered the message onto a second piece of paper. Though Scobell couldn't see the message, it must've been short because the process only took a few minutes.

The general seemed annoyed at the outcome. Straightening suddenly, he barked, "This message needn't have come to me at all. This is a matter for the quartermaster, a simple mix-up on an ammunition shipment."

Turning on his heel, Johnston strode out the front of the tent to the rider, who was still standing next to his lathered mount. "Corporal, take this message to the quartermaster down at Dumfries. He can handle this. And when you return to your unit," he said, pausing for effect, "instruct your commanding officer that he need only send such messages to me as require the most urgent attention. I do not wish to be troubled with ammunition being sent to the wrong camp, the quality of the bread at dinnertime, or whose pet hound has run off. Am I clear, corporal?"

"Yes, sir!" The rider snapped a salute and mounted his horse again.

"General, sir," one of the staff officers interrupted hesitantly.

Johnston wheeled to glare at him. "Yes?"

"Well, sir," the staffer said, "you'll recall that they don't have a cipher disc at Dumfries yet. They won't be able to decipher this letter without one, nor will they be able to encode their reply, sir." He looked as though he believed Johnston might slap him for speaking up.

For a moment, Scobell thought, Johnston looked as though he wanted to slap someone. Biting off his words, the general replied, "You are correct, Major. Quite correct."

He marched over to his desk and snatched up the cipher disc. Hastily stuffing it back into the leather pouch, he handed it to the rider. "Take this with you to Dumfries. When they've finished deciphering this dispatch and enciphering a response, bring it back here to me."

"Yes, sir," replied the rider. "Should I bring the disc back first or deliver the response first, sir?"

Despite his exasperation, Johnston considered the question. "I suppose you should deliver the response first. Your commanding officer will need to know when he can expect that ammunition to arrive."

"Yes, sir," the soldier replied, saluting again and then spurring his horse up the dirt path.

General Johnston gave his staff a withering look. "Let's just hope we don't get any encoded messages that the Yankees are attacking in the next few hours."

CHAPTER 10

Scobell finally packed up his handcart and left Johnston's headquarters tent. Moving to another part of camp, he tucked the cart up against the back of a wooden building where it was out of the wind. He then curled himself tightly inside a blanket and crawled under the cart for a cold and fitful night's rest.

Sleep was slow to come, however. For the second time this week, he'd been within a few feet of a cipher disc. Yet, once again, it had eluded him. Although stealing it from the headquarters lockbox might've proven impossible, it was now completely beyond his reach.

Worse, Scobell couldn't wait around Centreville for the disc to return. His cover story had bought him an excuse to be in camp overnight, but not much longer. With no supplies left to cook another meal, lingering in camp would either arouse suspicion, risk recognition by someone he'd met before his escape, or result in being pressed back into slavery in service of the Confederate cause.

Unwilling to submit to any of those outcomes, but not wanting to return to Washington without a cipher disc in hand, Scobell needed to leave camp. He needed another plan. Gathering the blanket even more tightly around his shoulders, he closed his eyes and shivered himself to sleep.

———————●———————

Bugles sounded before dawn and Scobell stiffly roused himself from under the handcart. It had been a miserable night, but perhaps a productive one. His sleeplessness had led him to a potential solution – the Loyal League.

He knew from his snooping at headquarters the previous day that there were other Confederate camps in the area. While some of them apparently didn't have cipher discs, others might. If he put the word out to the Loyal League, one of them might know where to find a disc. Perhaps, he thought hopefully, they might even help steal it.

Scobell surreptitiously made his way to where teams of slaves were working on the camp's defenses. Drifting among the men digging and piling dirt against the ramparts, he quietly asked each person he encountered, "What do you desire?"

It was about two hours before someone answered with the countersign, "Light and liberty."

Quickly and quietly, he explained to the Loyal League member that he wanted to arrange a meeting nearby in two nights. When he escaped the Centreville camp the previous fall, Scobell had hidden briefly in an abandoned farmstead nearby. They would meet there, in the dilapidated barn.

As he hurriedly gave directions to the place, he suddenly heard a familiar voice call his name. "Why, if'n it ain't Johnny! You dirty Negro!"

Turning to face the man, Scobell's stomach dropped. "Hello, Simon," he said in a subdued voice.

He glanced over Simon's shoulder to see whether the nearest overseer had noted the exchange. Fortunately, he hadn't. Yet.

The Loyal League man slipped quietly back to his work. Simon, though, continued loudly.

"Now, how long it been since I seen you? We was back down in Mississip' then. I heard you done run off!" The last declaration was loud enough that the overseer looked over at the pair. Scobell knew this wasn't by accident.

Simon and Scobell had grown up together. For a time, they had both been the property of the Scobell family, but when the boys were about six years old, Simon's father died. Master Scobell sold Simon and his mother to a neighboring plantation owner – one who had a reputation for abusing his slaves mercilessly.

A rivalry eventually developed between the two boys any time they encountered each other. As they grew older, it deepened into animosity, at least for Simon. Scobell guessed that Simon blamed him in some way for the many beatings endured at the hands of his master and perhaps even for his mother's death from the same cause. Jealousy over his own fate, and the fact that Scobell remained under the lighter whip hand of their original owner, eventually grew into bitterness on Simon's part.

Scobell had also learned to read and write. Though the practice of teaching slaves was illegal in Mississippi and had to be carried out in secret, Simon eventually learned that Scobell was literate. It seemed to fuel his hatred even more.

"I been around," said Scobell, hoping his voice would be loud enough for the overseer to hear his reply, but not so loud as to raise even more attention. "Massa done sent me down with a crew to another fort. Jus' got back las' night."

"S'at so?" said Simon, taking a sidelong glance at the overseer. Seeing the soldier had lost interest in their conversation and turned away, he shifted to another tack.

He asked in a more normal tone of voice, "You sticking 'round now?"

"Nope," Scobell replied. "Jus' here gittin' some building supplies. Headin' back to Dumfries after that."

"S'at so?" Simon said again. "I kinda figgered you'd be working as a house boy by now. Sumpin' that wouldn't rough up y'all hands. Mebbe keepin' Massa warm on these chill nights." He cackled at his own rudeness.

The insult glanced off Scobell, but he had to tread lightly. Simon wouldn't let this drop without getting in his jibes. Who could say how far his rival might push to bring trouble down on his head?

"No, suh, not me," Scobell replied. "Jus' workin' a pick and shovel, same as you an' them other boys. Pilin' that dirt and stackin' them logs."

"You two bucks quit yappin' and get back to work now," the overseer yelled at them. "Let's go."

Scobell grabbed a shovel and started slinging dirt with the rest of the men. Simon, determined to keep jabbing at his rival, took up a work spot next to him.

"I seen you talkin' to ol' Martin there over there," said Simon as he shoveled. "I didn't know you knowed him. He been heah since las' summer. You couldn'a met him while you was workin' at that other camp."

"We jus' met heah today," Scobell said. Without thinking, he picked up his speed to outpace Simon.

"Hmm," Simon grunted. "Seemed like you two's pretty chummy for jus' meetin.'"

"Seem't like a good fella," said Scobell. He didn't like where this questioning was going. "He say he from Mississipp' like us."

"Yep," replied Simon. He continued to dig, but stopped talking.

Scobell knew he had to get out of the Confederate camp and away from Simon. His longtime adversary would continue to goad him at every opportunity. He couldn't risk being drawn into that game.

After full dark had fallen, Scobell escaped from Centreville a second time – nearly six months to the day since he'd first bolted to freedom on a stormy night. This time, he slipped out of the camp's cramped slave hut on the pretense of relieving himself, then veered off and followed the road out of camp. When challenged by a picket on the outskirts of camp, he presented with the letter from his mythical master.

"Why are you heading back so late at night?" the soldier asked.

"My massa done told me to cook that food and get myself on home. Right quick, he say."

"Sure wish I could've had some of that food," the guard said. "I ain't had a decent meal in weeks."

"Well, I got jus' the thing, suh," said Scobell. Digging in his coat pocket, he fished out a large rectangle wrapped in a cloth. "Here's a hunk o' cornbread for you. Done made it myself."

Scobell had been saving the cornbread for himself, and he was sorry to see it go. But escaping camp without further questioning was a higher priority than a full stomach.

"Why, that looks right good," said the soldier. He took a huge bite and nodded emphatically. When he finally choked down the mouthful, he added, "That's real good."

"Glad you like it, suh," Scobell said, still a little disappointed at seeing the cornbread disappear. He drifted off down the road again. "I best be gettin' on home now."

"Just a second there, boy," the picket said. Scobell stopped and turned slowly back toward him. His nerves ignited instantly. He wondered if he'd have to jump the soldier and run for his life.

"Next time you're back this way with food, you need to bring me some more," said the picket. "My name is Private Glenn Wilson and I'm with the 10th Virginia infantry. Can you remember that, boy?"

"Yes, suh," said Scobell, relief washing over him. "Private Wilson in the 10th Virginny. Yes, suh, I'll 'member that, suh." He shuffled off down the road into the night.

———◆———

As he had so many times back in Mississippi, Scobell slipped through the darkness, spreading the word that there would be a meeting of the Loyal League. From his escape last autumn, he knew the rough lay of the countryside surrounding Centreville. He also knew which of the slave quarters held Loyal League members and where he could hide during daylight hours.

As blackness crept over the landscape on the appointed night, Scobell emerged from his hiding spot. He was once again a creature of the forest, waiting for twilight so he could prowl the land.

Although he'd slept less than a mile from the deserted farmstead, it took him over two hours to arrive. His caution was intense: frequent stops to listen for someone following him, multiple changes of direction to throw potential pursuers off course, and several backward loops to catch anyone who might be trailing him. But other than a few squirrels and a solitary deer, Scobell didn't see another living thing.

When he finally reached the abandoned homestead, he approached it with similar caution. He slipped silently up to the dilapidated house and peered inside to detect anyone hiding in wait. The dust on the ancient stairs was undisturbed.

After checking the three other rickety outbuildings with similar care, Scobell went into the barn. He spent twenty minutes scouring it, from hayloft to slab rock floor, before allowing himself to accept it was empty.

Finding a soft spot on a rotting pile of straw, Scobell finally sat down to wait for the other Loyal League members to arrive. The scent of dust and decayed wood filled his nostrils. Somewhere in the woods beyond the forsaken barnyard, a barred owl hooted its distinctive call: "Who cooks for you? Who cooks for you all?"

Though he was comfortable, Scobell didn't nap. Any gathering of slaves was illegal in the South. One held at night, in a hidden location, in the middle of the war, was unthinkable. If discovered, the punishment would only be limited by the extent of the cruelty and imagination of the captor.

Nearly three hours later, other men arrived. Though some carried lanterns or candles, not one was lit. The men flitted across the barnyard like wraiths, only visible in the occasional sparse shafts of moonlight, and even then, just for a split second.

As they approached the barn door by ones and twos, Scobell whispered, "Who comes?"

"Friends of Uncle Abe," each man replied.

"What do you desire?" said Scobell.

"Light and liberty," came the reply.

Over forty people soon crowded inside the old barn. All were slaves who had sneaked away from either nearby plantations or Secesh encampments. Most were like Scobell, men in their 20s or 30s. A few were middle-aged and there were a few ancient codgers as well, mostly toothless and bald. Still, they had mustered when the call went out.

There was also a boy. It surprised Scobell when the youngster materialized at the door next to his father, a local plantation slave named Lester.

"Why did you bring him?" Scobell demanded. "You know it's not allowed." The rules of the Loyal League strictly forbade children from attending gatherings. Besides the physical danger involved, children also were at risk of revealing damning details to the wrong ears afterward.

"I done wanted Peter to come, to hear what we all do," said Lester. "Y'all don' hafta worry none 'bout him telling a soul. He don' talk." Lester patted his son on the head as he spoke.

"Fine," said Scobell. He was still uncertain, but it served little purpose to turn them away now that the boy had seen the gathering.

Scobell started the meeting. He wanted to be as brief as possible, then let the group disperse again into the darkened countryside.

He quickly outlined who he was and the fact that he was spying for the Union. This revelation sent a murmur rumbling across the room.

He then explained the cipher disc and how it was being used to send and receive encoded messages between Confederate officers, as well as from Rebel spies in the North.

"The disc is about this big," said Scobell, touching the index fingers and thumbs of both hands in a circle. "There's one small circle, mounted on top of a little bigger circle. They both have letters on them, around the outside of the circle. I saw one made out of brass, but I suppose they could make them of some other metal or even wood. Has anyone here seen anything like that?"

Another murmur passed through the gathered group. No one spoke up to answer, however, and silence once again fell over the assembly.

Then, with jarring abruptness, a single gunshot in the barnyard interrupted the hushed tones of the Loyal League meeting.

"Are you niggers in there?" came a shout from outside. "This is Captain Matchett of the 1st Virginia Infantry. Come on out now or we're burning this place down and you with it!"

Scobell rushed to a window and looked out. He saw a mounted Confederate officer, surrounded by a dozen or more troopers on foot.

As he watched in horror, the soldiers ignited torches and encircled the barn. Then came another shock.

The glowing torchlight revealed a familiar face standing next to Captain Matchett's horse. It was Simon.

Scobell was stunned. He knew Simon hated him, but he couldn't imagine the man would stoop as low as revealing a secret meeting of slaves and lead a squad of soldiers right to it.

At that moment, Scobell heard Simon's voice above the din of the soldiers and the growing clamor of the men inside the barn. "He in there, Cap'n. Johnny's in there!"

Cursing, Scobell moved away from the window and scanned the inside of the barn. He could hear soldiers shouting just outside the wooden walls. Within a few seconds, he smelled smoke.

No sooner had he detected the scent than the crackle of burning wood reached his ears. The fire would devour the desiccated boards of the ancient structure in minutes. Not many minutes at that.

Scobell risked another peek out the window. He saw Simon point at the barn and shout, "He in there! Don' let him git out!"

Captain Matchett looked down at Simon from atop his horse. "Don't you worry, boy. We're gonna kill every single nigger here."

Simon looked up at the Confederate captain. "I...I thought you was jus' gonna arrest Johnny," he stammered, slowly backing away. "Them others ain't got nothin' in it. Johnny done put them boys up to it."

"There's not one black son of a bitch gonna walk away from here tonight," snarled Matchett, "Starting with you."

In one swift motion, Matchett drew his pistol and shot Simon in the forehead.

Scobell recoiled from the window in horror. The soldiers had no intention of letting anyone live. They would burn alive every man who stayed in the barn. Anyone who ran would be shot...or kept alive long enough for some other form of torture. It wasn't much of a choice.

He was dumbfounded. Smoke now filled the barn and the men inside staggered about in fear and confusion. The soldiers shouted to each other and Captain Matchett hollered for the slaves to surrender. A burning board clattered down from the barn's wall, igniting a pile of straw not ten feet from Scobell.

The noise and sudden flames startled him back to his senses. "We need to run," he shouted over the turmoil. "Don't go out the front door. Get out where you can and sprint for the woods. Don't stop for anything!"

The men rushed out in groups of twos and threes from any exit point they could find: a back door on the lower level, a side window, a gap in the wallboards. One slave, a giant of a man named Silas boosted several men on his powerful shoulders into the hayloft so they could jump out. As the men bolted from the burning barn, gunshots boomed above the fire's roar.

From his earlier reconnaissance, Scobell remembered a wagon loading entrance on the lower level. The door itself had long ago rotted and fallen off, but an old wagon and several wooden barrels were strewn just outside the doorway. He could use those to buy a few more seconds of cover before sprinting for the forest.

He scrambled over fallen boards and flaming piles of hay to get to the opening. Once there, he crept along the broken-down wagon and the row of barrels until he crouched behind the last of the cover.

He peered into the open barnyard beyond, searching for soldiers in the darkness. Seeing no one, he burst from his hiding spot and dashed into the open.

Just as he did, Captain Matchett wheeled around the corner of the barn atop his mount and nearly collided with Scobell. Matchett yanked on the reins and his horse skidded to a stop.

For an instant, the two men stared at each other. The soldier recovered first and drew his pistol.

At the same instant, Scobell jumped forward and grabbed the horse's bridle. Shoving with all his strength, he spun the beast's head back and to the side. The gelding reared, just as Matchett fired.

The bullet grazed Scobell's shoulder, but he barely noticed it. He charged at the horse again, intending to drag the captain out of the saddle before he could fire another shot.

The spooked gelding had other ideas. The blazing building and the sudden assault were more than he could bear.

He took a few prancing steps away from Scobell, accidentally moving closer to the barn as he did so. A section of flaming wall crashed down next to horse and rider, causing the horse to buck and crow-hop sideways.

With Matchett scrambling to regain control, Scobell flailed his arms and shouted at the panicked animal. The horse reared high in the air, sending Matchett flying.

Free of his rider, the gelding bolted past Scobell, momentarily obscuring where the officer had tumbled. When he finally spied the fallen man, Scobell saw Matchett had landed on his left side atop a flaming pile of boards from the barn. He lay motionless, the flames crackling around him.

The sound of a nearby gunshot jolted Scobell. "The captain's over here!" another soldier shouted. "He's hurt!"

There was another shot and the minié ball passed close enough that he could hear it whine.

Wheeling away from the barn, Scobell tore off for the woods. As he sprinted, he saw the bodies of fellow Loyal League members sprawled throughout the farmyard. Some writhed in pain while others lay completely still.

He reached the edge of the forest in a few seconds. Spotting an enormous magnolia tree, Scobell ducked behind its trunk.

He panted with exertion, then glanced back to see if he was being pursued. There were two figures scrambling away from the barn, but they weren't soldiers. It was Lester and his son Peter, running hand in hand.

Suddenly, Lester straightened awkwardly, arching his back and looking up toward the night sky. Peter, still clinging to his father's hand, stopped and watched as Lester spun to the ground, dead from a Rebel gunshot.

Scobell stared in dismay as the boy knelt and tried to lift his father. But Lester was gone. Peter didn't have the strength to do anything more than cause one of Lester's arms to flop awkwardly.

From across the barnyard, a Rebel soldier noticed Peter and started toward him. The soldier wasn't raising his gun to shoot the boy. Scobell knew this meant he had something worse in mind.

The man whistled for another soldier and pointed at Peter. Both men moved toward the boy.

Scobell hesitated. He'd been lucky to escape the first time. If he charged back to save the boy, both of them would probably die. He wanted to turn and run into the forest, then keep running until he found a way back to Washington. Getting killed here, in the middle of nowhere, would serve no one.

Still, he stared at Peter, now bent crying over his father's body. Maybe he could do it. Maybe Scobell could cover the open distance, snatch the boy up, and race back into the woods before he too caught a bullet in the back.

Scobell glanced at the soldiers, who had closed to less than fifty yards from the boy. They were close enough now that killing both Scobell and Peter would be easy. He'd be lucky to make it to where Peter knelt weeping, let alone grabbing the lad and escaping.

He made up his mind. Scobell shoved away from the tree trunk.

At that instant, a gigantic boom came from the barn, followed by flying debris and a shower of sparks. Silas, who had stayed inside the barn helping others escape, suddenly crashed through one of the burning walls, scattering flaming shards of wood in all directions.

The hulking man charged across the field and snatched Peter up in one meaty hand without slowing down. The Rebel soldiers were momentarily stunned by the appearance of this giant from the bowels of an inferno. It took them several seconds to recover and start firing volleys at his disappearing bulk.

Scobell thought one shot might have hit the fleeing giant, but Silas never slowed down and never gave up his hold on Peter. The pair disappeared into the woods, swallowed up by the brush and the darkness.

Scobell gazed across the farmyard, now lit by the towering flames from the barn. Confederate soldiers ran from place to place, shouting and rounding up the few Loyal League members who hadn't made it to cover. The corpses of those who fell short in their escape attempts lay scattered across the grass.

He surveyed the scene in stunned horror. Unarmed and alone, there was nothing he could do to help the captured or the fallen. He had just one recourse remaining.

He turned his back on the horrific tableaux and plunged into the woods. Back toward Washington, D.C.

CHAPTER 11

Scobell's return to the capitol was a disheartening one. Although he delivered word of the cipher disc's existence to Pinkerton, he also had to admit that he'd twice missed opportunities to lay his hands on one.

Worse, he had to relay the bitter story of Simon's betrayal and the tragic destruction of the Loyal League gathering. Captain Matchett and his graybacks had smashed the Loyal League around Centreville.

Pinkerton also questioned every element of Scobell's intelligence report from the Confederate camps. Not only was he convinced that Scobell had far underestimated the troop counts, but he completely refused to believe the existence of the Quaker guns.

Gazing down at the neatly written report from behind the desk in his I Street office, Pinkerton shook his head emphatically. "You must've been mistaken, Mr. Scobell. Logs painted as cannons? That simply can't be correct."

"I believe I know the difference between a log and a cannon," Scobell said.

Pinkerton lifted his eyes quickly, scanning his operative's expression. Scobell stared impassively back at him.

"Yes, I'm sure you do," the head of the secret service said, turning back to the report. "But there must be some explanation for this."

"There is," Scobell replied, maintaining his level tone. "They're using the Quaker guns to trick the Union army into believing they have more artillery than they do. I estimate nearly half their cannons at Centreville are nothing more than wood."

Pinkerton let the comment fall in silence. At length, he said in a confident tone, "They must be using those logs to measure and position where the real guns will go when they arrive. I'm sure that's it."

He raised his eyes to Scobell again. "We know from newspaper reports that the Tredegar Iron Works in Richmond produces up to fifty cannons each month. That's more than enough to fortify every Rebel encampment in the South."

Scobell opened his mouth to argue, but Pinkerton cut him off. "They're simply using the logs to measure out the ramparts where the cannon will go when they arrive. Centreville is too close to our troops here in Washington. They'd never risk leaving it so exposed. It's the first place they'll deliver new guns."

The Scotsman was talking faster now. "In fact, they probably put those guns in place shortly after you left the camp since it's so close to Richmond. Yes, I'm certain that's it. The logs you saw were simply...measuring sticks." Pinkerton chuckled at his own joke.

Scobell wanted to argue, to ask how Pinkerton could explain the comments of the Secesh soldiers about the Quaker guns. He wanted to push back and ask how the very technique of troop size estimation that Pinkerton taught him could've resulted in such wildly wrong numbers. The spy chief's attitude, however, had already demonstrated it wasn't worth the effort.

"Is that all, then?" Scobell asked.

"Yes," said Pinkerton. "Thank you again for your work in the field and your excellent report."

The agent nodded at the spymaster and excused himself from the office.

——●——

Scobell was done. After yesterday's frustrating, humiliating conversation with Pinkerton, he'd decided his spy career was over. He'd met his obligation and completed his mission; he would get on with his life and enjoy his hard-earned freedom.

No more would he serve the pompous chief of the secret service. He was finished with the man who'd sent him into harm's way and then refused to believe what he reported.

Nor was he interested in risking his life and freedom for Pinkerton's superior, General George McClellan. The previous evening, Scobell had heard from Pryce Lewis that McClellan, commander of the Union's Army of the Potomac, forcefully rejected even the inflated troop numbers fed him by Pinkerton.

"Somehow, he's convinced himself that the Confederate army is double or triple the size of his own," Lewis told Scobell, shaking his head at the thought. "It doesn't matter to him that they're pulling soldiers from states that have half the population of the North or that they don't have the benefit of a conscription draft."

It was inescapable, Scobell thought. McClellan had frightened himself into disbelieving the intelligence being gathered in the field, and Pinkerton was going to reinforce what his boss thought, whether that jibed with his operatives' findings or not.

Scobell had done his part. He had risked torture and death while dutifully gathering the intelligence his mission demanded. Now, he was on his way to the I Street office to tell his boss exactly that. He would leave Pinkerton's secret service with his head held high.

In his usual brusque manor, the spy chief launched into a discussion of the next mission before his operative could speak. Scobell wasn't listening, merely waiting for an opportunity to interject and announce his departure.

At last, the Scotsman paused in his soliloquy. Scobell seized the opportunity.

"Mr. Pinkerton, I am leaving your service," he announced. "I have met the obligation you placed on me and completed my assigned mission. You told me you would provide me with my free papers if I succeeded in that. I wish to have them now."

Pinkerton's demeanor shifted instantly. His steel-gray eyes hardened and he leaned forward, placing his arms on the massive desk.

"Succeeded?" he snarled. "Met your obligation? In what way, I might ask."

"Webster and I intercepted the Greenhow letters and returned them to you," Scobell began.

"An act that had little value without a method of decoding them," Pinkerton interjected.

Scobell could feel heat crawling up the back of his neck and bringing a flush to his cheeks. "I scouted the Rebel camps from Fredericksburg to Centreville and reported that intelligence back to you, as instructed," said Scobell. His anger briefly overcame his restraint and he added, "Whether you choose to believe them or not."

"You report to me that the Confederate troop strength is half of what I know it to be," said Pinkerton. "And then you tell me that the Rebels are guarding their camp – the one closest to Washington, no less – by logs masquerading as cannons!"

He paused, his harsh stare penetrating Scobell. "Now, tell me, how am I supposed to believe reports like this?"

Scobell clenched his jaw so tightly the cords in his neck stretched against his shirt collar. He spoke slowly and softly, as if in fear that talking at a normal pace and volume would release the fury inside him. "I am the one who discovered the cipher disc. Without me, you still wouldn't even know how the messages were being coded."

Pinkerton sat back in his seat and spread his hands, palms up, in front of him. "Where is it?" he asked. "Knowing it exists does nothing for our side."

He leaned forward again. His right hand clenched into a fist as he said, "I need to have one right here in my hand."

Scobell desperately wanted to leap across the desk and smack the smug expression off the Scotsman's face. Yet even as the thought of it welled up within him, he pushed it back down again. It would be satisfying, but it would also foreclose any chance he might have of gaining freedom instead of life in a contraband camp.

The degradation and resentment of the moment were emotions he knew all too well. He'd felt them each time he'd been forced to grovel to his master, each time he'd been tied to the lashing post. The mental torment was nearly equal to the physical pain.

Scobell returned Pinkerton's icy gaze with an equally heated one of his own. They stared at each other in silence for several seconds.

It was Pinkerton who finally spoke. "I will give you another opportunity," he said. "Another chance to earn your free papers."

Another chance? The image of his fist smashing squarely into Pinkerton's face leapt back into his mind. Scobell sat perfectly still, his gaze unflinching.

Pinkerton continued. "I'm sending two pairs of operatives south. We have sufficient intelligence regarding troop strength and placement in northern Virginia. But we need to know more about how their munitions are being supplied and learn what we can about their government operations."

He paused for effect. "Foremost, we need to get our hands on a cipher disc."

Though he still burned inside, Scobell's self-control was slowly returning. "And in return?"

"As I stated before, if you successfully complete your mission, I will attest to your liberation. You can use that documentation to get your free papers."

"I feel like I've heard this tale before," said Scobell. "What assurance do I have that you won't change the rules again? That you won't keep dangling my freedom in front of me each time you need my services, without ever granting it?"

"Change the rules?" Pinkerton sputtered. "I haven't -" Catching himself, the spy chief stopped and took a deep breath.

"Mr. Scobell," he said, "Arguing and distrust serves neither of us."

Scobell inclined his head in a barely perceptible nod.

"Allow me to propose a solution to overcome this," Pinkerton went on. "I will sign an affidavit right now verifying that you came to me as a freed slave and, as such, you are to be granted full liberty here in the North. I'll also execute an accompanying document stating that, upon your successful return from this mission, that affidavit will be to given to you. No questions or conditions."

"Successful?" Scobell said.

Pinkerton leaned across the desk again. "Bring me back a cipher disc, Mr. Scobell. And you can go free."

CHAPTER 12

The late January cold was harsh, and a biting north wind cut through Scobell's coat. As he drove the horse team, the wind forced stinging snowflakes down the back of his collar and reached up through the bottom of his coat to chill his spine.

To his right sat a slim woman, bundled tightly against the winter cold. Only the ends of her long blond hair were visible, peeking out below her bell-shaped, felt bonnet. A velvet ribbon descended from the brim, trussed below her delicate chin to keep the icy gusts from lifting the hat away.

Like Scobell, she was in her mid-twenties. Her clear, blue eyes gazed downward, tearing slightly from the biting wind. The fur coat and wool dress immediately identified her as upper class, but not extravagantly so. She appeared every bit the wife of a southern gentleman, which was exactly the countenance she wanted to present.

To everyone they met, she introduced herself as Mrs. Carrie Lawton, a widow from Corinth, Mississippi. Her real name was Kate Brackett, Kitty to her friends.

Scobell and Brackett traveled south through Leonardtown, establishing their cover as a moneyed Confederate wife and her personal manservant. They had stayed at the home of Washington Gough, an affluent secessionist who Webster had cultivated as a contact during an earlier visit.

The pair headed west across the Potomac, and once again plunged into secessionist territory. They purchased a wagon at Port Royal and from there traveled southwest to Bowling Green.

There, to help maintain their cover, Brackett delivered letters "smuggled" from the North to one of Webster's Secesh contacts. After delivering the messages – carefully read, copied, and resealed by the spies before they left Washington – they were on the move again.

Now, their path was due south, into the heart of the Confederacy. They were bound for Richmond.

Upon reaching the Confederate capitol, they checked into the Exchange Hotel. Timothy Webster had suggested it after one of his prior missions to Richmond.

The hotel was conveniently located just a few blocks from the office of Jefferson Davis, the president of the Confederate States of America. The Exchange was also just four blocks from the Confederate Army Intelligence Office and less than two blocks from the Signal Office of the Confederacy.

The location was so convenient, in fact, that multiple Confederate senators and representatives housed themselves at the Exchange. Brackett and Scobell would nestle snugly amidst the heart of the Rebel government.

Arriving at the hotel, the Pinkerton operatives settled in. Brackett took the large, well-appointed matron's room and Scobell deposited his bags in the tiny, spartan slave's room adjoining it. Since the gloomy January evening was already upon them, they decided to eat and turn in early. Tomorrow, the intelligence gathering would begin.

The following morning found Scobell standing atop the staircase of the Exchange's grand front porch. Instead of the rags he had worn during his years in bondage, he now sported the finery of a house slave. He had donned a starched white shirt with a high collar, a dark red vest with a paisley pattern embroidered into the silk material, a fine woolen overcoat, and leather riding boots, shined to a glare. He wasn't sure which slave outfit disgusted him more.

Pinkerton had given Scobell three objectives for his mission to Richmond. The first was to determine the production of artillery pieces from the Tredegar Iron Works. The spy welcomed the opportunity to back up his observation of the Quaker cannons at Circleville by debunking his superior's assertions that the armory was pouring out fifty cannons a month.

His second purpose was to identify and quantify the Confederate troops deployed in defense of the city. The spring of 1862 would almost certainly bring another Union incursion into Virginia. Lincoln had bitingly remarked on General McClellan's failure to move before now by sniping that if the general "does not want to use the army, I would like to borrow it for a time."

When McClellan finally did get around to attacking, intelligence on the number of troops and the details of Richmond's defenses would be critical.

Scobell's third objective was the most important – steal a cipher disc and bring it back to Pinkerton. Brackett and Scobell would work together to achieve the arduous task, the one that would finally earn Scobell his freedom.

As the pair of operatives departed his office, the spy chief reminded them, "We simply must have that disc. Our clerks can work out the messages, even if the Rebels change the combination. But they can't do it without knowing the disc's letter arrangement. That's the critical piece."

Then Pinkerton added, "If you should acquire a disc on your first day in Richmond, get it back here immediately. Regardless of your other objectives, the disc is the top priority."

———◆———

His first order of business this morning was to pick up a copy of the stranger's guide to the city or, as Richmond's version was called, the *City Intelligencer*. The *Intelligencer* contained helpful addresses that any traveler might need, such as the post office, telegraph office, and the city's five railroad depots. It also contained listings of various government offices; hotels, banks, and hospital locations; and every major Confederate Army department, from the Surgeon General to Army Intelligence.

The guide even listed every elected official of the Confederate States of America, up to and including President Jefferson Davis. It also revealed where each stayed while in Richmond. Potentially useful information for the out-of-town traveler; ideal for a newly arrived Union spy.

Brackett had initially planned to come with him to pick up the guidebook. Scobell had to explain to her that this wasn't a task a Southern lady would undertake. It was something she'd have her house slave handle.

"We're going to have to look the part and play the part, every moment," he said. "There is a certain order in the South that people follow, without fail. Anything that doesn't meet their customs or manners will make us stand out instantly."

"In Illinois, a lady can pick up a guidebook or buy a newspaper for herself," Brackett protested. "I've done it many times. In Washington, too."

"We're not in Washington now," said Scobell, "and we're sure as hell not in Illinois. You need to listen to me. I don't want to end up dead because you have your own ideas about what's right and wrong."

Brackett's expression said she wanted to argue further, but her only reply was, "Fine. Go get it then."

———⬥———

After asking directions to City Hall from the Negro doorman at the Exchange, Scobell set out through Richmond. Though his destination was northwest of the hotel, near the Confederate Capitol building, his first steps were in the opposite direction. The stiff soles of his shiny boots clacked on the brick sidewalks with each stride.

What he saw was a city that reminded him of Washington D.C. – only grimier. The wide streets bustling with horses, carriages, and marching soldiers; the fancy hotels teeming with well-dressed politicians, diplomats, businessmen, and their families; and the grand marble buildings and monuments towering above the surrounding structures. It all matched the feel of the US capitol a hundred miles to the north. Scobell could immediately tell that Richmond also shared Washington's almost tangible hum – an energetic blend of martial pride and boomtown commerce that lent a note of vigor and importance to every activity in the city.

However, where Washington was a city mostly devoted to the business of government, Richmond was also a center of industry. Flour mills, tobacco-drying facilities, and locomotive factories all belched smoke and soot into the sky, and black sludge into the James River. The web of railroads that met in the Confederate capitol carried not just travelers and soldiers, but also cotton, cowhides, and coal. They shipped out canvas tents, leather harnesses, and thousands of tons of iron. The difference was quickly apparent, from the sight of smokestacks erupting with black clouds and orange sparks to the sooty smell of burning coal that permeated the air.

Webster had reviewed his hand-drawn maps of Richmond with Scobell and Brackett before they left, so Scobell knew the general layout of the city. Just south of the Exchange Hotel, he came to the James River & Kanawha Canal. Teams of mules, straining endlessly against their leather bindings as they trudged along the adjacent towpath, tugged barges through the canal. The wooden barges, loaded with everything from cotton to bricks, ferried their loads to and from the nearby Petersburg & Richmond Railroad depot.

Scobell strode past the depot quickly, taking in as much of the layout as he could while trying to appear as though his mind was on important business elsewhere. He made a mental note to come back later and pump the slaves loading and unloading the railcars for information. They would certainly know the frequency of train traffic and might even share a nugget or two about military equipment shipments or troop trains.

Less than a mile beyond the railroad depot lay Castle Thunder and Libby Prison. Both prisons had gained notorious reputations, despite having been in use for less than a year. Having no interest in a visual reminder of that potential outcome, Scobell turned back before he reached them.

Turning corners every few blocks to vary his route, Scobell slowly zig-zagged his way northwest and found the Richmond City Hall. Not wanting to dawdle this close to the Confederate capitol building and its security detail, he requested a copy of the *City Intelligencer* from the designated clerk and departed quickly.

Once again, he began in a direction counter to his ultimate destination. His measured pace carried him up Capitol Street before swinging left onto 16th Street. He had just passed the busy shopping district on Main Street when he first spied the billowing clouds of smoke pouring from the Tredegar Ironworks.

The ironworks was not actually a single building, or even a standalone factory. It was a sprawling industrial complex that covered more than a quarter-mile of riverfront between the canal and the James River itself.

Tredegar was the largest ironworks in the southern states at the outbreak of the war. Besides the cannons, of which Pinkerton was so enamored, the complex produced steam locomotives and rifles for Rebel troops. The Richmond Armory, which made up about one-third of the Tredegar complex, produced those guns. They were already being called "Richmond rifles" by soldiers on both sides.

Ironically, the Richmond rifles were being cranked out on machinery that had once been used to make Springfield rifles for the United States Army. Webster had briefed Scobell about the Confederates shipping manufacturing equipment from the captured Federal armory at Harpers Ferry to Richmond.

Arriving at Front Street, Scobell looked out at the canal once again. The Tredegar works lay directly ahead of him. He had found his first target and wanted to scope it out.

To his right, however, just across a jutting arm of the canal, Confederate soldiers drilled on a stretch of open ground. The last thing he wanted was to be seen loitering there and have someone question why he was watching the men in gray.

He quickly spun in the opposite direction and proceeded down Front Street. A few blocks away, he came to a flour mill. The flurry of activity at the mill and on the surrounding streets would disguise his observations for a few minutes.

Slipping between rows of wagons loaded with flour barrels, he worked his way to a spot overlooking the canal. Just beyond the canal lay the sprawling grounds of Tredegar, engulfing the banks of the James River nearly as far as he could see in either direction.

Scobell marveled at the sheer magnitude of the complex. The sooty brick buildings towered three stories tall, their massive smokestacks jutting even higher. A railroad bridge stretched away from the factory across the James. A massive waterwheel turned inexorably next to one building, providing a portion of the power needed to produce the rifles and cannons. Dozens of enslaved workers shoveled coal dumped from railcars into furnaces to provide the rest.

Scobell quickly realized surveilling the mill was going to be more difficult than he'd hoped. Not only was the place too big to take everything in at once, but he immediately saw that access on the land side was restricted by high fences.

His initial plan had been to slip in amongst the many black faces in the plant, work a shift or two himself, gather what intelligence he could, and disappear back into the city. With only a few gates, each one heavily guarded, that couldn't work. He knew now he would need to cultivate sources from within the slave workforce at the plant to gather the required information.

He blew out a long sigh. Every extra day, every extra hour, was one step closer to being discovered. He pushed that thought out of his head and tried to focus on the matter at hand.

If he could talk to even a few slaves laboring at Tredegar, he could put together a fairly clear picture of its production. The slave laborers would know better than anyone how many loads of coal and ore arrived each day, and how many shipments of rifles and cannons went out.

A small noise behind him caused Scobell to start. Whirling, he saw a scrawny gray cat moving coyly toward him, rubbing its skinny ribs along the rough staves of an abandoned barrel.

As the gaunt animal approached, Scobell bent and rubbed his thumb and forefinger toward it. It came only close enough to sniff his hand, then meowed loudly and marched away. Scobell made a mental note to bring some food scraps the next time he observed Tredegar in case the feline appeared again.

He watched the activity along the waterfront for a few minutes more. Wagons came and went; barges disgorged their cargo and swallowed return freight whole. Both white and black workers hustled between the brick edifices. It seemed to Scobell as if some great being had kicked over an enormous anthill.

Carefully memorizing the guarded gates where workers might enter and leave, he slid back between the rows of loaded wagons and returned to the Exchange to meet Brackett.

CHAPTER 13

He went directly to her room. Though she'd given him a key, he rapped the oak door with his knuckles.

"Missus Lawton, ma'am. It's John," he announced loudly. "I done brung that item you sent me fo'."

Brackett let him in. Latching the door behind him, she said, "Is Mrs. Lawton supposed to be deaf? Why on earth were you shouting?"

"I wanted everyone on this floor to hear it," he said. "If anyone saw me walking around town by myself today, I wanted them to know I was on an errand for you. For another thing, no Negro man walks into a white woman's hotel room in Virginia without announcing himself, house slave or not."

Brackett made a face as if she'd tasted something bad. Ignoring it, Scobell handed her the *City Intelligencer*.

Flipping quickly through the pages, she nodded approvingly. "A ready-made list of our objectives," she said. "Names and addresses."

Scobell bobbed his head in agreement. "I've already been by the Tredegar Ironworks," he said. "It is massive. Takes up the better part of the riverfront."

He briefly recapped what he'd seen, sketching out from memory the buildings, loading docks, and railroad lines on a piece of paper. He shared his plan to contact slaves who worked there and piece together information to get the full picture of the factory's production.

"That sounds like an excellent idea," she said. "They're probably our best source of information from inside the works."

Pointing at the directory she still held in her hands, he asked, "Where do we start with that?"

Leafing through the booklet again, Brackett said, "We need a cipher disc. Which of these places are likely to have one?"

Under the heading Confederate States Directory, she read several department names out loud. "Treasury Office?" she asked.

"Maybe," said Scobell. "But if it's just being used for military and spy messages, they might not have one there."

"True," said Brackett. Skimming down the list, she read, "Surgeon General's Office?"

"Doesn't sound like a good candidate. What would they need coded?"

"True. Libby Prison?" she suggested.

"You can try that one on your own, thanks," said Scobell. "I'll pass."

Brackett glanced up at him with a slight smile, then read on.

"General Winder's office," she said. There was a thoughtful note in her voice.

"General Winder?" replied Scobell. "I don't know who that is."

"General John Winder," she said, reciting from memory. "Officer in the United States Army, resigned last year to become a Brigadier General in the Confederate Army. He was just recently made Provost Marshal of Richmond."

"Provost Marshal?"

"He essentially runs the city," she said. "At least from an enforcement standpoint. From what Webster says, Winder's in charge of everything from cracking down on gambling and prostitution to catching Union spies."

"Catching Union spies," Scobell repeated.

"Yes," Brackett replied.

"You're suggesting we infiltrate the office of the person charged with catching Union spies in Richmond and steal something from him, something he'll be under orders to protect at all costs?" asked Scobell.

"Think about it," she said. "He's in a new position and there's bound to be a lot of confusion around his office right now. People coming and going, material and letters moving in and out. Things can get discarded, misplaced in turmoil like that. Even important things sometimes go missing."

Scobell nodded slowly, her argument overtaking his skepticism.

"Besides," she continued, "he's responsible for so many things that he probably doesn't even know the full list right now. It won't be hard for us to cook up a reason to visit him, more than once if we need to."

Scobell carefully sifted through what Brackett was suggesting. He still didn't like the idea of walking into a lion's den to steal a lamb shank, but he had to admit that her logic was solid. Every Confederate office in Richmond would be carefully guarded and the cipher disc would be among its most valuable contents. Finding an office in disarray might give them the advantage they'd need to carry off this daunting mission.

"Well," said Scobell at last, glancing down at the directory lying open on the table between them, "his office is practically around the corner from here. Maybe that's a sign."

Brackett grinned. "Winder it is then," she said with enthusiasm.

"And if things go badly," Scobell continued as if finishing his prior sentence, "it's only a short stroll to Libby Prison."

Her grin faded. "Stop it," she said. "Don't say those things."

As he stood up from his seat, Scobell reflected that he hadn't even shared with her the next thought that had come into his head. Brackett would likely see the inside of a prison if Winder captured them, but there was little chance Scobell would live that long.

———◆———

The next morning, Brackett ate breakfast in the grand restaurant of the Ballard House. It was directly across the street from the Exchange and an elevated, enclosed bridge connected the two. Guests at either hotel could move between them a full story above Franklin Street, peeking out the windows at the bustling traffic below.

After helping Brackett settle at her table, Scobell glanced around the room. He took in the spotless tablecloths, topped by white linen napkins and frilly doilies lightly clasping the bottoms of long-stemmed crystal water glasses. Coffee cups with an intricate blue and gold print pattern around the rim nestled into saucers bearing the same pattern. They rested next to matching plates and silverware shined to a glinting polish.

The unwritten protocol of slavery dictated that he leave before her food was served, but Scobell's nose told him Brackett's plate would soon be filled with fried pork, glazed sweet potatoes, and biscuits. His stomach rumbled loudly as he helped slide her chair up to the table.

"Smells good, doesn't it?" she asked. Then she added quietly enough for only him to hear, "I feel bad that you can't sit down and eat here."

"I'll get some food," he said. "They'll have something for me in the kitchen." He knew, however, it wouldn't be the same menu presented to Brackett.

"Anything else, Missus?" he asked just loudly enough to be heard at the adjacent tables.

"That's all for now, John," Brackett responded. "I'll be back up to my room in an hour. I'm going out later, so have my things prepared."

"Yes, Missus." Scobell bowed slightly and removed himself from the dining room as inconspicuously as possible.

Retiring to the narrow alleyway behind the kitchen, he received a wooden plate of leftovers from the previous night's dinner. He shoveled a few bites of the gray mush into his mouth, then left to prepare for his day's work. He wondered if the leftovers not fed to slaves would be used to slop pigs this evening.

━━━●━━━

Two hours later, Brackett strolled up Main Street on her way to General Winder's office. To announce that she was a widow in mourning, she wore a black dress and a dainty veil covering the upper half of her face. The half veil, as well as her white collar and matching frilly cuffs, signified that the husband she'd lost had been dead longer than six months. More recent widows wore all black with full veils covering their faces.

Scobell trailed two steps behind, as custom dictated. He mentally rehearsed the story they had developed for Winder's benefit.

Brackett – or rather, the widow Carrie Lawton – was in Richmond searching for a long-lost relative. With her husband killed in the early days of the war, she had come north from Corinth, Mississippi to find her uncle. Uncle James was now her last living relative, and as a gentlelady who knew nothing of operating a business, she needed his help in managing the plantation.

But first, she needed Winder's help in finding Uncle James.

Carefully avoiding the dozens of horses and loaded wagons clattering along the cobblestones, the pair crossed Main Street. There they entered the brick building that housed Winder's office. At the end of a short hallway, they found a door with Winder's name painted on its glazed glass.

Brackett introduced herself to the secretary and requested a brief audience with General Winder. Clearly practiced at the art of deflecting visitors, the sallow, frail man peered at her over wire-rimmed glasses and asked disdainfully, "And what is the reason for your request, Mrs. Lawton? General Winder is quite busy."

Brackett launched into the story of losing her husband. He had, in her telling, died tragically but heroically during the glorious Confederate victory over the Yankees at Manassas. Scobell nearly had to suppress a smile, as she paused and dabbed a silk kerchief at the corners of her blue eyes.

She finished by explaining the need to track down Uncle James, focusing on her helplessness without a man to explain the plantation business. She punctuated the conclusion with another dab of the kerchief, seizing the opportunity to flutter her long, dark lashes at the clerk.

Brackett reached across the desk and lay her gloved hand gently on the back of the clerk's wrist. "I understand how busy General Winder must be right now," she said. "But if I could only get a few moments of his time. Uncle James came here to Richmond last winter and I haven't been able to reach him since. I was hoping that the general..." Her voiced trailed away in a sob, followed by another touch of the silk to her eye.

It was immediately clear that nothing in the clerk's experience had prepared him for this type of onslaught. His hardened gatekeeping demeanor melted immediately under exposure to Brackett's performance. The sadness in her pretty face, the teardrops, the soft touch of her hand on his. Scobell almost felt sorry for the chap.

"Yes, well...uh," the clerk stammered. "Perhaps we might get a few minutes with the general. Let me speak to him."

Prolonging the contact of her hand on his, he reached across with his other hand and gave hers a light squeeze. "I'll certainly do what I can," he said sincerely.

The clerk disappeared through the door behind his desk. When he reappeared after a few moments, he looked as if he was bearing the most wonderful news he'd heard in months.

"The general has agreed to speak to you, Mrs. Lawton," he said, his face radiating the excellence of the announcement. "Please follow me." He swept an arm grandly toward the door to direct her through.

Brackett furtively flashed a raised eyebrow at Scobell as she stood. The pair followed the clerk through the massive oak doorway into Winder's office.

The Provost Marshall was standing when they entered the office and took the hand Brackett lightly offered. Waving her to a seat opposite his desk, he hastily returned to his own wooden chair. Scobell retreated to a corner of the room near the door.

Winder was the picture of severity. The collar of his tightly buttoned uniform coat came nearly to his wide, square chin. His mouth was a taut line drawn across his face beneath a large, straight nose. His green eyes sat wide on either side of that nose, with worry lines gathering at the corners. A thick batch of wavy, gray hair swept back from his clean-shaven face. He might have appeared handsome, had the overall effect been less stern.

Glancing occasionally at the general from his corner, Scobell revised his initial assessment. It was more than sternness he saw in Winder's face. It was cruelty.

"What do you need, Mrs. Lawton?" Winder asked.

Brackett started into her tale of woe. "When the war came last year, my husb-"

Winder abruptly raised his hand. "Stop," he ordered.

Brackett went silent and leaned slightly back in her chair.

"Mrs. Lawton," Winder said, "I have many important tasks to address. I do not have time for stories. Just answer the question, please. What do you need?"

Pouting slightly at the affront on courtesy, she said, "I'm looking for my uncle. His name is James McLean. He came to Richmond last winter to arrange cotton sales and I haven't heard from him since."

She couldn't resist sneaking in another part of her well-rehearsed story. "With my husband killed at Manassas, I need Uncle James' help with our plantation."

Winder's hand shot up, stopping Brackett once more.

"I have no further time for this discussion," Winder said. "There are too many urgent items to deal with now." His voice, already hard-edged, had taken on an undertone of impatient anger.

The general pulled a piece of paper from a desk drawer and started writing. Brackett sat quietly, while Scobell wondered if they would need to find another route to the cipher disc. Winder extracted a second sheet of paper and made a quick notation on it.

"This first paper is a pass with my signature," he said. "You'll need it to move about Richmond now that we're under martial law."

Brackett thanked him and folded the paper into her bag.

Winder handed her the second sheet. "Go to this office upstairs. They are overseeing matters such as yours within the city of Richmond. My secretary will tell you how to find it. Good day, Mrs. Lawton."

It was clear the interview was over. Brackett thanked the general for his help, then retreated out the doorway as quickly as possible. Scobell slipped out behind her.

In contrast to the Provost Marshall's brusque manner, it seemed as if the clerk would've carried Brackett to the new destination on his back, if she'd only asked.

"It's just upstairs, ma'am. Third floor, two doors down from the staircase on the right side," he said when she showed him the paper. "I can lead you there, if you like?" It was a question rather than a statement.

"Thank you so much," said Brackett, her voice as thick and sweet as molasses. "I think I can find it, though."

"Yes, of course," the clerk said. His disappointment was palpable.

A note of hope returned to his voice as he added, "Please don't hesitate to stop by and talk to me again if you need anything. Anything at all."

"Of course," Brackett replied, gracing him with one final radiant smile. "Thank you again for your help," she said as they exited.

Brackett and Scobell stopped to confer in the hallway, a safe distance from Winder's office.

"That was a bust," she said. "If he has a cipher disc, there's no way we'll ever see it, let alone steal it. He'd never allow us time enough."

"True," Scobell acknowledged.

"I guess we'll go to this other office then," Brackett said. Her grim expression and flat tone announced her extreme skepticism that it would be anything other than a further waste of time.

Scobell shrugged. "I don't have any other plans this morning."

CHAPTER 14

When the pair reached the third-floor office, two doors down from the staircase on the right side, there were no markings on the door. No one answered when Brackett knocked politely. After waiting several seconds, Scobell rapped harder.

"C'min," came a grudging reply from inside.

Scobell followed Brackett through the tall wooden door frame, as always, trailing the proper distance behind.

In contrast to the military order of Provost Marshal Winder's headquarters, this office felt more like a saloon. A haze of tobacco smoke colored the air bluish-white. As thick as the nicotine cloud was, however, it didn't wholly mask the odor of sweat and bad breath.

Brackett stopped in the middle of the entryway, allowing Scobell just enough room to squeeze inside. There were tall roll-top desks to her right and left, and another door on the back wall opening into a smaller office beyond.

Though both desks were occupied, neither showed much sign of work being accomplished. There was a single curling, yellowed wanted poster pinned to the side of the one on the left, and a light detritus of paper scattered across its surface. The one to her right also had a wanted poster on it, depicting Abraham Lincoln's face as a gorilla. It read "Wanted for Treason" across the top.

The spittoons next to each desk showed signs of more active use. Tobacco juice stains on the wooden floors around them revealed both poor aim and indifference to the outcome.

The man seated on the left was the larger of the two. He had thick, powerful arms. His long beard descended over a broad chest, but it looked like the size of his gut would soon exceed it. A wave of belly fat crested over his thick leather belt.

The man on the right was smaller, but wiry. His shirt fit snugly around his taut muscles. He sat relaxed, his chair rocked back and boot heels perched on an open desk drawer. A cigarette dangled from his thin lips, which were barely more than a crease in the beard stubble that covered his face. The narrow mouth and unshaven cheeks gave his face a callous appearance that Scobell believed to be accurate.

The larger man had been honing a long, thin-bladed dagger on a whetstone when they walked into the room. He stopped now to test its edge by shaving a patch of shaggy hair off his forearm. Satisfied with the results, he stabbed the knife into the surface of the desk, its long blade wobbling a bit when he released it.

That task completed, he turned his attention to Brackett. His eyes crawled over her, from her boots to her curly blond hair, and back down again. His gaze finally settled on her chest, where he focused as he spoke.

"Well, now, what do we have here?" He punctuated the statement by spitting in the general direction of his spittoon. The trailing portions of the juice stream settled into his beard, joining the damp remnants of earlier attempts.

"General Winder sent me," Brackett started confidently. "He said that you could assist me."

Dropping the Provost Marshall's name did not have the intended effect. In fact, it seemed to have no effect at all.

"Did he now?" the big man said, still attempting to stare through the buttons of Brackett's coat.

"Yes." Brackett wavered for an instant under his scrutiny, then regained her footing. "Yes, he did. I'm looking for someone. His name is James McLean."

Scobell noticed that the other man had shifted his gaze to Brackett as well. His dark eyes were searching, assessing her. His expression was less one of lust than suspicion.

As she talked, he slowly lowered his feet from the desk and allowed his chair to rock forward and rest flat on the floor. The movement reminded Scobell of a water moccasin sliding from a tree branch into the water.

"And this James McLean is your husband?" the larger man asked, reaching between his shirt buttons to scratch a section of his prodigious belly.

"Oh, no," she said, sparking her radiant smile. "He's my uncle." Casting her eyes at the floor, she added in a lower voice, "I lost my husband last year at Manassas."

Clearly cheered by this bit of news, the bearded man said, "Is that so? You know, I might maybe be able to help you some after all."

Pausing to spit again, he continued. "I'm Deputy Agent Saunders."

Without getting up, he reached behind his seat and grabbed another chair by the leg. Skidding it noisily across the floor, he pulled it up beside his chair and patted its seat. "Why don't you jus' sit down right here and tell me more about it?"

Before Brackett could respond, a voice from the office in the back barked, "Saunders! Blake! What the hell is going on out there? Who are you talking to?"

The reaction was instantaneous. Both deputies immediately straightened in their seats. With surprising agility, Saunders swiped his knife off the desk and tucked it out of sight beside his chair.

Scobell also had an immediate reaction. The hair on his forearms stood up and a crawling sensation ran up the back of his neck. He'd heard that voice before.

A figure suddenly appeared in the doorway to the adjoining office. Gaunt, but still sharply upright and severe, the presence was unmistakable. It was Captain Matchett.

Scobell was stunned to see the man he thought he'd killed standing before him, very much alive. But he was nearly equally shocked at the captain's appearance.

An angry, red patch of alligator skin grew up from the high collar of Matchett's coat and spread across the side of his head and face. The scars continued past his left ear, now only a crumpled mass of flesh, until they disappeared under his broad-brimmed hat. They extended across his cheek and forehead, encircling his left eye until dying out at the bridge of his nose.

Terror surged through Scobell's body. He clamped his fists until his knuckles ached. Sweat sprung from every pore of his body.

Would Matchett recognize him? Would the entire mission – and with it, Scobell's life – end right here?

As subtly as possible, Scobell shifted his feet to hide behind Brackett. He slouched even more than his usual slave posture, trying hard to disappear in the wide open room.

It had been dark that night in the forest, he told himself. He'd only seen Matchett face to face for a few seconds. It was possible the captain wouldn't remember him from that fleeting encounter in the light of the burning barn.

He felt a drop of sweat trickling down his backbone; the sensation disappeared only when it reached his belted trousers.

Matchett focused on Brackett, fixing her with a look of disdain. "Who are you?" he demanded. "What do you want?"

"She's looking for her uncle," said Saunders, trying to show his superior that he'd been doing his job. "Her name is...uh..." He faltered, realizing he'd never done the most basic part of his job by asking her identity.

Matchett shot Saunders a withering look. The deputy quickly turned away, suddenly remembering he had something important to search for on his nearly empty desk.

Turning back to Brackett, Matchett slowly, acidly repeated his questions. "Who are you, and what do you want?"

"I...," Brackett hesitated. She was flustered by the interruption, as well as by the grotesque figure now interrogating her. "I am..."

"Ma'am, I have important matters regarding the security of Richmond to address," said Matchett. "I do not have time to be wasted. If you have business here, please state it. If not, please leave now so we may get on with our work."

Gathering herself, Brackett said, "Yes, of course. My name is Mrs. Carrie Lawton. I am here looking for my uncle, Mr. James McLean. I had an interview with General Winder this morning and he directed me to this office."

Matchett appeared disappointed at the mention of his senior officer. It meant he couldn't dismiss the woman's request instantly and without a moment's consideration, which had clearly been his intent.

"Fine." He fairly spat the word. "My name is Captain Matchett. Give your information to my deputies, and we'll make inquiries."

He turned toward his office, then stopped and faced once again toward Brackett. "I will make you no promises, Mrs. Lawton. We are charged with the security of this city and have many important duties. We will give your request the attention it deserves, but we likely will not find your uncle. There are many missing people during a war, ma'am. We cannot find all of them."

"I understand, Captain," Brackett replied. "And I can see that you and your men are quite busy."

Matchett stared hard at her, then wheeled toward his office. As he turned, Scobell saw the captain cast a glance in his direction as well. Had he seen a flicker of recognition in the man's eyes?

Scobell couldn't be sure as Matchett disappeared through the doorway.

Brackett sat down to give her story to the deputies, pulling her chair a more appropriate distance away from Saunders as she did so.

Scobell relaxed slightly after Matchett left the room. It didn't seem the captain hadn't recognized him. It was almost beyond belief, considering he was the one who had caused the angry scars across Matchett's face and neck.

As he thought back on that tragic night at the abandoned barn, he considered how this might be possible. Although memory made it seem like an eternity, the entire encounter – Matchett riding down on him, Scobell clawing at the horse, the Rebel captain crashing to the ground amid the flaming remains of the barn – had probably lasted less than a minute. Factoring in the darkness and rushing adrenaline of the moment, it was possible that Matchett hadn't gotten a clear look at him.

Not to mention the fact that Matchett wasn't the kind to distinguish one Negro from another. Scobell clenched his jaw. Not even while he was trying to murder them.

Brackett completed her tale for the two deputies and was gathering her things to leave when Matchett materialized at his office door again. He shot her a look demonstrating his disapproval that she hadn't left yet. Then Scobell once again felt the heat of the scarred man's gaze fall on him. He held his breath until the captain turned his attention to the deputies.

"Have either of you seen the pouch?" he asked curtly. "I need to write a letter."

Brackett shot Scobell a covert glance. The process of collecting her belongings slowed substantially.

Both deputies immediately disclaimed any knowledge of the whereabouts of the item in question, fearing blame for its disappearance falling on them. Seeing the anger rising in his captain's face, Saunders opined, "Lucy probably put it someplace."

This suggestion seemed to make Matchett twice as furious. "Goddam that darkie woman anyhow," he muttered as he stomped across to the front office door.

Jerking it open, he shouted down the hallway, "Lucy! Get in here!" Leaving the door ajar, he stalked back to the middle of the room.

A few seconds later, Scobell heard a door open down the hall, followed by soft footfalls in the hallway. The gait seemed measured, but sure.

Into the office walked an elderly black woman. She wore her white hair piled up in a neat bun behind her head, but there was hardly a line upon her face. She might've been anywhere from 50 to 100 years old, Scobell mused.

Lucy was short and thin to the point of appearing fragile. She also had a crook in her neck that permanently cocked her head slightly to the right. Still, she had an erect bearing and a competent air that made her appear both taller and sturdier than she was. She clenched a small wooden pipe between her front teeth, puffing it lightly as she walked.

Removing the pipe, she said, "Yes, suh, Massa Matchett. What can I do for y'all?"

"The pouch," said Matchett. "Where is it?"

Without hesitation, Lucy stepped over to a wooden filing cabinet against the wall. Removing a key from her pocket, she unlocked the middle drawer and extracted a leather pouch. Handing it over to Matchett, she said, "Here you is, Massa Matchett." She punctuated the statement by popping the stem of the pipe back in her mouth.

Even from halfway across the room, Scobell was certain she'd handed Matchett a cipher disc. The leather pouch was identical in shape, size, and color to the one he'd seen on the riverboat.

Rather than being mollified at the appearance of the pouch, Matchett was livid. "You goddam black devil!" he shouted. "How many times have I told you never to touch the things on my desk? I'm done with you and your shines. I'll have you sold South before the week is out!"

Unfazed by the tirade, Lucy removed her pipe again. "Aye, Massa, you did indeed say that. You also done said to Deputies Blake and Saunders that they shouldn't never leave that there pouch about. Well, Deputy Saunders done left it layin' out on his desk yesterday. I was cleaning up last evening and seen it. Weren't nobody 'round, so's I thought I best lock it in that there cabinet to be safe."

The rest of Matchett's face turned red enough to match his scars. The veins bulged in his neck and on the sides of his temples.

His eyes shifted from Lucy to Saunders as if unsure which one infuriated him more. The deputy fiddled with the corner of a sheet of paper on his desk, studiously avoiding Matchett's glare.

For a few simmering moments, the tension hung like smoke in the air. Suddenly, the silence shattered as Matchett smacked Lucy across the face.

Her pipe shot across the room and skidded to a stop at Scobell's feet. The blow was so sudden and sharp that Brackett gasped. Both hands shot up to cover her mouth.

"What's wrong, Mrs. Lawton?" asked the detective captain, turning his blazing glare on her. "You don't approve?"

Brackett, still in shock, stammered, "I...I just..."

"You just aren't used to seeing it, I suppose," Matchett sneered. "Your beloved husband handles that – or used to? Maybe your overseer? Conveniently away from you, though. So you don't have to see it or hear it."

"No, I-" Brackett began.

Matchett cut her off. "Well, it needs to be handled." He looked back at Lucy, and the puffy welt growing on her left cheek. "These darkies are slippery. If you don't keep them in line at every step, they'll take their liberties, get to thinking they can do as they please."

Matchett nodded toward Scobell. Did his gaze linger an extra second?

"You best hire someone to give your boy there a good beating," he said. "You don't want him getting out of line. Especially with you traveling and having no men-folk handy to deal with things."

"Yes, well, thank you for the advice," Brackett replied. She rose to leave.

"Captain Matchett, I appreciate all the help you and your men have provided today. Please let me know when you hear anything of my dear Uncle James."

"Of course," he said. His tone said he intended to do no such thing.

Scobell bent and picked up Lucy's pipe. As he and Brackett walked out, he paused and handed it to the older woman.

The swelling on her face was already red and angry. Their eyes locked briefly as she took the pipe from his hand; Scobell saw her expression was still resolute.

As they left the office, Scobell also noted that Saunders never glanced at Brackett again. Concern for saving his own skin had overtaken any salacious interest in hers.

CHAPTER 15

Back at the Exchange Hotel, Scobell sat in his room with a small lap desk making notes about their encounter that morning. Neither he nor Brackett had said a word since they left the detectives' office.

Twenty minutes later, there was a light tap at his door. It was Brackett.

"I'm sorry, John," she said in a low voice. "I wasn't prepared for that. For him to strike her the way he did."

She paused for a moment, then added, "They could've caught us. I could've gotten us captured."

Scobell nodded slowly in response. He swept his arm across the tiny room, inviting her in.

Brackett looked hard into his eyes. "Is it always like that?" she asked. "With slaves, I mean. Is it always so...rough?" Her voice quavered slightly on the last word.

Scobell released a deep sigh. "Yes," he said. "Often it is. There are some owners who treat their slaves better and some who treat them worse. But you'd be hard-pressed to find a Negro in Dixie who doesn't have whip marks or some other scars from being beaten."

"But she's an old woman!" Brackett objected. "I don't understand that."

"She's a slave," said Scobell. "His slave. She's not a woman. Her age doesn't matter. She's his property, simple as that."

Brackett shook her head, but Scobell continued.

"Would you think anything of smacking a dog that grabbed a piece of meat off the table or whipping a mule that wouldn't pull?" he asked. "That's all Lucy – or me, or any other Negro – is to these folks. Just a piece of property to be used when they're needed." He stopped for a moment, then added, "And tossed out when they're not."

"I'm sorry, John," she said again.

"It's alright," he said. "It didn't seem like they thought anything of it. There are probably a lot of high-bred women in the South who wouldn't involve themselves in disciplining a slave."

"That's not what I meant," said Brackett, still not taking her eyes off his. "I'm sorry that's how you've been treated. How your people are treated."

"I don't have people," he responded. "I've been alone since I was a boy. I've made my own way."

They sat in silence for a moment, then Brackett leaned forward and squeezed his hand. Her fingers looked even more slim and delicate as they wrapped around his gnarled digits.

As she rose to leave, Scobell said, "There's something else you need to know."

She turned back toward him with an inquisitive look.

"It's Matchett," he said. "Those burn scars on his face and neck?"

"Yes?"

"I gave them to him."

"What?" she gasped. From the look on her face, he wasn't sure she could take another shock today.

As Scobell recounted the night at the barn, the fire, and his encounter with Matchett, Brackett slowly made her way to his cot and lowered herself onto the edge.

When he finished, Brackett's face was ashen. He wasn't sure if she was more terrified by the tale of young men being shot and burnt alive, or by the implication that Matchett might already know Scobell was a spy.

"My God," she whispered at last.

"I'm not sure God was there that night."

"If Matchett recognized you," Brackett said, "we're already done. He and his men could already be on their way here to arrest us." She glanced toward the window, as if the detectives might suddenly burst through the curtains of the third-floor room.

"Yes," said Scobell. "I know. I have to find out whether he recognized me."

"But how? It's not like we can ask him."

"Lucy," he replied.

"How will she know?" asked Brackett. "She can't ask him either." She shuddered at the thought. "I don't even want her to be in the same room with that monster again."

"She doesn't have a choice about that," Scobell reminded her. "But she doesn't have to ask him either."

"How can she find out, then?"

"People like Matchett and his deputies talk in front of their slaves," he explained. "They don't think anything of it. You've already seen how it is with me, right? White folks don't even acknowledge I'm there."

Brackett nodded.

"Just like that dog or that mule, they forget there's even a Negro around most of the time," he continued. "And if they give the slave a moment's thought, they assume we're too ignorant to understand the conversation anyhow."

"You're sure Lucy will know whether Matchett recognized you?" she asked.

"Trust me," he said. "If there's a secret to be known, the black folks will be the ones to know it."

⎯⎯◆⎯⎯

Scobell stared at the ceiling of his hotel room that night, waiting for sleep to come. The actions of the day played back through his mind, as did that night in the flaming barn. He heard again the gunshots and screams, saw again men dying all around and Matchett's horse rearing in front of him.

Trying to chase the waking nightmares from his mind, he focused instead on what needed to be done.

They'd found a cipher disc. Unfortunately, it was guarded by the city's spy catchers, the very people charged with capturing people like Brackett and him. It was as if they'd found the disc lying amidst a nest of rattlesnakes. Their mission was to steal it, but even the slightest bobble would mean a deadly strike against them.

Lucy was the key. First, she'd have to determine whether Matchett recognized him. Then Scobell would have to convince her to steal the disc and hand it over to him.

That meant asking her to do more than eavesdrop on conversations. It meant asking her to betray her brutal master, which would risk her life as well.

Scobell sighed deeply. He'd turned it over enough times in his head. It was the only way. Without Lucy's help, there was no way to get the disc.

<hr>

The next morning, Brackett and Scobell strolled past the Tredegar Iron Works. They walked slowly, carefully noting the movement of people and materials from one part of the plant to another.

They realized they needed more detailed information than they could glean from walking public streets or scouring newspaper articles reporting the factory's outputs. They expanded Scobell's reconnaissance plan into a two-fold strategy to gather intelligence.

Brackett would cultivate relationships with Tredegar officials. The closer she could get to the top of the factory's management, the more information she could gather.

Scobell, meanwhile, would observe firsthand. He would find a covert place from which to observe the plant and spend as much time there as he could, documenting the activity he saw.

He would also look for opportunities to talk to the enslaved workers from the mill. Tredegar employed over one hundred slaves, either bought outright for their daily labor or rented from Richmond's ardent Rebel upper crust. If the chance arose, he would mingle with the workers and pump them for information.

Working from the top and bottom simultaneously, they could piece together an accurate picture of the mill's production today and its capacity for expansion if the war continued. At least, Brackett and Scobell hoped they could do so.

But first, Scobell had another mission angle to work. He needed to talk to Lucy.

<hr>

Waiting until evening, Scobell donned his slave rags and shuffled up Main Street to Matchett's office. He made his way past the building, noting the people moving about on the street outside and which office windows held flickering lights as darkness fell. A quick count of floors and windows revealed that there was a light emanating from Matchett's office window.

Scobell smiled to himself. Matchett didn't strike him as the type to spend late hours working in the office, and the thought of either of his deputies putting in late hours at a desk almost made him snort out loud. The most likely explanation was that Lucy was cleaning, which was exactly what he'd hoped.

He strolled two blocks past the office, crossed the street, and stopped for a few minutes to admire the horses at a livery stable. It was the least obtrusive way he could think of to linger while still watching the office door. Several people left the building, but none of them resembled his target.

Eventually darkness fell across Richmond and Scobell, worrying he'd lingered too long in that spot, moved back down Main Street. When he was across from the office, he ducked sideways into an alley. Just inside the shadowy opening, someone had stacked three barrels. He slipped behind them and turned to watch the building across the street.

An hour passed before someone doused the lights in Matchett's office. A few minutes after that, Lucy emerged from an alley beside the building. Scobell nodded to himself. She would've left the building by the slave exit in the rear.

Although it was dark, he could tell it was her immediately. Her thin build and crooked neck were distinctive enough, but the soft glow of the pipe in the evening gloom was a sure giveaway.

Just as William Ascot had taught him in Washington, Scobell waited for her to get halfway down the block before he slid out of his hiding place. Remaining on his side of the street, he moved casually and remained an unobtrusive distance behind Lucy.

Two blocks down, three men in long coats stopped Lucy. Scobell watched her produce a piece of paper from the pocket of her coat and show it to them. This seemed to satisfy them. She pocketed the paper back and moved down the street.

Though he stuck to his side of the street, the three men noticed him as well.

"Hey!" one of them shouted at him. "You over there. C'mere right now."

Scobell complied. When he reached the opposite sidewalk, one of them waved a gold badge marked with the letters "CS" and said abruptly, "Papers."

Scobell fished two pieces of paper from his pocket. One was a sheet signed by Brackett, identifying him as her servant. The other was a copy of the pass signed by Winder, giving Brackett – and by extension, Scobell – permission to be in Richmond.

"Where you headed?" one of them asked.

"Well, now," Scobell started, "The missus done axed me to check our hosses at the livery up the way. Then she axed me-"

"Yeah, yeah. That's enough, boy," another man cut him off. Examining his papers by the light of a streetlamp, the three deemed them satisfactory and waved him on his way.

Scobell strolled slowly away from the patrol, making sure to neither hurry nor linger where he might still be in their sight. After covering a city block, he sped up to catch Lucy.

Cresting a slight hill, he saw her just ahead. He slowed again to let her gain ground, wanting to stay at least far enough back that the sound of his footfalls wouldn't attract her attention on the quiet street.

As Lucy turned down Broad Street, Scobell noticed the houses around them getting progressively larger and more ornate. When the tall, white steeple of St. John's Church came into view, he realized they were in the Church Hill neighborhood. He'd heard slaves at the Exchange discussing this as one of the more upscale areas of Richmond, home to its upper crust citizenry.

It made sense, Scobell reasoned. If Lucy belonged to Matchett, it meant he was part of that gentrified class. That would explain how he became an officer at the outset of the war, and why Winder kept him on as a captain in the spy-hunting unit after his injuries.

Lucy turned down a side street. Scobell hustled to close the gap. Though there were no streetlights on this thoroughfare, he was close enough to see her slow as she passed the main gate in front of one of the more modest homes on the street. She took a few more strides, then stopped to open a side gate partially hidden by shrubbery: the slave entrance.

Scobell hurried up to her just as she went through the gate. "Lucy," he called in a hoarse whisper.

She paused and turned toward him, the glowing coals in her pipe flaring a bit.

"Yes, suh?" she said. Her tone seemed composed, despite the unusual interruption.

"I'm John," he said. "We done met yesterday at Cap'n Matchett's office. I was there with my missus."

"Yes," she replied, unperturbed. "I 'members."

"I needs your help," he said, cutting to the chase. "I needs to know something."

Lucy stood silently. The tobacco in her pipe flared brighter for a moment, then died down again.

"Has you heard the cap'n say anything?" Scobell continued. "'Bout me, I mean."

She was quiet for another moment, then said, "'Bout you, your own self? Don't s'pose I have. Can't recall it anyways. Why?"

Scobell didn't reply immediately either. He'd have to proceed carefully here.

"I done met him afore," he said.

"Why'd Massa Cap'n care 'bout that?" Lucy asked.

It was a reasonable question. Why would a prominent Richmond citizen and detective captain care about having crossed paths with a slave somewhere along the way?

"You know them burns on his face and neck?" Scobell said. "I done give 'em to him."

Lucy went silent again. Her pipe flared once more in the darkness.

"Hm," she said at last.

"He was tryin' to kill me," Scobell explained. "I didn't mean to hurt him. But that's what done happened."

"I wasn't with my missus then," he added. "She didn't have no part of that."

He saw the glow of Lucy's pipe move up and down as she nodded in response.

"I needs to know if he 'members me," Scobell continued. "If he don', that's good. If he do, though..." Scobell paused to let the thought settle in her head. "Well, that'd be bad. Real bad."

"What you wants me to do?" she asked at last. "Don't wanna do nothing agin the cap'n. I been with him since he's born. His daddy was my massa afore him."

"Don't need you to do nothin' special," Scobell replied, trying to keep his voice calm. "Jus' listen. See if the cap'n mentions me, like maybe he seen me somewhere afore."

He saw her glowing pipe bob up and down again. "S'pose I can do that," she said. "Don't see no harm in it."

"No harm at all," he said. "Jus' listening and letting me know."

"S'pose I can do that," she repeated.

"How 'bout I check back in a few days?" he asked. "See what you might've heard."

"Alright," she said. Without another word, she turned and disappeared into the night.

Scobell spun back to the sidewalk and headed toward the Exchange. He let out a deep breath. If Lucy heard nothing, it would confirm Matchett hadn't recognized him.

If that was the case, it would just be the first step. The next, a far more dangerous one, meant getting his hands on Matchett's cipher disc.

CHAPTER 16

S cobell entered through the slave doorway at the rear of the Exchange, then climbed the three flights of steep, narrow, and unlit stairs that the unwritten rules forced him to use. He was still catching his breath from the climb when he knocked on the door. Brackett whipped it open and waved him into the room.

"What's going on?" he asked.

"We have a dinner appointment tomorrow," she said with more than a hint of excitement in her voice.

"A dinner appointment?"

"With Joseph Anderson," Brackett said, a smile spreading across her face.

His eyes widened. "General Joseph Anderson? The owner of Tredegar Iron Works?"

"The very one," she said, still grinning.

"That should be interesting," he said. "How did you manage it?"

"I've been working on it since we got here. Pinkerton gave me the name of a Secesh captain named Michael Atwater and told me to contact him when I got here."

"Pinkerton gave you his name?"

"Yes. Webster connected with him last fall. Apparently, Captain Atwater is less than enthralled with the Rebel cause and is considering defecting back to the United States."

"Interesting," said Scobell. "Why didn't you share that information with me earlier?"

"Do you tell me everything you learn?" she asked.

He had to concede that he did not.

"Captain Atwater and his wife, Arlene, proved most helpful," Brackett continued. "The good captain served under General Anderson in the Tredegar Battalion that they formed last summer, shortly after the war broke out. When Anderson temporarily took command of the Cape Fear district in North Carolina last fall, they transferred Atwater with him."

She paused, confirming Scobell was following. He nodded for her to continue.

"Both of them were recently rotated back here. The general and his wife are keen to reestablish their places in Richmond society, so they're hosting their first dinner party since his return. The guest list included Captain and Mrs. Atwater."

"And Atwater secured you an invitation?"

"Well, more Arlene than the captain," Brackett said. "It seems she has family on her mother's side who live in Chicago."

Scobell perked up in alarm. "You didn't tell her you were from there, did you?"

Brackett raised her delicate hand to stop him. "I only told her that my widowed grandmother moved to Chicago in 1850. Which is true, by the way."

He let out a relieved sigh.

"Even though Pinkerton gave us this contact," Brackett added, "I don't know for certain where their loyalties lie right now. I'm maintaining my cover all the way."

"Smart choice," he said. His brief response didn't reflect his deepening appreciation for Brackett's discretion.

Returning to the subject at hand, Brackett picked up an invitation card. She read, "General and Mrs. Anderson request the pleasure of your company at dinner tomorrow evening, promptly at five o'clock."

"Dinner with the president of the Tredegar Iron Works," repeated Scobell. "Maybe the richest man in the city?" Scobell continued.

Brackett nodded and smiled. "The same."

"Well," he said, "I shall have to wash my socks."

⸻ ◉ ⸻

Their hired coach, pulled by a pair of jaunty gray steeds, pulled up in front of the Anderson's Franklin Street mansion. There was already a line of carriages waiting. General Anderson's enslaved coachmen, wearing gray uniforms trimmed in silver brocade, assisted each passenger as they alighted. The coachmen then skillfully guided the horse-drawn barouches around the corner to the stable.

The disembarking occupants, mostly couples, wore their finest evening wear. Women in their gaily colored hoop skirts, ranging from maroon to light blue to gold, glided down from the coaches. The gowns exposed a goodly portion of the ladies' shoulders and bosoms, but the crinolines virtuously hid the legs and feet of each.

The men wore a mix of clothing according to their service status. Civilians wore long gray or black coats over starched white shirts and bow ties, topped by wide-brimmed hats. Scobell observed that the stovetop hat favored by President Lincoln, and now wildly popular in Washington, was completely absent.

The Confederate officers among the guests were instantly recognizable in their gray uniforms. The spring evening being warm, the men wore shell jackets that rode just above their hips.

Captain Atwater, assisting his wife down from the carriage ahead of Brackett and Scobell, wore a gray wool jacket with a gold collar, broad gold lapels, and gold buttons. The jacket cuffs were similarly trimmed in gold, with gold braid extending up to the elbow. More senior officers wore plain jackets, although still with gold braid up the sleeves.

When their barouche reached the designated spot, Scobell hopped to the sidewalk, catching a whiff of sweet perfume on the still evening air. Clad in a neatly trimmed black suit, complete with black tie and black, narrow-brimmed hat, Scobell made a show of assisting Brackett as she stepped from the carriage. Brackett, still maintaining her role as a widow in mourning, wore a black silk dress trimmed with white collars and cuffs. She'd added a tasteful touch of black lace to embellish the presentation.

Scobell trailed behind her as she joined the Atwaters. They presented their invitation cards to one of the black doormen, then passed between the columns in front of the mansion and through the tall entryway.

The Anderson home exceeded even the most luxurious plantation "big house" that Scobell had seen in Mississippi. The ceilings towered ten feet overhead and dark wood trimmed every corner, doorway, and staircase. Thick carpets adorned with brilliantly colored, intricate patterns covered nearly the entire surface of the hardwood floors. Gas lighting, augmented by oil lanterns and candles, cast a flickering glow throughout the interior. The aroma inside was a combination of linseed oil, lamp smoke, and perfume from the female guests.

Scobell accompanied Brackett into the drawing room, where guests would briefly visit before dinner. He then retired to the kitchen, where he would remain with the other slaves throughout the evening. After asking the house slaves a few quick questions about the Anderson household, he found a seat in the hallway. He could sit here without raising suspicion and still overhear most of the conversation from the crowd in the adjoining dining room.

Since guests were still mingling in the drawing room, he peeked into the dining room. The massive wooden table was impossibly long and set with more places than he could quickly count. A small bouquet in a slender silver vase sat next to certain plates. Scobell assumed these denoted each lady's seat.

The men's plates also had flowers, arranged in the folds of the napkins. He knew from the few times he was called into assist with a banquet in the great house at the Scobell plantation that each gentleman would fasten the flower to his lapel once he sat down.

A dazzling array of knives, forks, and spoons spread beside the dishes. Plates were stacked four deep, one for every successive round of the banquet. House slaves had meticulously folded napkins on top of each pile of dinnerware.

A crystal water glass accompanied each place setting, along with an empty wine goblet. A plump black woman emerged from the kitchen to fill the water glasses. Her white apron, worn over a long black dress, was nearly a match to her white head of hair. A second house slave in a maid's uniform emerged from the kitchen to pour wine into carafes.

A polished wooden sideboard along the far wall held salad plates, waiting to be placed on the table. Scobell could see, and smell, a plate of bread waiting on the sideboard as well.

Main courses would still be in the kitchen. He'd seen a soup tureen next to the stove when he passed through earlier, and caught a whiff of the mouthwatering aroma emanating from it.

The war was taking its toll on Richmond. Wounded soldiers, women in somber widow's weeds, and displaced civilians from the surrounding countryside crowded the city's sidewalks more with each passing week. Newspapers described shortages of wool and flour. But here in General Anderson's house, it was pleasure as usual.

From the adjoining drawing room, he heard dinner being announced by the uniformed butler. The servers placed the first plates in front of the guests, starting with Mrs. Anderson, then the general. As soon as a guest finished their food, the quietly efficient butler pounced, removing the offending plate and utensils immediately. The moment they eliminated the last plate from a particular course, the butler began serving the next round.

As the initial din of guests being seated and the salad plates distributed came to a close, Scobell found he could hear the conversation from the dining room remarkably well. Shifting a bit, he realized he could even see some guests reflected in the glass of a breakfront cabinet across the hallway from his seat.

Brackett sat near him, but facing away. Scobell could only see the back of her head in the glass.

Arlene Atwater sat to Brackett's left. Captain Atwater's seat was on the other side of his wife. Sarah Anderson sat at the end of the table nearest the kitchen, while the general manned the head of the table opposite her.

Scobell had glimpsed General Anderson as he entered the room. He was a man of average height, with narrow shoulders and a high forehead. Anderson wore his wavy hair combed across the top of his head. He sported a neatly trimmed mustache, but eschewed the beard that so many Confederate officers cultivated.

"We've been able to increase production at Tredegar each month since the start of the war," General Anderson was explaining to a civilian seated opposite Brackett. "With so many men in the army, that's meant bringing in more slave labor, of course. We're even using Negro women now."

"Really?" asked the man, somewhat incredulously.

"Indeed," the general assured him. "They're proving quite handy at tasks that require more dexterity. The bucks, of course, we can only rely on for brute work. And even with those tasks, they require constant supervision, not to mention frequent lashes." He chuckled as if he'd made a clever play on words.

"Are they paid for their work?" asked Brackett.

"The owners?" said General Anderson, misunderstanding her question. "Oh, my, yes. We wouldn't think of using Negro labor without the owners being reimbursed. They require something to offset the loss of labor at home, of course."

"Of course," Brackett replied softly.

Conversation waned for a moment as the next course was served. As his guests dug in, General Anderson returned to what was clearly his favorite subject: the Tredegar Iron Works.

"We're nearly finished with a quite exciting new project at the manufactory," he announced in a conspiratorial tone.

"Do tell," Brackett said, a flutter of excitement in her voice. "What sort of project is it?"

"Well, naturally I cannot tell all," said Anderson, an unmistakable pride in his voice. "Two days from now, we will launch something completely unique. A new weapon that may very well win this war of Northern aggression." He paused for dramatic effect, then added, "We will rule the waters, for certain."

"Dear me," Scobell heard Brackett respond. "That does sound promising. I read about a ship that sails under the water. Is it something like that?"

"That was Mr. Cheeny's project," said General Anderson dismissively. "A gimmick, my dear. A novelty. This is a proper ship, mounted with 12 guns."

"Don't we have other ships with more guns than that?" asked someone else at the table.

"We do," replied General Anderson in a self-satisfied tone. "But none like this one. She is called the *Virginia*...and she is armored."

"Armored?" queried the voice of an unseen man.

"With iron. Tredegar iron." The satisfaction in Anderson's voice was conspicuous. "No cannonball can penetrate it, no torpedo can as much as dent it."

"Why, she'll be invincible!" someone cried joyfully.

"Indeed," said Anderson. "As I said, we will soon rule the waves. I'm certain a victory for our new nation won't be far behind."

Scobell's mind raced. Various newspaper reports had rumored the development of such a ship. No one knew it was this close to joining the fight.

Even as he pondered how to get this information back to Pinkerton, he realized it could never happen in time. They couldn't convey the intelligence of the *Virginia's* launch to Washington in only two days. Frustrating as it was, they'd have to rely on the southern newspapers, which Pinkerton and his team regularly collected and scoured for useful intelligence, to deliver the news.

The dinner party conversation returned to the success of the Confederate effort to date and what the invulnerable *CSS Virginia* would add to that effort. "We've already whipped the Yankees in every battle we've fought," said Captain Atwater. "With a ship like that, they'll be suing for peace before the year is out."

"Maybe before the summer is out!" someone added with a laugh.

"They'll be sorry once that happens," stated General Anderson with certainty.

"Why do you say that?" asked Brackett.

"Why, my dear Mrs. Lawton," said the general, "We'll control everything they need to survive." His tone was one an adult might use to explain something to a child.

"The North has staked their economy, nay, their entire future, on production from factories," he continued. "Our new nation, just like we have done for over a century, grows the food and the cotton that the Yankees or England, or any of a dozen other countries, need."

"I see," said Brackett. "I'd never considered it that way."

"Well, of course not, my darling," said Anderson. "These are the theories that gentlemen develop and evolve. Their grasp of economic interactions would be well beyond what you could be expected to understand."

"Oh, yes. Naturally," replied Brackett. Scobell knew she had a much pricklier response in her mind.

Another course arrived, and the conversation became muted once again.

General Anderson, having warmed to the matter of the promising future of the southern confederacy, returned to the subject after a few spoonfuls of soup.

"Those northern factories will never stay in business over time," he averred. "People just won't continue working in those filthy conditions, breathing soot and smoke for hours on end."

"Is that not a problem for Tredegar as well?" Mrs. Atwater asked.

"As I mentioned," Anderson said, "we've added more slaves to our workforce. With the institution in place, we needn't worry about the conditions. The darkies don't know any different. They have a place to sleep at night and something to eat, which is all they desire."

"They're such simple creatures," another man observed.

"Indeed," the general replied. "It's laughable that the Northern abolitionists wish to set them free."

There was a murmur of agreement around the table.

"The thought of it," said an army officer seated across from Brackett. Scobell could see the reflection of the soldier shaking his head in the sideboard. "It simply goes against nature."

"Of course, it does," said Anderson. "Why, if they set the Negroes free tomorrow, they'd be starving to death by the hundreds within a month. They don't have the slightest concept of how the world works or how to care for themselves."

The officer across from Brackett said, "Where else but here in the South do Negroes fare so well? Back in Africa?" He laughed derisively. "They live no better than the other beasts of the jungle there. Here, they have us to care for them. Feed them, house them. As you said, General, the thought of them existing without our care is laughable."

Another course of food was served, interrupting the conversation again. Scobell realized during the lull that he was gripping the seat of his chair so tightly that his fingers ached.

Shortly after the next course was set, the butler appeared from the front entryway. "General Anderson, suh. Cap'n Matchett is here, suh." The butler stepped aside to allow Matchett to stride into the dining room.

There was an audible gasp from a few guests at Matchett's grotesque appearance. Scobell heard a utensil clatter onto a plate.

General and Mrs. Anderson wouldn't invite a brutish man like Matchett to their home under the best of circumstances. With his burns now giving him a crocodilian appearance that caused people to avert their eyes, it was an intrusion they couldn't allow.

"Joseph, please," Scobell heard Mrs. Anderson say, equal parts horror and humiliation in her voice.

Recovering himself, the general said, "What is the meaning of this interruption, Captain Matchett?"

"I have news, General," said Matchett. "General Winder dispatched me to share it with you."

"What sort of news?" queried Anderson, his indignation at the intrusion overcoming his discretion.

Matchett glanced around the table, then announced, "We've discovered spies in our midst. Here in Richmond."

Another gasp went up from those seated around the table. Anderson suddenly recognized the risk of holding this dialog in front of his guests.

"Let's continue this conversation elsewhere, Captain." To his guests, he said, "Excuse me, please. I'll be back shortly."

Anderson stood and hustled Matchett back into the hallway. The army officers around the table rose and followed them out.

Scobell slipped out of his chair as well, easing up the hallway toward the front of the house. He hurriedly found a spot where he could overhear snatches of the conversation without being seen. He didn't dare risk being caught eavesdropping.

"Spies, you say?" he heard General Anderson ask.

"Yes." Matchett's rasping baritone was unmistakable.

There was an unintelligible exchange among some of the other men. Then he heard bits of Matchett's report: "A man and a woman...watching them for several weeks...staying at the Spotswood Hotel. Man...down with a malady. Two more arrived last week."

"How did you identify them?" someone asked.

"They delivered letters from the North to the *Richmond Enquirer* upon their arrival," came Matchett's reply. "We have people there..." The next part was muffled. "...they showed up at the hotel room of the man and woman. We had a man...in the room next door."

There was more murmuring that Scobell couldn't distinguish. Then Captain Atwater said, "How can you be sure they're spies?"

"The men...identified today by Mrs. Morton," replied Matchett. "...came to our office when they recognized them."

"What is the next step?" asked General Anderson.

"General Winder...warrant for their arrest," said Matchett. "...apprehending them right now...wanted to inform you."

A quick, unintelligible exchange followed, then Scobell heard someone ask, "What are their names?"

"Scully," Matchett growled in reply. "And Lewis."

CHAPTER 17

S cobell's whole body sagged. Somehow, Scully and Lewis had found their way to Richmond and would shortly be arrested.

Along with two more agents, a man and a woman. That could only be Tim Webster and Kate Warne. Pinkerton had sent them to Richmond at the same time as Brackett and Scobell.

Scobell didn't know the details of their mission, or why Scully and Lewis were now in the Confederate capitol, but it didn't matter. Someone had revealed them as spies. Could he and Brackett be far behind?

A shuffling of boots in the adjacent room told him the information exchange was over. He moved back toward his seat near the dining room. General Anderson returned to the party, followed by his officers, who slipped quietly back into their seats.

Anderson stopped and stood behind his chair.

"Well," he said, with a quick clap of his hands. "Rather more excitement than we foresaw this lovely evening, is it not?" A small murmur came from the civilian dinner guests.

The general slipped into his seat with a flourish. "Fear not, however. Our General Winder's detective force, including the skilled Captain Matchett, is more than capable of rooting out a few treacherous spies in the service of Mr. Lincoln."

"How frightening," came Brackett's voice. "And yet, what wonderful news that our detectives discovered them. Has someone captured them?"

Scobell marveled at the steady believability of her tone. He wasn't sure he could pull off the same authenticity in his current shaken state.

"You will read about it in tomorrow's newspaper, so there's no reason I can't tell you now," Anderson said. "Two of them are being imprisoned as we speak. It seems two more will soon follow."

A man's voice asked, "Imprisoned?"

"Indeed," said General Anderson. "Matchett will thoroughly question them, followed, no doubt, by the swift trip to the gallows that every Lincolnite spy deserves."

An abrupt quiet blanketed the dining room. Scobell saw the reflection of Captain Atwater's wife reaching across to grip her husband's hand under the table.

"But enough talk of spies and war for this evening, eh?" said Anderson with sudden cheer.

He snapped his fingers at a server who stood quietly along the wall. "Let's have dessert, shall we?"

———◆———

Brackett and Scobell rode back to the Exchange Hotel in complete silence. They dared not speak even a word of the spy ring's arrest in the rented carriage for fear of being overheard by the driver.

Once back in their quarters, Scobell told Brackett everything he'd overheard.

"Lewis and Scully were the ones they arrested?" she repeated fearfully.

"Yes," Scobell said. "It won't be long before Matchett has Webster and Warne arrested next."

Brackett gasped. The color drained from her face. She slowly turned her eyes away from him and stared at a blank spot on the wall.

The intensity of her reaction surprised Scobell. Up to now, Brackett hadn't struck him as someone who worried about her personal safety.

"It's upsetting, I know," he said. "It means Matchett's men are close to us, too."

"That's not-," Brackett stopped, her voice catching. "No, I'm fine."

Scobell let it drop. "Let's get some rest," he said. "Tomorrow will be an interesting day."

CHAPTER 18

YANKEE SPIES!

You could nearly read the *Richmond Enquirer*'s headline from across the street, Scobell thought.

The story was short, but conveyed the facts:

Two Lincoln spies, giving the names of John Scully and Pryce Lewis, were arrested at the Monument Hotel on Friday last, and are now in prison. The proof of their connection with the secret service of the enemy is most positive.

They were recognized on the street by a young lady, whose baggage they searched in Baltimore, while she was on her way to the South. Suspecting that they were detective officers sent by the Yankee Government to Richmond, she communicated her suspicions at Gen. Winder's office. Officers of our Government were immediately put upon the track, and discovered them in a private house. They became so much confused that they hastened away to the hotel, leaving their overcoats behind. They were followed, and captured by the detectives. Both of them claim to be English subjects, and they are in reality native born Englishmen, and have claimed the protection of that Government. But this will avail them little, since it is clearly shown, by evidence not prudent to detail in this place, that they are paid hirelings of the enemy.

Glancing furtively at the paper as he carried it to Brackett's room, Scobell realized it added a few things he hadn't overheard the day before. He mentioned this as he handed the newspaper over to Brackett.

"I heard Matchett say a Mrs. Morton identified Lewis and Scully," said Scobell. "That must be the young lady mentioned in the article."

"Mm-hm," Brackett mumbled as she read, then reread the article. When finished, she folded the paper and dropped it on her lap.

"Mrs. Morton is the wife of a United States senator," Brackett explained. "A former senator, anyway. From Florida."

"They were living in the North," she continued, "Before the war broke out, Mr. Morton traveled to Virginia. His family stayed behind in Baltimore."

Scobell nodded for her to continue.

"Mrs. Morton was vocal about her support for secession and the Confederacy, much like our friend Mrs. Greenhow," she said. "And like Lady Rose, Mrs. Morton soon caught Pinkerton's attention. He sent Scully and Lewis to search her house for any evidence to support his suspicions that she might be passing information to the Secesh."

"And?"

"They found nothing incriminating. Just a couple letters from her husband asking her to come to Richmond." She paused, then added, "Seems like she took his suggestion."

Scobell shook his head in disbelief. "She's walking down the street in Richmond and sees the same two Pinkerton agents who accused her of spying and searched her house. What are the chances?"

They sat in silence for a moment, both lost in their own thoughts. Brackett spoke first.

"The paper doesn't mention Kate and Tim," she said. There was a glimmer of hope in her tone.

Scobell gave a slight shrug. "Matchett probably didn't tell the reporters about them. He wouldn't want to spook them and put them on the run."

Her downcast mien returned. "Yes," she said. "I suppose that's true."

After another moment of reflection, she said, "I wonder if there's a way we can get word to them." Another spark of optimism.

It flashed through his mind to ask why she was so much more concerned about Warne and Webster than Scully and Lewis, who were already imprisoned.

Instead, he said, "And tell them what? They'll be reading the same news we are. Matchett said Scully and Lewis visited Warne and Webster. I'm sure they've already realized they're next on his list."

"Besides," he added, "the absolute last place we want to be right now is anywhere near them. They've been found out. Anyone they speak to will immediately be a suspect, too."

Brackett looked even more crestfallen than before, but said nothing. They lapsed into silence once more.

"I need to talk to Lucy," Scobell said at last. "I still need to find out if Matchett remembers me. If he does, I'll be next on the arrest list, whether they connect us with Scully and Lewis or not."

Brackett nodded in resignation.

"Besides," he continued, "maybe she can tell me more about the arrest, and about Warne and Webster."

Reviving a bit, Brackett said, "Yes, that's a good idea. While you're doing that, I'll talk to the Atwaters. The captain may know something more about what Winder and Matchett are planning."

They resolved to meet at the hotel that evening and compare their findings. Assuming, of course, they hadn't been arrested by then.

———◆———

Donning his sloppiest slave rags and a cotton cap pulled low over his eyes, Scobell set out for Matchett's office. Though he appeared to slouch along at an unconcerned pace, he timed the occasional stops to hitch his pants or scratch under his shirt to give him a clear view behind, ensuring he wasn't being followed.

Arriving at the building, he slipped into the alleyway behind it. When the odor of the outdoor latrine used by the slaves hit his nostrils, he knew he was in the right spot. He couldn't risk entering the building to talk to Lucy, so he would wait until she answered the call of nature.

He found a spot atop an empty barrel where he could lean against an abandoned shipping crate. From there, he could watch the rear door of the office building without being seen by anyone walking past on Main Street.

Settling in to wait, his thoughts immediately turned to the operatives who'd been arrested. It was a complete coincidence that Mrs. Morton spotted Lewis and Scully. Just as much a fluke as having Winder send Brackett and Scobell into the office of a man Scobell thought he'd killed.

And yet, both things had happened. Lewis and Scully were behind bars because of their bad luck. If Scobell's fortunes proved equally poor, he knew he'd never see the inside of a prison.

Who knew what kind of tortures men like Matchett and his deputies could devise? He tried to avoid it, but his mind drifted to the suffering they might inflict on him.

After a few moments, he noticed a dull pain in his right hand. Looking down, he realized he'd been grinding the back of his knuckles against a sharp corner of the crate while his mind raced. A small trickle of blood formed on his rough skin.

Shifting his thoughts to a different subject, his mind strayed back to the arrest of his fellow spies. From the moment he'd heard about Lewis and Scully's capture, his sole focus had been on the consequences. Now, for the first time, he pondered the reason for their presence in Richmond.

Why had Pinkerton sent them? He and Brackett were already on their mission in Richmond, and Pinkerton had told them beforehand that he was assigning Warne and Webster there on a different, parallel mission.

But sending two additional operatives into the Confederate capitol? Richmond was not a large city. Six agents operating within its confines would almost certainly draw attention at some point. It seemed an oddly reckless move by the spy chief.

Scobell turned the situation over in his mind, rehashing the newspaper article and the overheard conversation again and again.

Suddenly, it hit him. Matchett had said something about Webster being down with a malady. Perhaps Webster was on a mission in Richmond and took sick or got injured. If it was severe enough, Warne might've refused to leave him to fend for himself in enemy territory.

Once their return from Richmond was overdue, Pinkerton must have panicked and sent two more agents south to find out what happened. It was the only scenario that made any sense.

That didn't change the fact that it was a precarious decision by Pinkerton. Worse, it wasn't his own neck he was risking. Besides Lewis and Scully, sending more agents into Richmond imperiled all his operatives there.

The spymaster's Washington team would know soon enough from the southern papers that Matchett had captured Lewis and Scully. Brackett had noted the absence of Warne and Webster in the article, however. If he had no other intelligence source, Pinkerton still wouldn't know what became of them.

Would the spy chief realize the danger he'd already created for his two embedded teams in Richmond? Or would he double down on his mistake and impatiently send more operatives to search out Warne and Webster? Scobell pondered the possibilities, but couldn't be certain how Pinkerton would react.

The only thing he knew for sure was that he needed to get the cipher disc and get the hell out of this city. Until that happened, not a minute would pass when he'd feel safe.

Scobell started suddenly when the door into the alleyway opened. A small, thin woman stepped out. A short-stemmed pipe dangled from her lips.

"Lucy," he called softly.

Lucy showed no signs of surprise at being accosted on the way to the latrine. She simply turned her crooked neck slowly to look in his direction. It took a few seconds for her eyes to adjust to the dim light of the alley. Once they did, she inclined her head slightly to show she recognized Scobell.

"Getting so's an old woman can't even use the privy in peace," she said. Her tone was so flat that Scobell wasn't sure if she was joking.

He decided to play along. "True," he said. "I'm mighty sorry for catching you here. I jus' weren't for sho' it were safe to meet you in the open."

"Mm-hm," she said around the stem of her pipe.

"Been wondering whether you heard anything 'bout me from Cap'n Matchett," he said.

She shook her head from side to side in a slow, wide arc.

"Nothin'?" Scobell pressed.

She stared at him for a moment, as though insulted by the repeated question. "Nope."

"The cap'n or his men been talking 'bout Missus Lawton at all?"

Lucy considered this for a moment. "Nope. Can't say I've heard your missus' name neither. Guess Massa jus' ain't interested in y'all."

A wave of relief washed over him. Not only had Matchett not recognized him, but they hadn't tagged him and Brackett as part of the spy ring either. If they had, her name would've been on the lips of every man in the department.

"S'pose not," he said. "Jus' soon keep it that aways."

"I reckon so if you the one done burnt him," she said. Turning toward the outhouse, she declared, "Well, I come out here to take care of my business."

Scobell pressed his luck.

"I gots another question for you," he blurted.

She looked up at him, her eyes owlish behind the magnifying lenses of her spectacles. A quick puff flared the tobacco in the bowl of her pipe.

"That pouch what the cap'n was looking for when we was in the office?" he said.

Lucy nodded.

"You knows what's in it?" Scobell asked.

"Yep," she said.

A moment passed before he realized she didn't intend to say anything more. He stifled an exasperated grunt.

"What's in it?" he finally asked.

"Don't know as I oughta say. Cap'n Matchett say I shouldn't talk 'bout what I sees round him and his place."

"You seen it then?"

Another puff on the pipe. "Cap'n say I shouldn't talk 'bout what I sees."

Scobell thought for a moment. "How 'bout you don't have to talk?" he said.

She looked at him quizzically.

"How 'bout I axe you something and you shakes your head yes or no?"

Her pipe flared energetically as she considered this. At last, she nodded her head slowly.

"You seen what's in the pouch?" he asked.

Lucy nodded again.

"Is it a cipher disc?"

She stared blankly at him from behind her glasses. This was proving far tougher than he thought.

"A round thing, 'bout like this?" He made a circle with his thumbs and forefingers. "Gots another round thing on top?"

The pipe bobbed up and down as she moved her head.

He tossed in a test question. "Gots numbers all round it?"

Lucy shook her head no.

"Letters?" he asked. "Letters 'round the outside?"

She nodded once again.

He'd been right. Matchett had a cipher disc.

Now Scobell had to get it.

"Lucy, I needs what's in that pouch," he said urgently. "Can you help me get it?"

"No, suh!" she snapped, recoiling.

Damn it. He'd pushed too far, too quickly.

"Lucy," he said, "I needs it. I needs it to get free."

"No, suh." She turned and looked toward the outhouse. "I gots to do my business."

"Matchett done smacked you," he said. "Done kept you a slave your whole life long. Probably whipped you plenty."

Lucy suddenly turned back to face him.

"Cap'n Matchett been my massa since he were a boy," she said. "Probably thirty year, now." She pulled the pipe from her mouth, gesturing with it to punctuate her words.

"His daddy was my massa afore that," she said. "Since I been a little girl. Cap'n's daddy done gimme this pipe. Said it belonged to my granny afore she died." She took a step toward Scobell as her argument gained steam.

"Cap'n Matchett beat me some, sho'" she conceded, "'Bout like any massa would. But he done fed me and give me a roof. Done made me a house slave, too, so's I never had to work the fields. Never sold me South neither, where they work them Negroes to death."

Scobell had seen it before, but it still amazed him. The loyalty of a slave to their master. Despite every barbarous treatment imaginable – forced poverty, whipping, rape, even deliberately dividing mother from child and husband from wife – some slaves remained devoted to the people who deprived them of the most basic elements of human liberty.

It was all they'd ever known. The unfamiliar world beyond the veil of bondage was sometimes more terrifying than even the most horrific reality within it.

Scobell tried another tack. "So you gonna be true to him 'stead of helping free one of your own people?"

"My own people?" she said. "Didn't you hear me? The Matchetts is my people. And you being the one that done burnt the cap'n!" She gave a dismissive wave.

"But…"

"But nothin," Lucy spat. "You ain't my people. Havin' black skin don't make you nothin' to me. You jus' want something you can't get, so's you want my help. Don't you talk 'bout being my people."

With that, the proud old woman spun away from him and went back into the office. Apparently, her need to use the outhouse had gone away.

CHAPTER 19

"It's my fault," Scobell said in exasperation later that evening. "I let Lewis and Scully's arrest rattle me. I pushed too hard."

"It's understandable," Brackett replied. "All of this has me scared to death, too."

He shook his head. "Doesn't matter if you understand it. Lucy was our best chance – hell, our only chance – to get a cipher disc and get out. Scaring her off put an end to that."

A depressed hush fell over the hotel room as the two considered their situation. At last, Scobell said, "We just need to leave."

"What?"

"We need to pack up and get out of here," he said. "Get out of Richmond, out of the South completely. Get to safety."

It would mean sacrificing his liberty, but what good was freedom to the dead?

"But we haven't completed our mission," Brackett countered.

"We have the information we've gathered on Tredegar," he said. "We have troop numbers in the city to report."

"But no cipher disc," she interjected.

"So we're supposed to keep trying until we're caught?" he said. "Until you're thrown in prison, and I'm skinned and swinging from a tree?"

"We knew those were the risks when we came here," Brackett countered. "That hasn't changed."

He suddenly jumped to his feet and paced in agitation. "What's changed is they know we're here now!"

"You said Lucy hadn't heard us mentioned."

"They know the Union has spies in Richmond. How long until they link us to them and come knocking on that door? A week? A day? An hour?"

Brackett glanced at the hotel door before she replied. "You may be right," she said. "But we have an assignment. We need to see it through."

"So that's it?" he said. "You're leaving here with a cipher disc or not at all?"

"Are you that worried about saving your own skin?" she countered.

"And yours. I don't want either of us ending up in Matchett's hands."

Brackett set her thin jaw rigidly. He could see the muscles around it working as she forged her answer.

"Let's hope it won't come to that," she said after a moment. "But we have an assignment to accomplish. We need to see it through."

Another look at Brackett's expression told him she wouldn't be swayed. Any further discussion being pointless, he stalked off to his own room. Between frustration and fear, sleep would be a distant wish tonight.

⎯⎯◉⎯⎯

The next morning, things got considerably worse.

Another headline blared from the newspaper pages, this one from the *Richmond Dispatch*. Scobell's heart sank as he read the first line of the front-page story.

The Condemned Spies

We have refrained for several days past from mentioning that two men, Pryce Lewis and John Scully, had been tried before the Court Martial now sitting at the City Hall, and condemned to be hung as spies.

The news was upsetting, although not unexpected. The next section, however, was a gut punch.

The execution has been postponed for a short time on a respite granted the parties by the President, but we are assured will come off at an early day. It is intimated, and we believe on good authority, too, that the condemned have made disclosures affecting the fidelity of several persons, one or more of whom have been apprehended. If rumor speaks the truth, he will find himself, no doubt, in an uncomfortably hot place.

They had talked. Either Lewis or Scully, or maybe both, had stared at the gallows that awaited them and loosened their tongues to save their necks.

Scobell couldn't help but ponder whether he might do the same in their shoes. He shook the thought away and turned back to the article.

Who could the "several persons" be? It wouldn't seem to include Brackett or himself. Lucy had told him only the day before that Matchett and his men hadn't mentioned them.

That left only Webster and Warne. One of them was already in custody. If the other wasn't, it wouldn't be long until they were.

The Confederate government was unlikely to execute a woman, even one convicted of spying. But they had already sentenced Lewis and Scully to hang. If Webster was the one in custody, he would surely follow as quickly as they could pull together a jury to convict him.

Would the sight of the gallows sway Webster as well? Would the thought of that rope tightening around his throat, of dangling below the wooden deck, kicking and strangling as his last breath failed to come, chase away his loyalty to his fellow operatives, too?

Trading Scobell and Brackett to save his own neck would be an attractive proposition. If Webster wouldn't do it to save his life, would Warne do so to save herself from prison?

He posed this question to Brackett as he tossed the *Dispatch* to her. She quickly scanned the article, her face turning so pale he thought she might faint.

She rose from her cushioned chair and crossed the room to pour a glass of water from a ceramic pitcher. Brackett gulped down the water in one motion, refilled it, and nearly emptied it a second time.

She was still staring down at the glass in her trembling hand as she announced, "Warne won't talk."

"You're sure about that?"

Brackett whirled on him. "I'm telling you, she won't talk! I know it."

Scobell considered pressing, but her penetrating glare told him the topic was now off limits. He resigned himself to that reality and changed course. "What about Webster then?"

Brackett considered the question. "I don't think he'd talk either," she said after a moment.

"You don't sound as sure about him as you do about Warne," he observed.

Brackett fixed him with an icy look designed to remind him that the subject of Warne's loyalty was no longer open to discussion.

"I only meant that you don't seem as certain about Webster's integrity," he said.

"He's an honorable man, not to mention a brave one," she said. "I don't believe he would turn us in to save himself."

"Are you sure? Or are you trying to convince yourself?"

"I feel sure," she said.

Feelings, Scobell thought, won't make a difference. Only what came out under the forceful questioning of Winder and Matchett would matter.

———◆———

The next morning's *Richmond Dispatch* answered the question of which Pinkerton operatives they'd apprehended. A minor article on the bottom of the front page announced the arrest of Tim Webster on charges of spying in the service of the United States. The article noted that his wife, who was also under suspicion, remained in their room at a local boarding house.

While the espionage story might have been headline news just a day before, much larger events now took precedence: *YANKEES ATTACK YORKTOWN!*

McClellan's army had finally pushed south into Virginia again. They had landed at Fort Monroe, then marched on Yorktown. There, they'd fired the first shots of the invasion. From the Virginia maps he'd memorized, Scobell assumed McClellan's intent was to threaten Richmond by pushing up the narrow peninsula between the York and James Rivers.

Was it possible that the Federal army would reach Richmond in time to liberate all the Pinkerton spies? The mere thought kindled a spark of relief inside him.

He immediately tamped it down, however. There were too many variables that could slow the advance of the Union forces, and even one day too late would still be fatal. If Brackett and Scobell were going to get out of Richmond safely, it would be up to them to orchestrate it.

Scobell joined Brackett in her room to plan their actions for the day. It had become their daily custom after he picked up the morning newspapers. She opened the door with an expectant look on her face.

"What's the word this morning?" she asked.

"They've arrested Webster," he murmured, handing her the paper. "And McClellan has attacked Yorktown."

"What?!" She snatched the paper from his hand and quickly scanned the front page.

"They didn't arrest her," she said after a moment.

Scobell was confused. With another of their spy team arrested and a Union attack underway, that was the piece of information Brackett latched onto?

Before he could ask, she blurted, "I need to go see her."

Now it was Scobell's turn: "What?"

"I need to see Kate," Brackett said. There was no mistaking the urgency in her voice.

"You can't be serious," said Scobell. "Even if she isn't under active guard, they'll be watching her for sure. We can't be seen there. They'll know instantly that we're operatives, too."

Brackett turned away from him and sat silently. It wasn't until she sniffled and wiped her cheek with a handkerchief that he realized she was crying.

"You need to tell me what's going on here," Scobell said. "What is happening between you and Warne?"

Brackett drew in a deep, shuddering breath, then faced him again. Her eyes were rimmed in red and tears welled within them.

"She's my sister," she said. It was as if hearing her own words out loud made the reality worse. She began weeping uncontrollably.

Scobell sat upright in surprise. "Your sister?"

"Yes," she replied with a nod. "My oldest sister." This created another tearful outburst. Scobell waited once again for it to subside. This bout ended more quickly than the previous one.

"Why didn't you tell me before?" he asked.

"I haven't told anyone," she said. "And you can't either. No one can find out, especially Pinkerton."

Scobell didn't understand, and told her so.

"If Pinkerton ever found out we were family," she said, "He'd fire me immediately."

She blew out a long breath that ended in a wry laugh. "Exactly because of situations like this."

"I see," Scobell said. "Because someone might put concern for their sibling above loyalty to his secret service, above completing the mission."

Brackett nodded again. "Exactly." She took another trembling breath and started again.

"Kate met Pinkerton in Chicago," she continued. "She worked for him for about five years and did so well that he asked her to create a department of female detectives within his agency." She stopped to dab her eyes and wipe her nose.

"This was all before the war?" Scobell asked.

"About a year before," she said. "When she became the superintendent of Pinkerton's female department, she wrote me a letter asking me to join."

"Even though Pinkerton wouldn't allow it?"

Brackett nodded. "She knew from the outset that he had a rule against employing multiple family members, especially with two women. But I needed a job and Kate thought I'd be perfect at the detective agency, so we agreed to keep the whole thing a secret."

"When the war started," she continued, "Pinkerton brought some of us east when he was hired to spy for General McClellan and President Lincoln. By chance, he brought both Kate and me."

"Well, not totally by chance," she added with a feeble smile. "I was the only woman who could put on a believable southern accent."

Scobell leaned back in the cushioned chair, pondering the effect of this revelation. "I understand why you're worried and why you want to see her," he said at last. "But you also have to understand why we can't possibly do that."

"I have to talk to her," she pleaded. "I must know she's alright."

"She's not in any danger right now."

"How can you say that with everything that's happening?"

"They're talking about hanging Lewis, Scully, and Webster," he said. "And they very well might." He saw Brackett cringe.

"But they won't hang a woman," he continued. "Not even for spying."

"You can't know that! You saw how vicious Matchett can be. He'd do anything to punish someone for spying in his city."

"I do know that. I've lived among these people my whole life. No matter how brutal they are to people like me, they still have chivalrous ideas about white women. Even if Matchett wanted to hang Kate, Winder and the others in the Confederate government would never allow it."

She paused momentarily. "That may be true. But she's still my sister. I need to see her, to know that she's alright. I'll go by myself. I'm willing to take the risk."

"It doesn't matter if you go alone, Kitty. Once you're arrested – and there's no doubt you will be – how long will it take before they nab me, too? You're risking both of us if you go there, whether I'm with you or not."

Tears once again leaked from Brackett's eyes.

"I understand how you feel" he said. "But we have to accept that Matchett is using Kate as bait. They threw Webster in prison, but left her on the outside. He's hoping any other Union spies will try to contact her or even rescue her. What better way to draw them in than a woman in distress?"

"It doesn't matter," she insisted, her breathing coming in ragged gasps. "I need to see her, to know that she's alright."

"Kitty, you need to listen to reason," he said. "Kate is already trapped. There's no way of getting her to safety now. You can't help her. And if you even attempt to contact her, you seal our fate, too. Are you willing to do that?"

She whimpered into her handkerchief for several long moments, her hands shaking as she held the small cloth to her face. At last, in a barely audible voice, she sighed, "No." She shook her head without looking up at him and added weakly, "No, I'm not."

"Alright then," he said. "We need to get out of Richmond and get home, where we can be safe. To do that, we're going to need to get our hands on that disc."

"I thought you were ready to leave without the disc?" she asked.

"I've had some time to think about that," he said. "I don't want to go back if I can't be free."

"What do you mean?"

"Pinkerton is using my free papers to keep me as an operative. He'll only grant them to me if I come back with a cipher disc."

"What? I can't believe he'd do that!"

"It's true," he said. "Believe me. And it's also true that I don't want to die here, especially at the hands of Matchett." He saw Brackett shiver at the thought.

"I've risked my life a dozen times or more to get free," he continued. "It's the thing I want most, what I've craved my whole life. To stop now and go North to live as a contraband, knowing I could end up back in slavery if the Secesh win this war..." His voice trailed off.

"I understand," said Brackett.

"I'm not sure you can," he said. "Not truly. But that makes no difference now. What matters is that we get the cipher disc and get out of Richmond."

CHAPTER 20

Over the coming days, the Federal troops' first offensive movement since the previous fall dominated the headlines. McClellan's troops, stymied in their initial attack at a place called Lee's Mill, shifted their focus to Yorktown. Having landed the invasion from the waters of the Chesapeake Bay, the general had barricaded the city.

As he read of the siege, Scobell mused that McClellan, aided by a compliant Pinkerton, had probably convinced himself that the Rebels outnumbered him five to one. Having seen firsthand the number of troops the graybacks had in Virginia, and the relatively few more that had since moved through Richmond, Scobell knew the opposite was closer to the truth.

Buried below the news of the invading Yankees, though not much below, was the tale of captured spy Timothy Webster. Provost Marshal Winder, humiliated by the infiltration of a Union agent within sight of the Confederate capitol, moved rapidly to end that tale.

In custody for less than two weeks, they tried and convicted Webster on April 22, 1862. His sentence was death by hanging. One week later, despite a letter of protest from President Lincoln himself, the Rebels executed Webster at 11:22 AM.

A few key details from the article in the *Richmond Dispatch* caught Scobell's attention. The first was that "owing to defective cotton rope," the initial attempt at hanging failed and Webster tumbled to the ground below the gallows. Scobell couldn't help but wonder what ran through the Welshman's head as they trundled up the ladder to face the noose a second time.

The *Dispatch*'s article about Webster stated that Lewis and Scully "let the cat out of the bag on him after their conviction." That could hardly be more damning. Still, he contemplated again whether he might not do the same to save his own skin.

The newspaper continued that they'd arrested Warne, still being referred to as "Mrs. Webster," and imprisoned her at Castle Godwin. The report noted that she "will no doubt be sent out of the Confederacy." Scobell was quick to point out that passage to Brackett when he showed her the account, though her only reaction was a silent nod.

The last quote that stuck with him was a reference to the outcome of the trial. They'd convicted Webster, the article said, of "lurking about the armies and fortifications of the Confederate States in and near Richmond." This particularly concerned Scobell, because that's exactly what he was currently doing.

In fact, he'd spent much of his time in Richmond lurking about the armies and fortifications, especially those at the Tredegar Iron Works. Tonight, he found himself there once again, tucked away between packing cases and barrels on the hillside overlooking Tredegar. He watched the workers as they bustled about like so many ants; counted the soldiers of the Tredegar battalion as they mustered, marched, and drilled on the perimeter of the manufactory; and documented the number of trains as they rolled in with raw materials and rolled out to the battlefront laden with cannon and Richmond rifles.

Brackett and Scobell had already documented the production from Tredegar, completing the first phase of their mission. He had spent many hours tucked away in this hiding spot, watching activity at the plant.

He'd been here so many times, in fact, that he and the gray cat had formed a regular ritual for his visits. It would appear within a few minutes of Scobell's arrival and he would reward it with a small morsel of food scraped from his own plate at the Exchange.

Despite its obvious hunger and the frequent rewards Scobell provided, the cat would never trust him enough to eat from his hand or come within petting distance. At most, it would brush coyly against his leg or swat a paw at his hand until he released the food.

Each time he reached out to stroke the cat's back, no matter how gentle the movement, it would shy away. Apparently, no amount of food or tender treatment could earn its trust.

As the cat disappeared among the debris again, Scobell's thoughts turned back to Tredegar. He'd also met enslaved workers from the plant, blending in with them as they walked back from their daily labors and pumping them for information.

Brackett, meanwhile, had conducted her subtle interrogations of General Anderson and his subordinates. Between them, Brackett and Scobell determined that about a thousand rifles shipped from Richmond each month, along with about twenty-five cannon – half of what Pinkerton estimated prior to their mission.

Yet here Scobell sat, watching over Tredegar. This was mainly because he didn't know anymore how to get his hands on a cipher disc.

Until they devised a new plan to get one, he had simply gone back to something he knew, something that made it feel like he was making progress. Plus, surveilling Tredegar gave him time to sit alone and think. Maybe that would lead to a scheme to grab a cipher disc.

Tonight, though, it hadn't. Every scenario he'd run through in his head resulted in a dead end. Some of them literally so.

He watched the Tredegar workers trickle out the front gates at the end of their shift, the white workers first, followed by the slaves. He noted that the enslaved workers not only veered off in a different direction from the white workers as they left, but that there were no guards overseeing their exit.

As he'd found out when he'd talked to the black workers earlier, they didn't need a guard. Anyone who didn't return to their owner's quarters would quickly be missed and Tredegar supervisors immediately noted anyone not checking in at the factory first thing in the morning. Bonded to servitude here in the heart of the Confederacy, where else did these people have to go?

Scobell rose stiffly and plodded back to the hotel. He normally moved slowly when in his slave guise, but this evening, he dawdled even more. As much as he hated to admit it, Webster's hanging had affected him. The walls of the city felt as though they were closing in, preparing to trap him there forever.

When he reached the suite at the Exchange, Brackett pounced the moment he entered. Bounding out of her seat to greet him, her eyes shone with a light he'd never seen before and her cheeks were pink with excitement.

"Oh, John!" she said, her voice thick with emotion, "You won't believe it!" She moved so close to him that Scobell took half a step backward.

"Believe what?" he asked, baffled at the giddiness that had suddenly replaced her recent melancholy.

"There's someone here to help us!"

Brackett looked like she might want to hug him. He took another half-step back.

"Help us?" Scobell was having a hard time comprehending. "Who?"

"His name is Samuel Joseph," she replied, finally reining in her excitement a bit. "Pinkerton sent him. He's here to help us get home!" Another flush of pink surged into her cheeks.

Scobell shook his head and said, "You need to back up and tell me what on earth you're talking about. From the beginning."

Brackett took a deep breath. "He approached me downstairs at the restaurant this evening," she began. "He introduced himself as a businessman dealing in whale oil. I thought that odd at first, since there's so little of that industry here in Richmond."

Brackett produced a small scrap of paper from her pocket and handed it to Scobell. "Then he gave me this."

He held the fragment up to the light. It held only eleven words, written lightly in charcoal: *sheet iron, olive oil, scrap iron, sweet oil, logs, tamarac, coffee.*

"It's our code, John," Brackett said. "It's the mission code for you and me."

When he'd set up his secret network of operatives, Pinkerton developed a code to use when transmitting messages. Unlike the Confederate cipher, which replaced each letter in a message, Pinkerton's code substituted whole words. Without knowing the words to swap, any coded message read like gibberish. Each agent in the Pinkerton network was required to memorize the entire code, which contained over 170 substitutions.

The code served another purpose as well. Before sending them into the field, Pinkerton gave each team of agents a mission code, known only to him and the agents. Just as the Loyal League had their call and response recognition code to identify members, Pinkerton's mission code would identify anyone who presented it as part of his team.

He glanced at Brackett, then looked again at the piece of paper. Mentally replacing the nonsense words with their code equivalents, he read: *white, woman, black, man, disguised, cannon, Richmond.* There was no refuting it;

this was the exact string Pinkerton had them memorize before they left Washington.

"You're right," he said. "It is our mission code."

"And 'whale oil,'" she said, her voice quivering with excitement again, "means-"

"Union," Scobell finished.

"Exactly!"

He processed this information, turning it over carefully in his mind. To receive such good news after so many weeks of horrible events felt like someone had thrown them a lifeline. But was this news too good?

"Can we be sure about this?" he said. "How do we know it isn't a trap?"

Brackett's expression immediately shifted to one of exasperation. "Don't you think I've thought of that?" she said. "Look, Lewis and Scully could've identified us as operatives to the Confederates. Maybe Webster might've, too."

Scobell nodded.

"But they wouldn't have known our mission code," she continued. "Only someone sent directly from Pinkerton to help us would have that."

Grudgingly, Scobell had to admit it was true.

"Did he tell you what we're supposed to do?" he asked.

"No. But I'm going to meet him again tomorrow morning. And I want you to come with me."

Her bright attitude had returned. Grudgingly, Scobell could feel a certain lightness seeping in as well "Where are we meeting him?"

"At Peebles Watchmakers & Jewelers."

Scobell raised an eyebrow at her.

"I didn't choose the place," she said defensively. "Besides, we have to maintain my appearance as a wealthy widow. Where else would you have me meet him, the billiard saloon?"

"I didn't say a word," he said, raising his hands to feign surrender.

"Nor should you," she said with mock indignation.

Scobell noticed it was the first slight hint of humor Brackett had shown since the news of Webster and Warne had broken.

CHAPTER 21

The next morning, at the appointed time, Brackett was browsing the various necklaces, brooches, and bracelets adorning the shelves of Peebles Watchmakers & Jewelers. She was clad, as always, in the black dress of a grieving widow, but today she also wore a light gray bonnet and matching gray gloves.

Scobell, wearing his black houseman's suit and hat, followed attentively behind. He carried her parasol hooked over his forearm, and quickly jumped in to assist when the black skirts of her dress needed navigational support in the store's narrow aisles.

They had deliberately arrived early. This allowed them to make a leisurely pass up both sides of the street to reconnoiter the area while ostensibly window-shopping. Neither of them identified anything out of the ordinary.

Brackett decided aloud to, "step into the jewelry store and see if I can find a gift to take home for Mother." A few minutes of browsing inside resulted in a visual evaluation from a decrepit old man behind the high counter. A horseshoe of gray hair wrapped around the frail man's bald head and thick, wire-rimmed spectacles perched on the end of his nose. Mr. Peebles, apparently.

His evaluation of Brackett must have led to a favorable outcome since he approached her and offered, "How may I assist you today, ma'am?" As was to be expected, there was not even an acknowledgement of Scobell's presence.

Brackett, not wanting to be occupied with the jeweler when Joseph arrived, replied, "Why, thank you, sir. That's quite kind, but I'm only browsing right now."

"Is there anything in particular you're interested in perusing?"

"I'm visiting from Mississippi and I'd like to take something home to my dear mother when I return," she said with a voice dipped in honey.

Peebles shifted his weight as if to take a stride toward the display case in front of her. Brackett cut off his move by saying, "I just do not know what I want yet. Perhaps even a fur instead of jewelry. But I will let you know if I see something I like."

"Of course, ma'am." Suitably chastened, he retreated a few steps to let her shop in peace.

Gracefully haughty, thought Scobell. She wears the role well.

The bell above the door chimed softly as someone entered the store. From where he stood, Scobell could only see a hat moving above the shelves, its narrow brim and low, rounded crown seeming to bob along the aisles on their own.

"Good morning, Mrs. Lawton!" the voice belonging to the hat suddenly rang out. "What a delightful surprise to find you here on this fine day."

As the hat rounded the last tall shelf, Scobell could finally observe its owner. He was a thin man, perhaps in his mid-thirties. He was at least six feet tall, but he somehow looked shorter. His narrow shoulders slouched forward, and a paunch protruded under his coat.

As tall as he was, his skinny arms and legs appeared too long for his body, and his hands and feet were too large again for those appendages. The latter impression was enhanced because he shuffled his feet instead of lifting them with each stride. Overall, he gave the appearance of being assembled from mismatched spare parts.

"Why, Mr. Joseph!" Brackett responded. "This is indeed a pleasant surprise." While the surprise was manufactured, she appeared genuinely excited to see him again.

Joseph bowed and doffed his hat in her direction. Scobell saw that his hair was parted in the middle and slicked onto his skull with an extra helping or two of pomade. His drooping mustache also appeared to have received a dollop of the greasy stuff. Scobell didn't know whether it was the hair tonic or some other body treatment, but Joseph carried the unusual aroma combination of lavender and creosote.

Brackett gestured toward Scobell and said, "This is my man, John."

Joseph looked at Scobell and away again so quickly that it barely qualified as a glance. Scobell suddenly felt heat rise on the back of his neck.

"Yes," said Joseph, focusing once again on Brackett. "What brings you here this morning?"

"Just looking for a little something to take home to my dear mother when I leave," she said. "But I just don't know what to buy her. She has so many pretty things already." Brackett punctuated her statement with a pout that, had it still been wintertime, might've melted snow off the sidewalk outside.

Joseph cleared his throat and adjusted his collar. "Yes, uh. I see," was the best he could muster in response.

"Perhaps you might know of another store nearby where I might find something for her?" Brackett offered.

Finding his composure again, Joseph said, "Of course. I believe I know just the place, only a short stroll down the street."

Joseph brushed past Scobell as if he were invisible and grasped Brackett lightly by the elbow, then guided her up the aisle toward the door. Scobell cast a quick glance back toward Peebles, who looked offended at the sudden redirection of a potential customer.

If the aged storekeeper knew the truth, he'd be glad to see all of them gone, Scobell thought.

The bell above the door jangled again as they exited the store. The trio moved down the brick sidewalk, Joseph clinging to Brackett's elbow and Scobell following a few paces behind.

Because social protocol wouldn't allow him to follow any nearer, a frustrated Scobell could only hear a few brief snatches of the conversation's low tones. At one point, he caught the word "Richmond" and at another, the phrase "help you." He noted Joseph did most of the talking, while Brackett mostly nodded and occasionally turned her radiant smile toward her gangly companion.

Although they stopped in front of a few more store windows, there was no need to continue the pretense by going inside. In fact, because of the chance of being overheard, this would've limited their ability to converse.

Strolling the noisy streets of the city, they could talk in a near whisper, adjust the content of their conversation when any stranger approached near enough to hear, and carry on a covert conversation in broad daylight. To the extent anyone noticed them at all, the worst assumption they might've made was that the tall man was taking a slightly ungentlemanly interest in the young widow.

Returning at last to the Exchange, Joseph left them at the grand front entrance with an exaggerated bow and another doff of his hat.

"It has been a genuine pleasure, Mrs. Lawton," he said. "I look forward to the time when our paths cross again."

Scobell caught another whiff of lavender and creosote, heavier on the creosote this time.

Neither Brackett nor Scobell spoke until they reached the security of their room. Once inside, Brackett removed her bonnet, then quickly turned to Scobell. "Well," she asked, "What do you think?"

"What do I think about what?" he snapped, annoyance in his tone.

"About Joseph, of course," she answered. "Do you believe now that Pinkerton sent him to help us get out?"

Scobell flung his black derby hat onto one of the cushioned chairs. "How would I know?" he exploded. "I couldn't hear a damn word either of you said once we left the store."

"I'm sorry," Brackett said. She looked genuinely saddened. "I didn't realize you couldn't hear any of it."

"Yeah, well, I couldn't," he said. At length, he added, "What did he have to say?"

"He told me again that Pinkerton had sent him to help us, that he thought we might need assistance to get out."

"He was certainly right about that."

"He wants to help us escape, John. To get a cipher disc and get back to Washington. To get home."

"How?"

"He said it will take a little while, maybe a week, to arrange."

"While we sit here waiting for Matchett and his goons to snatch us up?"

"Why are you acting this way? We finally have someone willing to help us instead of trying to lock us up and you're fighting it every step."

He blew out a long breath. "I didn't like being treated that way, not by another operative from our team."

"I'm sorry that happened. It wasn't right."

"How can you be so sure Joseph isn't working for Matchett?"

"You mean besides the fact that he knew our mission code?"

"Yes," Scobell said, "Besides that."

"John, he knows everyone we know," she said. "Pinkerton had told him about Scully and Lewis, and Webster, of course. But he also knows Seaford and Gardner, and even Harry Davies. He was with them in Washington before he came to Richmond."

"Kate?"

"He knows her real name," she said. "He doesn't know she's my sister. I told you before, no one knows that." Then she added, "Except you."

"He knows everything he should then, to prove he's a Pinkerton agent."

"Yes," she said. "He does. He is one of us."

"One of you, maybe," Scobell said. "Pinkerton or not, to him I'm nothing but another Negro."

"John!"

"You saw it," he said. "You already said so." He paused, then added, "I have to admit that the other Pinkerton agents always acted like I was part of their team. But not this fellow. He treated me like a pile of horseshit in the street, something to be avoided and ignored."

Brackett was quiet for a moment. At last, she said, "Will that matter, if he can help us get a disc and get home safely?"

"Not if he succeeds," he conceded. "But some sacrifices might have to be made to achieve that success. If it comes down to it, I have a feeling I'll be the first offering."

⟢ ● ⟣

The next afternoon found Scobell back in his hidden nest overlooking Tredegar. He had little left to observe here, but at least it felt as though he was doing something useful. Otherwise, he'd be sitting in his hotel room, either staring at the door contemplating when Matchett, Blake, and Saunders might come bursting through, or enduring further arguments about Joseph. He wasn't sure which of those prospects he found less appealing, but he was avoiding them both at the moment.

After a few minutes passed, the gray cat poked its head out from between the slats of a broken crate. It slinked over to Scobell, brushing deliberately against his lower leg.

The cat continued their normal ritual by working its way up to his extended hand and sniffing for the morsel of food he held there. As always, though, it refused to take the tiny piece of meat from his hand and waited for him to drop it.

Scobell slowly reached out to pet it as it chewed, but it shrank from his touch. With an offended glare, the feline strolled off into the trash-strewn lot.

Cats can't be bought or bribed. They truly have no masters, he admiringly thought again.

He turned his attention back to the grounds below. Just as they had the day before and many days before that, workers moved about the factory.

They unloaded coal and iron ore from incoming barges, and loaded crates of rifles, cannon, and steel rails for railroad construction on outgoing railcars. Scobell watched as he had for weeks, but his mind was elsewhere.

Their shift over, the workers queued at the gate to leave. As always, the white workers left first, with the black slaves following behind.

Inevitably, the workers broke into small groups who strolled home together, chatting among themselves. Each day as they left, a few of these clusters would pass Scobell's hiding spot. They would walk within a few feet of him as he remained unseen amid the piles of debris.

Today, a group of white workers came up the path, followed by a band of slaves. Scobell shifted positions so he could watch them approach. When they were finally close enough to observe through the gathering gloom, Scobell was stunned.

Those eyes.

The last time he'd seen them, years ago, they'd blazed with loathing and spite. It was a look of hatred he'd never forget.

And then, as quickly as the realization hit him, they were gone again. The workers continued on their path, enveloped by an evening mist that slowly climbed its way up the hillside from the James River.

Scobell jolted backward, jabbing a stave into his ribs as he did so. He hardly noticed.

Could it be possible? After all this time?

It had to be. He could never forget that face. He'd remember it to his dying breath.

The thought stirred a long-buried hatred in his own breast. Buried long perhaps, but not very deep.

The hatred rose in him like molten steel, threatening to roil its way out in an act of violence or sear through his being, scorching him from the inside out. He arrived back at the hotel's slave entrance without even realizing he'd been walking.

When Brackett let him into the suite, he strode straight past her and into his own room without speaking. He spent the next three hours sitting on the foot of his bed, staring into a darkened corner and reliving the worst day of his life. He ignored Brackett's knocks on the door until they stopped, focused solely on the rage that welled within him.

At last, from the haze of fury, came the realization that what was done could not be undone. Instead, he needed to decide – here and now – what he would do next. Only that mattered.

He considered his circumstances and the few avenues available to him. If he acted on what he'd seen today and righted the terrible wrong from his past, he'd need to bolt from Richmond immediately. There would be no waiting for Joseph to come up with an escape route for him and Brackett.

In fact, there would be no Brackett at all. If he did what he was contemplating, she would have to be excluded completely and left behind when he ran.

He considered this. Brackett had Joseph to look after her now. She was enamored with him, so excited that Pinkerton had sent him to save them.

But not them, he corrected himself. Not really. Joseph was in Richmond for her. Whether Scobell lived or died, or earned his freedom, would be of no consequence to Joseph whatsoever.

Earning his freedom. There was that.

If he went forward with what he was contemplating, there would be no cipher disc and no letter from Pinkerton certifying that Scobell was a free man. In fact, there would be no reporting back to Pinkerton at all, probably not even a return to Washington.

No, the best case was that he'd end up in the contraband camp at Fort Monroe. There, he'd no longer be a slave, but he wouldn't be free either. He'd remain nothing more than an indentured servant until this miserable war was over.

If the Federals won, who knew what would happen to the contrabands? Would they ship them back to their masters? Keep them in the North in some sort of half-free purgatory?

And if the Rebels won, there was no question what would happen. The two sides would negotiate for the contrabands to be returned to bondage. There, the slave owners would beat them to death or work them to death, under conditions far worse than what they'd originally escaped. Just for having the arrogance to take a sip of liberty, however limited, for the first time in their lives. For the first time in generations, in fact.

The contraband camp was risky, for certain. If Scobell didn't make it out of the South, though, there were other ways it could end. Much worse ways.

He could head west, into the mountains. There he'd live as he did before he crossed the Potomac; hiding like a prey animal, constantly searching behind the next tree for slave hunters who would slap him in irons or kill him as he tried to run.

That was assuming he escaped Richmond at all. Of the potential outcomes, he had to admit that the most likely one was being captured right here, never even getting out of the city.

They'd slap him in Lumpkin's Jail, the city's slave prison. The place was so mercilessly brutal that even whites referred to it as "the devil's half acre." They'd hold him inside, manacled and rotting in his windowless cell, until the day he earned the reprieve of being auctioned off and returned to hard labor.

Of course, even that miserable fate would be better than what awaited him if he fell into Matchett's hands. He'd already imagined, too many times, what horrors might lie in store for him if that happened.

All bad conclusions. No waving grass in rolling fields, no life of freedom. Perhaps no life at all.

Yet he already knew what he must do. He had to face the risks, daunting as they were.

He had to set things right.

CHAPTER 22

The following afternoon, Scobell stationed himself once again in his hiding spot overlooking Tredegar. Unlike the past several watches, though, he was completely attuned today to every action visible within the plant.

He mentally logged each group of workers as they moved wheelbarrow loads of coal to the furnaces and drove wagons loaded with iron ore for smelting. His sharp eyes registered each barge's arrival and departure. He carefully noted every string of empty train cars pulling in, each loaded train pulling out again, and the duration of time spent sitting in the siding.

From this distance, he couldn't see faces. He tried to pick out individuals by height or body movements, but he was too far away for that as well. He had no way of knowing whether his target was there in front of him or not.

Scobell had devised a plan for his ambush. Well, the outline of a plan. The shreds of a plan, really.

Not that he hadn't wanted to perfect the scheme more fully. But much of it would have to be improvised, depending on what was happening around him at the moment and what the immediate reaction was when he pounced.

Some of it relied on pure luck. For instance, the very first step in the plan. Would he see that face – those eyes – passing his hidden position once again? Fate would decide.

Scobell pulled his watch from his pocket and checked it. It would soon be time for the Tredegar laborers to line up and leave for the day. A horse knickered nearby as Scobell slipped the watch back into his pants.

The queue started forming, as always, with the white workers at the front. Scobell's jaw clenched. His heartbeat quickened.

Slowly, the crowd spilled from the front gate of the mill. Straining his eyes, he still couldn't distinguish one from another. He shrunk back into the shadows of the crates and casks.

A mist rolled uphill from the James once again. He listened to catch a hint of footsteps approaching up the path. It was hard to hear anything at all, though, over the thrumming pulse in his ears.

Minutes passed like hours. Sweat beaded under the brim of his slouch hat.

A footstep crunched on the gravel path.

Holding his breath, Scobell eased closer, though still hidden in the shadows. He peered down the hill, where spectral forms slowly materialized out of the evening mist.

He counted five of them. They walked in a group, but not together. They moved single file and there was no conversation.

His hands shook. A tear slid from his left eye, forced out by the strain of staring without blinking.

At last, the faces became clear. The first two he didn't recognize. Nor the third...or the fourth.

His jaw ached from clenching it like a vise.

The last face swam into focus. It was one he knew; the one he sought.

Scobell jerked back into the shadows once more.

He took a deep, silent breath. It felt like the first one he'd taken in minutes.

A few more seconds passed. He could hear the group approaching his hiding place. They were less than a few dozen feet away now.

He slipped farther back into the jumble of material, picking his way through until he emerged in the narrow alleyway beside it. The horse he'd tied there hours ago still waited, yoked to the cart that he'd loaded with baskets of food. Purchasing these items, ostensibly on the orders of Mrs. Lawton, had cost him the last of the gold coins he'd carried south from Washington.

Rounding the back of the cart, Scobell pulled the locking pins and dropped the tailgate. Then he moved up alongside the horse's left flank. Grabbing a small stick he'd left on the seat, he quickly poked the animal's haunch.

The horse neighed and reared slightly in its yoke. Scobell poked it again, harder this time, then smacked the rod across its backside just above the tail.

The nag whinnied again and bolted down the alley. It charged out onto the footpath just as the group of workers reached the corner, baskets full of bread, vegetables, and salted meat bouncing out the back of the cart in all directions. Scobell dodged back into the maze of packing crates.

The crowd of five scattered, shouting in surprise. As the horse crossed the path and started down the grassy bank toward Tredegar, it suddenly veered left, overturning the cart. Panicked now, the animal picked up speed. The cart dragged on its side and pulverized itself bouncing along the hillside.

As the cart dissolved into splinters and the frightened horse galloped off, the laborers' attention turned to the bounty of food spread on the ground before them. Recovering from the shock of the spectacle, they scrambled around the slope, grabbing up what they could and stuffing it into their clothing.

The last laborer in line was the slowest to react. It was a costly delay.

Like a wraith, Scobell slipped silently out from his hiding spot. With two quick strides, he was behind the lone figure.

With lightning quickness, he slid one sinewy arm around the worker's neck. The other he clamped rigidly over the mouth.

A sudden backward jerk yanked the laborer off balance and Scobell dragged his victim back into the darkness of his hiding spot. The kidnapping took less than five seconds.

Forcing his body against his captive to decrease the struggling, Scobell kept his hand clamped over the victim's mouth. He couldn't afford a shout that would bring help running.

After a moment, the struggling stopped. The pair were face to face, just inches apart.

Once again, after so many years, Scobell looked into those eyes. He remembered them as he'd last seen them, filled with bitter hatred.

Now, they only registered fear. And then, in a flash of recognition, shock.

"Marie, it's me," Scobell whispered. "It's John...your husband."

In an instant, he felt her body give way under his. For a moment, he thought she might go completely limp. He adjusted his grip from one of restraint to one of support.

He slowly lifted his other hand away from her mouth. Her breathing came raggedly through her lips.

One breath. Two.

Suddenly, she launched herself at him, engulfing him in a passionate kiss. Though Scobell wanted to give in to the moment, body and soul, he pulled himself away.

Looking back toward the footpath, he asked quietly, "Are they going to come looking for you?"

"No," she whispered back. "I barely even know them. We just walk home in the same direction each night."

"They'll be so busy gathering all that food that fell," she added, "They might not even notice I'm gone."

"That was the plan," he murmured. "I needed a distraction so no one would try to stop me."

"You found one."

"Made one," he corrected.

She stared lovingly up at him, absorbing him into those gorgeous dark eyes. Giving in to the flood of emotion, he drew her into another deep, loving kiss. He felt her entire body crushing against his.

Many seconds passed before they pulled apart again. Both of them panted from the effort and emotion.

"We can't stay here and do this," he said, glancing about. "Though God knows I want to."

"But, John," she said, shaking her head, "How did you find me? Where did you come from?"

"That's a long story," he said. "A really long story. But there's no time to tell it now. We have to get away."

"Where to?" she asked, still refusing to unlock her gaze from his.

God, those beautiful eyes.

"Excellent question," he said. "I hope I have the right answer."

Scobell grasped her hand in his. Despite its hardened calluses, he'd never felt anything so tender. He led her out the side exit of the lot and into the narrow alleyway.

A few loaves of bread and heads of cabbage were still strewn on the cobblestones. He snatched up a loaf and handed it to Marie, who tucked it inside her coat.

The spring evening had given way to dusk. Scobell welcomed the gathering darkness. They'd need it to get where they were going.

If one of Winder's detective squad stopped and checked them, his papers would be no help to Marie. He assumed she had her own papers, but they would only allow her to move to Tredegar and home again. There would be no explaining why she was halfway across the city in the company of a strange man.

Hand in hand, they scrambled from the shadow of one building to another, working their way east. For a short distance, they paralleled the Kanawha Canal, then looped around the canal basin.

The streets in this industrial area were poorly lit, except for lights from the factories. When they came upon a gas streetlight, Scobell either led Marie across the street or they pressed themselves against the uneven fronts of buildings to avoid the cone of light.

They moved as quickly as they dared, but their progress was slow. Much slower than Scobell wanted.

He led Marie back toward the river again, dipping downhill and darting around the stone piers of Mayo's Bridge. It was nearly black down here. Picking their way through the rubble of discarded factory material and trash dumped from the bridge above hindered their pace even more.

At last, they reached the docks behind the city's gasworks. Skirting the orb of light cast by the gasworks, Scobell led her to a steel ladder mounted to the edge of the wooden dock.

The ladder curved down from the dock. Its black metal rungs disappeared into the gloom. They could hear water sloshing against the piers in the dark below.

Peering over the edge, Marie came to a rigid halt. "John," she whispered, "Where are we going?"

"We have to go down the ladder."

"I can't. It goes down to the water. I can't swim."

"I can't either," he said with obvious pain in his voice.

"We can't go down there," she protested again.

He pulled her into the shadow of a large crate that perched on the dock, waiting to be loaded tomorrow morning.

"Believe me," he said, "I don't want to do this either. But it's the only way out."

"Out to where? Where are you taking me?"

"Out of Richmond."

"What? How are we going to get out of Richmond from here? We're in the middle of the city, down at the river...and that ladder goes down into it."

"I know," he said. "But where we'll go into the water is just a few feet from where Shockoe Creek comes out."

"How does that help?"

"The creek is only a few feet deep. It has walls on both sides, like a man-made canyon running through the city. We can wade up it without being seen, as long as we stay close to the side walls."

"Wade it? To where? Where on earth are you taking us?"

"About a half-mile up Shockoe Creek is Broad Street. The channel gets shallower and there aren't any walls. We can get out of the creek there."

Marie stared at him.

"Once we get there," he continued, "We'll be next to the Central Railroad station."

"What then?"

"We're going to hop a train."

"Hop it?"

"There's a freight train sitting at the station right now. This morning, I talked to a slave who works at the railyard. He told me the train is due to pull out..." He pulled the watch from his pocket, squinting to read it in the dim shadows.

"...in one hour. We'll stow away on that train. According to my railyard friend, it'll take us north as far as Fredericksburg."

"What then?" she asked, her tone softening a bit as she considered his plan.

"I know that area," he said. "I can find a way across the Rappahannock River from there."

"To the Federal side?"

"Yes, to the Federal side. We won't have free papers, so we'll be contrabands, but at least we'll be out of the South."

"No overseers," she said warmly, running her hands across his chest.

"And the entire Union army to protect us," he replied, wrapping her hands in his. "But first, we need to go down that ladder."

Marie scrunched the front of his coat into her fists.

"Do you trust me?" he asked. He gazed down at her, although the shadows hid the details of her features.

"Trust you?" she said. "John, I haven't even seen you in seven years. Seven long years." Her voice trailed off.

"Yes," she whispered after a moment. "I trust you with my life."

He hugged her close, pulling her entire body against his as if he could hide her from danger by enveloping her.

"Then we need to go," he said, breaking away. It required no small effort. "Now."

"OK," she said.

She walked back across to the ladder. Scobell followed her.

"I'll go down first," he said. "If you slip, I'll catch you. And there's a little drop at the bottom. I'll have to help you down from there."

Marie nodded her understanding. He mounted the ladder and disappeared down its rungs into the inky blackness below.

CHAPTER 23

Scobell shimmied quickly down the first several rungs, then paused while Marie started down. Her approach was shaky and her feet pawed at the emptiness as she tried to locate the next rung below her.

The mist off the river had left a heavy dew that coated everything along its banks. The moment Marie put weight on her foot, her leather bootie slipped off the rung. She fell.

Scobell lunged upward. He clung to the metal side of the ladder with his left hand, while trying to grab her leg with his right.

Marie dangled precariously for a moment, clinging with one damp hand to the rung above her head. At last, she found purchase again with her foot on the hard metal. With support from Scobell's powerful hand below, she righted herself.

"I got you," he assured her. "You're alright."

Marie said nothing, but continued her unsteady descent.

When Scobell could feel no more steel rungs below him, he stopped. The water looked shallow enough here when he'd scouted it in the daylight.

But the river was murky with pollution from the docks and the boats that frequented them. Could he really be sure?

Clenching his jaw, he dangled for a moment from the last metal bar. Goddamn rivers, he thought.

He let go.

The distance from the bottom of the ladder to the water was about eight feet. Free falling through the darkness, it felt like a hundred.

With a jarring splash, his feet hit the water. Scobell submerged to his knees, and then to his waist. He could feel something more solid than water around his feet, but he continued to sink.

Once the shock of hitting the water wore off, he realized he was slipping into the silty bottom of the river. He strained to pull his feet up out of the muck.

His left foot suddenly pulled free. The right remained embedded, however. The unexpected torque of this action pitched him face first into the black water.

Panic hit him instantly. He flailed the filthy water of the James with both arms and tried to leap back up to the ladder. This only stirred up more muck and embedded his stuck leg even deeper.

"John!" Marie called down to him. Her voice was urgent, but she kept it at a low volume. "John, are you alright?"

The sound of her words penetrated his panicked mind. It calmed him instantly, reminding him why he was there.

"Yes," he said, still panting from his momentary terror. "Yes, I'm fine."

Recovering his senses, he said, "Hang on a minute. I have to get my feet under me."

"OK," she said, although there was a tremor in her voice.

Scobell inhaled deeply and steadied himself, both physically and mentally. Pushing down gently with his left foot, he slowly extricated his right from the muck.

Free from the underwater trap, he scanned the immediate area and spied a short length of board jammed against the dock support. Lining himself up under the ladder again, he pushed the board underwater and stood on it to spread his weight. This worked much better, with the board sinking only a few inches into the river's silty bottom.

He softly called to Marie that he was ready.

"Just lower yourself to the bottom rung and hang there for a second," he said. "Then drop straight down. I'll catch you."

"Alright," she replied uncertainly.

Marie dropped to the lowest rung, dangled for a few seconds until her body stopped swinging, then let go without saying a word. She plummeted, falling with a splash into Scobell's outstretched arms.

Though he tried to cushion her landing, his perch on the board was precarious. For an instant, they both teetered. He skidded one foot back to keep his balance. This wasn't enough, so he shifted it a few inches farther.

The slight alteration caused him to slip off the back of the board. As he tried to catch himself, the plank shot forward, taking his other foot out from under him.

Still holding Marie firmly around the waist, Scobell toppled over backward, dragging both of them underwater. They thrashed for a few seconds in the shallow water, each trying to stand upright without pushing the other under.

At last, Scobell locked his hands on Marie's arms and pushed her upward. With this support, she finally gained her footing.

Winded from fear and exhaustion, he could only bring himself up to his knees. It was enough, though; the water lapped around his chest. He threw his arms around Marie's waist and hugged her.

Panting from exertion herself, she stroked his head, pushing the river water from his hair as she did. They held each other like this for a few seconds, then she burst into laughter.

"Shh!" said John urgently. "We have to be quiet."

"I know," she said, catching herself at last. "I'm sorry." Suddenly, another laughing fit overtook her.

Standing up at last, Scobell said, "What the hell is so funny?"

"Look at us," she said at last. "We almost drowned in water no deeper than a washtub!"

Suddenly, from above them, a man's voice called out, "Who's there?"

Fear instantly struck both of them silent. Scobell put his finger to his lips and gently nudged her toward the dock. Holding onto one of the support beams, they eased underneath it.

They heard footsteps on the boards above them. Then the voice called out a second time, from directly overhead.

"Hello? Is somebody down there?"

Holding the pier with one arm, Scobell kept the other wrapped tightly around Marie. She also gripped the pier with one arm and him with the other.

Long seconds passed as they waited to see what the man on the dock above would do. There were more footsteps on the creaky, weather-beaten boards. The iron ladder groaned slightly as someone leaned against it to look over the side.

"Hello?" the voice called again.

A second man spoke. "There's nobody down there. You're hearing things."

"I'm telling you," said the first man. "It sounded like a woman's voice."

"Coming from the river in the middle of the night?" said the second. "You wish."

A soft glow of light suddenly reflected off the river. One of them was dangling a lantern from the dock to get a better look.

"See?" the second man said. "Nothing there."

"Yeah," the first voice conceded. "I don't see a thing."

"Maybe it was a mermaid."

"Go to hell." Their footsteps receded across the dock and faded away.

When a few minutes passed, Scobell and Marie dared to breathe again. He took her gently by the arm and guided her away from the dock. They waded silently toward the mouth of Shockoe Creek.

———◦———

Shockoe Creek looped around the northern side of Richmond. Passing the Shockoe Hill Burying Ground and the poorhouse, it wound its way south, entering the main part of the city. From there, it was essentially an open sewer splitting the upper part of the city, where the Confederate Capitol Building and White House sat, from the lower section.

Near its outlet into the James River, Shockoe Creek was perhaps thirty feet across. But instead of banks, steep retaining walls rose fifteen feet or more on each side, directing it where the city's engineers wanted it to flow.

From those precipitous walls protruded pipes of varying sizes. These carried effluent from Richmond's storm drains, house sewers, and outlets from industrial buildings of all types.

During a rainstorm, the water of Shockoe Creek might approach the top of its retaining walls. Tonight, however, the water was closer to its normal level, less than three feet deep at its mouth.

Marie and Scobell stayed out of the stream's main channel. Hidden in the weird, dancing shadows thrown by the city's gasworks above, they inched along, backs tight against the creek's western wall.

The spring evening was chilly, but despite the drenching they'd received in the river, neither one felt the cold. The only sensation they knew was an overwhelming fear, barely interrupted by the warmth of their clasped hands.

A few dozen yards after they'd passed the gas plant, a gurgling noise emitted from a pipe overhead. Scobell yanked Marie by the hand as they dashed across the creek and pinned themselves against the far wall.

A burst of water poured from the pipe, dousing the far side of the stream in a foul, chemical-smelling discharge. Watching the hundreds of gallons pour down on the spot where they'd stood moments before, Scobell shivered.

"Hold your breath," he said to Marie. They moved off upstream again.

Traveling up the creek took far longer than Scobell planned. They clung to the shadows against the walls, dodged discharging pipes, and stopped under each street bridge to make sure no one spotted them from above. It was a time-consuming business.

When he'd checked at the docks, they had an hour until the train departed. He doubted his watch was still working after being dunked in the river, but his mental clock told him they were running out of time.

The water was getting shallower. But there were also more rocks and debris hiding below the surface here, which slowed their progress even more. It was maddening.

More minutes slipped by as they stumbled and splashed through the stream, all the while trying to stay hidden along the walls. Finally, they passed under the fourth bridge. Scobell knew they were finally nearing the railroad station.

The waters of Shockoe Creek were only a foot deep now. The stone walls tapered away to muddy banks here. This opened the way for their escape, but also meant they had to creep on their hands and knees in the cold, murky creek to avoid being seen.

They were just a few dozen yards from the spot Scobell had scouted for their getaway route. It would keep them hidden in shadow until they were nearly at the train station.

Even as the chilly water splashed over them, drenching their clothes again, his heart rose. They were so close. They were going to make it.

The loud blast of a steam whistle suddenly sounded.

Scobell froze. Marie stopped beside him.

A second long blast sounded, followed by the clear peal of the train engine's bell. A loud bang rent the night as the locomotive lurched forward and the cars behind it leapt ahead to follow it.

Dear God, no, he thought. We won't get there in time.

He grabbed Marie by the arm. In one motion, he jumped to his feet and snatched her onto hers.

"Run!" he shouted.

They both tried to scramble out of the shallow stream, but Marie slipped and fell back on her knees. Scobell wrenched her up again.

"Come on!"

They hit the bank simultaneously, and both immediately slipped and fell in the slick mud.

Scobell swore under his breath. Marie cursed even louder.

They clawed their way through the muck until they found dry enough footing to stand again. The train was rolling out of the station now, the last car twenty yards ahead of them and picking up speed.

"Let's go!" he said, pulling her forward.

Climbing the last few feet of stream bank, they finally reached the level of the railroad track. The pair broke into a dead run, chasing the departing train.

As they passed the station house, a shout came from inside.

"Keep going!" Scobell yelled over the din of the clattering train cars.

It wasn't necessary, though. Marie was already sprinting faster.

"Stop!" came a cry from the station behind them. "You there, stop!"

They were nearly even with the last train car now. It was a flat car with two cannons strapped to its open deck.

The train was picking up speed. In a few seconds, it would outpace them and be gone forever.

He reached for the metal handle next to the car's stairs. As he did, a shot rang out.

The rifle ball rang off the iron just a few inches above his fingers. Reflexively, he jerked his hand back, nearly stumbling as he did.

Catching his balance, he leapt forward, grabbing the handle and planting one foot on the bottom step of the car's short ladder. In the same motion, he swung around and reached back for Marie. She was close enough that he could hear her panting as she ran.

For one terrifying moment, they fumbled their grip. Marie lost her balance and pitched forward toward the rumbling wheels of the train.

Pulling with all his strength, Scobell yanked her upward and flung her onto the flat deck of the car.

She rolled twice and came to rest with a thump against the wheel of a cannon. She gasped for breath and latched onto the wheel with both hands to make sure she didn't slide off the other side.

Scobell climbed onto the car and ran over to her. "Are you alright?"

"Yes," she panted. "I'll be fine." Catching her breath, Marie added, "No thanks to you. You almost threw me off the other side of the train."

Scobell sank down on the wooden deck. A relieved smile spread across his face.

"We made it," he said, still panting himself. "We're getting out of Richmond."

CHAPTER 24

John Scobell woke in the morning in the arms of the woman he loved. Slowly and gently, he pulled himself away and rose so as not to disturb her slumber.

He looked down at her lithe form, curled inward against the chill of the morning. How long he had waited to be with her, to be united as husband and wife. He might not have the freedom he'd dreamt of for so long, but having Marie by his side would be enough.

Scobell padded across the dirt floor of the slave cabin. Pulling back the canvas curtain that covered the doorway, he looked out onto the plantation of his master, William Scobell.

It was the day after Christmas, 1855. Following the tradition of most plantation owners, Master Scobell gave those living in bondage on his property a few days off from their ceaseless workload over the holiday.

For the enslaved, it was a time of revelry. Each year, the plantation owners designated one planter to provide a Christmas meal, not only for their own bondspeople but also for those from surrounding plantations.

With up to five hundred slaves attending, it meant singing, dancing, and feasting. They gave thanks for enjoying a single heartier meal than the bread and dried pork they subsisted on the rest of the year.

Men washed their best shirts and coats. Women bound their hair in a kerchief they'd purchased months prior, just for the holiday celebration. Some ladies added a flaming red ribbon or piece of yarn to tie up their hair. Others wore one around their neck, above the collar of their finest dress.

While the Christmas celebrations were the highlight of every year, this one was exceptional for Scobell. He and Marie had taken advantage of the brief respite from their endless toil to get married.

John had approached Master Scobell for permission to marry Marie several weeks earlier. In fact, he asked Master Scobell before he'd even broached the topic with her. He didn't want to ask for her hand until he knew he'd be permitted to take her as his wife.

Master Scobell was initially sour on the idea. "You're a good hand, John," he said. "I'd like to let you have a woman. But I have as many slaves now as I can support. You know I take good care of y'all here and that costs me a lot of money."

John looked down at the tattered hat he held in his hands. Through a two-inch hole in the crown, he could see his right big toe protruding from the burlap wrap that served as his shoe.

"Yes, suh. You and the mistress done taked good care of me."

"Aside from that," Master Scobell continued, "I'd have to buy Marie away from Mr. Suggs. That'd be even more money out of my pocket."

"Yes, Massa," John said without looking up. He didn't turn and walk away, although that was clearly what his master wanted him to do.

A few seconds of silence went by. Master Scobell felt the awkwardness of it first.

"What if you were to marry, but both remain where you are?" he asked. "You stay here and she stays with Suggs. You could see each other all you wanted on Sundays, or evenings when the work's done early."

He smiled at the wisdom of his proposed solution. John wanted to smash his fist into the grinning face.

He knew that many slave couples lived separately on nearby plantations. Because of the cost associated with buying and selling human beings, and the unwillingness of plantation owners to bear that cost without some clear monetary benefit to them, it was probably the most common arrangement for married blacks in the South.

Still, he'd harbored hope that things could be different for Marie and him. He thought perhaps the master would recognize what a strong worker she was, what value she'd add to the plantation if he was to buy her. Now that hope was dead.

John bit back the bile that rose in his throat. He thought he might tear his worn hat in half with his bare hands.

Despite his yearning to live with Marie as his wife, he'd already considered the possibility of this arrangement. And he already knew his answer. It would be better to spend some time with Marie than none, or worse, to lose her to someone else.

"Yes, suh, Massa Scobell."

John forced a smile onto his face as he finally looked up at the man in front of him. It must've looked more like a grimace, considering the effort required.

"Well," said Master Scobell. "That'll be just fine." He was clearly pleased with himself.

"Congratulations, John," the plantation owner said, a broad smile spreading across his face. "Why, I'll even talk to Suggs myself and get his permission for the arrangement." His tone announced just how magnanimous an offer he considered this to be.

"Thank you, Massa," said John. He made sure not a hint of bitterness crept into his voice. "I thanks you much, suh."

———◆———

Now that the Christmas Day wedding was over and he'd spent the first night together with his wife, John considered again whether it was worth it.

His love for Marie burned strong. Though they were both just twenty years old, he knew it was impossible for him ever to love anyone else as much.

Beyond that, their first night together had been magical. The other slaves that shared the cabin with John had moved to different quarters for the night, leaving the two of them alone. He felt a warmth come over him in an instant as he recalled the tender moments of the previous hours.

But he knew that was all about to change. The other slaves would need to return to the cabin tonight, so the newlyweds' hours alone were at an end. Worse, Marie would have to go back to the Suggs plantation in a few days.

He tried not to think of it, but he knew the pain of that moment would be excruciating. It was already glowing like a burning ember in the pit of his gut. When the time came for her to leave, it would erupt in a ball of flame inside him.

Still, he reminded himself, it was better to have her part of the time – even such a small part of the time – than not at all. To reinforce the idea, he gazed across the cabin at her tranquil form.

Yes, he thought, this is better.

He crossed the tiny room in three strides and went outside to bring in more wood for the fire. Winter weather had come to Mississippi and frost clung to both the inside and outside of the cabin's log walls.

John had lived on the 800-acre plantation since he was born. Twenty years he'd lived under the lash, every minute dreaming of an escape to emancipation.

His parents had both lived out their brief existences on the Scobell plantation as well. John had never known his mother, who'd died just hours after bearing her only child. He still had vague recollections of his father. Papa D, as John called him, contracted yellow fever and died when John was just six.

From that time, he'd been on his own – at least to the degree that any person subjugated on a cotton plantation could be. The other slaves had collectively raised him after his father passed. He had dozens of parents, but also none.

Scobell gathered more firewood from outside the log cabin and stacked it inside, near the back wall. He tossed a couple logs onto the smoldering fire to ward off the chill of the winter morning. Staring into the wisps of smoke as they rose through the hole in the roof, he thought back on the early days of his life.

Most of it was a blur: never-ending field labor with too little rest, curled in a corner of a drafty cabin, wrapped in the same dingy, tattered cotton blanket he'd used since birth. The unending images of drudgery changed suddenly, though, when M.J. came to mind.

John was thirteen years old when M.J. McGinnis appeared one Sunday at the Scobell plantation. John couldn't remember the details anymore, but he was sure it was the Sabbath because the slaves weren't working in the field when M.J. arrived.

McGinnis's appearance was extraordinary in several ways. First, he was the only black man young John had ever seen wearing a suit. Until then, the Scobell family only had women working as servants in the great house, as did the other nearby plantations John had visited. When they held a party in the great house, the female house slaves who served the meal and cleared the table wore elegant black and white uniforms. Scobell had heard that some masters and mistresses had male house slaves who dressed similarly, but he'd never witnessed it firsthand.

McGinnis strolled up the dirt road to the plantation wearing a black suit, white shirt, and a shiny black bowler perched on his head. A neat string tie completed the outfit.

He arrived shortly after the slaves returned to their quarters after morning services. As on many southern plantations, Master Scobell made it a point to deliver a Bible reading to his bondservants each Sunday morning. Afterward, they had the rest of the day to tend to their own needs. Because the other six days were consumed with work in the fields from before sunup until well after nightfall, this meant baking enough bread, cutting and splitting enough wood, and mending tools and clothing to last the entire week.

A murmur went up among the enslaved people on the Scobell plantation when McGinnis wandered into their midst. As he introduced himself, a somewhat louder rumble spread across the gathering crowd.

"My name is M.J. McGinnis," he said in the deeply resonant baritone that Scobell would come to idolize. "I am a free black man who has come to Kosciusko, Mississippi, to live."

The proper English, erect bearing, and neat appearance of the 35-year-old McGinnis immediately grabbed people's attention. In particular, it ensnared the imagination of an inquisitive young boy named John.

"I am opening a barbershop in town," McGinnis continued. "I'll be barbering for white gentlemen to make my living. But I've come here to tell you that any Negro slaves who wish to have their hair trimmed can come to my shop. I will provide that service at no charge, along with free shaves for men."

Yet another murmur. "Do 'no charge' mean what I thinks?" asked one of the older men.

"Yes," McGinnis assured him. "It means it won't cost you anything." This time, the tremor of sound was one of approval.

By now, the excitement among the slaves had attracted the attention of Sipe, the plantation's overseer. The crowd of blacks clustered around McGinnis parted suddenly as Sipe strode into their midst.

"What's this business?" he demanded in his customary snarl.

Sipe was a short, thick boar pig of a man. With a frayed cigar stump perpetually clenched between his blackened teeth and an unkempt grayish beard, he ruled the fields with an iron hand and a leather bullwhip. Too dumb to save enough money to buy his own property and too volatile to last at any other job, Sipe seemed born to the overseer role.

McGinnis repeated his introduction, tactfully neglecting the part about providing free haircuts to Negroes.

"Freeman, huh?" Sipe grunted. "Lemme see your papers."

McGinnis produced his free papers for Sipe to inspect. He did so without complaint or argument, Scobell noted. In fact, he appeared to show no emotion at all in response to the overseer's demand.

Thinking back on the moment years later, Scobell doubted Sipe could read. Not wanting to admit that shortcoming in front of his charges, he stared at the official-looking pages for a few seconds before handing them back to McGinnis.

Sipe spat on the ground, splashing mud and tobacco juice onto McGinnis's leather shoes. The latter didn't flinch. He simply folded his papers and tucked them back into his interior breast pocket.

Clearly disappointed that he hadn't provoked a reaction, Sipe said, "Mebbe you're free, but you ain't welcome here. We don't want nobody coming 'round here and stirring up our niggers for no reason. 'Specially not some cheeky buck from somewheres else."

"I understand," said McGinty. "I'll be going then."

He nodded to the black faces gathered around him. Touching the brim of his hat in Sipe's direction, he turned to leave.

"I sure hope you understand," said Sipe to McGinty's back as he walked off. "You ain't welcome back here. If I see you on this place again, you'll be a freeman in a pine box. You get me?"

McGinnis came to a full stop and turned to face Sipe again. For a moment, young Scobell held his breath, wondering what might happen next.

"As I said," intoned the deep voice once again, "I understand."

Sipe, searching for the slightest hint of argument in the reply, couldn't discern any. At a loss for any other response, he simply grunted again. McGinnis turned away and proceeded down the dirt road.

CHAPTER 25

Marie stirred briefly on the rough-sawn wooden plank that served as their wedding bed, snapping Scobell back to the present. He looked over, thinking she might awaken, but she merely mumbled a few unintelligible words then slipped back into a deep sleep.

Scobell stoked the fire, and dropped another log onto it. He stared into the dancing orange flames, allowing the childhood reverie to creep back into his mind.

More flashes of McGinnis washed through Scobell's head: relaxing in the shade of a mulberry tree on a Sunday afternoon, watching black men and women get shorn and trimmed, receiving his own first haircut. These took place in the small yard behind McGinnis's shop. If he'd served his black clientele inside, the white customers would've disappeared and the flourishing shop would've closed overnight.

Scobell's thoughts drifted eventually to the quieter moments he'd spent with McGinnis. On tranquil evenings, long after the other slaves had finished with grooming and returned to their rude cabins for the evening, the older man taught the young teenager to read and write.

Sometimes other slaves gathered in secret behind the barbershop to take lessons from McGinnis, "learning their letters." But nobody attended as faithfully as young John.

Nor did any of them take to it like him. For the young orphan who was about to grow into a man, the world opened by reading changed his life.

McGinnis put ever more challenging books into his hands. When John exhausted McGinnis' personal library, the instructor had new volumes shipped to him from bookstores in New Orleans, Atlanta, and even Philadelphia.

The two became fast friends, despite the difference in their ages. McGinnis shared that, like John, he had been born on a plantation. The name given to him by the plantation master was Mingo Joe. He came to hate the name as he grew up, eventually dropping it in favor of his initials.

An older slaveholder named McGinnis bought M.J. away from the plantation where he was born when M.J. was just a boy. When Master McGinnis passed away a few years later, his wife moved to New England, where the rest of her family lived.

Before she left, she freed every person in bondage on their plantation. M.J. McGinnis, still just a teenager, was now a freeman.

The young McGinnis drifted north, working odd jobs along the way and stashing every penny he earned. When he reached Ohio, he found a school that specialized in teaching black students. There he became a student just as eager and industrious as young John thirty years later.

Before he really even understood what a college was, John knew McGinnis had graduated from one in Ohio. They offered McGinnis a teaching job at the first school he had attended, but he was determined to return to the South. There, under the guise of barbering, he would teach those with no other access to education how to read and write.

Because educating slaves was illegal across the South, he knew he could only remain in one place for so long before raising suspicion. McGinnis would stay for a year or two, pass on what knowledge he could to the local black population, and move on to another location. Kosciusko was the fifth town he had lived in since his return from the North.

Scobell smiled to himself as he recalled it was McGinnis who introduced him to the Loyal League – or its precursor, at least. At first, it was just a few dedicated people in a loosely affiliated network that passed news among the enslaved population of the Deep South. It would be years before it grew into the covert organization in which Scobell became an active participant.

McGinnis had been in Kosciusko about eighteen months when it all came to a sudden, tragic end.

John and the other workers had come in from the cotton fields well after dark when a woman from a neighboring plantation arrived at their quarters. She was on an errand to the Scobell plantation for her mistress. Before leaving to return home, she veered off briefly to share the news that someone had killed McGinnis and burned his shop to the ground.

It was an open secret among the slave population of the region that McGinnis had been educating Negroes. Somehow, that information had reached the wrong ears. It had cost McGinnis his life.

Sitting beside the fire in the same cabin seven years later, Scobell tried to recall how he'd felt when he heard the news. It had hurt, to be sure, losing his friend and mentor.

But punishment, loss, and death were part of the daily life of a slave. He remembered feeling anger at McGinnis' murder, but couldn't recall grieving over his friend's passing.

Marie stirred again on the wooden bed plank. Scobell shifted his gaze to her and a grin once again crept onto his face.

One of her eyes opened just a sliver and their gaze met across the room. She smiled in response to his expression, but a sudden yawn interrupted it.

"Good morning, sleepyhead," he said when her mouth closed.

"Good morning, husband," she replied.

From shortly after their introduction three years earlier, John had been secretly teaching Marie to read and write, as well as how to speak proper English. To avoid detection and a repeat of what had happened to McGinnis, they never used such language when anyone else was nearby.

When they were alone, however, they spoke it exclusively. It was their own special secret, one that drew them even closer.

"Husband," he said. "I like the sound of that."

"How do you like the sound of 'wife'?" she asked. As she did so, she lifted herself up on one arm, coyly letting the blanket slip down to her waist and fixing him with a look from those mesmerizing brown eyes.

"I like the sound of it," he said, crossing the room to join her once again on their rough wedding bed. "And I love the look of it."

⎯⎯⎯◉⎯⎯⎯

For more than a year, Marie and John lived the separate life of a married slave couple on different cotton plantations. They begged passes from their masters and mistresses at every opportunity, running the three-mile distance between the Suggs and Scobell properties at top speed just to spend a few extra minutes in each other's company.

Though he wouldn't have thought it possible before he met Marie, John's work burden seemed lighter. Looking forward to a few hours with his wife on Sunday made the grinding pain of working the cotton fields slightly more tolerable. Even the occasional whipping by Sipe or Master Scobell, for not hoeing fast enough or turning in a cotton bag that was lighter than they judged it should be, was slightly more bearable when he knew Marie would tend his wounds.

They talked of having a family, and of approaching their owners again with a proposition of allowing them to live together on one of the two plantations. John had sorted out how such an arrangement could work to the benefit of all parties, but the couple were too afraid to present it for fear of revealing his understanding of finances.

Instead, they bided their time and saved whatever meager income they could generate. When slaves were forced to work seven days a week to bring in a cotton crop before the weather turned, masters allowed them to keep the few pennies they earned for their Sunday work. During busy times that didn't conflict with work on the cotton plantation, Master Scobell loaned John out to the local sawmill or to load goods at the riverboat landing. Sunday work at those businesses also contributed to their savings, as did occasional sewing projects Marie did for other slaves.

The goal was to purchase freedom for one of them, who could then go to work earning regular wages. With that money, they could purchase the other spouse's freedom, making both of them independent.

It would be a slow process at the rate they were accumulating savings, but it gave them a goal. The plan allowed them the slightest glimmer of hope for the future. It was during this optimistic time that John first began dreaming at night of a farm with grassy hillsides waving in the breeze.

Then came the auction.

It always seemed that the people bound in slavery knew beforehand when a slave auction was going to be scheduled. Sometimes word traveled so quickly that it seemed like they knew before the white slave traders who arranged it.

Word had spread a week earlier that an auction was going to be held in nearby Durant. Sure enough, handbills soon followed, announcing the date and time of the event.

Auctions were a constant source of dread among the bonded population of the South. Sometimes, a slave might be sold into better circumstances, but those instances were uncommon.

Much more often, auctions tragically disrupted the slaves' lives. They separated mothers from their beloved young children, never to be seen again. They divided siblings from their brothers and sisters, torn away bawling and screaming.

They tore away husbands from their wives.

Two nights before the date of the Durant auction, Marie materialized in the doorway of John's cabin.

"John," she called softly, trying not to wake the other slaves around him. "I need to talk to you." Her voice caught, and she could barely finish her sentence.

He snapped awake at the sound of her voice. Catching the urgency in her tone, he slipped out of the cabin, tip-toeing around other slaves who lay sleeping on the dirt floor. A few of the lighter sleepers grumbled at the interruption to their already limited rest.

Once outside, Marie pulled him away from the door and farther into the darkness.

"Marie, what are you doing here?" She was risking punishment just by being off the plantation at night.

"John, I -" She broke off her sentence and a choking sob burst from her throat.

"What's wrong?" he asked. A gnawing anxiety suddenly sparked in his gut.

"I..." she stopped again, then finally forced out, "One of the slave women in the great house overheard Master Suggs talking."

Her voice cracked, followed by another sob. In the pale moonlight, he could see tears sliding down her face.

Marie gathered herself and continued, "John, he's going to sell me at the auction." The words were a more brutal blow than he'd ever received from Sipe's bullwhip.

"Why?" he asked. He could feel tears burning in his own eyes now. "Why would he do that?"

"He said he needs money," she said, wiping her face on her sleeve. "Probably drank or gambled it away," she added bitterly.

"But why you?" he asked, though he already knew the answer.

"He doesn't want to give up any of his top men so he can keep the cotton money coming in. He figures out of the women, I'll fetch the best price."

They both knew what this meant. Suggs was old and had never shown an interest in Marie beyond how many pounds of cotton she could pick. However, with her shapely figure and arresting features, Marie would be the instant object of desire for any white man with more lecherous intentions.

"We can't let this happen," was all he could muster. His mind was racing with scenarios to get her away.

"I don't know what we can do," she said, wringing her hands as she spoke. "I went over it a hundred times on my way here. There's no way to stop it."

"We've got to run," he said. "Run now."

"To where?" she replied. "We'll never escape."

"We have to try," he said, pleading. "We can't just give up. What if you're sold away and we can't see each other again?"

"I've already thought this through," said Marie, her sad tone now turning gentle. She put a trembling hand behind his head and pulled him close.

"John, I love you. I need you to remember that."

"Of course, I know that."

"If we run without a plan or a way out, we will get caught," she continued. "I may survive, if only because Suggs won't want to sell damaged goods."

John started to interrupt, but stopped. He didn't know what to say.

"But if we get caught running, they'll kill you," Marie said. "If the dogs don't rip you to pieces, Master Scobell will turn Sipe loose on you afterward. You may be his top hand, but they'll want to make an example of you."

"Marie, it doesn't matter. If I can't be with you, I might as well be dead anyhow."

She pulled his head down to hers and whispered in his ear, "It matters to me."

With that, she kissed him, then pushed away and disappeared into the woods. John, feeling as though all strength had ebbed from his body, collapsed to the ground. There he sat for the next hour, his head held in his hands and tears pouring in a steady stream from his eyes.

CHAPTER 26

On the morning of the auction, every slaveholder in Holmes and Attala Counties gathered at the local horse racing course for the sale. Most, including Master Scobell, brought their overseers along as well. If an owner made any purchases, he might need an extra hand to get the new slave back to the plantation.

John and the other enslaved people of the Scobell plantation were, as always, in the field before sunup. After they had labored for an hour, however, it was clear Master Scobell and Sipe would not be there to crack the whip that morning.

As soon as that realization dawned, John left. Telling the workers nearest him he would be back as soon as he could, he dropped his hoe and bolted for the woods.

He sprinted through the brushy forest, briars tearing at his forearms and branches stinging his face and ears as he ran. Rather than running away, though, John was running toward something.

At one spot, he had to cross a dirt roadway. As he did, he noticed a broadside tacked to a tree advertising the sale of "More than 45 Slaves in Prime Condition" that day. Only one of those 45 mattered to him now.

John reached the racecourse, panting from the exertion of his run. Concealed in the brush, he skirted the grounds until finding the point where the woods extended nearest the raised platform being used for an auction block. His hiding spot was perhaps 100 yards away from the platform.

From there, he could see male slaves being pushed or dragged onto the auction block. He saw the auctioneer strip off the men's clothes and turn them about so their entire bodies were on display. A few potential buyers jumped up onto the block to examine them more closely, sometimes checking their teeth by wrenching back their lips and poking fingers inside their mouths.

At this distance, he couldn't hear the auction clearly. The only sound that reached him was the singing cadence of the auctioneer. The words and numbers he called out were unintelligible, but an occasional roar of excitement from the crowd followed the bang of his gavel. John knew this signified the end of a sale, but couldn't tell whether the animation was because of an especially high price or an especially low one.

When the men were done, the women and children began mounting the auction block. John could see a few sold together in groups, but they divided others and sold the children separately from their mothers.

In these instances, the shrieks of agony from both mother and child reached John's ears clearly and painfully. When some parents clung too long to their offspring, he could also hear the crack of the whip being applied.

He searched the slave pen behind the platform as carefully as the distance would allow, but couldn't catch sight of Marie. Not until they steered her onto the platform.

She was one of the last people led to the auction block. John instantly knew her slender build, erect bearing, and graceful movements.

The bidding went on for several minutes before it paused. One bidder, a younger man in a light gray suit and wide-brimmed hat, hurried onto the platform to get a closer look.

Grabbing Marie by her long hair, he tilted her head back and pulled her chin down to get a better look inside her mouth. Satisfied with what he saw there, he seized the front of her shirt with both hands and tore it open to expose her bare upper body.

The man took a step back to better admire the view of her bare breasts, then grabbed her arm and spun her around to see her back as well. John seethed with fury and shame, although Marie stood straight and tall throughout.

The man turned to say something to the auctioneer, then dismounted the stand, nodding as he did so. Marie shouldered back into her shirt and the bidding resumed.

After a few more minutes, John heard the bark of the gavel, followed by a small roar from the gathered crowd. They pulled Marie down from the auction block and she disappeared from his view.

He sat down on a bed of leaves and leaned back against the tree trunk he'd been hiding behind. Every muscle in his body was taut with rage and his breath came in ragged bursts.

What now? He'd dropped his work and sprinted to the auction with no plan in mind other than seeing his wife once more. He'd seen her, from a distance at least, but didn't know what to do next.

As minutes passed, John's seething anger slowly receded. His breathing became more regular and conscious thought returned.

He needed to see her up close one last time. He needed to speak to her. The heartbreak of this moment would never leave him, but he had to tell Marie he loved her just once more before she left his life.

With only that thought in mind, he leapt to his feet and ran back the way he came. A quick glance at the racecourse told him the auction was breaking up, so he'd have to move fast.

———◆———

John crouched in the brush by the side of the road, near where he'd seen the handbill announcing the slave auction. Carriages and carts rumbled past. A team of horses or mules pulled each one, with a plantation owner or overseer driving, and a cargo of newly purchased human beings onboard.

He examined the human merchandise carefully. At last, he spied a buckboard approaching with Marie in the back. Tucked in between two other black women, she sat facing three unknown black men across the open back of the wagon.

John bolted into the road in front of the wagon and raised both hands above his head. The buckboard's driver kept up his team's speed as they bore down on him.

When they were just a few yards away, John shouted, "Stop!"

The driver reined up, drawing the team to a dust-slinging halt just short of running over him. The horses stood near enough that John could feel their labored breath on his face.

"What's this business?" demanded the master. It was the same man John had seen mount the auction block to examine Marie.

Up close, he appeared to be in his early thirties. A tailor had carefully fitted his gray suit, and dirty blonde hair poked out from under the matching wide-brimmed gray hat. A skiff of a beard covered the man's cheeks and chin, an obvious but unsuccessful effort to look more mature than his years.

"I won't tolerate no shines from a Negro," the young man said. "Whether he belongs to me or not."

"Ain't no shines, Massa," John said, lowering his hands and removing his hat from his head in a single motion. "Jus' wants to say something, is all."

"Say something?" the man replied in disbelief. He turned to look at the burly ape of an overseer seated next to him. "This boy wants to say something, Henderson. What do you make of that?"

Henderson spat over the side of the buckboard. "Not much, Mr. Landry," he said. It was barely more than a growl.

The slaveowner turned back to face John. "Henderson here doesn't think much of you saying something. Not sure I do either. We need to get these new-bought slaves home to Franklin tonight. That's a long ride and you're holding us up, boy." Landry's tone started off light, but ended on a decidedly ominous note.

"Won't take a minute, Massa," said John. "Jus' wants to say goodbye to my wife."

"Your wife?" The buckboard shook as Landry let loose a derisive laugh.

"Yes, suh. You done bought her at the sale. Jus' wants to say goodbye is all."

"Ain't this something?" he mused. Landry looked back at the three women seated behind him in the wagon. "Which one is she?"

John moved around the side of the wagon where the women sat. From there, he could see their wrists encased in iron manacles, each woman shackled to the next. He pointed at Marie. "That'd be her there, suh."

"Well," Landry said, his attention now fully on Marie. "You have good taste, boy. That one there's a beauty. High spirited, too."

Marie stared straight ahead, refusing to acknowledge the lascivious stare from the seat above.

Before John could speak, Landry said, "Don't you worry none, though. We'll take care of her just fine. Won't be but a few weeks before she's sharing a blanket with one of these bucks I just bought, or maybe one of the other boys back home."

He paused for a moment and ogled Marie once more from head to foot. "Then again," he said in an oily voice, "Maybe I'll be taking care of her myself."

At this, Marie raised her head to look Landry full in the face. John could see the look of venomous hatred that clouded her beautiful brown eyes.

Unsettled by the fierceness of her stare, Landry turned back to Henderson. "Drive on," he commanded.

The overseer flipped his reins and called, "Giddup!" The team jumped and the buckboard lurched forward.

"Marie!" John shouted. "I love you!"

She had returned to staring straight ahead. He wasn't sure whether she'd even heard him over the noise of the clattering wagon.

He wanted to stay there and watch her, if only to prolong their time together for a few seconds more. But he could hear another wagon approaching and couldn't risk being caught away from the plantation, particularly if the next carriage belonged to Master Scobell.

With one last, longing glance toward his wife, John bolted into the woods and raced back to the Scobell plantation. Once again, he barely noticed the tearing briars and stinging branches that smacked him as he ran. This time, however, tears streamed down his face.

John was certain he'd never see his beloved Marie again in this lifetime.

CHAPTER 27

John Scobell woke in the morning in the arms of the woman he loved. They were tucked together under the wheels of a cannon on the flatbed car, hidden from sight as the train rolled through the pre-dawn Virginia countryside.

The train rumbled along the tracks, the soft swaying and regular clack of the wheels against iron rails almost hypnotic. His wet clothes were cold in the breeze sweeping over the open car, but the warmth of their bodies afforded enough comfort for a couple of brief hours' rest.

There was a warmth inside him as well. With the urgency to get Marie out of Richmond, he'd hardly allowed himself a moment to reflect on reuniting with her. Now that moment was here. He could hardly believe that they were together again, over seven years since he'd been so sure he'd lost her.

With his arm still draped over her body, Scobell gave Marie a light squeeze. It was almost as though he needed to feel her again to convince himself this was a reality.

Marie gave a sleepy murmur in response to his hug. It was definitely real.

Now Scobell's mind turned to the task ahead of them: escaping from the Confederacy. While it would be far from easy, he believed there was a way they could get safely to the North. For the last time, he thought.

An hour later, with dawn brightening the eastern horizon, Scobell softly roused Marie. She looked up at him dreamily. "I can't believe it's you, my love," she said. "I can't believe we're together again."

"I know," he replied with a gentle smile. Then, with a look at the surrounding countryside, he added, "But we're not safe yet. We still have a ways to go."

"It's alright," she said, pulling him close to her once more. "We'll do it together."

They enjoyed a few more moments of warmth with their bodies intertwined. Suddenly, the train slowed noticeably. A few seconds after that, they heard the locomotive's whistle sound.

Scobell knew what this meant. His confidante at the railroad yard had told him the locomotive would stop to take on water and coal for its steam boiler just south of Fredericksburg. They had to be nearing that stop.

If the men who'd fired at them in Richmond wired ahead, the notification would've already reached this water stop. They would search every car for the two runaways.

They had ridden the rails nearly 50 miles through the night, but now the excursion was over. Scobell and Marie had to get off the train.

They crawled out from their spot beneath the cannon's wheels. Scobell led her by the arm to the edge of the flatcar, where they crouched in readiness.

"When it slows enough," he said, shouting over the noise of the train and wind, "We'll jump. When you hit the ground, don't try to stop. Just let yourself tumble."

"Got it," she said, without looking at him. She fixed her eyes on the rushing ground below.

Looking ahead, Scobell saw a suitable spot approaching. There was a gentle, grassy slope on their side of the tracks with a patch of trees at the bottom.

They could hear the metallic squeal of the train's brakes. The grassy slope was nearly under them now. The train was rolling fast, but waiting for a safe speed might mean having to jump off onto rocky or steep ground. Or worse, having to dodge through occupied houses and buildings as they escaped.

Here was a manageable landing spot and cover to hide them. It was now or never.

Grasping Marie's hand tight, Scobell shouted, "Let's go!" The pair leapt hand in hand from the car, then immediately parted as both involuntarily pinwheeled their arms while they fell.

Marie's feet hit first. She staggered two strides down the hill before momentum overtook her and she pitched forward. She soared for a few feet, then, gracefully as an acrobat in a circus, tucked into a ball and somersaulted twice before sliding to a stop on her back.

Scobell, distracted by watching to make sure Marie landed safely, fared worse. His first foot landed cleanly, but as the other struck the ground, it caught on a hidden clump of dirt. He shot straight forward, hands thrust out in front as if he were trying to fly.

In fact, he did fly...if only for a few feet. Then he landed with a thud on his chest, snapping his head forward and knocking the air from his lungs.

Stunned by the blow, he skidded another twenty feet down the dew-slicked hill on his stomach. He slid past Marie, who was already brushing herself off, and finally came to a stop on top of some thorny blackberry canes near the edge of the woods.

Scobell could feel small trickles of blood forming on his chest and belly where the blackberry thorns had raked through his shirt. Still, with the wind knocked out of him, he couldn't even muster the strength to roll off the spiky stems.

Marie rushed to his side and tried to roll him over. "John, are you alright?" The fear in her voice was palpable.

He tried to lift his arm to show he wasn't injured, but couldn't even muster that. Instead, he raised the index finger on his left hand, signaling he wanted her to wait a minute.

The next few seconds took an hour to pass. At last, he managed a small, squeaking breath, followed by a slightly longer one.

After another moment of recovery, he gently rolled off the stabbing blackberry branches and onto his back. He looked up at Marie and she gently laid a hand on his chest.

"That was graceful," she said. "I thought I remembered you being nimbler on your feet."

"I...caught my...foot," he panted, still trying to suck air into his lungs.

"It looked like you caught your whole body."

He rolled away from her, but she caught his shoulder and pulled him back.

Leaning down, she planted a gentle kiss on his lips. "Don't be that way," she said. "I'm just glad you're alive."

At that very moment, he was too. In fact, he was happier to be alive than he had been in years.

He savored the taste of her lips for a moment, then forced himself into a sitting position. "Let's go," he said. "We need to move."

Marie helped him the rest of the way to his feet. Holding hands once again, they hustled into the woods.

The train had disappeared, coming to a stop somewhere in the distance. In its absence, an eerie quiet settled over the lightening forest. There was no wind and even the birds hadn't yet awakened.

Scobell once again called to mind the maps of Virginia he'd so carefully memorized. He hadn't been through this exact area previously, but he knew where he needed to go and how to get there.

They'd leapt from the train just a few miles south of Fredericksburg. From here, they would work their way east and north to reach the Potomac.

He could envision the spot where the great river dividing Virginia and Maryland narrowed, opposite Smiths Point. The distance from here to that spot wasn't far, perhaps ten miles as the crow flies. But they weren't crows.

Their path would be an irregular one. They'd stick to brushy, wooded cover where possible and avoid at all costs encounters with soldiers, slave catchers, or anyone else who might request to see a pass.

Scobell knew that even a white person too poor to own a single slave had the right demand a pass. In fact, a destitute white might be even more predisposed to do so, since they could claim a reward for catching a runaway.

All of this meant a return to the animalistic ways of his first escape from the South; hiding in the brush, moving only at night, and ready to bolt at the slightest hint of danger. This time, he had Marie to worry about as well. It was an additional burden, albeit a welcome one.

Determining which direction was east was simple enough. The rising sun was just creeping above the horizon.

"We're going to head this way for a bit," he said, pointing toward the sunrise. "I don't really want to move during the daytime, but we need to get away from the railroad line."

"I understand," Marie said with a nod. "If the railroad comes looking for us, we don't want to be anywhere near here."

"Exactly," he said.

He'd forgotten how connected he felt to Marie, how their thoughts meshed, how he rarely needed to explain things to her. My god, it was good to be with the woman he loved again.

Hands still clutched together, they stole to the edge of the forest, then sprinted in an awkward crouch across the edge of an open field. From there, they dropped into a narrow stream channel. The wooded banks hid the couple from view as they eased down the rocky creek.

They picked their way downstream, keeping sharp watch on the hills above. The spring leaves were already sprouting, providing some additional cover, but they hadn't yet reached the lush summer growth that would have hidden the fugitives completely.

Just over an hour later, they reached a point where the banks flattened and the stream widened into a wide, flat swamp. Brushy willow branches rose above their heads and the broad, green leaves of skunk cabbage sprouted in scattered patches.

"Let's stop here," Scobell said. "We should be able to find a spot to hide through the day. When it gets dark tonight, we'll move out again."

Marie looked doubtfully down toward her feet, hidden in ankle-deep water. "You want to spend the whole day here, hunkered down in the water?" she said.

He laughed softly. "We should be able to find a little rise somewhere that won't be wet." This time, she turned her doubtful look at him.

"Well," he said, "Somewhere that won't have standing water, at least."

About twenty minutes later, two hundred yards deeper into the swamp, they found a suitable spot. It was a small, mossy hummock rising a couple feet above the surrounding water.

Two trees had fallen across the hummock, forming a V with their trunks. Nestled on the soft bed of moss between the fallen trunks, Marie and Scobell would be nearly invisible to anyone passing more than a few feet away.

Exhausted by the exertion and excitement of the past twenty-four hours, the pair snuggled together and immediately fell asleep. Around them, birds flitted among the branches, insects hummed, and frogs grunted their approval as a warm spring day enveloped their sodden home.

CHAPTER 28

When they awoke in the early afternoon, they made love. If the mental connection the couple shared resurrected a warmth in Scobell's heart, renewing their physical connection stirred a passion he no longer thought he could feel.

The heart-rending experience of losing Marie at the slave auction had charred his soul. He hadn't been with another woman since, wouldn't allow himself the pleasure of even one fleeting night because the connection might strike too deep.

Now, in a swamp in the Virginia countryside, he rediscovered the depth of feeling he carried for his wife. Their time apart had been so long that their love-making felt both familiar and new at the same time.

Exhausted again, they dozed, locked in an embrace, for another hour. At length, they rose and ate a bit of the food they'd brought. Then they made love again.

At last, the sun reached the far side of the swamp and settled amidst the tree branches on the western horizon. The surrounding shadows lengthened and the light slowly dimmed.

"We'll stay here until it's full dark," Scobell said. "Then we'll start moving."

"How far do we need to go?"

"It's only a few miles from here to the Potomac," he replied. "I think we can make it there by dawn if we don't have to veer off too far to stay hidden. We'll need to cross the north fork of the Rappahannock first, but there's a ford nearby where we should be able to wade over."

"Then what?"

"There are Federal troops stationed at Smiths Point. The Potomac is narrow enough there for us to yell across to them. We should be able to convince them to row over and rescue us."

"Why would they want to rescue us?"

It was a fair question. In all his time in the South, Scobell had hardly experienced a kind word from a white person, let alone a rescue attempt. He was sure Marie's encounters had been similar.

"Things have changed with the war on," he said. "The Federals know every black slave they take from the South is one less person the Rebs can rely on. One less person working the plantation or, like you, at the cannon factory."

"And maybe a little step closer to winning the war," Marie said with a nod. "Makes sense."

Suddenly, the image of Henry Wyant popped into Scobell's mind. "Believe it or not," he said, "Some of them just want to help because they're good people."

As they waited for the night to grow darker, they talked about how they'd spent their time apart. He told her about his ensuing years on the Scobell plantation, catching her up on friends they'd known. That led to the tale of John traveling north with Master Scobell at the outbreak of the war, his escape to Washington, and recruitment by Pinkerton to serve as a spy.

Marie then recounted her time enslaved on the Landry plantation. Even with the wretchedness and anguish she described over her three years there, Scobell felt she was withholding the most hurtful details. He didn't prod her for more.

"I ran away four times," she said. "When they caught me and brought me back the last time, Landry decided I wasn't worth the trouble anymore and chose to sell me." She paused, then added, "I think he finally got tired of beating me."

Scobell said nothing. Their eyes locked together for a moment before Marie looked away.

"By then, the war had started," she continued. "A fellow named Tatum was buying slaves to work in the factories in Virginia. When we were riding north on the boat, I heard him say he could turn a tidy profit by buying slaves cheap way down south and renting them to war manufactories in Virginia for five dollars a day."

"A real supporter of the Confederate cause," commented Scobell.

"No doubt he was a dollar bill patriot," Marie agreed. "But at least he left us alone."

"How was working at the mill?" he asked. "Any worse than the cotton fields?"

"Mostly, it was just loud. With all the machinery clanging and the furnaces roaring when they dumped the hot metal, you couldn't hear anything else. I could've been as close as we are now, screaming at the top of my lungs, and you never would've heard me."

He shook his head. He'd heard such stories from other slaves in Richmond, but never experienced it firsthand.

"It was hot, too," Marie continued. "Especially in summer. If you worked anywhere near those furnaces, it would just about burn you up. You could only work in there for about an hour at a time, then that crew would come out and another one would go in. I don't care how tough you thought you were; there isn't a soul alive that could work in that heat for very long."

"I thought picking cotton in August was hot," he said, "Doesn't sound as bad as that, though."

"None of it's good," she observed. "But Tredegar wasn't terrible. Less whippings, at least. As long as you did what you were told and kept up production, they let you be."

"Sounds lovely." He smiled to show he was joking, but it was so dark now he wasn't sure she could tell.

"Just wonderful," she said. "Once we get North, I might go back and visit after a couple months, just to see how they're doing."

"Speaking of getting North," he said, rising to his feet, "We best get North."

He extended a hand and pulled Marie to her feet. They both stretched and moved around a bit. It was the first time all day they'd stood.

The night was clear. With the overhead branches not yet in full leaf, they could see well enough to navigate by the stars. In a short time, they came to the Rappahannock and waded across the shallow ford without incident. Scobell said a brief prayer of thanks when they reached the north bank.

Just on the other side of the Rappahannock, they struck a road. Relying on his earlier map study, Scobell decided to save some time by following it.

It was a gamble. The public road was the most likely place to encounter another traveler, or worse, Confederate soldiers. It was also the fastest way for the fleeing pair to proceed. Traveling overland through the forests and fields would be much slower, not to mention increasing the chances of getting lost.

If they didn't reach the Potomac by morning, it meant another day hiding and waiting to cross. Another day when even a chance meeting with a passing stranger could mean imprisonment, separation, or death. They would stick to the road.

They followed the edges of the road, avoiding the roadbed itself except where a stream crossing forced them to scurry across a bridge. The rest of the time, they walked the brushy margin, ready to bolt into hiding at the first hint of another human being.

They made remarkably good time using this method and by midnight had reached a three-way intersection. Scobell confidently pointed to the left fork, a route he knew would lead them to the south shore of the Potomac.

When they reached another intersection an hour later, they were close enough to the river that they could smell the brackish water in the night air. Somewhere far across the water, a bell clanged.

Scobell pointed to the right, and the pair continued their journey. After a short distance, he pulled up.

Gesturing toward the forest on their left, he said, "I'm pretty sure the river is just a few hundred yards through these woods. I think we should duck in here and hide until it's closer to daylight."

"Isn't there a road off of this one that will take us right to the river's edge?" Marie asked. "Seems like there should be."

"There is," he said. "But I don't want to take it."

"Why not? We're making good time this way."

"That's the problem. I don't want to get there too soon."

"Too soon for what?"

"Too soon for the Federals to see us. If the sun's not up, they won't know who's yelling at them. They might think it's some kind of trap and stay away."

"Oh."

"Worse," he added, "there might be Confederate pickets guarding that road. We don't want to stumble into them in the dark."

Marie considered his logic for a moment, then made a sound that seemed to imply agreement. However, she said, "Are you sure you're not just trying to lure me into the woods in the dark?"

"Why, Marie Scobell," he replied. "I cannot believe you'd suggest I'm capable of such skullduggery."

She gave him a quick hug. Before pulling away, she whispered in his ear, "I know all the things you're capable of."

They slipped off into the woods. Scobell still clenched her hand tightly in his.

Picking their way downhill through the forest, they eventually found another deadfall to hide under. Huddled together against the predawn chill, they tried to rest, but neither could. The night's cold, combined with the excitement of being so close to escape, was too much to allow sleep to come.

Instead, they talked. In barely audible whispers, they did their best to catch up and somehow erase the seven-year gap in their relationship. Scobell told her of his first mission through the South and how he'd discovered that the Confederates were using the cipher disc to encode messages. He recounted his narrow escape from the *Celeste*, and the tragic night when Simon's betrayal resulted in his own death and scarred Matchett for life.

Marie listened quietly through most of the tale, although she gasped and covered her mouth when she heard of Simon's violent end.

"It's so sad about Simon," she whispered when he'd finished.

"Matchett is a brutal man," Scobell replied.

"I meant Simon betraying you like that. Not just you, but all the others from the Loyal League."

"He hated me for a long time. In some strange way, he came to blame me for Mater Scobell selling him and his family off. And for every bad thing that happened because of that."

Marie looked away from him. "I never told you this, but Simon came sparking after me at one time. I told him I wasn't interested. Then a few months later, I met you. There was never anything between him and me, but I think he was still jealous when I married you."

"One more reason for him to despise me, I guess," said Scobell.

"Still, to lead Matchett to you like that..."

"I don't think he knew their full intent. I'm sure Matchett gave him a few dollars for his information. They probably told him I'd be arrested and punished, and the other Loyal League men would be let go."

"Still," she said, shaking her head.

"It's surprising what some people will do for the promise of money," he said. "Or out of hatred."

She reached over and gently squeezed his biceps. "It's surprising what some people will do for love, too." He felt the warmth spread inside him again.

It was Marie's turn to talk. Avoiding any more discussion of Landry, she focused on her time in Richmond. She talked of the other workers she'd known at Tredegar. She'd interacted mostly with other blacks in bondage at the factory, but also with a few white laborers.

"They were alright, I guess," she said of the whites who toiled alongside them on the factory floor. "They didn't much care to talk to us, but they might've just been afraid."

"Afraid of what?"

"General Anderson runs that place hard. They didn't whip us much, but you best not get caught chatting when you should be working. I don't think they liked the black and white workers getting friendly with each other."

"Easier to control both groups that way," Scobell observed.

"Exactly," she said. "Better for management to keep us apart and looking over our shoulders."

"They had people there watching us every minute, too," she added. "There was one fellow that sat up on a balcony looking out over the factory. He had a pair of field glasses he used to scan all the workers and make sure we weren't slacking."

"Really? He was using field glasses inside?"

"I guess he didn't want to miss anything. We started calling him The Hawk because of the way he was always spying on us from up there. He was tall and skinny, and sort of awkward looking, so the name fit him."

"What did he do if he saw something he didn't like? Did he handle the punishment?"

"Oh, no," Marie said. "The Hawk would never get his hands dirty. He'd just run to General Anderson and tattle. Then the general would have his security men handle the punishment."

"I met Anderson," said Scobell, quickly relaying the details of the dinner party at the general's house. "Seemed like a wonderful gentleman," he added drily.

"A real peach," she agreed. "The Hawk loved him, though. Followed him everywhere when the general was walking around the ironworks. It was funny to see because The Hawk was so tall and he had this funny way of shuffling along behind with these big, old feet."

A flicker of recognition jolted him. "Do you know this Hawk's real name?" he asked.

Startled by his sudden urgency, Marie paused to think. Not waiting for her to respond, Scobell pressed. "Tall and thin, in his thirties? Oil-slicked hair and mustache?"

"That could be him," she intoned. "I never really saw him up close. John, what is this? What's wrong?"

"Think hard," he pressed. "Did you ever hear his name?"

Marie grew quiet for several seconds. Suddenly, she snapped, "It was Joseph!"

Then, in unison, they said, "Samuel Joseph."

CHAPTER 29

S cobell leaned back and blew out a long breath.

"I knew it," he said. "There was just something wrong about him."

"You know him?"

"He reached out to Brackett, claiming to be another Union operative. He told her Pinkerton had sent him to help us escape after they captured Webster."

"That's definitely not true," Marie said. "He worked at Tredegar before I started there. That's nearly a year now."

"He has to be working for Winder and Matchett," Scobell replied. He turned over the scenarios in his head.

"He was Anderson's toady, spying on the workforce at Tredegar," he continued, thinking out loud. "When they found out Scully, Lewis, Webster, and Warne were spies, it revealed the identities of Matchett's detectives, too. Their names were even in the newspapers."

"Yes," she said. "I remember that. A few workers at Tredegar even mentioned that detectives had been at the factory before."

"That's not too surprising," he said, the pieces falling into place. "Anderson is close with Winder and Matchett. That's why they showed up at his house the night Brackett and I were there. He was one of the first people they alerted when they found out about the spies."

"Winder and Matchett needed someone else to spy for them," said Marie, catching on to the thread Scobell was pulling. "Someone who wouldn't be recognized as part of their detective force."

"Exactly," he said. "Lewis and Scully must've blown on us and told them we were spying in Richmond."

He stopped for a moment and thought back to the point when Brackett introduced him to Joseph. The Matchett spy – The Hawk, as Marie called him – hadn't seemed to realize Scobell was anything other than Brackett's actual slave.

"They told him Brackett was spying in Richmond, at least," he added. "Once Matchett found that out, he realized he needed a new face to play the role of a sympathetic spy sent from by Pinkerton to help. So Matchett, or maybe Winder, went to their friend Anderson to ask for a volunteer."

"And who better to send on a spying mission than someone who spends all day watching over other people?" Marie asked rhetorically.

"They wouldn't need Joseph to do much," Scobell said. "Just cozy up to Brackett a little to determine how much she knew about Confederate operations, and whether there were any more operatives in Richmond they didn't know about."

"I'll bet The Hawk said yes even before Anderson finished asking," Marie said emphatically. "Besides being a sneaky son of a bitch, he'd do anything for the general – as long as it didn't put him in any personal danger."

"I'm sure they all thought tricking a young woman who's alone in an enemy city, with her circle of associates already collapsing, would be as safe as a trip to the store," replied Scobell.

"It looks like they were right."

"Yes. It does look that way."

They both fell silent. Finally, Marie asked, "Are you worried about her?"

"Why should I be?" he said, a hard edge discernible in his tone even at a whisper. "She's a grown woman who needs to take care of herself. I tried to tell her not to trust Joseph and she wouldn't listen. That's her problem, not mine."

Marie laid her head against his shoulder and gently ran her hand across the banded muscles of his chest. "I'm glad you're here with me instead of back there in that nest of vipers," she said.

"I am, too," he said, squeezing her close. "We have a couple more hours before daylight. Let's try to get a little rest."

Marie was soon asleep on his shoulder. Her soft snores reminded him of a purring cat.

Scobell dozed only fitfully. When he finally fell asleep, he dreamed again of swimming across the Potomac, with skeletal Union soldiers once more clawing at his legs and arms.

Staring down into the black depths of the river, he saw that one skeleton wasn't a soldier at all. As the wraith sank toward the bottom, he saw it wore a widow's black dress and bonnet. Long, blonde hair trailed out the back.

<hr>

The couple rose at the first hint of light in the eastern sky. Silently, they stretched their limbs until the blood returned.

Scobell led the way downhill from their hiding spot until the wide expanse of the Potomac was visible below them. From there, he turned right and guided Marie parallel to the river, remaining concealed by the wooded hillside.

The eastern sky was turning from pink to orange by the time they stopped. Though the landscape's features weren't yet discernable, a large mass of land was visible on the Potomac's north bank. They could see flickering light from campfires and bobbing lanterns across the river as the soldiers rose to start their day.

Hunkering in the brush on the south bank, Scobell pointed toward the moving lights. "That's the Federal camp at Smith's Point. That's where we need to go."

Turning his attention to the open riverbank in front of them, he whispered, "First, we have to make sure there aren't any Secesh troops on this side." He grinned at Marie and added, "Wouldn't do to come all this way and get caught five feet from freedom, right?"

She tried to smile back, but it didn't quite penetrate the look of concern on her face.

"You stay here and keep out of sight," he said. "I'm going to climb up on that little knob right there." He pointed at a small rise just above them.

"From there, I should be able to see the whole riverbank. By the time I get up there, it'll be light enough to see if there are any troops on this side of the river."

Marie said nothing, but gripped his hand with the strength of a vise. The lines of worry deepened across her face. "It'll be alright," he said. "I won't be gone long."

He thought for a moment, then added, "If anything bad happens, run for the river. Head for Smiths Point and start yelling for help. Those Yankee soldiers should row out to help you if you make enough noise." He didn't bother to address what would happen if they didn't.

He gave her hand a last squeeze, then pulled free and slipped up the hill. Moving silently as a deer, he picked his way carefully up to the little rise. Once there, he lay down on his belly and eased forward through the sticks and leaves. Within a couple minutes, he was in a spot where he could scan the entire riverfront for a half-mile in each direction.

It wasn't quite full daylight, but it was bright enough to detect motion along the river's edge. Definitely enough light to see whether a troop of Confederate soldiers was camped directly across from their enemy counterparts.

There were none. Other than a half-dozen mallards paddling quietly in the shallows near the shore, there wasn't a hint of movement. He waited another ten minutes to be sure. It required a forcible effort, overcoming the impatience that welled within him from being this close.

At last, convinced that there were no Confederates nearby, he left his perch and scrambled back down the hillside to Marie. "Let's go," he said, grabbing her wrist and almost forcibly lifting her out of her hiding spot. "It's time."

They clambered down to the water's edge, then moved to a spot where the brush parted to create an opening for an ancient, disused wagon trail. Scobell cupped his hands around his mouth and shouted, "Halloo! Halloo the camp!"

Marie quickly chimed in as well. "Halloo, Yankees! Halloo over there!"

After a few seconds, the sounds of metal equipment clinking drifted across the water to them. A shout of "Who's there?" replied.

"We's a husband and wife!" Scobell hollered. "Done escaped from the Rebs and wants to come across." Then he added what he hoped would be the magic word: "Contraband!"

Seizing on the term, Marie repeated, "Contraband! Help us!"

They could see a small knot of blue-coated soldiers forming on the opposite bank. One of them pulled out a pair of field glasses and aimed them at Scobell and Marie. Arms gestured toward the couple, followed by agitated discussion among the men.

At last, the voice called out again, "Are you alone?"

"Yes, suh!" John yelled back. "Jus' the two of us, suh! We jus' wants to get North."

"Please, suh!" Marie chimed in, "Please, help us. We don't wanna be slaves no mo'." Scobell wondered how much of the urgency in her voice was playacting and how much was real.

"How do we know you're not bait?" the soldier shouted. "That some damn Secesh aren't gonna start shooting at us if we row over to get you?"

Scobell was growing frustrated...and worried. While there were no Confederate troops in the immediate area when he'd scouted it, they couldn't stand here all day. The shouting was going to attract attention eventually.

"Please, suh. It jus' us, me and my wife!" he yelled back. "Please come save us! We wants to be contrabands!"

This time, he questioned how much of the quaver in his own voice might be real.

Marie's voice rang out again, with even more desperation this time. "Please help us! Please, suh, come and gets us. Contraband! We wants Uncle Abe to save us!"

When he glanced over at her, she raised her eyebrows and turned up her palms as if to say, I'm trying anything I can think of.

They could see the group of soldiers deliberating once again on the far shore. In that moment, in a conversation they were no part of, their fates would be decided.

Finally, they saw one of the blue-clad soldiers cup his hands to his mouth. "Stay right there!" he hollered. They watched as three other soldiers moved up the bank. They untied a rowboat and dragged it down to the river's edge.

"Oh, thank god," he heard Marie say under her breath.

"Thank you, suh!" John yelled back. "Thank you, Lawd!"

It took nearly thirty minutes for them to get the boat launched and row across the river. Two soldiers pulled on the oars. Two more sat, one in front and one in back, with their rifles trained on the south bank.

They slowed nearly to a stop about fifty yards offshore, scanning the riverbank cautiously for a surprise attack. Spotting no Confederates, they resumed rowing. The hull of the wooden boat soon crunched in the gravel as it reached the southern shore of the Potomac.

The soldier in the bow quickly hopped out and tugged the boat up the bank. Rifle in hand, he scanned the hillside once more, then turned his attention to Marie and Scobell.

"Get in," he commanded. "Let's go!" He continued to watch the surrounding ridge, his back to the boat.

Marie stepped forward to the bow of the rowboat. The two rowers dropped their oars and came forward to help her. Scobell lifted her over the gunwale and into their arms. They got her settled on one of the plank seats.

The soldier guarding the operation motioned to Scobell. "Help me shove us off," he said.

The two men put their shoulders against the hull of the boat, and it eased off the gravel. The soldier nimbly hopped over the gunwale, then turned and reached a hand over the side to help Scobell aboard.

Standing in water up to his shins, Scobell ignored the extended hand. Instead, he put both hands against the boat's bow and gave it a hard shove, pushing it out into the swirling current of the Potomac.

"John, no!" Marie exclaimed as she realized what was happening.

"I have to," he said, staring into her eyes. Remembering his cover, he added, "Gots to go back. Gots to help."

"No!" It was all she could muster.

"You gets yourself to Washington, Marie. You gets there and I'll come for you. I'll find you. I swears it."

"I understand," she said. A tear leaked out of the corner of her eye and rolled down the curve of her cheek. "I'll sees you there."

"You will," he said, but he wasn't sure she heard him over the splash of the river and the creaking of the oarlocks as the soldiers rowed away.

CHAPTER 30

I t took Scobell five nights to get back to Richmond.

Sneaking out had been difficult, but they'd managed it in a single night. There was no timesaving train ride on his return journey, though. With no opportunity to scout the train schedules and stops, he couldn't risk hopping a ride on the rails.

Other circumstances had intervened as well. A discarded copy of the *Richmond Gazette* found just outside of Fredericksburg told the tale.

The siege that General McClellan had established weeks ago at Yorktown had finally caused the Rebels to pull back and abandon the city. The following day, the two sides battled at a place called Williamsburg. From the *Gazette*'s account, Scobell gleaned that the battle was more or less a draw. The Confederates, however, had pulled back when it was over.

As Scobell guessed when he'd first read of their landing, the Yankees were moving up the peninsula between the York and James Rivers. The two armies were located southeast of Richmond, far from where Scobell was traveling. But having McClellan's Yankee army only forty-five miles from the heart of the Confederate capitol had raised alarms across all of Virginia.

Although most of the Army of Northern Virginia was dedicated to fighting against McClellan on the peninsula, small patrols of Confederate soldiers still prowled the countryside. Supplementing them, local rangers armed with squirrel rifles and antique muskets roamed the fields and woods on the lookout for invading Yankee hordes.

These small bands slowed Scobell's return, forcing his movements to be both nocturnal and painfully slow. Even at night, armed soldiers roamed the routes he wanted to follow. More than once, alerted by lanterns bobbing in the distance, he hunkered in a marsh or forest for hours waiting for the troops to pass.

At last, however, he reached Richmond again. Ironically, back within the capitol of the Confederacy, he no longer needed to travel in secret.

Still armed with his copy of the papers Brackett had secured from Winder – carefully stretched and dried after his dip in the James River – all he needed to move safely within the city was a new pass from his mistress. He'd kept a blank sheet of letterhead from the Exchange Hotel folded in his pocket in case such a need arose.

He commandeered a pen and ink from the unguarded front desk of a low-rent boardinghouse near the edge of the city. With a few quick strokes, he had a pass sending him across town to pick up a package on behalf of his mistress, Mrs. Carrie Lawton.

It was early morning when Scobell slipped through the slave entrance of the Exchange Hotel, quietly climbing the rear stairs to the third floor. As he approached their suite, the thought occurred to him that Brackett might no longer be there. They might have already apprehended her; she could be sitting at this moment in a cell near her sister.

Brushing the thought aside, he knocked lightly at the door. He heard rustling inside the room, then Brackett's wavering voice called out, "Yes? Who's there?"

A powerful wave of relief swept over him. Leaning close to the door, he said, "It be me, Missus. It's John."

Before he could add, "Open up," Brackett flung the door open. "Good lord, John!" she said. "Where have you been?"

Before he could respond, she latched onto the front of his coat and pulled him inside, swinging the door shut behind him. "I've been worried sick about you," she scolded.

He could tell it was true. In the week since he'd left, Brackett had grown thinner and wan.

When he didn't respond immediately, she repeated, "Where have you been?"

The entire trip back to Richmond, he'd considered how to explain the events of the past week to Brackett. Now, none of the words he'd so carefully planned would come to mind.

"It's a long story," he started.

"Tell it!"

He drew in a deep breath and tried again. "I found my wife."

"Your what?!" Without taking her eyes off him, she slowly backed up and plopped into a chair.

"My wife. We were separated years ago, when they sold her away from me. I found her here in Richmond, working at Tredegar."

"You're married?" she interjected. "I can't believe it. You never told me!"

Scobell stopped and looked directly into her eyes. "You asked me to tell you where I've been. Are you going to let me?"

"Yes," she said, flushing slightly. "Yes, of course. I'm sorry. I'm just...I'm overjoyed that you're back safely."

He launched into the story: how he'd married Marie in Mississippi, then lost her through the sale to Landry; how he'd found her again at Tredegar; and finally, his decision to rescue her and take her North.

When he'd finished, Brackett leaned back in her chair.

"That's quite a tale," she said. "It's wonderful that you found Marie and rescued her. It's just so sad how the two of you were torn apart for all those years."

Then a quizzical look crept onto her face. "But why are you here? Why didn't you go North with her?"

Scobell blew out a sigh. "There's one more thing I haven't told you."

"What is it?"

"How much have you told Joseph?" he asked. "About our mission?"

"Joseph? Not much, I suppose. I mean, he already knew that Pinkerton sent us here, and that we were gathering intelligence for the Union."

"You said 'we.' Does he know I'm a spy?"

She considered the question. "Well, he knows you're here with me..."

"Yes, but does he know my role? Or does he think you're actually the agent and I really am your houseman?"

"I don't know, John. Why does any of this matter?" There was more than a hint of suspicion in her voice.

"He's a spy, Kitty."

"I kn-," she began.

"A spy for Matchett," he finished.

"This again? He can't be. We've been over this."

"He is. There's no question," said Scobell. He quickly recounted how Marie had identified Joseph as being The Hawk from Tredegar.

"You think he got the background on us from Scully and Lewis?" she asked.

"Yes. They gave up Webster and Warne to save themselves. They must've told Matchett about you, too."

"How did Joseph know our mission code?"

"I've been considering that. Pinkerton must've given it to Lewis and Scully when he sent them to Richmond. They were coming here to check on Webster and Warne. They must've had orders to contact us, too, so Pinkerton gave them our mission code to confirm he'd sent them. When they spilled the beans to Matchett, they also gave up the mission code."

Brackett nodded thoughtfully. Though she was reeling from the shock of learning Joseph was an impostor, he could tell the news also confirmed some suspicions of her own.

"I have a feeling maybe he didn't tell Joseph about me, though," Scobell continued. "Judging by the way Joseph acted when you introduced me, I believe he thinks I'm just your servant."

"What does that mean to us now?"

"Not much, I suppose," he admitted. "But we're in danger here, Kitty. Serious danger. Any advantage, regardless of how small, might help."

"Help with what?" she asked, desperation in her voice. "They know we're operatives, or at least that I'm one. They're just waiting to close the net."

Maybe close the noose, Scobell thought, although he didn't say it out loud.

"They are waiting," he said. "There must be a reason for that."

"I think they're trying to find out whether there are any more Pinkerton agents in Richmond," she replied. "Joseph has been asking me questions, hinting about other contacts I might've developed since I've been here. He said Pinkerton wants to make sure the entire network stays intact after the arrests."

"What have you told him?"

"Nothing yet." She paused. "With Tim being hanged and Kate jailed, I was so relieved at the thought of someone sent here to help. I practically jumped into his arms. But the more I talk to Joseph, the more he just seems...off."

"I know what you mean," he agreed. "Besides the fact that he's an arrogant ass, he just didn't seem like someone who'd be part of Pinkerton's team."

"Exactly. It's funny that Marie calls him The Hawk, though. He does kind of resemble some sort of weird, giant bird."

They both laughed, but it faded quickly in the air between them. The urgency of their situation, the idea that Matchett's trap could snap shut on them at any moment, was settling over them like a shroud.

"John," Brackett said quietly, "I want to thank you."

"For what?"

"Coming back for me."

"No need to thank me."

"I think there is. You could've stayed with Marie, gone on to safety. But you decided to come back here, into the belly of the beast, just to help me."

Brackett was staring hard at him. Scobell avoided her gaze, looking off into a far corner of the room.

"If I didn't know better," Brackett continued, "I'd almost think you cared."

Now it was his turn to blush.

Finally, he said, "Don't flatter yourself too much. It's just another in a long string of poor decisions on my part."

"Don't worry," she said with a forced smile. "It won't be your last."

"I hope you're right," he said.

———◉———

Scobell flattened himself against the brick rear wall of the Exchange Hotel, trying to hide from the steady drizzle under the building's narrow roof overhang. As the droplets clinging to the brim of his hat attested, that effort was only marginally successful.

He didn't need to stand in the rain. He'd stepped outside to clear his head and think about their situation. When he did so, the overcast sky was not yet spitting rain. After just a couple minutes, though, the mist had started. Scobell could've ducked inside the hotel's slave entrance at that point, where at least it was dry.

But the iron-gray clouds hanging just above the rooftops and the rain that had now increased to a steady downpour matched his dour mood. He stayed where he was. Right then, the miserable weather suited him.

Now that Scobell had revealed Joseph's true assignment, they needed to work out their next move. And there was precious little time to do so.

His first instinct was to pack their things and run, just as he had with Marie. Brackett quickly pointed out, however, that escaping together wouldn't be nearly as simple.

"You got away last time because they were watching for me to leave rather than you," she'd said. "When you went missing for a few days then reappeared, it definitely alerted them that something's up. They'll be watching for both of us now."

She was right, of course. To make things worse, getting out of Richmond was only part of the problem. If they returned to Pinkerton without the cipher disc, he'd likely send them out again to secure one. That would mean more time behind enemy lines, more danger, more days away from Marie, and worst of all, no release from bondage.

Scobell looked into the dark sky overhead. As he did, a large drop of water slid off the brim of his hat and splattered on his nose. He quickly doffed the hat, shaking both it and his head to shed some of the annoying raindrops. Jamming it on his pate again, he turned back to his thoughts.

They needed a plan that would allow them to escape with a cipher disc in hand. Even though the only one they knew about in Richmond was in the hands of Matchett's spy-hunters.

Another rogue raindrop came off his hat brim. This one dripped off the back and slid down the inside of his collar. He pressed his back against the wall to mash the exasperating droplet into his shirt and keep it from running the entire way down to his pants.

He was soggy and agitated. Worse, he was out of ideas. And nearly out of time.

At that moment, the answer came to him. Not as an abrupt inspiration, but rather in the shape of a short, thin black youth who padded up the alley toward him.

Scobell watched the teen walk, seemingly unconcerned about the rain falling on his uncovered head and thin, sloping shoulders. He had longish hair, at least by Richmond slave standards, and intermittent puffs of facial hair sprouted across his jawline and upper lip.

"You Mistuh Scobell?" the young man asked. He had the calm, confident demeanor of someone who was used to dealing with strangers. Someone who lived by his wits more than by straining his back.

"Yep," Scobell replied, wondering how the teen knew his name.

"Name's Laddie," he said. "Miss Lucy done sent me."

Scobell was stunned. He was sure he'd heard the last of Lucy. He'd burned that bridge with his clumsy demand for her help.

"Lucy?" he asked. "What she sent you here for?" His words came out more rushed than he intended.

Laddie looked over Scobell's soggy form from his damp boots to his dripping hat. "Said she had sumpin' for you," the teen said. His expression said he wasn't sure Scobell was worth either his trouble or Lucy's. "Sumpin' you wanted."

Scobell's heart raced. Was it possible? He tried to steady his nerves and pretend to be calm.

"Yeah?" he said. "What's 'at?"

"Don't know," said Laddie with a shrug. "Miss Lucy didn't say. She jus' say she gots it and you wants it."

"That so?" Scobell replied, his mind racing. "You gots it now?"

"Nah," Laddie said with a backward swipe of his hand. "She wanna talk to you first." He paused, then added, "I think she worried 'bout it. Like mebbe she a little scared 'bout it."

Scobell pondered this. It had to be the cipher disc. Had she already stolen it?

Worry immediately overtook him again. If she'd snatched the disc and hid it, it wouldn't be long before Matchett realized it. He would immediately suspect Brackett and Scobell of the theft. The chance to get the disc and escape Richmond might already be slipping away.

"She gonna come see me too, then?" he asked.

"Miss Lucy want you to come to her," the youth responded. "Not at her work, though. And not at Cap'n Matchett's house neither."

Scobell silently agreed. "Where 'bouts then?"

"She say to meet her back of the Friends Meetinghouse," said Laddie. He was still eyeing Scobell suspiciously. "You knows that place?"

Scobell suddenly realized that Laddie's misgivings about him were rooted in the boy's concern for Lucy. "Yeah, I knows it," he said, trying hard to keep an indifferent air to his voice.

"She say she'll meet you there tonight," Laddie said, reciting details he'd obviously practiced multiple times. "Right after the church bells sound seven. Round the back, jus' inside the gate."

"She gonna have this thing I want then?" said Scobell.

Another shrug. "Don't know."

"Alright then. You tells her I'll be there." The young man nodded and turned back the way he came.

"Laddie," said Scobell. "She pay you?"

The youngster turned to face him, squinting through the sharpening rain. "No, suh," he said. "Miss Lucy was a friend to my mama 'afore she passed. S'pose I'd do 'bout anything for Miss Lucy if she asked."

"I can see that," he said. "Here." He pulled a coin from his pocket and flipped it to the teen, who caught it one-handed through the raindrops. "For your trouble."

Laddie's eyes lit up as he looked over the coin, then back at Scobell. "Many thanks, suh," he said, unable to hide the excitement in his voice.

Scobell nodded in response, which caused a small cascade of water to fall from the brim of his hat down over his face and the front of his coat. He didn't mind at all. Things were suddenly looking up.

CHAPTER 31

Scobell lounged against a wrought-iron fence across the street from the Richmond Quaker church, known as the Friends Meetinghouse. The meetinghouse was located away from the other churches, which were mostly clustered near the majestic buildings of the capitol complex. By comparison, the Quakers shared a neighborhood with Libby Prison.

Scobell tried to appear disinterested as he scrutinized his surroundings for even the slightest flutter of unexpected movement. As he slouched against the fence, he wondered if the fact that Quakers opposed slavery had led to their poor real estate situation.

On the way from the hotel, he'd stopped and looped back on his own path multiple times. Before he settled in across the street, Scobell had walked a complete loop around the block where the meetinghouse was located. The prison's brick walls and armed sentries gave him chills as he passed.

Finally satisfied there was nothing unusual, he'd stopped at his current location to watch the narrow walkway that disappeared behind the building. He'd taken every precaution he could imagine. Now that Joseph knew they were Federal spies, Scobell could nearly feel the noose tightening around his neck.

The evening bells from St. John's Episcopal Church, whose parishioners enjoyed a location a block away from the Confederate Capitol, rang out. Scobell jumped slightly as the peals rolled down the hill and across the city, jostling him from his morbid thoughts.

He waited until the bells' last echoes had receded across the James River. Seeing nobody coming or going from the meetinghouse, he did as Laddie had instructed.

Casually, he pushed away from the fence and slouched across the street. Giving one more glance down the deserted thoroughfare, he pushed through the church's front gate, then moved down the passage leading behind the building.

He crept silently along the walkway, which was crowded by a brick wall on his left and the evergreen shrubs against the church wall on his right. At the back of the building, he stopped and peeked around the corner.

There, seated alone on the back steps of the meetinghouse, was Lucy. He scanned every crevice, but didn't see another soul. Still cautiously glancing about, Scobell stepped into the open and advanced toward her. After a couple of steps, she heard him and turned toward his approach.

As soon as he got close enough to see Lucy's face, he froze.

Even for Scobell, who had seen some of the worst beatings a human could endure, her appearance was appalling. Both eyes were blackened, with the right one swollen firmly shut. Her left eye was a narrow slit, kept open only with a visibly painful effort.

Her nose was flattened and looked to be shifted out of line. It was hard to tell, though, because it had distended to twice its normal size. Dried blood scabbed across the bridge of her nose where the beating had split the skin wide open. The blood formed a tiny trail down the side of her nose and disappeared into the puffy folds below her left eye.

Her mouth was also swollen, her lips grotesquely fattened. More dried blood crusted around them and spread across her cheeks. Yellowish liquid oozed from an open wound on her bottom lip.

Scobell cursed to himself. He didn't have to wonder who'd done the damage; it was obviously Matchett's work.

His shock ebbed, slowly being replaced by anger. "How that happen?" he asked.

Lucy answered, but her response was so distorted that he had to sit down and put his face inches from hers. "What's that now?" he asked.

"Massah done beat me," she croaked. "Beat me good," she added unnecessarily.

"Why he do that?" He suddenly worried that Matchett might've been trying to extract information about him and Brackett. It was perhaps the only thing that could make him feel worse about Lucy's condition.

"Spilt his inkwell," she said. "Weren't nothing, really. Got on some of his papers is all."

"He done beat you like that for spilt ink?"

"Sure enough did," she said. "Massah mad a lot these days." She looked like she wanted to add something else, but the pain of speaking caused her to stop.

Scobell could feel his own temper rising. Matchett was angry because he'd found a nest of spies operating in his city. He'd calm down when they were all captured and hanged, no doubt. Nothing would satisfy that monster except more injury and death.

Scobell considered this for a moment. It probably meant they would put him and Brackett under surveillance. Matchett would want to know if they were in touch with even more Yankee spies in Richmond.

"So that's why you wants to help me now?" he asked.

Lucy shook her head no. "He done beat me plenty afore."

"Why then?"

She drew a laborious breath through her shattered nose to prepare her answer. "He done broke my pipe."

Her appearance was so shocking that he hadn't noticed her ever-present wooden pipe was missing. "Broke it?"

She nodded slightly, looking down at the ground. "Snatched it out my mouth and snapped it," she mumbled. "Then he done crush the rest with his boot. Nothin' left."

She stopped speaking to gather herself. A tear leaked out of her damaged left eye and slid down over the abrasions and bruises on her cheek.

"Was my granny's," she choked out.

She paused again. "Gone," was all she could manage. A few more tears escaped her damaged eye.

Scobell didn't know how to react. Seeing this woman, who was tough as saddle leather, battered and crying pained his soul. He squeezed her knee gently in silence.

A few moments passed. "Wanna get him," Lucy said at last. "Hurt him."

Scobell nodded. Now he understood.

This wasn't about helping him. It was about avenging the loss of the only valued possession she'd ever owned.

Stealing the cipher disc from under Matchett's nose would harm him in a way she never could otherwise. He'd be personally and professionally humiliated, even more so if it became known that a Union spy had made off with it.

"You gots the disc now?" he asked.

She shook her again. "Gonna though." She pulled her shoulders back and sat upright as she said it.

Scobell was relieved she hadn't already made off with the disc. He would have a chance to control the timing. His mind immediately started turning on a solution to the next problem.

"He gonna kill you if he know you took it," he said.

"Don't matter none," she said, looking into the distance.

"Mebbe there's a way he don't find out who stole it," Scobell said.

She turned her head slightly toward him, but didn't speak. He nodded, confidence growing as a plan coalesced in his mind.

"There's mebbe a way," he repeated. "You go on back now. Don't say nothin', don't do nothin' till you hears from me."

She peered at him through the open slit of her left eye.

"Don't you worry none neither," he reassured her. "We gonna hurt him."

<hr>

"Lucy has agreed to get me the disc."

The words seemed to hang in the air. Even to Scobell, who was the one that spoke them.

"What?" asked Brackett in astonishment. "I can't believe it. Why now? What changed her mind?"

"Matchett did," he replied. He repeated the story of Lucy's beating at the hands of her master and the broken pipe. Tears formed in Brackett's eyes as she listened.

"That poor woman," she said when he'd finished. "How has she lasted this long, enslaved by that evil man?"

Scobell shrugged. "It's what we black folks do. Push on, push through. Hope that tomorrow will be better. If not tomorrow, then another day down the road." He paused for a moment, then added, "It's the only way to survive it."

She nodded silently. After a moment, a small smile came to her lips. "We?" she said. "I thought you didn't have people?"

He allowed a smile, too, despite himself. "Yeah," he acknowledged. "We. Maybe I have more people than I thought."

"You have Marie waiting for you in Washington. You came back for me. And now, Lucy," she said. "I'd say you have a few people."

He nodded, then sat quietly.

"We need to make sure they can't trace the disc back to Lucy," Brackett said, interrupting the silence at last. "They can't tie her to this at all. If they figure she's involved, Matchett will beat her to death, for sure."

"True," he said. "But I think I have a way to deal with that."

Brackett looked at him inquisitively.

"When I was working with the Loyal League down in Mississippi, we sometimes had to move papers from place to place," he said. "Things you couldn't just hand someone in broad daylight. Forged passes, freedom papers, and such." She nodded for him to continue.

"We'd pick a certain spot: a hollow tree, between a couple rocks, someplace like that," he said. "One person would leave the papers in that spot, wrapped in something to make it hard to see. Then they'd leave a sign at another place to let the second person know it was ready to be picked up."

"What kind of sign?"

"Something nobody else would notice. A strip of cloth hung in a window, or a certain piece of clothing hung out to dry. Sometimes something as little as a broken branch on a specific bush."

"Then they'd know the package was there, and go pick it up," Brackett finished. The appreciation for the simple genius of the system was clear in her voice.

"Exactly. The best part was, the two people didn't need to see each other or even be in the same place at the same time. Once one dropped the package and sent the signal, it might be days before the second person saw it and picked them up. There was no way to figure out a connection between them."

"But we don't have that kind of time now," she said. "This needs to happen quickly."

"Don't worry," he said. "I'll let her know through Laddie. It'll be clear that we need the disc right away."

"Where are you going to have her drop the disc? And what will the signal be?"

"I think I have that pretty well sorted out, but I have to take one more look at the spot to be sure. I can't tell you, though." She looked at him with surprise, and not a little hurt.

"Don't be offended," he said. "If this goes badly and either of us gets caught...the less you know, the better. You'll be able to answer honestly that you don't know where the disc is."

"I see," she said. A hint of disappointment still hung in her tone.

Getting her back on track, Scobell resumed outlining his plan. He laid out how they could get the disc and hustle it out of Richmond without it being seen. Just as important, he outlined how they could accomplish it without Matchett and his henchmen suspecting they were behind it.

Brackett quickly picked up on the details and suggested a few refinements. Scobell promptly agreed to them.

"There's just one part I haven't sorted yet," he said at last. "We need another person."

"For what?"

"We need someone else who could carry the disc out of the city for us. Joseph knows you're a spy, which means Matchett does, too. They won't let us just ride out of Richmond, especially if they realize the disc is missing first."

Brackett pondered this silently for a few seconds. Suddenly, she said, "I think I know the right person. If the timing works out, that is."

"Who?"

"I met a gentleman at dinner yesterday," she said. "His name is Mr. Featherington. An older gentleman. He carries a hickory walking stick with a brass head on it."

"Yes, I think I've seen him downstairs once or twice."

"Though he hasn't spoken about them too loudly here in the capitol," she continued, "it's clear he has certain ideas that would seem to...well...align with ours."

"Interesting," said Scobell. "Can we trust him to help with something like this?"

"I'm not sure," she said, drawing out her words. "But I know he's planning to leave Richmond the day after tomorrow. Heading west, over the mountains. He already has his pass in hand."

"That does present an opportunity, doesn't it?" he said.

"Yes," Brackett replied. "It does." Her tone was distant. He could tell her mind was churning on something.

Brackett suddenly slapped her hands down on her lap. The sound was so loud in the small hotel room that Scobell jumped in his chair.

"I have an idea," she said. "Let me suggest a minor alteration to your plan."

A broad smile played on her face as she explained her strategy. A similar smile spread to Scobell's face as she walked him through it.

"What do you think?" she asked when she'd finished. Her eyes beamed with excitement.

"I think that's a grand idea," he replied. "Let's do it."

CHAPTER 32

When he came out of the Exchange Hotel's slave door the next day, Scobell peeked out onto Franklin Street before stepping onto the sidewalk. He'd developed this habit after they arrived in Richmond. He usually saw little of interest.

This morning, however, he spied Blake's thin, wiry form coiled into a doorway of the Ballard House across the street. Matchett's deputy gazed at the front entrance to the Exchange, no doubt waiting for the pair of Yankee spies to make an appearance. Scobell and Brackett were now under full-blown surveillance by Matchett's men.

He retreated into the side street. Hoping the deputy hadn't spotted him, Scobell retraced his steps back past the slave entrance. Turning a corner, he came out on the other side of the hotel, onto Fourteenth Street. From there, he peered out from the shadow of the hotel and scanned the street for more observers.

Instantly, he spotted the portly form of Deputy Saunders. Unlike Blake's watchful attitude, however, Saunders slouched on a crate tucked between two barrels. His hat was tugged down over his eyes to shade against the sun – or perhaps to hide the fact that they were closed.

Scobell watched the deputy for a few minutes. He noted the deep, regular heaving of the man's ample belly with each breath. He couldn't detect it from across the busy street, but Scobell was pretty sure if he crossed to the opposite sidewalk, the sound of snoring would be emanating from under Saunders' hat.

Scobell waited until a small cluster of black men walked past, then slipped out onto the sidewalk behind them. He followed them for three blocks, strolling just a few steps behind and trying to blend in with them without actually joining the group.

As they slowed to a stop at the bottom of a hill, Scobell eased between them and kept moving forward. At the next corner, he snapped a quick left turn and disappeared around the corner. It was opposite the direction he wanted to travel, but he didn't want to cross the open street anywhere near where Matchett's deputies might be lurking.

Scobell took extra caution during his walk, changing directions multiple times and ducking behind more than one wagon to check behind him. Eventually, he made it to his destination and found Laddie loafing by the wharf, exactly as Lucy said he would.

Scobell made a pretense of buying a pack of playing cards from the teen while they talked. To a casual passerby, it would look like a minor business transaction between two slaves. He doubted anyone would bother to linger near enough to hear their conversation.

As Laddie dug through his pack to find the playing cards, Scobell quickly explained what he wanted Lucy to do. He stressed that time was critical. They needed to get the disc and leave Richmond immediately, not only to protect themselves but also to shelter Lucy from suspicion.

Laddie nodded his understanding at that part. "Don't nod," Scobell said. "I jus' buying cards from you, 'member?"

The boy looked down into his bag again. "Sorry, boss," he said under his breath.

"After she leave the disc where I said," Scobell went on, "Lucy gots to signal me."

"How?"

"Tell her she gots to go to the Bosher Hall Hospital on Main and Eighth. You know how them windows on the Eighth Street side be down low to the street?"

"Yeah, boss. I knows where you means."

"Tell her she gotta put this here bottle on the windowsill by the door." Along with the money for the playing cards, Scobell slipped Laddie a small flask made of thick, blue glass. It was half-full of a dark liquid.

Laddie glanced suspiciously at it, even as he slid it into his bag.

"Don't worry," said Scobell. "It ain't nothing but dye and water." Laddie started to nod, then stopped himself.

"Prob'ly won't nobody notice it," Scobell continued. "But if'n they do...well, ain't many gonna wanna grab a bottle of something sittin' outside an army hospital."

Laddie grinned, then quickly wiped it from his face.

"You got all that?" Scobell asked.

"Yessuh," the boy replied. "I gots it."

"Good man," said Scobell. He passed the teen one of Pinkerton's gold pieces that Brackett had given him.

Laddie's eyes lit up. He instantly palmed it into his pocket.

"Thank ya, suh," he said. "Thank ya."

"You ain't gotta thank me," Scobell answered. "Jus' make damn sure Miss Lucy gets it straight."

He paused for a moment, then added, "And be sure you tells her thank you for me."

With that, Scobell turned away. Studying the box containing his new deck of cards with feigned fascination, he started back toward the hotel.

Saunders was awake this time, but appeared only slightly more watchful than when he'd been asleep. Besides, he was looking for Brackett or her manservant to exit the main lobby of the Exchange Hotel. He had no interest in yet another black man slouching down the alley to enter the hotel via the black folks' entrance. Scobell slipped unnoticed into the rear alley.

After checking in with Brackett and confirming that he'd sown the seeds of their plan, Scobell returned to his room. He wanted to rest, but knew sleep would never come.

The knowledge that Matchett might send his deputies crashing through the door at any second was pressure enough. Now, the tension of waiting for Lucy's signal was a second stressful layer atop the first.

He lay awake through the night, turning over in the bedsheets as he turned over every detail of their plan in his mind. There was so much that could go wrong.

The whole thing relied on stealth and misdirection, not to mention near-perfect timing. To make matters worse, it was no longer just Brackett and Scobell in the game. They'd have to rely on others playing their parts as well.

Could Lucy get the disc away from Matchett? Could she drop it and set up the signal without being detected? Would Featherington do exactly what they needed? There were no answers to any of these questions, at least not now.

Eventually, he realized that every muscle in his body was taut. Though the night was cool, a light sheen of sweat coated his skin. It wouldn't be long now until the light of dawn peeked under the door from the adjoining room.

Today will tell, he thought.

———◉———

Scobell rose shortly after first light. It wasn't worth staying in bed any longer.

It was much too early to check the signal location at Bosher Hall Hospital. Lucy wouldn't have had time to nab the disc, if Laddie had even delivered the message to her.

To kill time, Scobell picked up his things and loaded his bags. They might need to leave on an instant's notice now. He wanted to be packed and ready.

The only thing he didn't pack were his ragged slave clothes and his shabby overcoat. These he would wear into the city today, hoping they would allow him to disappear among the many other slaves on the streets. He would be too easy to detect sporting the fine suit he wore when accompanying Brackett.

He sat on the bed for a while longer, staring into a corner of the tiny room and mentally reviewing the plan again. At last, when he could wait no more, he arose, blew out a long breath, and slipped into the adjoining room. He gave only a grim nod toward Brackett, who was packing her bags as well, when he passed through her room.

He wasn't hungry, but stopped to get some breakfast from the Exchange's slave allotment anyhow. Listening to the hotel's black staff and guests' slaves chat over their morning meal would provide a minor distraction and pass a few more minutes before he left. A small piece of salty cornbread was all he could stomach. He nibbled it slowly as he stood by the rear door.

At last, Scobell had waited as long as he could. He slipped out the door into the back alley. He once again headed for Fourteenth Street and stopped to survey the surroundings before turning the corner. What he saw made him pull up short.

Saunders' chubby form was nowhere to be seen. Instead, it was Joseph watching the Exchange's door. The spy was tucked unobtrusively into a doorway across the street, but his lanky form was an immediate giveaway.

Jerking his head back, Scobell considered this development. Though the streets were busy with pedestrians and horse traffic this morning, Joseph would be much more watchful than Saunders. Sneaking past him undetected was unlikely.

This would change the plan he and Brackett had created. But, he thought as he ran through a variety of scenarios in his mind, it could still work. Perhaps even to their advantage.

Deciding at last on a course of action, he steeled himself and swung onto the sidewalk of Fourteenth Street. As Scobell crossed the street half a block below where the Confederate spy lurked, he pretended not to see Joseph signaling to someone else farther up the street.

Scobell dodged around two young boys pulling a cart full of live chickens at the next intersection. He glanced backward as he did and confirmed what he suspected.

Joseph was following him.

CHAPTER 33

It was almost disappointing how easy it was to lose Joseph. He may be good at ingratiating himself, thought Scobell, but he doesn't understand the street.

He had led Joseph about halfway across town before making the decisive move. Matchett's agent was half a block behind him when Scobell noticed a team of mules struggling to haul a wagonload of coal up the street toward them. The teamster cracked his whip and cursed at the mules as they strained to move the heavy cargo up the grade.

The moment the load of coal passed him, Scobell darted into the street. When he cleared the far side of the wagon, he dodged left to put it between Joseph and himself.

Coming up alongside the wagon, Scobell leaned in to help to push it along. The mule skinner was either too preoccupied with swearing and whipping his animals to notice or too aggravated to turn down help.

Peeking around the wagon's seat, Scobell saw Joseph had stopped on the sidewalk, gawking about to see where his target had gone. Not finding him on the opposite sidewalk after the wagon passed, Joseph now started across the street himself.

Scobell dodged ahead of the mule team, looping in front of the two lead animals just as Joseph passed behind the wagon in the opposite direction. Still keeping the wagon and team between Joseph and himself, Scobell made a show of grabbing the bridle of the mule closest to him and pulling on it. The teamster continued to bellow and curse at the top of his lungs.

At that moment, the mule team finally reached flatter ground and quickened their pace. Scobell backed away from them as they did, then hurried to the side of the street where he'd started. Mingling with other people as quickly as he could, he hastened off in the direction from which he and Joseph had come.

When he came to a display of crates in front of a dry goods store, Scobell slipped behind them and looked back. He was rewarded by the sight of the gangly spy standing with his hands on his hips, looking back and forth in vain along the crowded street.

Frustrated at having lost his quarry, Joseph finally yanked his hat off his head and swiped it toward the ground as if he might throw it down and stomp on it. Scobell allowed himself a quick grin at The Hawk's expense.

With that, he moved back among the pedestrians on the sidewalk and returned the way he came. It was time to go to the hospital.

⸺◉⸺

Though he'd shaken Joseph, Scobell took his time and relied on his usual random walking pattern. If he could, he would've sprinted all the way to the hospital to check for the sign. But now was no time to get careless.

Eventually, he made his way to Eighth Street. Crossing Main, he was nearly within the shadow of the Confederate Capitol Building. Ignoring the sense of foreboding the building cast over him, he eased down the sidewalk on the opposite side of the street from Bosher Hall Hospital.

He cast a quick glance at the window sill nearest the door and his heart fell. There was no bottle in sight.

Hiding his disappointment, Scobell shuffled down the street. He didn't stop until he reached the banks of the James River. Needing a place to stop and think, he found a wooden apple crate discarded between two bushes and used it for a seat.

What now? Did the missing signal bottle simply mean Lucy hadn't had time to get the disc yet? Or had they had caught her? While the latter scenario was far worse, the former wasn't much better.

The fact that Joseph was the one watching Brackett and Scobell instead of the bumbling Saunders implied things were escalating. Surely, Joseph would realize Scobell had ditched his tail deliberately. If he hadn't already notified Matchett, it wouldn't be long before he did. Once that happened, the spy-catching captain would immediately unleash a swarm of deputies across the city to apprehend the Yankee spies, just as he had with Webster and Warne.

Then again, Scobell reflected, maybe Joseph wouldn't be so quick to report his failure to Matchett. The vicious Confederate captain was not exactly inclined toward forgiveness. Further, Joseph would be loath to admit anyone had gotten the best of him, least of all a woman and a Negro.

The more Scobell considered this angle, the more he was convinced that the smarmy agent would try as hard as possible to right his mistake without letting his boss know. The longer Joseph had to search, the more frightened he'd be of Matchett's reprisal if found out. That was an element Scobell might use against him.

It was something, at least. With the deck stacked as steeply against him as it was, even one good card to play was a bonus.

With this in mind, he shoved himself off his uncomfortable seat and rose to his feet. He headed back up Eighth, intending to return to their hotel by blending into the crowd on Main Street.

As he walked past the hospital again, his eyes were inevitably drawn to the empty window sill. At the last instant, something small and blue caught his eye.

Scobell's heart skipped a beat. Forgetting his desire to avoid attention, he darted across the street to get a closer look, nearly getting run down by a horse and carriage as he did.

Sure enough, tucked far back on the wide sill, sat a small blue bottle. It was still half-full of the dark liquid.

Though elated, he had to laugh at himself for missing the bottle the first time. Following his instructions, Lucy had left the bottle on the windowsill. Wanting to keep it inconspicuous, she had slid it all the way back in the corner where the window sill and frame came together and, in the process, hidden it from view in one direction.

She'd done it. Lucy had not only stolen the disc from Matchett's office but also dropped it and left the signal for Scobell. Bless her heart, he thought.

Despite her initial reservations, Lucy had helped him and Brackett achieve the most critical part of their mission. And exacted her revenge on Matchett.

Now, he had to make sure her vengeance was complete by getting the disc out of Richmond.

The sweet, earthy aroma reached Scobell even before the Public Tobacco Warehouse came into view. There were at least a half-dozen tobacco warehouses along the city's canal basin – known collectively as 'Tobacco Row' – so a perpetual hint of the rich smell hung in the air nearly all the time.

Scobell had chosen the Public Warehouse as the drop site for several reasons. First, between the activity of the warehouse itself and its proximity to the canal, it was one of the busiest areas of the city. Today there was a tobacco auction underway, which created even more activity. Merchants, dockhands, plantation owners, and slaves mingled together to create a constant, chaotic bustle of activity that would help hide the drop and pickup of the cipher disc.

Second, between the slaves who worked there, and those that came and went constantly with loads of tobacco, there were more black faces moving in and out of the tobacco warehouse than white ones. When Lucy made her drop and when Scobell picked up the package, neither would stand out due to their skin color.

Lastly, the Public Warehouse was positioned on the far western edge of Tobacco Row. That put it directly on Scobell's frequent route to the Tredegar Works, so he had observed the site and its activities multiple times. This location also put the drop site farther from the Exchange Hotel and the watchful eyes of Matchett's henchmen.

Arriving at the warehouse, Scobell timed his pace so he would enter at the same time a gaggle of dockworkers started unloading a barge full of coal. He slipped through the large barn doors among them, then peeled off once inside. He turned toward the back wall of the building, where tobacco was stored in huge casks.

The casks were nearly four feet in diameter and lay stacked on their sides, four layers high. They formed a solid wall that reached high into the rafters of the tall warehouse.

He drifted down the narrow opening between the waist-high piles of dried tobacco dumped in loose mounds on the warehouse floor and the massive stacks of tobacco drums. Feigning interest, he occasionally stooped to examine a pile of loose leaves more closely. In reality, though, his eyes were poring over every inch of the stacked barrels, searching for the mark.

At last, he spotted it. On one of the massive poles that held up the building's roof, just a few inches above the floor, was a small, black smudge of charcoal.

Scobell's heart leapt into his throat. He glanced around to make sure no one was watching, then took a subtle stride toward the towering pile of wooden casks. Another quick look backward assured him that all other eyes in the warehouse were on the auctioneer and the bustling activity of the sale. He turned sideways and slid, as quickly and quietly as possible, into the cramped space between two piles of casks.

It was harder to see back here, with the towering barrels blocking out most of the already diffused light of the building. Scobell strained his eyes as he scanned the end of each cask.

Suddenly, he stopped short. There it was.

Another black splotch – made by the piece of charcoal he'd given Laddie to pass to Lucy for exactly this purpose – marked the round wooden bottom of one cask.

He slipped his hand into the gap formed where a cask in the second row sat atop two in the bottom row. For a moment, he felt nothing, and his pulse quickened as his fingers skittered more hurriedly inside the opening.

Then, just before panic set in, his hand brushed something soft. It felt smooth and pliable...like a leather pouch.

Scobell snatched the leather bag from between the casks. Prying it open, he peeked inside. Even in the dusky light between the towering walls of stored tobacco, he could see well enough to discern what the little sack held.

The cipher disc.

Scobell's hands suddenly trembled. It took a substantial effort just to pull the bag's drawstring closed without dropping it on the warehouse floor.

The disc had cost Tim Webster his life, and Kate Warne her freedom. It was the key to saving Brackett's life and his own and, almost more important to Scobell, the key to his freedom. Now he clutched it tightly in his hand.

The enormity of the moment took hold of both his mind and body. His heart hammered and his vision began to blur and darken around the edges. He had the feeling that he was lifting out of his physical form and watching himself from the outside.

Temporarily losing his balance, Scobell teetered backward, jabbing the hard edge of the cask behind him into his spine. The sudden pain jerked him back to the reality of his situation.

He forced himself to get his breathing under control. Still rattled, but at least able to function, he slipped the bag containing the cipher disc into the deep side pocket of his overcoat.

It was time to get out of Richmond and back to Washington, DC. First, though, he had to get out of Richmond's Public Tobacco Warehouse and back to the Exchange Hotel.

He shuffled his feet to work his way out of the crevice between rows of casks. When he reached the end of the row, he glanced around the warehouse. All eyes were still diverted from him, focused on the auctioneer's stand and a pitched bidding war for the current lot of tobacco.

Moving into the open warehouse again, Scobell worked his way toward the rear door. He had to restrain himself from breaking into a run. It took continual reminders to tamp down his flight instinct.

Along the back wall, he grabbed a block and tackle looped with a length of thick rope from a shelf and slung it over his shoulder. Camouflaged to blend with the other dockworkers, he marched out the warehouse doors and into the warm sunshine of a spring morning.

CHAPTER 34

Scobell discarded the block and tackle at the end of the dock, then turned to work his way up Tobacco Row toward the hotel. He needed to get back to the Exchange in time to connect with Featherington.

But there was one more thing he needed to do on the way. He needed to find Joseph.

Odd as it seemed, he had to attract the attention of Matchett's spy. It was going to take misdirection for Brackett and Scobell to escape safely from Richmond – and creating misdirection meant drawing attention to himself first.

Scobell did the mental math on where he'd left Joseph, how long the operation at the tobacco warehouse had taken, and how far the Matchett spy might have wandered since then. He narrowed it down to roughly a two-block area between the Confederate Capitol Building and the canal basin.

Inhaling deeply to brace himself, he turned down the street in that direction. Right to where the enemy agent most likely waited. One who wouldn't waste a second before proudly turning Scobell over to his cruel, murderous leader.

Scobell only covered a short distance before he spotted Joseph moving toward him on the opposite side of the street. The lanky Southerner wasn't hard to find. He weaved quickly along the crowded sidewalk, his shuffling gait exaggerated as he shouldered frantically between the other pedestrians.

Scobell grinned to himself as he moved parallel to the Confederate spy. Nearly an hour had passed since he'd disappeared from Joseph's surveillance. That was plenty of time for panic to set in as Joseph pondered an explanation for how a dim-witted slave had slipped away.

To attract Joseph's attention, Scobell waited until they neared each other, then weaved to the curb as if he might cross. From the opposite side of the street, Joseph's head snapped sideways as he caught sight of his quarry.

Scobell slid back into the crowd, picking up a little speed. He needed to stay ahead of Joseph long enough to get back to the hotel and his rendezvous with Featherington. He made a sudden turn at the next corner and sprinted a few steps to put some space, but not too much, between himself and the opposing spy.

About halfway down the block, Scobell crossed a side street. As he did so, he allowed himself a quick backward glance to confirm Joseph was still following.

He was. The Hawk's long legs ate up the ground as he crossed the side street several seconds after Scobell.

Another quick glance a few moments later confirmed that Matchett's agent had settled in a dozen paces back. Exactly as Scobell hoped.

There was just one more stage to complete in the plan that Brackett and he had pieced together. The final and most difficult part, where one misstep or slip of a finger could bring the entire plot to a sudden, and deadly, conclusion.

At the next corner, he turned once more, this time toward the Exchange Hotel.

━━━◉━━━

As Scobell approached the front entrance of the hotel, he saw a coach in the loading area. A pair of black men were lifting trunks onto the platform in back and stowing smaller bags inside. A gray-whiskered man in a brown overcoat and Homberg hat emerged from the hotel to oversee the loading. He carried a cane with a brass head on it.

Featherington.

Scobell's timing was perfect. He measured his paces, ensuring that his route and speed over the last few yards would put him precisely where he needed to be.

At that moment, on the far side of the bustle in front of the hotel, he spied yet another of the ubiquitous Confederate widows walking slowly down the sidewalk. Donned in black from head to toe, she wore deep mourning widow's weeds, complete with black crepe and a long veil covering her face.

She appeared older than many of the widows he'd seen on the streets of Richmond. Gray curls peeked out from the back of her black hat and fell over the high-necked collar of her dress.

She walked slightly bent, as if age and the weight of her loss were combining to pull her toward the ground. Moving at a slow, but dignified pace, the widow was walking toward the hotel, which would put her directly in the middle of the loading activity.

This presented an additional complexity for the plan. The peculiar calculus of Southern civility demanded that a black man passing a white woman on a sidewalk either step aside to let her pass or give her the widest berth possible. Doing either right now was impossible for Scobell.

He picked up his pace slightly, attempting to carry out the planned maneuver without drawing unwanted attention. He crossed a small alleyway just before the Exchange, using the opportunity to glance back and confirm that Joseph was still tailing him.

He was.

Scobell looked ahead at the bustle of activity. The two black porters scrambled between the hotel and the coach, hoisting Featherington's bags and trunks with audible grunts. Featherington barked out directions as they loaded, adding emphasis when needed by pointing his cane or rapping its head atop a trunk lid.

Scobell took a deep breath and plunged forward.

One of the enslaved porters had latched onto an especially heavy trunk and was dragging it toward the rear of the coach. Scobell hurried over to him.

"Lemme help you, brother," he said. He hustled into the fray, grabbing the handle on the other end of the trunk. The pair hoisted the trunk onto the back of the coach, loud grunts accompanying their efforts.

The porter nodded his thanks to Scobell as he lashed the trunk into place. Scobell returned the nod, then turned toward the remaining loading activity.

Featherington held a red and black carpetbag at his hip as he watched the process. Spying it, Scobell made his move.

"Lemme help you there, Massa," he said, snatching at the bag. "Lemme get that there bag for you."

The old man pulled back on the bag's handle. "Easy there, boy," he said. "I'll take that bag myself."

"No, suh! No, suh!" Scobell protested. "I gits it for you, Massa."

Tugging on the bag, he pulled so hard that the two men briefly bumped into each other. In the same motion, unseen by the audience in front of the hotel, Scobell slipped a small leather pouch into Featherington's coat pocket.

"I say now!" Featherington protested. "I'll keep that bag myself, you rascal. Any more of that and I'll put my cane upside your skull!"

"Sorry, suh," Scobell said, releasing his grip on the bag and backing away with his hands raised. "I'm sorry indeed. Didn't mean no harm, Massa. No harm at all."

He glanced in the direction he'd come from and saw Joseph closing in. Scobell had to hurry now.

He spun around, as if to start again in the direction he'd been walking. As he did, he nearly collided with the black-clad widow.

"Pardon ol' John, ma'am," he said, "Begging your pardon, indeed." He doffed his hat and bent in an exaggerated bow, so deep that he brushed the hem of her dress as he did.

She slowed for a moment, long enough to glance haughtily at the black man practically groveling at her feet. With a lift of her head that simultaneously conveyed pride and disgust, she continued on without another look at him.

Allowing himself another quick glance back at the oncoming Joseph, Scobell hurried off down the sidewalk. He reached the next cross street when he heard the Confederate spy calling from just a few yards behind him.

"You there," Joseph cried. "Stop right now."

Scobell turned suddenly and zipped up the side street. He could hear Joseph's boots clomping on the sidewalk as he broke into a run.

Scobell pivoted again, darting up the alley behind the hotel. After just a few strides, he found his path blocked by a wagon unloading food for the Exchange's restaurant.

He spun back the way he'd come. As he did, Joseph entered the alley, blocking Scobell's path.

Huffing slightly from the exertion of catching up, Joseph drifted to a stop. "Alright," he said between deep breaths, "Where is it?"

Scobell looked at him with a mystified expression. "What's you looking for, suh?" he asked innocently.

"You know damn well what I'm looking for, you black son of a bitch," Joseph retorted. "Where's the disc?"

"Don't know nothing 'bout no disc, suh."

"God damn you," Joseph sputtered. He took two long strides, closing the distance between them to just a few inches.

Scobell raised his hands in the air and took a couple of shuffling steps backward. He needed to buy time to allow Featherington to get away.

"I ain't got nothing but what's mine, boss," he protested.

"I know you have that pouch," said Joseph. "I want it. Now!"

"That pouch is mine, suh." Scobell continued to hold his hands up on either side of his head.

"We'll see about that," Joseph snarled, charging toward him again. The two men danced around the dead-end alley for a few moments as Scobell dodged the taller man's attempts to snag him. Though there was an instant when Scobell could've darted past and run up the alley toward freedom, he didn't.

Finally, Joseph cornered him, grabbing the labels of his coat with those long fingers. The Hawk clutched the coat with one hand and reached into Scobell's coat pocket with the other. The black man immediately began wriggling away.

Grasping Scobell's lapels with both hands again, Joseph hissed, "Stay still, you goddam darkie. I've had enough of your shines. I'm gonna see what you've got stashed in here."

He spun Scobell sideways, tugging the shorter man's coat off his arm as he did so. Pulling hard on it, Joseph twisted Scobell around backwards and yanked the coat the rest of the way off.

"That's more like it," he said, holding it draped over his arms. He panted slightly at the effort.

"Boss, I tell you there ain't nothing in that there coat that ain't mine," Scobell protested.

"We'll see about that."

Joseph rifled through the coat pockets, pulling out everything his fingers touched.

The first thing he found was Scobell's paperwork, giving him permission to run errands through Richmond on Mrs. Lawton's behalf. The second item was a copy of the pass that Winder had signed for Mrs. Lawton, allowing her to move around Richmond. Both were summarily tossed onto the mossy cobblestones of the back alley.

From the bottom of another pocket, Joseph produced a balled-up bandana. He cursed under his breath and flung it aside when he realized it wasn't the object of his search. Scobell tried not to smile.

Finally, from a lower side pocket, the Confederate spy produced a worn leather pouch. He carelessly dropped Scobell's coat onto the muddy street and held the pouch high.

"What's this now?" he asked, triumph in his voice.

"That's mine, suh," Scobell said, making a half-hearted reach for it.

Joseph glared at him. "I doubt that." He pried open the drawstring and plunged his slender fingers into the leather bag.

Fishing the object out of the bag, Joseph held it aloft. As he stared at it victoriously, a look of bewilderment stole its way over his face.

In his hand was a piece of wood, about three inches in diameter and a half-inch thick. It appeared to have been sliced from a cross-section of a tree branch. On the front was a detailed engraving of a horse's head. Each hair on the horse's mane seemed carved individually, and its eyes were detailed in relief.

Flipping it over, Joseph found a carving of a woman's face in profile. Her long hair was pulled back from her face, highlighting the elegant curve of her neck.

He continued to stare for a moment longer, then finally muttered, "What the hell?" He shook the wooden carving in Scobell's face, demanding, "What the hell is this?"

"I tries to tell you, boss. That'd be mine," said Scobell. He added with a hint of pride, "Whittled it out my own self."

Joseph's hands shook. "No!" he shouted. "No, God damn it! Where's the goddam disc?"

Scobell raised his hands once again in a show of innocence. "Don't know nothing 'bout no disc, boss."

Joseph quickly snatched up Scobell's coat and ran his hands through it once more. It was still empty.

He took a threatening stride toward Scobell, who backed against the outer wall of the Exchange. His hands were still in the air, but he braced himself for a punch. It appeared Joseph was ready to snap.

Suddenly, the Matchett agent stopped and stood stock still. "That man out front," he said, only half aloud. "The one loading his bags on the coach."

Scobell lowered his hands, then turned them palms up, shrugged, and shook his head. "You alright, boss?" he asked. "Don't know what you talking 'bout."

With dawning realization, Joseph slowly shook his head again. "You black son of a bitch," he said. His tone was mostly one of surprise, but Scobell thought he detected the slightest hint of admiration, too.

"You slipped the disc to him, didn't you?" Joseph said, his voice suddenly growing louder.

"No, suh!" Scobell protested. But Joseph had already turned away and started running back toward the front of the hotel. Even after Joseph turned the corner out of the alley, Scobell could hear his heavy footfalls retreating down the side street.

Hurrying after him, but staying far enough back to not attract his attention again, Scobell followed. Reaching the corner at Main Street, he peeked around to see the front of the hotel.

Featherington, the coach, and all his bags were gone. In fact, the sidewalk was completely empty...except for Joseph.

In frustration, the tall man shifted his eyes from the spot where the coach had stood, to the front doors of the hotel, then down Main Street in the direction the coach had gone. Scobell snickered to himself as he watched the opposing spy repeat the process twice more.

Joseph suddenly whirled, his eyes meeting Scobell's. Scobell stepped into full view on the sidewalk, still maintaining body language that implied both innocence and ignorance.

"I'll deal with you later!" Joseph shouted, pointing a bony finger in his direction. "I know you didn't come up with all this on your own, so I'll take care of that bitch missus of yours, too!"

With that, Joseph bolted across the street. From the direction he was headed, Scobell guessed he was going to Matchett's office, most likely to gather up Matchett and his deputies to track down Featherington and recapture the disc.

Scobell allowed himself one more self-satisfied smirk when he realized that Joseph and the deputies would have to return to the hotel to inquire about Featherington's travel plans. Joseph had been so frustrated at being duped that he'd neglected to ask the hotel staff about the old man's destination before he left.

That much more time for us to disappear. With that thought, he rushed off toward the slave entrance at the back of the hotel. Stopping to pick up his coat, he hurried inside.

CHAPTER 35

"If we're going to get to Wilson's Landing tonight, we have to leave now." Scobell's voice was low, but so forceful it caused Brackett to start. "Where's your pistol?"

The pair had carefully studied reports of the Union troop movements in the Richmond newspapers over the past few days. Comparing what they read with Scobell's mental map of the region, they decided Wilson's Landing was their best target for an escape.

The land across the Chickahominy River was firmly in Yankee hands at that point, and McClellan was rumored to have established his headquarters along its southern banks. Some reports had the bluecoats already with a stronghold on the northern shore. If the pair of spies could make it that far, they would be safe in the arms of the Federal army.

"The gun's in the lockbox," Brackett replied.

Scobell nodded.

"As long as it's handy," he said. "If we need to make a stand, we're gonna want it close."

Brackett nodded and handed him the small iron box. As he held it, she snapped the lock and made a show of slipping the small metal key into the bosom of her corset. "No Southern gentleman would ever search there," she said with a grin.

"Let's hope," he said. The grim note in his voice was unmistakable.

He shoved the last items into his duffel and said, "I'll load the horses. The lockbox will be in your right saddlebag. If we hit trouble and need to leave the horses, grab it and run."

The sun was setting when they climbed into their saddles and set out. This gave Scobell a little confidence that they could make the long ride to Wilson's Landing, though it was slight. With the Union forces fighting their way up the peninsula, the pair might encounter soldiers from either side. A midnight encounter on a dark road in a war zone could end badly, whether at the hands of friend or foe.

They set out at a quick pace to put as much distance as possible between them and Matchett's men. The road was wide and flat as it stretched through the surrounding farmland. The spring moon cast enough light across the open fields to allow the riders to canter without fear of veering off the road.

After an hour of hard riding, Brackett finally spoke. She only talked loud enough to be heard above the horses, but the night was so quiet that it sounded like a shout at first.

"I think we're going to be alright, John," she said. "I know we still have a few hours' riding ahead, but it doesn't look like anyone's following us. Maybe they don't even know we're gone."

"I hope you're right," Scobell said. "We still have a way to go and there could be patrols out here...from either army. And I'd say they're about equally likely to shoot first and ask questions after we're lying in the dirt."

"Let's at least slow up a bit and give the horses a break," Brackett suggested. "If we find trouble, we'll want them fresh."

They slowed to a walk. The moon still lit their way, and the only sound was the clopping hooves of their mounts.

Despite the trepidation, it was hard to envision they were riding through a war zone. There were no soldiers' encampments in sight, no campfires, no boom of cannons in the distance. The silence was almost more frightening than the sound of gunfire. Brackett and Scobell once again picked up their pace.

At last, a small crossroads broke their path through the unending farm fields. From the maps, Scobell thought it was the road to Charles City. If he was right, they were only about five miles from their destination. They pushed on into the night.

A few hundred yards past the crossroads, the road narrowed as it went into a copse of pines. The riders instinctively slowed, wary of a surprise attack from the woods. The soft moonlight that had been their companion all night abruptly vanished, dispersed by the overhanging branches.

"Seems like a good place to get ambushed," Brackett observed.

"Yes," Scobell said in a low voice. "It certainly does."

The pair slowed their horses to a walk, both out of fear of what lay in wait in the forest and from the lack of visibility. They strained their eyes to pick out figures hidden behind the trees, but it was in vain.

And then, just as suddenly as the forest had swallowed them, it spit them back out again. The trees fell away on either side and they were once again in open fields.

Scobell let out his breath in a long sigh. He didn't even realize he'd been holding it.

"Thank goodness," said Brackett, also sighing audibly. "I'm glad that's ov-"

Before she could finish her sentence, they saw four glowing lights moving toward them from ahead. They couldn't make out details at a distance, but the movement and height of the lanterns meant four riders on horseback.

Scobell quickly weighed their choices. Fleeing back up the road wasn't an option; they would have to move so slowly through the dark woods that the horsemen with their lights would be on top of them in no time.

He considered racing off through the field, but he recalled a maze of streams and marshes on the map. While he might struggle through the morass and find a way to the landing, he wasn't sure Brackett could. And even if she could, their pursuers might have fresher mounts and run them down anyway.

The only genuine option was to continue forward. Play their roles once more and hope their cover would get them through.

The six riders came together on the gloomy road. Each of the horsemen riding toward Brackett and Scobell carried long poles with oil lanterns dangling from metal loops at the end.

As they moved within the circle of flickering light, Scobell knew immediately they were trapped. The first face he saw was hideously scarred on its left side.

Matchett.

The four men reigned up next to the fugitives. At that distance, Scobell recognized Blake and Saunders as the riders to Matchett's right. The man to Matchett's left lifted his head so the brim of his hat no longer hid his face. It was Joseph.

"So where are y'all headed on this lovely night?" asked Joseph, his sneer apparent even in the dim light of the lanterns.

Brackett gasped. Her horse, sensing the anxiety, pranced in place.

"I allow you didn't expect to see us here tonight, did you?" Joseph said. "Not after you sent us off chasing your friend Featherington halfway to Kentucky."

"I don't know what you're talking about," Brackett protested.

"That's what Featherington said when we caught up to him," sneered Joseph. "Of course, *he* really didn't know. He couldn't even explain how that leather pouch with the carving of a horse on it got in his pocket."

"Didn't matter how hard we beat him," Blake snarled.

Scobell felt a pang of remorse stab his gut. The older gentlemen had only been a dupe, used to misdirect their pursuers. Despite Featherington's anti-Confederate leanings, Brackett had never said a word to him about their plan.

"It took me a while to piece it together once we realized he was telling the truth," said Joseph. "I just couldn't figure it. If the old man didn't have the disc and this buck didn't have it," he said, pointing at Scobell, "where did it go?"

He paused and looked at Brackett with a smug smile. "Then I remembered that old widow woman passing by the hotel. She walked right by that buck on the sidewalk, close enough to touch. Close enough, I'll bet, to hand her the cipher disc."

Scobell wasn't about to explain that it was considerably more sophisticated than that. Brackett had actually sewn an extra pocket near the hem of her black dress so that Scobell could slip the disc into it when he brushed her skirts outside the hotel.

Joseph pointed at Brackett's saddle bag. "I'll bet there's a gray wig tucked in there somewhere," he said. "You'd make a pretty fair actress, Mrs. Lawton. Or whatever your name is."

Brackett glared at him. "You know very well my name is Carrie Lawton," she insisted indignantly. "I have no idea what nonsense you're talking about here, but I demand you let us go right now."

Ignoring her response, Joseph continued. "It was a good plan you devised. We never would've caught up to you, except that Captain Matchett wired General Winder, who got us on an express train back here."

Joseph started to say more, but Matchett cut him off.

"We don't have time for any more nonsense," barked the captain. He gestured toward Blake. "Get that darkie down off his horse now. Beat him till he gives up the disc and be done with this."

Blake rode up next to Scobell. In a flash of motion, the deputy belted him across the temple with a blackjack he'd concealed in his hand. The blow knocked Scobell sprawling from his horse, landing him face first in the dusty road.

Getting down from his own horse, Blake stood over Scobell. The spy writhed in pain, holding the side of his head and trying to blink away the bright lights that flashed inside his head.

A searing pain in his ribs temporarily replaced the pain in his head as Blake delivered a kick to his side.

"Where is it?" the deputy demanded. "Where'd you hide it, boy?"

"Don't know, boss," gasped Scobell, "Don't know what y'all talking 'bout."

The point of Blake's boot found Scobell's side again, slightly lower this time, in the soft area below his ribs. It felt as though the kick might go all the way through him.

Scobell tried to repeat that he knew nothing about the disc, but could only muster a garbled cough. He flopped over onto his back as he did.

"Stop it!" Brackett yelled from atop her horse. "You're going to kill him!"

"Yes," said Matchett evenly, still staring down at Scobell. "We're definitely going to kill him. The question is how much pain we'll deliver first."

Then he slowly lifted his menacing gaze to her face. "And then we'll see about you."

Still on his horse, Saunders pulled his long-bladed knife from his belt and pointed toward Scobell. "Why don't you let me have a crack at him, Captain? Let's see how he likes this here Arkansas toothpick. I'll split him from his balls to his neck, a little at a time. That oughta jog his memory."

"Just a minute," ordered Matchett. Scobell turned his head almost imperceptibly to see the captain.

"I know that buck," Matchett murmured. His left hand raised unconsciously to the alligator skin scars on his neck.

"'Course you do, captain," said Blake. Pointing at Brackett, he said, "He was in our office when she came in."

"No," Matchett growled. "That's not it." He stared hard at Scobell. "That's the goddam nigger that burned my face. I realized it when I saw him in this light. It's the same son of a bitch."

"You sure?" asked Blake, now staring at Scobell as well.

"Your damn right I'm sure," said Matchett. He addressed Scobell for the first time. "I'll carry these scars for the rest of my life. Your life won't last more than a few minutes anyway, but we can end it quick or slow. If you don't tell us where that disc is right now, I'll have Blake smash that oil lamp on you."

Scobell's glance flitted to the lantern, then back to the captain.

"It'll kill you, for sure," Matchett continued. "But it'll be slow and it'll hurt like nothing you've ever known. Trust me."

"You can't –" started Brackett, but she froze when Saunders drew his pistol and pointed it at her face.

Matchett continued as if she'd never spoken. "You tell us where that disc is, buck, and I'll put a bullet in your head. It'll be quick. And you'll never know the difference."

Scobell blubbered, "Please, don't, Massa. Please don't burn poor John."

"Burn him," said Matchett abruptly. "We'll get her to tell us where the disc is."

Blake snatched his lantern from the end of the pole and raised it high, ready to smash it onto the prone man. Scobell knew when it hit him, the glass would shatter, splashing flaming oil all over his body.

"Wait, boss, wait," he pleaded to the deputy. "I'll tell."

Blake looked up at Matchett. The captain nodded slightly, and the deputy lowered the lantern.

"She gots it, Massa," Scobell said to Matchett. "Please don't burn me, Massa. My missus gots the disc."

"Where?" Matchett demanded.

"Right there in her saddlebag. She done got it locked in a box."

"John!" shouted Brackett. "No!"

Matchett motioned toward Saunders, who dismounted and walked over to Brackett. She aimed a kick at the deputy's chin as he approached her horse, but he was prepared for the move and dodged it easily, despite his bulk. He grabbed her leg and pinned it to her horse's side with a powerful hand.

With his free hand, Saunders felt the outside of the saddlebag, then reached inside to pull out the lockbox. "It's here," he said. "Just like the buck said."

Matchett turned his gaze from Scobell to examine the prize. "Open it," he commanded. "Make sure this sneaky black son of a bitch isn't lying to us."

Saunders tugged at the small lock, but it wouldn't budge. Lifting the box over his head, he flung it to the ground. Still, the iron box held.

The other three men all watched as Saunders struggled to open the box.

"Just smash the lock off," said Joseph.

"Pry it off with your knife," suggested Blake.

"Good Christ, Saunders," barked Matchett. "Just break the damn thing open!"

At last, Saunders set the lockbox on the ground. Using the butt of his knife, he smashed the hinge and lock off the front.

"It's empty!" he shouted, holding up the dangling box in the flickering lamplight. "It's not here!"

Suddenly, from behind Blake, a deep voice spoke. "Pardon my mistake, gentlemen," said Scobell. "I had it right here all along."

The confusion created by his calm tone and perfect diction lasted less than three seconds. In that moment, Scobell's right hand flicked into his boot, as quick as a striking rattlesnake, and pulled out Brackett's Smith & Wesson.

Blake spun back to face Scobell, raising his revolver to fire as he did.

CHAPTER 36

Scobell was faster.

Firing as he sprung to his feet, his first shot hit the deputy high on the right side of his chest. The impact spun him partly around, but he still lurched forward, swinging the lantern toward Scobell with his left hand.

Matchett pulled his pistol and swung it toward the fracas. He fired just as Blake took another staggering step toward Scobell.

The shot hit Blake in the left forearm, shattering it and sending his lantern crashing to the ground. On impact, a ball of flame burst into the air.

The horses immediately pranced and reared. Joseph pitched sideways out of his saddle and hit the ground hard.

Blake struggled fiercely to fire a shot at Scobell. He dropped to one knee and lifted his pistol with his right arm.

In one swift motion, Scobell stepped to within arm's reach of Blake and brushed aside the revolver with his left hand. Then he put Brackett's pistol to the deputy's forehead and fired.

Blake toppled over backward, dead before he landed. As he fell, Scobell snatched the deputy's pistol from his lifeless grip.

Saunders recovered from the shock of the scene first. His revolver was still in its covered holster, so he lunged to grab Brackett's horse, hoping to use it as a shield until he could draw the gun.

In the confusion, however, he lost his hold on Brackett. This time, it was Saunders who received a hard kick from a boot.

Brackett's pointed toe caught him flush on the nose, crushing it instantly. Blood spurted onto Saunders' lips and chin as he staggered backwards.

He didn't suffer long. As soon as he cleared Brackett's horse, Scobell shot him dead.

Firing two more quick shots toward Matchett, Scobell raced to Brackett's side. Snatching the cipher disc out of his left boot, he pressed it into her hand.

"Ride!" he shouted. "Ride to the landing! I'll be right behind you."

"You took it?" she asked, still processing everything she'd seen.

"Just go!" he shouted, slapping her horse's flank. "I'll explain later."

Recovering herself, Brackett spurred the horse and sprinted past Matchett and Joseph. Joseph was still sprawling on the ground and Matchett was trying to control his mount, which was spooked by the tower of flame rising into the night. Brackett was gone down the road before either man could react.

Emptying Brackett's pistol at the struggling horsemen, Scobell sprinted to Saunders' prone body and snatched the revolver from his holster. Stuffing it into his belt, he leapt onto his horse, still carrying Blake's pistol in his other hand.

Scobell tore after Brackett, which took him between the two remaining Confederates. Joseph was still on the ground, but he'd risen to one knee and seemed to be recovering himself. Matchett had finally calmed his horse and Scobell saw him raising his sidearm again to take aim.

Scobell leveled Blake's pistol. In the dark and galloping full speed, he couldn't afford to miss. Matchett surely wouldn't.

He chose the bigger target and fired. Matchett's horse staggered a few steps, then pitched onto its right side. Blood spouted from the side of its head.

Scobell leaned forward over his horse's mane and they dashed into the night. He hoped he'd arrive at the landing and find Brackett safely waiting with their Union rescuers.

Instead, he found her just a few hundred yards ahead. She had hidden behind a small patch of brush just off the trail. As Scobell rode past, he heard her shout, "John!" He reined his mount to a stop.

"I told you to ride for the landing," he said, a touch of anger in his voice.

"I was worried about you!"

Seeing it wasn't worth arguing further, Scobell dropped the subject. "Come on," he said. "Let's go find our ride home."

Brackett glanced back the trail in the direction they'd come. "Are they chasing us?"

"I'm sure they will be," Scobell said. "But I left them a little disorganized."

The pair of operatives started toward the river again. Even as they rode, Brackett couldn't resist asking.

"You took the disc from the box? And my gun?" Her tone was a mix of surprise and disapproval.

"I didn't want them to find it on you," Scobell said. "If I died, and they found you with the disc, you would've ended up in prison for sure. If not worse."

He paused for a moment, then added, "I figured to end up dead either way if they caught us. I thought if I had the disc, they might let a lady like you go."

They rode in silence for a few moments. At last, Brackett asked, "How did you unlock the box? I still have the key."

"I've been a slave my whole life. You think I haven't picked a lock before? A bent horseshoe nail works really well."

Scobell, who'd been continually checking their back trail, glanced behind them again. This time, however, he thought he saw two riders charging after them through the dim moonlight.

"No more talking," he shouted to Brackett. "They're coming up behind us. Time to ride like hell!"

Picturing the landscape in his mind, Scobell figured they were about a mile from the landing. There was a sharp left turn a few hundred yards ahead, and then they'd enter another thick forest. From there, it was a gradual descent to the landing at the river's edge.

He hoped that meant safety, although the nagging idea that the graybacks had come from that direction crept into his head. Would they find Union troops when they reached Wilson's Landing? Or had the Rebels retaken control of it?

There was no way they could know and damn little they could do about it if they did. Their only option now was to ride as fast as possible to the spot they'd picked and hope fortune was on their side.

Just as that flashed through his head, Scobell suddenly pitched forward and flew over the head of his horse.

He turned a full somersault in the air and landed hard on his hip. His left leg ricocheted off the hard ground and he heard more than felt the bone in it snap. Brackett, whose horse had been a few strides behind, reined up just in time to avoid the same fate.

A small stream cut through the road at this spot. It was only a foot lower than the road surface. In the daylight, or even if the horses had been walking, they could've negotiated it easily. Instead, Scobell lay writhing in pain in the dusty road.

Brackett was down off her horse in an instant and bent over her partner. "Can you get up?" she asked, her voice quavering.

"No," came the grunted reply. He sucked in his breath through gritted teeth. "My leg's broken."

"You must get up!" she insisted. "We have to go now!"

"You need to go," Scobell replied. "I can't." He gestured toward his horse, which was up again but dangling its own broken ankle. "He can't either."

Brackett grabbed the front of Scobell's shirt and tried in vain to lift his dead weight. "You have to get up," she repeated. Scobell could feel tears dripping off her cheeks onto his.

"You have to go, Kitty," he said. "Get the disc back to Pinkerton. If you don't, everything we did, everyone we lost, will be a waste."

They could now hear the rumble of their pursuers' hoofbeats from the north. "We can both ride my horse," she argued weakly.

"They'd be on us by the time I got in the saddle," said Scobell. "Even if we got going, they'd catch us in no time."

He squeezed her arms with both powerful hands. "It's up to you now," he said. "Make all of this matter."

The sound of the two approaching riders grew louder. "Go!" Scobell said. "Now!"

Brackett leaned over her prone partner and hugged him tightly. "You're a good man, John," she whispered in his ear. "Maybe the bravest I've ever known."

With that, she leapt into the saddle. Chancing one last, mournful look down at him, she wheeled and spurred her horse to a full gallop toward Wilson's Landing.

Scobell watched her disappear into the murky darkness. He mentally measured the distance from here to the river. Her mount had traveled hard all night and would be tired. He doubted Brackett could outrace the two men who now bore down on him.

He had to buy her some time.

With a hugely painful effort, he rolled onto his stomach. As he did, the pressure at his waist reminded him of Saunders' revolver stashed there.

Scobell pulled the revolver out, which made it easier to haul himself forward on his belly. Using his elbows, he dragged through the dust and gravel to where his injured horse now stood.

A few feet before he reached his mount, he was relieved to find the other revolver lying in the dust. He grabbed it with his other hand, then finished dragging himself to the horse.

He peered under the animal's belly to see the two Rebels riding down on him. They were only about a hundred yards away now. He could see their horses clearly, although the darkness still hid the riders themselves from view.

Scobell set his teeth against the pain. Lying flat on his face, he reached behind and tucked one of the revolvers into his belt. Then, using his free hand, he snagged a stirrup and hauled himself upward.

The injured horse whinnied and shied away from the pressure. The wounded spy clung to the stirrup with every fiber of his waning strength. Through the agonizing pain, he gradually lifted himself.

Sweat pouring down his face and neck from the exertion, he finally reached a point where he could plant his right foot on the ground. With a muffled groan, he put all his weight on the uninjured leg and forced himself upright.

Steadying himself with the saddle horn, Scobell snagged the reins with his left hand to keep the injured horse in place. He would need it if he was going to stay upright.

He saw the riders had discarded their lanterns to move faster. They were now only a few dozen yards from him.

Scobell snatched the other pistol from his belt. With the reins wrapped around his left fist and a pistol in each hand, he braced his arms over the saddle.

How many shots had he fired earlier? Two? Three? He couldn't recall.

Was that gun in his right hand or left? In the chaos, he couldn't remember that either.

It didn't matter now. He knew he was going to die here on this lonely road.

Still in the South, the place he hated more than any other. The place that had cost him his freedom, his love, at least one of his fellow operatives...and now his life.

If he couldn't stop the two men now flying toward him, they would catch Brackett before she got to safety; before she could get the cipher disc out. All that loss would be for nothing.

Scobell steadied himself on his good leg. He cocked both hammers.

Matchett and Joseph bore down on him, guns drawn. At about twenty yards, they both started firing. It amazed Scobell how bright the muzzle flashes seemed in the dark.

A bullet whined past his ear. Another slammed into his horse's midsection with a sickening thunk.

Scobell pulled tight on the reins and waited. On the riders came.

When they were so close that he could distinguish their features – Joseph to his right and Matchett to the left – the horsemen fired another volley. He tried to stay steady, even though the muzzle blasts were so close it seemed they might singe his face.

At last, Scobell fired.

The revolver in his right hand barked. Joseph tumbled backward out of his saddle for the second time that night. This time, he wouldn't be getting up again.

Swiveling his head to aim down his left arm, Scobell cracked off a shot with his other revolver at Matchett. The captain kept on as if nothing had happened. Scobell noted with disappointment that Matchett's horse cleared the small stream without a stumble.

Matchett was now passing Scobell on the road. They tried hurried shots at each other, but both missed.

Forgetting his broken leg for an instant, Scobell attempted to spin toward his target and get off another shot. The move instantly caused him to crumple to the dirt in pain.

Looking back over his shoulder, Matchett saw his foe struggling on the ground. Foregoing his pursuit of the disc for the moment, the Confederate captain turned his mount and went back to finish the man who had caused him such pain.

Searing agony coursed through Scobell's body. There was no way for him to stand again, let alone run. The best he could do was force himself into a sitting position, facing the lone approaching rider.

Scobell had dropped one revolver when he fell. He couldn't find it right now. And right now was all that mattered.

Matchett slowed his horse as he approached the fallen man. From his sitting position, Scobell couldn't get a clear shot past the horse's head. With no idea how many rounds he had left, he didn't dare waste one.

When Matchett was just a few yards away, he wheeled his mount to one side and aimed his own revolver at Scobell. "You're finished, nigger," the captain said.

Both men fired at the same time.

Scobell felt a burning stab in his left biceps. He saw Matchett sag slightly in his saddle.

The wounded captain struggled to thumb back the hammer for a second shot.

Holding the trigger down, Scobell swiped the hammer of the revolver with the palm of his other hand three times in quick succession. Just as he'd practiced with Scully.

All three shots caught the Rebel spy-hunter in the torso. At the third one, he slumped forward onto his horse's neck for a moment, then slid to the ground with a dull thump.

Not sure whether Matchett was dead, Scobell tried to fire once more. The result was only a metallic click. The pistol was empty.

Matchett didn't move. Relieved, Scobell let himself topple onto his back again.

CHAPTER 37

His strength was gone. All he could feel now was the unbelievable pain. He couldn't be sure how long he lain there in agony, drifting in and out of consciousness. It might've only been minutes, although it felt like hours.

Then he heard it. Faintly at first, but then clearly and growing louder. Hoofbeats.

Scobell struggled to dial in his scattered senses and focus on the noise. Which direction were they coming from?

At last, his concentration overcame the pain, and he located the sound of the riders. His heart sank at the realization they were coming from the north, not from Wilson's Landing.

That meant Confederate riders. They would've already found the bodies of Blake and Saunders. When they arrived here, they'd find Scobell lying in the road next to two more dead Confederates.

He would've been better off if Matchett had killed him. At least that would've been quick. A black man who'd killed four Rebels would suffer a slow, painful death at the hands of their compatriots.

Scobell tried to push the thought out of his head, but it wouldn't leave.

The sound of the riders grew nearer. There were more than a couple of them. It was an entire squad.

He turned his head to the side and spied the other revolver lying in the road, just a few feet away. At most, there were five shots left in it.

It would take another grueling effort to reach it. Scobell dug his elbow into the road and pushed. He crunched his jaws shut to keep from screaming as he rolled onto his side with his injured leg beneath him.

Pausing for a moment to suck air through clenched lips, he rocked forward and flopped onto his chest. He could taste the dust and feel the grit in his teeth as a small cloud billowed around him.

He used both arms to push and pull himself along the ground. The pistol wasn't far, only a couple paces if Scobell could walk. Instead, it seemed like miles.

Lacking the strength even to lift his head, he dragged the side of his face through the grit and pebbles. After only a couple feet, he could feel the dampness where the skin had worn off his cheek and blood flowed.

Still, he inched along. The hoofbeats pounded ever closer.

With a final herculean shove, his body shifted close enough that the fingertips of his outstretched right hand touched metal. Straining as far as possible, he grasped the barrel of the revolver between two fingers and pulled it toward him. When he finally had the pistol in his hand, he clutched it to his body for a moment.

Scobell thought of Marie, realizing that he'd never look into her magnificent brown eyes again. A tear slid down his cheek.

In that instant, a sudden fury took hold of him. He would die here; without his freedom, without the green fields he'd dreamed of, without the love of his life.

As he lay facedown in the dirt and gravel of enemy territory, Scobell decided he would sell his last few minutes of life as dearly as possible. The oncoming Confederate squad would be the ones who paid the price.

No longer able to sit up, he forced himself onto his elbows. If he let them get close enough, he might knock a couple out of their saddles.

One, for sure, with a well-aimed shot. For Webster. Maybe two, for McGinnis.

Hell, maybe even three. The thought almost brought a smile to his face.

He peered through the darkness, trying to pick out his targets. Sweat, tears, and blood mingled to blur his vision. He swiped at his eyes as best he could from his awkward position.

At last, the ghostly forms of the riders appeared out of the gloom. There were at least a dozen of them.

One rode a few paces ahead of the rest. Scobell focused his attention on that one. If he could kill that rider with one shot, the surprise might create enough confusion to pick off a couple more before they killed him.

He had to focus. He strained to pick out the rider's face, where he'd aim that critical first bullet.

They slowed to a trot as they approached. They'd seen the bodies, both men and horse, lying in the road.

Scobell stared at the lead rider, still waiting for the right moment to strike. He clicked back the revolver's hammer, worried that they'd hear the sound if he let them get any closer.

Just a few steps more. Scobell aligned the sights on the rider's face. His finger slowly tensed on the trigger.

A half-second before twitching it, Scobell froze. Something wasn't right.

He'd focused on his target's head, but something else caught his attention. Something was fluttering in the night. Gradually, the realization came to him.

The Rebel rider was wearing...a dress.

"John!" Brackett's voice rang out as she saw him lying in the road. "John, are you alright?" For the second time that night, she slipped from her saddle in an instant and was at his side.

"Oh, my God," she cried, examining his filthy, bloody face. "Oh, my God. You're alive!" She bent to hug him, but Scobell immediately protested with a groan.

"Don't," he whispered. "Please don't."

"It's alright," Brackett said. "I found these Federals camped at the river. Right by the landing, just as we thought." She grasped his hand and squeezed it, which elicited a pained grunt from Scobell. "We're here to help you. You're going to be safe now."

The Union captain barked, "Private Hanson, give that man some water. Clausen, examine his wounds."

The two men dismounted and moved to Scobell's side immediately. Hanson handed his canteen to Brackett, who was still bent over Scobell. She cradled his head to pour a few drops over his dusty lips.

"We need to move quickly," the captain said, swiveling in the saddle to look up the road behind them. "The boat is waiting for us at the landing. We're too exposed if the Rebs find us here in the road."

As the soldiers bandaged the bullet wound in his arm and improvised a quick splint for his broken leg, Brackett gave Scobell some more water. His pain was still excruciating, but seeing Brackett cheered him.

"I don't understand," he said to Brackett finally. "If you went to the landing, how did you come here from the other direction? I thought you were Confederate riders." He paused for a moment, then added more quietly, "I almost shot you."

"We were hurrying to get back to you," she said. "One of Captain Reed's men knew a shortcut through the woods. But we didn't know exactly where I left you." Her voice caught as she said the last few words.

"We rode until we found Blake and Saunders," she continued. "When we realized we were too far north, we lit out back this direction to find you."

"I'm glad you did," was all Scobell could muster.

"You left quite a mess back there," Brackett said, gently wiping blood from his cheek. Turning to survey the surrounding scene, she added, "And a bigger one here."

He nodded slightly and grunted a reply.

"I leave you alone for one hour..." Brackett said, shaking her head.

Scobell hurt far too much to laugh.

"Can you ride, Scobell?" Captain Reed asked.

"I don't think so, sir," said Scobell.

"His leg's broken, sir," Clausen chimed in. "He'll need a litter."

"Get him on one now," Reed ordered. "Use a couple of those small trees there. Hanson, use your coat to make it."

"My coat, Captain?" Hanson hesitated. "Use my coat for...one of them?"

Reed's glare bore holes into the private's skull. Several seconds passed. Hanson shuffled his feet uncomfortably.

"Private, this man nearly gave his life tonight to save Miss Brackett and complete their mission." The captain spoke slowly, as if he were talking to a wayward toddler.

"He also killed more Rebs in two hours tonight than you've shot in six months in this army." Reed's voice was still quiet, but the pace of his words quickened.

"If I tell you to carry Mr. Scobell out of here on your goddam back, you will do as you are ordered. Do you understand me, private?"

"Yes, sir!" came the reply, and Hanson scurried off to help Clausen construct the litter.

Scobell could hear some of the other soldiers chuckling softly amongst themselves. Even in his battered state, he found himself grinning up at Brackett. She giggled and wiped tears from her face.

The soldiers loaded Scobell onto the litter. Suspended between two men's mounts, one behind the other, he bounced along in agony as they trotted toward Wilson's Landing.

From there, the Union gunboat that would take them down the Chickahominy River to the safety of McClellan's headquarters, where they would deliver the Confederate cipher disc to Pinkerton. Where Scobell would claim his freedom, forever.

It was the most painful, wonderful ride of Scobell's life.

EPILOGUE

Bells pealed from seemingly every church tower. Clutches of people rushed about the streets, clapping each other on the back and offering warm wishes. It was like nothing Scobell had ever seen.

Scobell walked down Pennsylvania Avenue, arm in arm with Marie. They were bundled in their winter finest, warding off the chill of the New Year's morning. His leg was healing nicely from the break, but he still had a trace of a limp.

Strangers, both black and white, rushed up to shake their hands and extend congratulations, hurrying off again to share greetings with the next people they encountered. From the naval yard on the banks of the Potomac, the boom of cannons rang across the city.

An elderly white man, his face enveloped by a bristling mass of white hair sprouting from both his head and chin, strolled up to the couple. A broad smile split the ancient creases of his face.

"It's a historic day," he said, grabbing Scobell's hand and pumping it up and down. "Congratulations, my son."

"Thank you, sir," John said. "It's a historic day, indeed."

Tipping his hat to Marie, the gentlemen moved away, then quickly turned back to the pair. "Here," he said, extending a folded newspaper toward them. "You might want to keep this."

"Why, thank you, sir," said Marie as Scobell accepted the paper. "That's very kind."

Scobell unfolded it and read aloud the headline: *EMANCIPATION DECLARED.*

He turned to look at her. As their eyes met, smiles crept across both of their faces. Looking back at the newspaper, he said, "They published the whole thing."

"Really?"

"That on the first day of January," he read, "in the year of our Lord one thousand eight hundred and sixty-three, all persons held as slaves within any State or designated part of a State, the people whereof shall then be in rebellion against the United States, shall be then, thenceforward, and forever free."

He stopped, his voice catching. Marie reached out and stroked his arm.

"I never thought we'd see the day," he said.

"I know," she replied softly.

At the next corner, they passed a group of young men singing at the top of their lungs. Each pedestrian who had the misfortune to walk within arm's reach received a hearty pat on the back from the crooners. Scobell absorbed his clap on the shoulder with a nod and a smile.

As Scobell and Marie moved down the avenue, they could see a crowd had formed in front of the White House. Again, blacks and whites gathered together, marching the broad sidewalk in front of the mansion and calling for President Lincoln to speak.

They were still more than a block away when a loud cheer went up from the throng. People pointed toward the White House, hopping and shouting, "There he is! Come out, Abe! Freedom!"

Lincoln didn't come out, choosing instead to wave from a balcony, then disappear again inside. Appropriately, he left the celebration to the people.

Not wanting to force their way through the rowdy crowd in front of the White House, Marie and Scobell crossed to the other side of Pennsylvania Avenue. There, they were intercepted by another pair of well-wishers, two black men in their early twenties.

"Some day, ain't it?" said the taller of the two.

"It is," said Scobell. They'd been accosted so many times on their short walk that he'd run out of fresh responses.

The shorter man pointed at the paper folded under Scobell's arm. "You read it yet?"

"Only part of it so far," Scobell admitted.

"It don' jus' free them blacks still down South," the first man said, sticking his chest out. "It say we can fight."

Pointing at his friend, he said, "We gonna join up. I reckon we got a few scores to settle."

"I reckon so," said Scobell with a slight nod.

"You gonna join up?" asked the shorter one.

"No," he said, looking down at Marie. "I've already done my part."

Tapping the brim of his hat, Scobell led Marie down the sidewalk again. They could both feel the quizzical looks of the exuberant young men on their backs as they walked away.

Marie tugged his arm close and squeezed. "Do you miss it?" she asked. "It's been over six months since you left Pinkerton's secret service."

"Not at all," he said. "Brackett and I finished our mission and got him his cipher disc. He was good to his word and signed my free papers."

"Mine, too," she reminded. "It was good of him to do that."

"It was," he agreed. "He didn't have to do that. Although, he was so happy that the Rebs exchanged Scully, Lewis, and Warne from prison that he probably would've agreed to free half the slaves in the South."

"Now he doesn't have to," Marie said with a smile. "Mr. Lincoln's taken care of that for him."

Scobell grinned back at her. "I reckon he has."

They walked in silence for another block. Then Marie asked, "If you're not going to war and you're done spying, what are you going to do? We can't live forever on the secret service money you saved."

"I've been meaning to talk to you about that," he said. "I'd like to buy a farm."

"A farm?"

"Yes. I have a particular place in mind. Rolling hills, green grass, a little breeze blowing across the fields."

"It sounds wonderful. Where is it?"

"Well," he said, "I'm not sure. I've heard Pennsylvania is nice."

AFTERWORD

You've reached the end of *In Freedom's Shadow*. Since the book is advertised with that well-known but still vague phrase "Based on a True Story," I'm assuming you have some questions. Primary among those is probably, how much of what I just read is true?

Since you went to the time and expense of purchasing my book – for which I am sincerely grateful and thank you immensely – I feel I owe you some answers. Here you go.

Q: Is John Scobell a real person?

A: Yes. Well, at least we think so. Allan Pinkerton wrote about Scobell, and his missions to Leonardtown and Richmond, in his 1883 memoir *The Spy of the Rebellion*. There have been numerous articles and analyses of Scobell and his exploits since that time, but they all trace back to Pinkerton's book. There's no other contemporary mention of Scobell, so *The Spy of the Rebellion* is all we have to go on.

One problem in uncovering Scobell's reality is that he was a spy. By definition, much of his identity was hidden. In addition, Pinkerton loved to change the names of his operatives in his post-war memoirs (more on that later). Lastly, of course, Scobell had been a slave prior to the Civil War. Individual enslaved people were poorly documented, if at all, in written records.

So, is it possible that a slave who became a spy, and whose only written reference probably didn't use his real name, could exist without his true identity ever being known? Definitely.

In fact, a majority of serious historians over the last 160 years have stated that Scobell was very much a real person who became an operative for the Union cause. One of those researchers worked for the CIA (yes, *that* CIA) and wrote a monograph on "Black Dispatches" that became my inspiration for telling Scobell's story.

In the interest of full disclosure, however, it should be noted that some historians dispute his existence. At least one has been quite insistent that Scobell was fictional from the outset. Another suggested that Pinkerton created the operative as an amalgam of the many escaped slaves he relied upon for intelligence about the Confederacy.

To be clear, I am not a historian. I am a storyteller who relies on serious researchers to do the heavy lifting of establishing facts, which I then attempt to weave into a tale that you'll enjoy.

In this case, I'm going with the preponderance of evidence and the decades of researchers who have made their opinions known: John Scobell was very much a real man, who really did become a spy for the Union cause against the Confederates.

Q: OK, so Scobell was real. What about the rest of Pinkerton's operatives?

A: Real people, real spies. Every one of them. Again, I drew on exceptional research by multiple historians to get the names and backstories of the Pinkerton agents identified in *In Freedom's Shadow*.

And yes, Pryce Lewis, John Scully, Kate Warne, and Tim Webster were all captured while spying in Richmond. Even the newspaper stories in the book were taken directly from contemporary accounts of their incarceration. Sadly, it's also true that Webster was tried and hanged as a spy, the first of the Civil War. The remaining three were released in prisoner exchanges later in 1862.

Q: Were Kate Warne and Kitty Brackett really sisters?

A: Yes, although that fact remained hidden for over 150 years. As noted above, Pinkerton liked to change the names of his operatives when he wrote about them years later. He didn't do this for people who'd been named in public records, such as Webster or Scully, but for those whose identities remained hidden throughout the war, he used pseudonyms to continue that layer of protection.

It worked. In *The Spy of the Rebellion*, Pinkerton referred to Warne as Hattie Lawton and Brackett as Carrie Lawton. These references confounded historians for decades. Was he talking about one person or two? How could she be in two places at once? Was Pinkerton just a lousy writer in need of an editor (he absolutely was) or was there a deeper meaning?

Until the publication of the exceptionally entitled book *Pinkertons, Prostitutes and Spies: The Civil War Adventures of Secret Agents Timothy Webster and Hattie Lawton* by John Stewart in 2019, these questions lingered. Stewart's excellent research answered them by revealing that Hattie and Carrie Lawton were, in fact, sisters Kate Warne and Kitty Brackett. As his title suggests, there were a few other secrets revealed in Stewart's book, but I'll leave that additional reading to you.

Q: Was Scobell married to Marie?

A: Yes. Well, sort of. There is one reference in *The Spy of the Rebellion* that mentions Scobell's wife, stating that she had "obtained employment in Richmond, while he had made his way to the Union lines." Since there was no other discussion of her, I decided to take it from there.

Q: Alright, then what happened to Lucy?

A: I know this is a question on some readers' minds because they have asked me in real life. They're usually quite disappointed when I tell them the answer is...nothing. She is a completely fictional character. Therefore, her fate is entirely up to imagination. Perhaps with her master deceased, Lucy fell into the hands of his gentler sister and served that household until being liberated with the rest of Richmond's slaves at the end of the Civil War. For the first time in her life, she was free. Let's go with that.

Q: Speaking of Lucy's master, what about that jerk Matchett? Was he real?

A: No, thankfully. Although there were doubtless many like him throughout the Confederacy, Matchett was a product of my imagination. Scobell needed a powerful and evil adversary. I gave him Matchett and, to stack the odds a bit more, his deputies and the spy, Joseph.

Matchett's boss, the infamous General John "Hog" Winder was very much a real person, though. He was also very much a vicious martinet. In his role as Provost Marshall of Richmond, he was charged with uncovering spies, finding and punishing deserters, and overseeing prisons. In 1864, he was put in charge of the Confederate Bureau of Prison Camps. These camps included the hellish Andersonville Prison, commanded by Winder appointee Henry Wirz. Wirz's oversight of Andersonville was so horrific that he was hanged for war crimes in November 1865.

Which brings me to the final **Q:** Was Henry Wyant a real person?

A: Definitely. In fact, I wouldn't be here and you might've never read a book about John Scobell without Wyant; he was my great-great-great grandfather.

When I set out to write this historical spy thriller, I made one overarching rule for myself. If I was writing about an actual person, they would only appear where (and when) they were in real life, if that was known. Wyant was the single exception I allowed myself.

He really was from western Pennsylvania and did enlist as a private in the Civil War (Company G, 103rd Pennsylvania Infantry) in January 1862. However, the 103rd didn't come to Virginia until March 1862, well after the Battle of Balls Bluff. Wyant, along with most of the rest of his regiment, was captured at Plymouth, North Carolina in April 1864. He died of dysentery in Andersonville Prison on June 15, 1864.

Don't miss out!

Visit the website below and you can sign up to receive emails whenever Robert Hilliard publishes a new book. There's no charge and no obligation.

https://books2read.com/r/B-A-UJQM-XDBKB

BOOKS 2 READ

Connecting independent readers to independent writers.

About the Author

Robert Hilliard has written on sports, history, and the outdoors for over three decades. Rob started as a reporter for the *Pittsburgh Tribune-Review* and has since written articles for outlets such as *Upland Almanac*, *Pennsylvania Wildlife*, and *Pittsburgh History Magazine*. He has the distinction of having feature articles in three different sports Halls of Fame: Baseball, Basketball, and Pro Football.

In 2000, Rob was asked to contribute to his first book project, a history anthology entitled *Rivers of Destiny*. In 2012 his first individual book, *A Season on the Allegheny*, was published. It quickly hit the Top 10 in two Amazon categories and has garnered national attention since its publication.

Rob recently completed his first novel, entitled *In Freedom's Shadow*. The historical novel is based on the true story of slave John Scobell, who escaped the Confederacy during the Civil War, only to return to the South as a Union spy. *In Freedom's Shadow* will be published on November 17, 2023.

9 7 9 8 2 1 8 2 8 9 3 6 2